TIDES OF YOUTH

The second volume in the Pencarrow family saga. The Pencarrows are now prosperous farmers, with Miles, the eldest son, becoming a lawyer in the newly developing township of Wellington. But there are turbulent emotions sweeping through the family as the grandchildren develop their own characters, not always to their parents' liking. Only Bessie understands them, but Bessie is now growing old and fragile. Who will keep the family together when Bessie dies? The years pass by with their joys and sorrows, and on to the First World War.

NELLE M. SCANLAN

TIDES
OF YOUTH

Complete and Unabridged

ULVERSCROFT
Leicester

First Large Print Edition
published September 1982
by arrangement with
Robert Hale Ltd.,
London

© Nelle M. Scanlan 1933.

British Library CIP Data

Scanlan, Nelle M.
  Tides of youth.—Large print ed.
  (Ulverscroft large print series: romance)
  I. Title
  823′.914[F]   PR6069.C3

  ISBN 0-7089-0849-7

Published by
F. A. Thorpe (Publishing) Ltd.
Anstey, Leicestershire
Printed and Bound in Great Britain
by T. J. Press (Padstow) Ltd., Padstow, Cornwall

To
DAN
who lies in France
AND
MARY

Take on this summer noon the ribbon way,
White with spread shells or drab with clay;
Over a tea-tree ridge it curves, and down
Dips to a narrow swamp with rushes brown.

So on, past paddocks trim and ferny rise;
Here where success its bright green banner
  flies
There where the ever watchful scrub has
  crept
To win back land while tired sentries slept;
Past stout straight fence or tangled trailing
  wires
Poplars that stand against the blue like spires;
Squares of dark pines about a hillside home,
Set for the time the wild nor'-easters come.
A pleasant road, with many a wide-ranged
  sight
Of mountains' purple empire, and the bright
Tranquility below; a new world touched with
  old,
Brave with the making, beautiful and bold.

Golden Wedding—ALAN MULGAN

1

THE flush of dawn glowed like a curtained candle over the eastern hills. A night of biting frost had passed its darkest and chilliest hour, and the midnight glory of the stars had paled. Hoar frost whitened the fence-rails and painted the shabby gate, and it coated the grass like snow. Roof and ridge and stump and the furrows of the ploughed land were almost robbed of their contours.

Nothing stirred. A deathlike stillness wrapped the sleeping countryside. High among the inland ranges, winter lingered into spring, yet the crisp mountain air was already scented with the wild fragrance of the uncut bush.

As the dawn spread and rolled back the dark night sky a horse's hoofs rang out on the frozen road. The horse stopped suddenly at a gate, and the rider bent down and lifted the iron clamp that held it closed. The horse went through and turned so that the man might shut the gate, dropping the clamp into position. It was an instinctive movement, a concerted action born of frequent repetition.

As the horse, with the bridle hanging over his neck, walked up the path to the stable door two jets of vapour gushed from his nostrils.

Frost lay thick on everything: the pump, the water-trough, the plough, the upturned barrow. An empty sack was frozen hard as iron.

Kelly Pencarrow unsaddled his horse, patted his flank, and threw a cover over his back. The horse whinnied as Kelly closed the lower half of the stable door. Stamping his cold feet on the frozen ground, he swung his arms to warm up a little before turning into bed for an hour's sleep.

The sun was high when he awoke with a start, and all the familiar, clattering sounds of the farm were at their noisiest. He sprang up, annoyed at having overslept, and puzzled that no one had called him. He stretched luxuriously, his young, healthy body responding to the pull and thrust. Tired? Sleepy? What are a few hours' sleep when you are young? He could dance all night, ride twenty miles there and back, and plough next day without betraying a sign of weariness.

Vincent Crawford was not the man to pamper him. He worked hard himself, and expected his men to do the same. He had no objection to Kelly dancing, provided it did not interfere with his work.

"You can't dance all night and work all day at my age, but b'God, I did it in my time, and was none the worse."

The milking was finished, and they were having breakfast when Kelly appeared, confused and apologetic.

"Why didn't you call me? I've never overslept before."

"It's all right, boy. Have your breakfast now."

There was a kindlier note in his voice. Mrs. Crawford said nothing, but in her face was a look of tenderness, a maternal understanding, that stabbed to quick response some warning instinct. They had let him sleep on. Why? There must be some reason. Something had happened; something was wrong. He was now consciously aware of an atmosphere of suspense; an acute wave of sympathy flowed towards him. It startled and unnerved him.

"Finish your breakfast, boy. Finish your breakfast."

"There's something wrong, I know," and

3

Kelly glanced quickly from Crawford to his wife.

"A telegram; it came late last night. Harrison was passing and brought it over from the post office."

Crawford was a stout, slowish man of sixty, with sparse sandy hair. His deliberate manner of speech was as unhurried now as ever.

"From home?" Kelly asked, quick apprehension darting from one to the other. His mother, father, Genevieve, Pat?

"Yes; from home."

"Not . . . not Father?"

"No; nor your mother. It's your dear old Grannie who is ill. They want you to go down at once, as it's only a matter of days now, and she's asking for you."

Grannie! Somehow he had not thought of Grannie. She seemed immortal. Though she was so old, she was intensely alive; one did not associate her with death. To Kelly she had always seemed old; old and lovely and wonderfully wise. The passing years made no change in her to his young eyes. When he was a baby Grannie's hair was white, and her face all tiny wrinkles. One could imagine other people dying, but not Grannie.

The sun was high, spreading a clear, crisp

light over the broken country. The frost, crystal white, sparkled like a myriad jewels as house or tree or fence-rail intercepted the pale warmth of the spring sun; but sharp patches of green patterned the landscape where it had caught the early rays and thawed. The plastic mud of winter, trampled and deeply grooved by wheels, was still frozen hard.

Soon a distant cap of snow emerged from the white mist that vanished before the mounting sun. The day was opening up. It seemed to grow higher and wider as the clear atmosphere added miles to the view. In winter, rain and fog made it a small world: a world of little intimate things that centred round the farm. But on this day, as Kelly Pencarrow packed his bag and strapped it behind the saddle, and with a terrible fear in his heart set out for Wellington, he felt that his destination was almost in sight, or just behind that last barrier of hills on the horizon.

From the eminence of the farm, a great sweep of country was spread out: rich, rugged, broken country with its rutted roads of frozen earth, and the simple, scattered homesteads. It was a heavenly day, as he said: clear, cold, brilliant; the sunlight intensifying

5

every colour; the air like wine. How he would have loved that long, lonely ride, but for the thought of what lay ahead! Bessie Pencarrow was dying.

Kelly urged his horse along the bush track. At the end of five miles he came to the main highway, a wider metalled road that linked the district with the railway.

At noon he stopped for dinner at a farmhouse, and ate hungrily of roast mutton, potatoes, cabbage, apple pie and cream. And he drank three large cups of strong tea.

Finding that he had made good time in the morning, he let the horse jog along easily after dinner.

If Grannie died! She was getting old, he knew, but this tiny, frail, white-haired Grannie who had stood by him after the quarrel about Duffield, he could not believe that she was dying.

As he rode more slowly now, his mind travelled back to that stormy scene three years before. He saw them all gathered in the big drawing-room of Miles Pencarrow's house on the Terrace. Grannie, so happy, her erect figure, tiny but dominant, as she looked with pride at the expanding clan. His grandfather, twisted with rheumatism, but sharing her glow of triumph in what they had achieved. His Aunt Kitty, whose whole world centred in Robin Herrick, her only child. For him she renewed the ambitious but abandoned dreams of her youth. And all the others.

The party was celebrating the launching of a new generation, the third: the marriage of his cousin Ella to the Englishman, Philip Gentry. He recalled the joy in Michael's face at having solved the problem of keeping Ella with him at Duffield, despite her marriage. He had made Gentry a partner in Duffield station—Gentry, who didn't care.

It was in a blind passion of rage, a sudden madness of disappointment at finding that Gentry, and not he, would share Duffield with Michael, that Kelly had struck the blow. Gentry had laughed at him and his wild love for the big, lonely sheep farm. It was a blow that had shattered the unity of the Pencarrow family. That night Grannie had had her first heart attack. A sense of guilt, that he was responsible, could not be dispelled, and, deep though his regret for her sake, he could not bring himself to make his peace with Philip Gentry or his Uncle Michael. He would do anything for Grannie, almost anything; but he could not apologise. To-day, Kelly, maturing into manhood, was the outgrowth of those youthful tendencies; hot-headed and impulsive. He could, however, be generous. He had an odd attractiveness, and was spasmodically a leader, but he was too quick to take offence and throw everything to the wind in a flash of temper. He could be stubborn also, and refuse to see things from any but his own point of view.

The same rash impulse which would one day precipitate a quarrel might as suddenly wipe out enmity with an equally unreasoning and generous atonement. But it must come about naturally. No argument, or punishment, no pleading or persuasion could bring it about prematurely. Sometimes the break was final. Yet Kelly could forgive largely, even if he baulked at some obscure point that he alone could see; some imaginary injustice that would brook no interference or mediation. It was this reef of rock in him on which so many chances of happiness were to be wrecked.

In family councils after the quarrel, the cold logic of his father left him unmoved. This stubborn attitude once again opened the breach between father and son, the breach caused when Kelly refused to take law and join his father in the firm.

His father was ambitious for him; his mother loved him; his sister, Genevieve, worshipped him; but it was his Grannie who understood him. She had the gift of divination. She saw the tumult in his troubled mind; the warring in his heart. No one else realized quite how much Duffield had meant to Kelly; no one, perhaps, but Michael. And it was Michael who was so bitterly hurt over the incident. With the one stroke he had kept Ella, but lost Kelly. They did not cancel out each other. Yet, had he foreseen the consequences, he might have hesitated. Since his wife's desertion in Ella's childhood, everything in life had centred round his little daughter. Into that channel he had poured all his love and devotion. To keep Ella now became the supreme purpose of his life. Tormented by the thought of losing her, when she and Gentry talked of taking up land in Hawkes Bay, he had been blind to everything else. To keep her near him was the one thought in his mind when he gave them, as a wedding gift, a half-share in Duffield. So engrossed had he been in his personal problem that it had not occurred to him what this change would mean to Kelly.

Kelly and Gentry had worked amicably together before the wedding. As a new cadet, working under Kelly, who was his uncle's right hand at Duffield, no difficulties had arisen. Kelly, with his passion for the place, his ambition to make the Pencarrow station a model, and see its sheep and cattle carry off the blue riband in competition with other breeders, set up an ideal to which Gentry did not subscribe. Duffield, or Hawkes Bay, it was all one to him, provided he prospered.

Kelly saw what the change would mean. Gentry, as part-owner in authority; and he, a paid man, subject to orders. The indignity, as well as the inevitable conflict that must follow, made it impossible. He could not go back to Duffield under those conditions. At first he felt that Michael had betrayed him, betrayed Duffield and the Pencarrow heritage, by handing it over to a stranger; to one who didn't care. Later, in calmer mood, he knew that Michael was not guilty of deliberate treachery towards him. Still, he could not forgive his uncle.

As he struck Gentry's smiling face that night, Kelly had sworn that one day he would own Duffield. It was a wild, foolish threat, but he was determined never to set foot on that beloved land while Gentry had any share in it.

He had refused his father's offer, indeed, demand, that he should become a lawyer and carry on the firm after him. Here was ready-made prosperity for him; a secure place into which he could step. But not even this promise of easy wealth could divert him from his determination to farm the land. Even Jack's tragic death, making him the eldest son, and the harsh year on the Taranaki dairy farm to which his father submitted him, failed to change his mind. His heart was set on Duffield, and the happiest days of his life had been spent there with Michael Pencarrow, and the relations between uncle and nephew had been ideal. Then Gentry came as cadet, and Ella married him and, to keep her near him, Michael had given them a half share in the estate.

When first one and then another of the family had tried to patch up the quarrel, and "knock some sense into Kelly", as they put it, Kelly had found his sole refuge in Grannie.

"You're a fool, Kelly," Genevieve had said. "Chucking away a jolly good chance like that. Uncle Michael was going to leave you the other half—"

"I don't want the other half. It isn't that. You don't understand," and he turned wearily away.

But Grannie understood. She knew it was not the material loss that worried him. He did not begrudge Gentry and Ella their half share in the profits. But they didn't care, as he repeated over and over again. They didn't care where they lived. Hawkes Bay or any other place would do. But to Kelly, the Pencarrows had made Duffield. It was something almost sacred and apart. He loved every ridge of the hills, every curve of the valleys, every sweep of the pasture, and the beauty he had brought about with his own hands; the trees he had planted, the gardens he had made; the experiments he was trying, and the improvements he was accomplishing. Gentry didn't care. Often he had laughed at the passionate enthusiasm with which he had worked. But Gentry was an English cadet then, and didn't understand. Now he was part-owner . . . and didn't care.

How could Kelly carry out these almost sacred rites of improvement and experiment under such blasphemous indifference? It was not the money, though he now found himself with little enough, and no prospects. He would have to begin again somewhere else. He refused to stay and manage the Home Farm for his grandfather. The small, mixed farm in the Hutt Valley was the joyous holiday land of his childhood, but it was constricted and limited. It did not offer the scope he demanded. It was, one might say, perfected and complete, for his grandfather was an admirable farmer, and he could see himself getting into a rut and just following in the path laid down. His grandfather was getting old, and, less flexible than his wife, was slow to adopt new ideas. The conservative pioneer would not be swayed by Kelly's modern theories. Such a life had no attraction for him. He would wake in the night with some wonderful scheme, and was up in a fever of impatience to try it out, and his uncle had always encouraged him. Gentry laughed at this fervour. Now, as part-owner, he might find a malicious pleasure in thwarting Kelly; in forbidding the experiment. For these reasons he could not return to Duffield, nor could he work on the Home Farm. He had tried to make them see, but they would not.

"It's not the money, Grannie. I'm not jealous of Gentry, as Father said."

"I know, my dear. You have a lot of your grandfather, John Kelly, in you, but you have enough of me to make me understand."

"It was my fault, upsetting you last night. I'm terribly sorry, Grannie."

"The old heart is a little tired, my boy. But it is not the first shock it has had, and it won't be the last, so don't blame yourself for that."

"But I do."

"Tell me, what will you do now? You have quarrelled with your father again."

"Yes. I'm sorry, Grannie, but I couldn't help it. He will never see my point of view. He talks to me as if I were a criminal he was prosecuting!"

"Don't say that, Kelly."

"He does, really, Grannie. I don't think he likes me much. He's ambitious for me, I know, for the Pencarrow firm, but not for me as I am. He resents me because I want to go my own way—"

"Some day, Kelly, you may marry and have sons of your own. Remember it then.

Don't try to force them too hard. But you will; you will. If you owned Duffield, and your son wanted to be—a doctor, shall we say?—and sell the farm, what would you say then? What would come of all your planning and contriving?"

Kelly was silent. He knew she was right, and yet he could not surrender.

"Tell me, what are you going to do now?"

"I'll get on some up-country place, and later I may be able to pick up a bit of new country cheap, and clear it. Father says he'll never give me a penny. But I don't care."

Bessie Pencarrow saw the stinging tears held back. He was stubborn. Of all this turbulent brood of grandchildren, Kelly was dearest to her. He was laying the foundations of a stormy life, but no words or entreaties could save him.

Kelly thought of it all now as he rode through the short afternoon, hastening to see her once again before she died.

He was obliged to spend the night at the railway hotel in order to catch the train next morning. There was another hard frost, and he sat in the bar and drank beer with a couple of cow-cockies, while the last day of September went to join history. To-morrow would be the first of October, the heart of spring in New Zealand's calendar, where June brings rain, not roses, and Christmas treads on the heels of the longest day.

2

GENEVIEVE met Kelly at Wellington station.

There was a frank fearlessness about Genevieve that was almost boyish. She was tall, like her father, moving with an athletic grace, but her interests, to the despair of her mother, were not domestic. She drove and rode well, but she sewed with a "homeward bound" stitch, as sailors say; there was neither neatness nor permanence about it. She had a quick wit and a sharp tongue, and was hard to beat in an argument. Sir Miles Pencarrow had learnt that his daughter Genevieve was the only member of the family who dared to contradict him. She was not afraid.

"Curb your tongue, my girl. No man will marry a shrew."

"Who wants to get married?"

"That's no way to speak to your father, Genevieve."

Lady Pencarrow made the remark automatically. She spent much of her time preserving the troubled peace of the house. Her ready interposition with a mild rebuke between father and child saved his dignity and turned the point of his anger. Sometimes he pursued the theme, but often he was glad to evade a new and distressing feature of family life: the deliberate thwarting of his plans by his children, and their defiance. Defiance he called it. The amusing, kindly, devoted father of their early childhood had become, after Jack was drowned, a brooding, disappointed, temperamental man, with a grudge against fate. True he was wealthy, and retained his place at the head of the Bar; was knighted for his services to the Government, and had a devoted wife and six healthy children. What more could a man ask? Yet he had a sense of failure.

Kelly had stubbornly refused to take his elder brother's place and carry on the old firm of Kelly and Pencarrow. This first bitter disappointment broke the framework of his ordered existence. Then Mary, his eldest daughter, took her pretty face into a convent, instead of making the brilliant marriage he had hoped for her. Kelly had not only refused to take up law, but had precipitated a family quarrel that had split them asunder, and now defiantly went his own way, refusing all efforts at reconciliation. That accounted for the eldest three. Then young Pat flashed into the limelight.

As one of the younger he had been merely a cipher. He fed and fought and took the biffs and bangs of his elders in the rough and tumble of that infantile democracy, the nursery.

Patrick Aloysius Pencarrow was the youngest of the main brood, a gap of several years dividing him from the last child, Peter. Margaret, who was his immediate senior, was a soft, pliant child, and the one who would conform to her father's demands. But for her he had no special ambition.

"No brains, but a nice disposition," was Kelly's verdict on her in later years.

She lacked the vital qualities which Pat demanded. Genevieve, who was eighteen months older than Margaret, had allied herself with Kelly, whom she adored. A sharp line of demarcation cut the family in two, ranging the Big Ones on one side and the Little Ones on the other. This was drawn between Genevieve and Margaret. Kelly and Genevieve now constituted the Big Ones, and Margaret, Pat and Peter were the Little Ones.

Margaret, or Meggie, as she was called, was a nice child, but ineffective, and not adventurous, and Pat resented being eternally classed with her and the much younger Peter. It left him in resentful isolation from his elders.

"Oh, Mother, make the Little Ones go in; they're such a nuisance."

"Clear out, you youngsters! You're too small; you get in the way."

The crushing weight of this classification had long irked Pat. He wanted to be in things; to join with Kelly and Genevieve, and skip over Meggie. The little girl had more in common with the baby, Peter, whom she mothered.

In this way Pat was cut adrift. When he complained, his father would say: "Keep to your lessons, my boy. You're too young yet."

From this, Pat was driven to seek adventure in books. Not having Kelly's pugnacious disposition, he had not yet asserted himself as an individual within the family, but a passionate development was going on inside the boy's mind during his entry into the teens. He feasted on books of adventure, and revelled in thrills of the sea, which woke a wild longing to share in these dare-devil doings before the mast. He would sit deep in a tale of storm and wreck, of coral islands and strange fascinating ports, without thought of time or place. He was transported hither and thither by the wild rush of words, which built new and enthralling worlds for him. He could almost smell the very spice of Eastern cargoes, and his flesh would creep with the curl of the lash.

Into this little world apart came crashing one day his father's chance statement, which he overheard in the curtained corner where he read. It sank deep into his childish mind.

"Kelly will do what I tell him, or I shall know the reason why. I'll not be thwarted by my children. I have worked and planned for them, and I know what is for their good."

"But Miles, dear, Kelly has set his heart on being a farmer with Michael at Duffield." It was his mother's voice pleading.

"I say he is to come into the office and take his place in the firm. And don't you encourage him in his foolish ideas."

"He can be very stubborn, Miles. And he loves Duffield; and, remember, Michael has no son."

"I know, I know all that." His father's voice had been impatient. "Pat will go to

21

Duffield with Michael. I planned that long ago."

"I don't think Pat wants to be a farmer," his mother had ventured timidly.

"My God, Norah, must I consult every whim of these children, and be dictated to by them? I say Pat is to go to Duffield, and that settles the matter."

The small boy, reading his *Treasure Island*, was stunned by this unexpected blow. They were going to send him to Duffield and make a farmer of him, and he didn't want to go. He wouldn't go.

It was after Kelly had defied his father, and taken the consequences, that Pat, in the secrecy of his heart, made his decision. If Kelly could break down his father's opposition, and go to Duffield with Uncle Michael, might not his father insist upon Pat going into his office instead, and taking law? Farming was a dreary enough outlook when your head is full of the wild fascination of the sea, but a dull, dry lawyer's office was an unspeakable prospect.

Kelly's revolt had caused open conflict in the house, but he had succeeded. Pat knew that he had not Kelly's resistance to persuasion and entreaty. He took no one into his confidence. But after a specially unpleasant scene at home, when his father was more vehement than ever in his determination to bend his children to his will, Pat, with the glamour of romance luring him on, packed his little bag and stole out one evening. He had made his plans cautiously. One of the Colonial clippers belonging to the Circular Saw Line, which took timber from New Zealand to Sydney, was in Wellington. Her usual ports were Auckland and the Bay of Islands. When she sailed at dawn Pat Pencarrow was on board. He had run away to sea.

No one had dreamt that Pat was a rebel too. They had not bothered much about the likes and dislikes of this fifteen-year-old schoolboy. His sudden departure came as a terrible shock.

Relief followed the first panic when a note to his mother revealed the fact that he had decided to become a sailor. He knew his father would not listen to him, or give his permission, so he had run away.

Miles made every effort to get the boy to come home, but, once away, it was easy to be firm. His vessel did not come into Wellington again, so Pat was spared a personal interview. In the end, when convinced of the lad's determination, Miles was compelled to give in. Patrick Aloysius Pencarrow was properly indentured for four years to the New Zealand Shipping Company's vessel *Waitangi*. Sailing to London by the Horn, and coming out via the Cape, he was the first Pencarrow to return to England.

Now Genevieve was showing signs of revolt. Mary had been gentle but firm in her desire to enter a convent. Kelly had been silent but stubborn—damned stubborn, his father said. But Kelly's stormy nature could not sit soberly under his father's dictatorial manner. Words meant quarrels, and Kelly was no good with words. He had plenty to say at times, but that was the humorous, irresponsible Kelly whom they so loved and who made them laugh. But to put serious thoughts into words, and frame effective arguments under the withering effect of his father's ready tongue—the tongue of a brilliant advocate—was quite beyond him. He met it in silence, and nothing goaded his father to such lengths as this rocklike imperturbability of Kelly's. It drove him to fury, and he said harsh things, of which later he was ashamed.

Pat just took the matter into his own hands, and did not argue. He went.

Genevieve's revolt was incipient, but anyone could see that she had ideas of her own; advanced ideas not in consonance with her parents'.

Norah saw it from both sides, and tried to keep peace among them. She loved her husband, but sometimes she longed for those early days when he came-home-in-a-cab, walking unsteadily into the hall, and slashed at the Cockie with his walking-stock. She had hated that ugly, stuffed green parrot under its glass case. But how trivial it all seemed in retrospect. Yet that occasional indulgence, marking the close of a big trial, was her one worry at that time.

Plump and matronly, Norah had lived her full life of domesticity and social activities without much change. She had mellowed, but neither weakened nor hardened under the constant friction of later years.

To mothers of her period their duties were clear-cut and inflexible, and the taint of modernism opened up terrifying prospects. She was shocked at much because she felt it her duty to be shocked. But why be shocked? This was the challenge that Genevieve was constantly flinging down.

Norah was shocked at her freedom of

speech; her candour. Impudence, Sir Miles called it. That a girl should openly demand reasons for her parents' actions and opinions was preposterous. Why? That's why? But it was not enough for Genevieve. Perplexed, Norah turned to her husband to see if he could explain why they were objecting. Personally, she felt sure she ought. But Genevieve demanded to know why.

"Children did not ask why when I was a child."

This recurring "why" of Genevieve's irritated her father also. With a word he could silence the others, but Genevieve persisted.

"It's not ladylike."

Genevieve laughed.

"How dare you laugh!" snapped Miles.

"Oh, I'll dare a lot more than that."

As she drove to the station to meet Kelly her mind was busy running over the things she must tell him. He would want to know so much all at once; the things you can't put in letters.

As he stepped from the train, she thought he looked older; yes, distinctly older. And thinner.

"How is she?" he asked anxiously.

"Just keeping herself alive until you come. The doctor said she couldn't last, but I knew she would. She's marvellous."

"Poor Grannie! It doesn't seem possible. She was always . . ."

His voice trailed away. Kelly found it difficult to express in words his troubled, emotional soul.

They drove on in silence. A wet wind came whipping across the harbour with a searching cold that was more penetrating than the hard frost of the mountain country. The sky was grey, and a gloomy shadow hung over the city.

The Hutt Valley, green under the veiling misty rain, opened before them. The familiar road was crowded with associations that linked him with the old Pencarrow home.

"Has—have any of the others come?" Kelly asked as they left Petone behind.

Genevieve knew what he meant.

"Uncle Michael and Ella came down three days ago, and Aunt Hester is over from the Sounds."

Apparently Philip Gentry had stayed at Duffield. That was what he wanted to know. His grandmother had been kind to Gentry, but he had not captivated her like that earlier

Englishman, Robert Herrick, whom Kitty married. Bessie Pencarrow had loved that gentle, amusing, courteous failure like her own sons. She had no fault to find with Gentry, yet she felt an arid quality even in his love for Ella. This dryness was the unproductive soil in which no great and passionate relationship could strike deep roots. With Kelly the rocks were on the surface, but he had secret depths that were rich and fertile.

Kelly's mind was a tumult. Not since his defiant departure to make his own way had he been back to Wellington or the Hutt. From the annual gathering of the Pencarrow clan each Christmas Kelly was absent. It was a special grief to his grandmother, the great matriarch on those occasions, around whose table they assembled—three generations of them now. But Christmas was midsummer, and a busy time on the farm, and Kelly made this his excuse. But Bessie knew. There had been no healing of the wound, and Kelly would not embarrass her or introduce a discordant note. He could not and would not pretend a friendliness he did not feel. The others might dissimulate, but not Kelly.

Day was closing in and dusk was falling when Kelly arrived at the Home Farm. It was all so familiar; the square, friendly house, squatting so comfortably in the midst of that rambling old garden which Grannie had planted. A rush of memories came crowding into his mind as he drove through the wide, hospitable gate. Grannie had insisted on a wide gate and a wide door. She said a narrow entrance had a grudging look.

He saw the orchard flushed with spring, the early blossoms and tender leaves almost too delicate to face the ruthless lash of the spring storms. The reason for his coming made poignant all this loveliness. He could not imagine it without her. She was woven into the very fibre of it. At every turn he saw her hand at work; her thoughts and hopes and love were embroidered on the very surface of the land she had come to as a bride more than half a century before. It was then a new and savage land; now a beautiful and fertile country. She had given it the priceless example of her courage and her faith, which was to be seen in the simple, great accomplishments around her.

When the warning was sounded to the clan that Bessie Pencarrow, the great little

Grannie, was nearing the end, Norah went out weeping.

"Don't waste your tears on me, Norah. My day is over. I am old and tired, and God will rest my weary bones. I have had much to be thankful for, so much love and kindness from you all. I want to tell you now, that at first I was afraid about your marriage. Miles was a headstrong boy, and I did not know if you would manage him rightly. I know now that no one else could have done half as well. You have been a splendid wife to him, Norah, and it has not always been easy. If only poor Michael had chosen as wisely. Poor Michael!"

Proud of this final judgment in her favour, Norah wept on.

One by one they had been in to see her, Michael and Miles, Hester and Kitty; and the grandchildren. Now Kelly had come.

"She is sleeping," Kitty said, as she met him at the door.

They talked quietly as they had tea. Kelly noticed how rapidly his aunt's hair was turning grey, that black, rebellious curly hair of the gay Kitty Pencarrow.

"Your father and Robin are coming out again this evening." Kitty thought it better he should realize that he must inevitably meet them all here at Grannie's bedside.

"How is Father?" Kelly asked.

"He's well, but—different."

Kelly understood, and knew that she blamed him.

"And Robin?" he asked.

Kitty's eyes lighted up at the mention of Robin.

"He is such a darling, Kelly. Not a bit grown-up, and yet he has only his final examination to pass."

A momentary twinge of envy darkened his mind. Here was he, Sir Miles Pencarrow's eldest son, a penniless farm hand, and his cousin, Robin Herrick, whose father had been a failure and ended by keeping a country pub, had stepped into his place as Sir Miles's successor. Yet it was his own fault. He knew that. He had sacrificed everything to go his own way.

Of course he had expected to spend his life at Duffield with Michael; to succeed Michael. Oh well, it was no good harping on it now. It was disturbing to think that here, at his Grannie's deathbed, he must meet them all for the first time since the quarrel with Gentry at the wedding party.

He suspected there had been a lot of talk about his coming. Would Grannie insist upon a reconciliation before she died? Would Kelly, who was devoted to her, refuse such a last request? Would Philip Gentry come down to the Hutt? Would the gallant little woman still exert her influence over them from the grave, binding them by promise of forgiveness?

Of course they had talked of it.

Norah and Kitty had spoken of it every day since Grannie's illness.

"I am sure it is worrying about Kelly that makes Miles so difficult. He imagines that all his children are determined to disobey him, and that Kelly is at the bottom of it. If only they could talk it over quietly; but they can't. Kelly is so obstinate. He won't say a word, and it drives his father to fury. Genevieve answers him back, and I believe he likes it better."

Norah's problems were many, but the greatest of all was keeping peace between Miles and the children.

"You are lucky, Kitty. I don't believe Robin has caused you an hour's worry in his life."

"He is a darling. But he is all I have, and it

sometimes makes me afraid." Kitty revealed for the first time the secret fear that haunted her days.

"Nonsense! He looks the picture of health," said Norah.

"It's not that. He has outgrown the old weak chest he inherited from his father. It is some unknown threat. It's foolish, I know, but I am always afraid that I will lose him."

"Kelly is fond of Robin. I think he likes him best of the cousins; better than Hester's two," said Norah.

"Yes, and Kelly is generous too. He doesn't bear Robin a grudge for taking his place."

"I wonder if Mother will ask for Philip Gentry?" Norah speculated. "I mentioned it one day, and she put me off."

"How?" Kitty was curious, too.

"She said that with Michael and Ella here, someone would have to stay and look after Duffield."

"I don't think she likes him very much." Kitty put the suggestion cautiously.

"No. Yet he's a nice man."

Norah was not one to find fault easily.

"I'd back Mother's judgment any time."

"Then you don't think she will make Kelly

patch up the old quarrel? She could. He would do anything for her, especially now."

"It is hard to say what Mother will do. And yet, she is usually right."

Miles, without saying so, was counting on his mother's intervention. If she took Kelly in hand, and made him promise, it could all be fixed up yet. Memories of his own childhood here at the Hutt, and the wonderful holidays the children had spent, came back vividly as he paced the garden path, smoking and thinking. The secret wound that never healed was the death, here on that summer New Year's Day, of Jack, his handsome eldest son, who was to have followed in his footsteps. Well, there was time yet. Kelly was in his early twenties, and young enough to begin. The years he had spent roughing it might not be lost if they taught him a lesson in values. There would be room for them both in the firm, Kelly, and Robin Herrick. If Grannie would only use her influence! Perhaps he might drop her a hint.

Michael, too, hoped that his mother would have a word with Kelly. He missed the boy.

True, he had kept Ella with him, but Kelly had gone. Not even to Ella had he confided how deeply he missed Kelly's enthusiastic companionship. Kelly, of course, would inherit his half of Duffield. But then it might be too late. It would be impossible for Gentry and Kelly to work together. Each would be hardened in his own way, and Gentry, no doubt, would resent Kelly's desire to change and improve and reorganize everything about the place. Kelly's passion, also, might be spent, and he would have ceased to care. Of course, one might sell out to the other. Michael did not like to think of Duffield, the fine station that he and his father had given so much of their lives to make, being left to the indifferent care of Philip Gentry.

All his life Michael had been chasing a will-o'-the-wisp, for the thing on which he set his heart evaded him. Or, when he captured it, there was merely an empty shell; the core had vanished.

If Grannie intervened and asked Kelly now. If Kelly came back, how different life would be at Duffield; like the old days before Ella married. He longed for that happy companionship; riding over the farm, with that cheerful, impetuous boy at his side; planning, dreaming. He might suggest it to his mother. Only she could do it, and a word from her might be enough.

3

ON the big four-poster bed, beneath the crochet quilt, a tiny, frail old woman lay waiting to say her last good-byes on earth.

The white hair was parted in the middle; the pale, knotted hands lay at rest on the quilt into which, in the winter evenings long ago beside the fire, she had crocheted her thoughts and hopes, as the growing family talked and squabbled and laughed around her.

One by one they came in to see her, and wept.

"I have been very rich in the love of my children," she thought.

These were no sham, deathbed tears, induced for the occasion. Bessie Pencarrow had been a dominant figure, but never had she tried to impose her will upon them, not since her failure to prevent Michael's foolish marriage to Vi Cumberland. True, she had planned and schemed a little, smoothing here, quickening there; adjusting and reconciling. But the family subjection to her was a voluntary tribute to a great mother—great in love and understanding, in patience and in the simple wisdom of the heart. From childhood they had come to her with their problems. Even Miles did not despise her kindly counsel. More than once he had felt a light hand on the guiding-rein at a critical moment, when ambition threatened to overwhelm him.

Robin, the lonely little boy in Marlborough, had found her singularly companionable. Kelly's tempestuous outbreaks were often spent before her. She seldom tried to check him, and the storm left him ashamed. It was then that a little healing philosophy was not only balm, but drew them closer, for he knew how deeply she saw into his heart, and understood.

Bessie Pencarrow lay in her big four-poster, and all around was grief and the turmoil of warring elements.

Both covertly and openly, her middle-aged sons, Michael and Miles, had sought for the last boon of her influence in healing the breach, and bringing Kelly to a reconciliation with the family. Norah had asked it, too, so that her husband and son might come together again. Kitty had urged the value of a promise made at such a moment. Hester, the quiet elder daughter, who had married the Scottish Macdonald, did not neglect her opportunity to put in a word in the cause of peace.

Matthew, father and grandfather of them all, now severely crippled with rheumatism, played no part in this drama of reconciliation. Bessie was going, and he would follow soon. They were both old and tired, and longed to be at rest.

After a fitful sleep, Bessie woke.

"Has Kelly come?" she asked again.

"Yes, Mother. He is waiting to see you," and Hester hurried out to fetch him.

The big grey eyes, that had retained a hint of starry wonder even at death, turned towards the door. With a movement of her hand she signalled Hester that she wanted to be left alone with him.

"Oh, Grannie!"

The stinging tears slipped down his cheek as he saw how she had changed—smaller, whiter, gentler; like a wisp of thistle-down, he thought. And yet there remained the same compelling quality that had held them all.

"My boy! My boy!" she said, and her

fingers brushed back the hair from his forehead as he knelt beside her bed.

"Kelly, dear, would you do something—something very difficult—just to please me?"

She saw the quick apprehension flash in his eyes, and then retreat, conquered, as he took conscious control of himself.

"Yes, Grannie, I'd try."

Dim as her eyes were growing, Bessie Pencarrow had seen that first flash of refusal. For days she had been keeping herself alive by sheer force of will in order to see Kelly before she died.

"If I asked you to apologize to Philip Gentry for striking him?"

Kelly had not expected that. Grannie had always been so fair; so just.

"I'd—I'd speak to him, and try to be friends, if that's what you mean."

"And would you go back to Michael and help him at Duffield, and not mind Philip being there?"

How many times she had rehearsed these questions in her sleepless nights!

"Perhaps he wouldn't have me now."

His answer came slowly, painfully. To refuse her this, her dying request, was

40

impossible. Yet to bind himself to it might mean further disaster, and she would not be here to release him from his promise. Sweat broke on his forehead.

"Or would you give up farming, and go back to your father, and take law, as he has always wanted?"

Here in the presence of death he was being asked to bind himself by a promise; to take a decision, to negative all that he had made so great a sacrifice to obtain—his freedom to order his own life; to do the work he loved.

He fumbled with the crochet knobs on the quilt, and his mind seemed to dash about like a trapped animal, seeking escape. Then his eyes met the steady grey eyes of his grandmother, watching every phase of the battle.

"Would you, to please me, make up this old quarrel, and do as your father asks?"

Something rose into his throat and choked him. He could not bear to refuse, to disappoint the one person who had truly understood and believed in him. She had done so much for him; now it was his turn. But he saw what it meant; all the cramped unhappy years in his father's office, at a task he loathed. As an alternative, taking orders from

Philip Gentry at Duffield. Steadily her eyes watched the battle fought out to a finish.

"Would you, Kelly dear?"

The lump in his throat was choking him; tears blinded his eyes. Plunging his face into the coverlet beside her hand, he said chokingly: "Yes."

There was silence in the room. Kelly felt her hand against his forehead in a feeble gesture. He did not look up; he could not see her face or know the change that had come over it. The minutes passed, then Kelly raised his head. She felt his movement and opened her eyes.

"Thank you, dear. But I shall not ask you to. A wound that heals first on the outside festers within. I believe if I had exacted that promise you would have kept it, but at a terrible cost. I have tried not to be a tyrant to my children when I was alive. I shall not tyrannize over you from my grave. All I ask is that you will try to forgive the old hurts, and understand each other better. I am asking no promise, but until my sons are all at peace with each other I shall not be at rest. It must come from the heart. But remember, Kelly dear, the will can often guide the heart."

Kelly kissed her, and, his eyes blind with tears, he stumbled from the bed.

In the big living-room the family waited— waited for Kelly. Kitty was there and Hester, and Sir Miles and his wife, Norah. Michael had come in with Ella. Robin Herrick and Genevieve stood by the window. They all talked in hushed voices, and waited. No one dared to put into words the thought in each mind. Some delicacy, some reticence, had kept them from blundering openly in speculation as to what was being said behind that closed door.

It was dark now, a cold, crisp night, with a slice of pale moon just above the hills. Silence fell as the door opened and closed. They waited, their eyes turned to the wide passage. They saw Kelly, hatless, rush out of the front door and disappear into the night.

"I'll go in now," said Hester. She was, you might say, a neutral member of the family, and far less involved in the problem Kelly had precipitated than the others. She alone of the family had not been present at the wedding party and the quarrel.

"I'll see how she is," she added, and the family sat in that curious hushed atmosphere which surrounds the house of the dying.

"Is Robin here?" Bessie asked when Hester went in.

The tiny figure seemed more spent, and her voice was feebler. She spoke with an effort.

Robin, slim, handsome, gentle, with her own grey starry eyes, bent over her. To her wandering mind he was again the little lonely boy in Marlborough, whose games and imaginings she had shared. Kelly and Robin—so different and yet each with something of herself. In a special way she loved these two. Hester's sons, the Macdonalds, were good lads, but she did not feel so close a bond with them. Perhaps she had seen less of them in their remote farm down the Picton Sounds. It was more than that, however. She could not find much Pencarrow in the young Presbyterian clergyman, Hector Macdonald, now married in Dunedin. And even less in the rather self-centred, Dr. Neil Macdonald, who was taking a post-graduate course in Edinburgh. She loved them all, these grandchildren of hers, but in a special way Kelly and Robin came first.

"Robin, dear, in a few years you and Kelly will be head of the family." Bessie paused and her breath came in little gasps. "Stick together. Life isn't always easy, and though I

44

hope you will prosper, don't set too much store by success. Ambition is good, but don't let it rule you. Money can be a tyrant."

She spoke slowly, in broken sentences.

"Some day you will marry. If you have a son, call him Pencarrow. I think Pen Herrick would be a nice name for him."

A faint shadowy smile shone in the dim eyes, as though once again she was seeing an infant son, like Robin, laid in her arms.

She closed her eyes and lay silent.

Robin hurried out to his mother, and Hester, Kitty and Norah went in. They poured a little brandy between the pale lips and adjusted the pillow, but she had lapsed into unconsciousness again.

"You had better go to bed. Norah and I will stay with her," Kitty said. She addressed them all—Miles, Michael, Robin, Hester and Genevieve.

"I'll put a couple of logs on the fire, it is going to be a cold night," said Michael.

"If there isn't enough in, you'll find some in the woodshed," Kitty told him.

Michael poked the fire, broke the back of a log that was nearly burnt through, and heaped it together. It sprang into new leaping flames. Taking the hearth-brush, he swept in the ashes and coals tidily, straightened the fire-irons, and went out for more logs.

The air was sharp, and Michael shivered as he crossed the path leading to the woodshed. Suddenly he stopped. A pear tree laden with white blossom grew where the kitchen garden was joined by the lawn. Leaning against it, his head resting on the trunk, his body drooping wearily, stood Kelly. No one had mentioned his absence from the room. They thought he had avoided them and gone to bed.

Michael watched for a moment, all the affection he felt for the boy surging in his heart at the pathetic figure of Kelly's unhappiness. Kelly had not heard him. He was looking down the valley, away and away past the trees and the hills. His mind was in turmoil; his soul was tormented. He was trying to see the way ahead, the future, when Grannie was gone. She had asked him if he would make the first effort at reconciliation, but she had not bound him by promise; she had left him free. She had seen the fight and understood. No promise was asked, yet she told him she would not be at rest until her sons were at peace. But it must come from the heart; must heal from the inside. She was too

wise to be deceived by a stage-managed reconciliation at her deathbed. She knew her children too well. The bonds were strong but the
breach was wide. It must come naturally, and
be based on sincerity. To compel Kelly to go
into his father's office on a pledge extracted
from him now would be accentuating the
trouble. It could only lead to disaster. Kelly
would be unhappy, and, because he hated the
work, a failure, and that would add further
bitterness to his relations with his father. To
have Kelly refuse was bad enough, but to be
the father of a failure would have struck
deeper at Miles's pride.

Duffield! Much as he loved it and longed to
go back, life could never be the same with
Gentry there. Michael had given him a com-
paratively free hand, and had loved the boy
for his passionate enthusiasm. Michael had
longed for a son to carry on after him. When
his wife left him, he knew it to be a vain hope.
Then Kelly had come, and they had worked
and planned together.

As Michael watched Kelly—Kelly, whom
he had not seen for three years—his heart felt
warm with the rush of affection for the boy
and the old longing for companionship.
Gentry was Ella's husband, an easy-going

young man, but lacking in vital qualities; the warmth and depth, the fiery temperament of Kelly.

Motionless, Kelly leant against the tree, numb with misery, and heedless of the cold. He knew he must face them all. He could imagine their kindly searching eyes, trying to divine what had passed between him and his grandmother. But he could not face them now; not yet. He ought to, he knew. He had seen his mother and Genevieve, but not his father; nor Michael. His father would resent this evasion, but he couldn't help it. To-morrow, perhaps. He would like to do what Grannie wished, but she would not burden his soul with a false promise. He was trying to adjust himself to the future, to bring peace to her soul, and yet retain his integrity. For Kelly's loves and hates were fiercely defined, and he could not temporize.

Michael guessed something of the conflict. He knew Kelly so well, and understood this uncompromising attitude. Pity stirred him and a great yearning to win back for Kelly and himself something of that old happy comradeship. There had been so much conflict in his own life, those years of his early marriage; the brief hours of glamorous contentment, of briefer ecstasy, and the long periods of petty conflict, of hurt and humiliation, of bitter taunts and denials. Vi, who hated the Duffield that he loved, and to whom the hills were an encircling prison; what spelt serenity and peace for him was boredom unutterable for her. Michael had learnt a great deal in those unhappy years. Impelled by this impulse, Michael crossed the garden, treading softly on the turned earth. Gently he laid a hand on Kelly's shoulder, but did not speak. The boy started as though suddenly awakened.

"Come in, Kelly, you're cold," he said.

Kelly was frozen; his hands were numb. A sudden shiver shook the sturdy frame. In the intensity of his absorption he had not noticed the cold. It was not the chill of the frost, but some icy dread of the future that had gripped him.

For the moment their eyes met. Kelly did not disguise his gratitude to Michael for the little vibrating note that throbbed in his voice; that had coloured the simple phrase.

"Come in, Kelly." It was as though he were asking him back into his heart, into his life. He couldn't go back because of Gentry, but he was glad that Michael still wanted him.

Michael's hand slid down his arm, and their two hands met and gripped in silence.

"They've all gone to bed. I was just getting a couple of logs for the fire."

Michael made it easy.

They piled on the logs, and Michael mixed Kelly a hot whisky. He was white and chilled. For a while they sat beside the fire and smoked. No word was said. The bold-faced clock on the mantelpiece ticked loudly.

At a crisis, as when death throws into truer perspective the changing values of life, memory becomes acute, and past events appear in sharper outline than the happenings of to-day.

Michael was haunted by memories of Vi; of the first time he had brought her out to meet his mother, in this room; of the night when he had quarrelled with her in Wellington, and his mother had come to him, and he had repulsed her intrusion. Of his impetuous marriage when Vi's father, Charles Cumberland, had shot himself rather than face failure. He retraced all the sad events in his life, and always, now, he could see his mother hovering over him with wise counsel and tactful intervention, trying to avert the final catastrophe of his marriage. Experience, he knew, brought wisdom. He, in his turn, would gladly have told Kelly of the bitterness he had endured, brought about by his own headstrong action. But Kelly must go his own way, and learn the lesson that experience alone can teach.

Like Kelly, he had never been able to ease his burden by confiding in others. He, too, had found words impossible. He was tongue-tied about the locked secrets that a man keeps in his heart. Miles could storm and rage and find vent for his disappointments, and Norah soothed and comforted him. But to neither Michael nor Kelly could the balm of words bring healing. It was because he too had suffered that Michael respected Kelly's silence.

About midnight, when he was thoroughly warmed, Michael persuaded him to go to bed. He was exhausted by the long journey and the emotional strain.

As the day was dawning, and the thrushes and blackbirds were singing in the garden, Bessie Pencarrow sighed a longdrawn,

51

quivering sigh, and slipped into eternity. So softly had she passed that Kitty and Norah, who kept watch beside her bed, scarcely realized that she had gone.

4

PHILIP GENTRY came down for the funeral. Not only was it right that he should be there, but it was felt that this was the opportune moment for healing the quarrel. If the two met at Grannie's graveside the poignancy of his grief must surely soften Kelly. He could not, at such a moment, refuse to be reconciled. After all, Kelly had been the aggressor.

Like a bright thread running through the fabric of their grief was the hope that peace might be restored.

Miles's brood no longer spent the holidays at Duffield with their Uncle Michael. Ella did not stay at Miles's house on the Terrace when she came to town; she and Gentry went to an hotel. They met at Grannie's at the Hutt for Christmas, but there was strain beneath the civility. It was not the same. Unless the quarrel were made up now, with Grannie gone, they would inevitably drift farther apart. They were still in the dark as to what she had said to Kelly in that last inter-

53

view. He had not spoken, and no one had dared to ask.

The whole Hutt Valley came to pay tribute to the little woman they had loved, and who had been one of the gallant pioneers of the Province. Flowers poured into the house, simple garden flowers, and gorgeous wreaths from the florists'.

Kelly had gone to the farthest end of the Valley. He wanted to be alone. As he walked back across the paddocks in the evening Robin came to meet him. There had been no quarrel between these two, and Robin had not taken sides. All his loyalty, however, was with Kelly.

They talked about the lambs, and the creek that was flooding part of the land and needed clearing. They never mentioned Grannie.

Robin, who was the taller, put a hand on Kelly's shoulder, they fell into step, and turned out into the Hutt road. It was as though Robin's hand had piloted them.

They walked at a swinging pace, the spring evening cool and inviting. Kelly felt he must keep moving. He could do nothing at home but talk or listen, and either was distasteful to him. All the preparations for the funeral were now complete. For a while he had sat with his grandfather, and heard once again the tales of their early hardships. Age had dulled the edge of his sorrow, and Matthew Pencarrow, now practically crippled, his big frame bent and twisted, waited for the day when he would join Bessie. He was tired and old, and his body wracked with pain. He had surrendered to age before his wife, for to the end she had kept high courage and loved life with all its complexities.

"Gentry has come," Robin said at last.

"I see." Kelly understood.

For a while they walked in silence.

"What are they all saying? What are they expecting me to do? Whenever I go in they stop talking suddenly. I know it's about me, and I hate being discussed. Why can't they leave me alone?"

He spoke without bitterness, but a note of anguish, of pleading, struck Robin.

"I think they were hoping that you—that Grannie—that . . ."

Even Robin did not like to put it into words.

"Well, she didn't. But if they're afraid I won't meet Gentry, they're wrong."

"Would you go back if Michael asked you?"

"No!" His answer was final and definite.

"I wish you had taken law, Kelly. It would have been lots more fun if you were there."

It was the first time Robin had ventured on such dangerous ground.

"I'd hate it, and be a failure. And that would make Father angrier than ever. I'm not such an ass that I don't know my own limitations."

"But messing about on farms, where's it getting you?"

"I'm learning my job."

Robin was conscious of being a usurper. His Uncle Miles had welcomed him partly because he liked the boy and found him companionable, but also he hoped that by showing favour to Robin he might awaken Kelly's jealousy. He thought the boy would resent his cousin's position both at home and in the office. The point had not escaped Kelly, but, after the first flash of resentment, he accepted it. After all, it was his own choice and he could not complain.

Kelly and his father were not together ten minutes without some violent dispute arising. They clashed on every subject, and such a thing as a quiet discussion between them was impossible.

Robin, too, had fixed ideas of his own, but he could voice them without dispute. Miles would listen patiently, with admiration for the incisive quality of the boy's mind. He was not combative. And when he disagreed with Miles he did so courteously.

"Well, perhaps you're right."

But Kelly could never wring such an admission from his father. He was too conscious of parental superiority to admit that one of his own children could teach him anything. Since the first revolt in the family Miles had met defiance with thunder.

"Rows, rows, more rows!" Genevieve would say, and walk right into the middle of it.

"What's the row about to-day?"

"I'll have none of your impudence, miss."

"I'm not impudent, Father. I'm merely asking what the row is about to-day. I might arbitrate the question, if you asked me nicely."

"Genevieve, that's no way to speak to your father."

Norah's rebuke thrust a buffer between them.

"You've a damn' sight too much cheek."

"Not cheek, Father—brains. I'm the only

one of the family with brains; I'm like my brilliant father."

Nevertheless, Miles secretly admired her fearlessness. If only she had been a boy!

Miles's indulgence towards Robin did not wake jealousy in any of his own children. Robin never took advantage of the position, and he was always loyal to Kelly.

These two cousins, one half-English—tall, handsome, inheriting the courteous manner of his father—and the other, dark, sturdy, with vivid blue eyes, rebellious black hair, and his Irish grandfather's heavy eyebrows, were linked by that something which Bessie Pencarrow had recognized as her own special gift to them.

"I wish—" Robin began as they turned home.

"Oh, cut it out!"

"But it's not fair, Kelly. I hate to see you the only one not getting a chance."

"I'm not complaining, am I? It's my own fault, I suppose, but I'm not blaming anyone. Only I wish to God they would leave me alone."

Miles, at his age, would have staged a theatrical reconciliation. He would have enjoyed the notoriety; being the entire of a scene. It would have fed his importance to know that, when he was out of the room, they were all talking about him and speculating what he would do.

To Kelly it was a hideous intrusion into his privacy. The very fact that they were watching and waiting, preparing the spectacle, as it were, made it impossible for him to do anything. Neither in word or gesture could he make the first advance under their eyes, though all his soul was yearning to bring that final peace to Grannie that only reconciliation could achieve.

It was in this mood of conflict that he had set out across the valley. As they walked home, still keeping step, the serenity of the night in the valley and the talk with Robin had somewhat laid the stress and tumult.

Boys find an exchange of sentiment difficult. In sport and games and the gossip of the stables they have adequate resources. But shyness shuts out all talk of things felt. Of football, yes; but not of feelings. Poetic imaginings and the responses of the senses and the soul are not themes for discussion. It was in this lonely world apart that Kelly Pencarrow decided his battles, and no eye save his own witnessed the carnage or shared the bitter-sweets of conquest. On the Hutt road that spring evening, with Robin silent beside him, Kelly offered the little dead mother of them all the first fruits of her victory.

"Hullo, Gentry!" Kelly's voice was toneless; a sound empty of emotion. He had come in so quietly they had not heard him. Most of the family were gathered in the big living-room talking, but a queer hushed murmur, like the beat of wings, trailed off into silence.

"Hullo, Kelly!"

Gentry was taken by surprise, and felt at a disadvantage. He had no time to prepare either words or expression. He had not expected this from Kelly, despite the fact that there had been much speculation as to what Grannie had said to him.

They were all sure that Kelly was merely fulfilling his promise, perhaps reluctantly. No one gave him credit for the voluntary action. He could feel it all around, as though they were saying. "He promised Grannie; that's why." It angered him, and checked the impulse. They would not understand that he could not bring himself to make this submission if his heart had not sanctioned it. Grannie was right. To close a wound on the outside first was dangerous. He had fought it out alone, and had brought his will to bear upon his stubborn inclination. He had made the first move. He knew this was right, for he was under no delusion about who was to blame. Now they were all thinking that he had acted under compulsion, bound by a promise to his grandmother.

Kelly did not wait, but, feeling a new tenseness in the air, he said a general good night and went to his room, releasing as he did so the damned-up flood of happy approval behind him. But that he could not face.

This was only the first step, they thought. How much further had Grannie gone in her demands? Michael and Miles exchanged looks—wondering looks. They both wanted the boy, but from different motives. Would he come back?

Kelly stood at the window for a while, looking out at the dark shoulder of hill that blotted out the dim night sky.

He felt desperately tired. Did she know, and was she happier for knowing?

"I did it for you."

★ ★ ★

The sombre group in their deep mourning sat

61

round the big table after the tea-things had been removed. Bessie Pencarrow had been laid to rest in the valley she loved, and her children were feeling, for the first time, the desolation of the old farmhouse. At every turn some reminder of her clamoured at memory and woke a fresh gush of tears.

From their early days the proceeds of her personal labours, the profits from her garden and orchard, her calves and chicks, had been Bessie's own money; Matthew had insisted on this. And as the pence grew to pounds, and the pounds to hundreds, Miles invested it for her. It was from this personal source that so many charities were helped, and those five-pound notes, folded and knotted, that found a way into the birthday letters to her children. Each one of them had had cause to remember these timely benefactions.

Miles read the will, and also the letter in her shaky hand, written a short time before she died.

I have no great wealth to leave you, but my gratitude for all the love and happiness my children have brought me. I have said this before, but I say it again: Do not put too much value on material success. I would rather see you happy than merely prosperous. Not that I despise success, but it is often bought at too high a price. You are as different from each other as the flowers in my garden, and each has its beauty and its season, but I have loved you all. Be tolerant; be kind to each other, and do not condemn what you cannot understand. The little I have to leave I have disposed of as I deemed wisest, and if some get more than others it is because their need was greater, and must not be taken entirely as the gauge of my affection.

So Kelly got two thousand pounds. That was the outstanding feature of the will. To the others she left little gifts and smaller sums, but everyone got something.

Hester's children, the Macdonalds, would be comfortably off. Ella was quite wealthy. Miles was a prosperous man and could provide amply for his whole brood. Robin, as Kitty's only child, would not be short, and with his place in Kelly and Pencarrow he had an excellent opportunity.

But Kelly! Miles had said that Kelly would not get a penny of his money so long as he disobeyed him and wasted his time on back-block farms. Grannie was afraid that Miles might keep his word and Kelly would be left without land or profession or inheritance.

Miles had not drawn her will, so the terms of it were unknown to him when he read it. Twice he broke down as he read her last letter of admonition, so much of it, he felt, was meant for him. Kelly got two thousand pounds. Miles had said he would not give him a penny, and, by God, he had meant it. He was going to punish him for wrecking his hopes and inspiring the rest of the family to defy him. Now Grannie had provided him with a start. Miles had an uncomfortable feeling of failure. Money, social position, professional reputation, knighthood, yet he had failed with his family, and in her firm yet gentle way his mother had made that clear. She had sounded a warning.

He ceased reading, but no one stirred. They all looked at Kelly, but he did not see them. His mind had travelled far beyond the room, and a rich gush of happiness welled up. The darling, she had understood and was standing by. She would not have left him this money if she had wished him to go back to Duffield—or into his father's office. It was her gesture, telling him that he was free; it meant a chance to start on his own, and with her blessing. It struck a shattering blow at the fiction the family had woven around that last conversation. Grannie had listened to all their hints and pleas to intercede for peace and make Kelly promise to be guided by his elders. The fact that she had not agreed with them, or been persuaded by their arguments, came as a shock. This was her answer; Kelly was free to make his own choice.

Robin was the first to speak, and the starry eyes, so like his Grannie's, smiled as he gripped Kelly's arm.

Then Genevieve. "I'm so glad, Kelly, so glad."

Norah kissed him and wept. Michael said nothing, but put a hand on his shoulder in the gesture he knew so well. He could feel the pressure of his fingers saying so much more than foolish words. Yet the bequest had come between them.

To Hester and Kitty there was a tinge of regret that their sons had not been equally chosen. But, then, it was because poor Kelly was such a failure, and pride in their own off-spring supplied ample compensation. So they, too, offered congratulations.

They had all drifted away, leaving father and son together.

"Well, my boy." Miles tried to combine paternal pride with a warm solicitude. "Your grandmother has been generous to you—most generous. What will you do with the money?"

"They are cutting up the Tapuwai. I think I'll take up land there, and start on my own."

"The devil you will!" An angry frown knotted Miles's face. He had hoped Kelly would ask his advice. Here he was stating his plans without consultation with anyone.

"What do you know of the Tapuwai? You've never been up there, have you? You can't start off like that, up there, alone. You're mad, boy."

"Grandfather knew nothing about New Zealand, and he came out alone."

"That was different."

"I don't see it. I'm a pioneer of a later generation. I must do in the interior what he did on the coast. I can't afford to buy improved land, so I must take up a block of bush, and do as he did, clear it."

"I absolutely forbid you to do anything of the kind. You might as well throw the money into the sea."

"I'm sorry, Father, but I'm over twenty-one, and Grannie has left me the money."

Kelly felt her moral support. She would not have left it to him unless she meant him to use it.

"You and your damned defiance have upset the whole house."

"Who's being murdered now?" and Genevieve came in at a bound.

"Hold your tongue, will you?"

"I'm sorry, Father, we can't agree, but I must make my own life." With a desperate effort Kelly was restraining his anger.

"You've caused more trouble than enough; more than all the rest put together."

"I won't cause you any more. I shan't be here."

The strange, repressed quiet of Kelly's tone frightened Genevieve.

"Yes, go skulking into the country now that you've caused dissension all round."

Miles was losing his temper properly now. He was wrong, and he knew it. But something of the gentle rebuke in his mother's last letter had stung him, and he blundered on. He knew Kelly felt that his grandmother was supporting him in this.

"Your quarrel with Gentry and Michael—"

"Don't drag that in; it's all over and forgotten," said Genevieve.

67

"Clear out, Veve. You needn't get into this."

"No fear. I love a scrap."

"What's all this! What's all this!" Norah came hurrying in. "Haven't we trouble and sorrow enough without father and son quarrelling?"

"Don't worry, Mother, it's all right."

Kelly noticed that she was trembling. "I'm going. Father doesn't understand why I want to take up land of my own. I'm putting in for a piece of the Tapuwai."

"Tapuwai! Oh, Kelly!"

His mother's voice echoed the dismay in her face.

"It's a bit far in, but remember what it was like here when Grannie came out to the Hutt. And she survived and was happy. Why can't I?"

"And look here, Kelly, when you've got a whare built, I'll come up and keep house for a couple of months in the summer, and bring some of the others. We'll make Tapuwai hum!"

Kelly smiled at Genevieve's enthusiasm. "Righto!" he said.

It was the first time Kelly had ever discussed anything with his father. It seemed as though the security of Grannie's money put him on a different footing. Or perhaps the thought that she was still near them, listening maybe, restrained him.

"Tapuwai!" Norah repeated the name despairingly.

"Don't worry, Mother; I'll be all right. Well, good-bye; I'd better be off."

"But you are coming home for a few days, dear, aren't you?"

Kelly paused. He had intended to, but his father's violent outburst had changed his mind. He looked at Miles.

"Oh do, Kelly; you must, mustn't he, Father?" and Genevieve thrust an arm through each of theirs, and challenged them to draw away.

"Yes, my boy, your mother and I hope you will."

"Very well—thanks. Till Monday."

His mother sighed with relief, and Genevieve dragged Kelly out before there could be more trouble.

5

THE shadow of Grannie kept peace during the few days that Kelly stayed at home. A truce had been declared. While Norah bought him a too-lavish outfit, heaping useless equipment with maternal desire to soften the harshness of his chosen life, Genevieve made a point of always being present when Kelly and his father were together. She had a gift for scenting danger between them, and diverted them from topics that might lead to friction.

Miles had clung to a faint hope that the hardships and buffetings would teach Kelly a lesson, and that he would eventually come to his senses, admit his folly, and join him in the firm. Miles was confident that he had the ability, but was too lazy. Up till his mother's death he had hoped that she would use her influence. Instead, she had encouraged him by leaving him enough to make a start.

Now he relinquished the last faint hope. He made no further protest, realizing that it was useless. But he took no part in Kelly's plans for the future. He had decided to go his own way. Well, let him. During meals the name of Tapuwai was studiously avoided. Though all legal matters in connection with acquiring a part of Tapuwai were dealt with by Kelly and Pencarrow, it was Robin who acted as intermediary. Miles outwardly ignored the transaction, but Robin knew that he gave it the closest attention.

"You're a stubborn pair," Robin said, laughing, one day, as he impressed upon Kelly how deeply concerned his father really was in his venture, and with what meticulous care he had looked into every aspect.

"That's the trouble; I'm his son. I suppose I'll belt the hide off my own youngsters, if I have any, when they disobey me. I wonder."

After Kelly's departure for Tapuwai, life on the Terrace flowed as much as usual.

Kitty still lived at the Hutt with her father, while a manager ran the farm. Here the loss of Bessie was more acutely felt. They were sad days that summer, and little by little the old habit of "going out to Grannie's" dropped off. Robin alone spent a great deal of his leisure at the farm. He was devoted to his mother. When he could persuade her to go,

71

he took Genevieve with him. They were a comradely pair, and having her with him always intensified Robin's pleasure. In many ways she was like Kelly, but she had not his quick temper. If she were hurt or annoyed she would not dash off in a flare of anger. She would have it out and argue. She generally won on sheer weight of words. Robin, who had a keen analytical mind, enjoyed a bout with Genevieve; they might not agree, but they never quarrelled.

To Michael, out at Duffield, his mother's death had brought back sad memories. Whenever he thought of her now it was as he had known her more intimately in his youth. It reawakened all the tragic misery of his foolish marriage, and the old wound quivered with stabs of pain as his mind drifted back.

His solitary life made for introspection. No man can do long-tots in a ledger, or measure cloth or weigh groceries and meet his fellow man in the deep or trivial intercourse of commerce and yet give his mind to brooding. But the squire of many acres, with the long hours he spends alone in the saddle, or in solitary occupations which, while requiring attention, do not engage his whole mind, is often prey to morbid thoughts. If he is a happy man—

happy in his work, in his home, in his personal life, this mental leisure gives room for the growth and expansion of contentment. But to the unhappy mind, this solitary life breeds regrets to feast on older follies.

Michael had kept Ella with him. She was still the central joy in his life, but as the years passed he saw her drifting from him. She had more of her mother than the slim, dark beauty that she inherited from Vi. She belonged to a newer age which was bored by tales of its parents' hardships. She could see nothing heroic, but, rather, stupidity, in burying yourself alive in the backblocks when you could afford to live more comfortably in town. The country was pleasant in summer. She had been brought up at Duffield, and had known every pleasure it could yield, and they were many. Kelly had intensified every phase of its beauty by his enthusiasm. He compelled her to see it through his eyes. Much that she had shared with him—mustering in the early morning on the misty hills, and duck shooting on the Lake—retained something of the old delight. But it had waned with his going. Her husband, Philip Gentry, had a city soul, which encouraged that element in her. To him the country was a place where you made money, and the town where you spent it. All country was alike to him, provided it was profitable. He could never enter into and share those sentiments of Michael and Kelly which spread a special glamour over Duffield.

"I can't get lyrical about the blasted place," he had said more than once. "Farming is a job like anything else; something you do to make money. If I could make more in town I'd sell out to-morrow."

Ella did not quite share this view. Yet, once removed from Kelly's eloquence, and curbed only by her father's silent rebuke, for he would not dispute the question with his son-in-law—she gradually fell under Gentry's sway. Deep down was much of her mother's attitude to life, but it had been overlaid by training and the Pencarrow tradition. Grannie had sought to correct that irresponsible attitude towards life and one's special obligations. The Gentry influence was now in the ascendancy and the Pencarrow on the wane.

Ella agreed with her husband, and Michael was driven more and more into a silent acceptance of the position. He might have asserted himself more vigorously, but he hated conflict. He had had too much of it already in his life. And he could see the consequences of it in Miles's household.

His mother had accurately gauged the situation at Duffield. She did not question him, but it was quite apparent that the repeated disappointments of his life had sapped his vigour and undermined ambition. Michael had smiled proudly on all Kelly's schemes to make Duffield the prize station of the Wairarapa. He had been a much-needed spur, and had talked and dreamt dreams for Duffield which woke a response in Michael's heart. They were an echo of much he had hoped for in the beginning, when he had brought Vi Cumberland out as a bride.

Gentry's lack of interest, his general apathy towards anything that would not bring in quick returns, soon dampened Michael's ardour. He needed the spark of Kelly's high hopes to keep the flame alive. Gentry was a wet blanket. Why bother? Why plant trees? Trees didn't pay. Why bother about show cattle and sheep? They were more bother than they were worth. Couldn't the men do this? Or that?

At first Michael persevered, but he was soon worn down. The Pencarrow name no longer headed the prize list at shows; nor did the Pencarrow brand fetch top prices. And Ella sided with Gentry.

They were often away now. Gentry was keen on races, and though Michael had never missed the Wairarapa meetings, he did not feel that it was wise to follow them all over the country, as Gentry did. They always went to Christchurch for the Grand National in the spring, no matter how busy they were at Duffield.

"Get another man; get two, if you like," he would say when Michael voiced a mild protest.

At Christmas they went to Manawatu meeting at Awapuni. This permitted them to have Christmas dinner at the Hutt, and go north for Boxing Day. After Bessie's death, that obligation no longer held, and they now went to Auckland, which meant a week or ten days' absence.

Once, after Ella had been ill with influenza, they decided that nothing less than a trip to Sydney for a month would repair the damage. It was their own money they were spending, of course, and Michael could not complain.

This lack of interest in the place, and total indifference to his feelings in the matter, made him regret that he had sacrificed Kelly to keep them.

In these lonely days, when even the joy of Duffield was dimmed by Gentry's lack of co-operation, he longed for Kelly. To feel the boy beside him, to see his blue eyes shine and hear him planning in a tempestuous mood, for to Michael alone he revealed that passionate quality that others silenced. And Michael, towering above him, would put a hand on his shoulder, a gesture of approval and affection they both understood.

While Bessie lived she had managed to keep things in check. Respect for her opinion, as well as affection, permitted few breaks. Her death left Michael, always a little vacillating, without one firm anchorage for his lonely heart.

Hester had returned to her home in Picton Sounds. Now that Hector had his parish in Dunedin and Neil was finishing medicine in Edinburgh, there was only Jessie.

Macdonald's Scottish pride in intellectual achievements had found compensation for his sons' desertion of the land. Unlike Miles Pencarrow, he did not strive to force them, to hinder them in their choice of professions. But often he looked at the adjoining farm over which he had taken an option, the gift for his lads the day they left school. But they never knew. He hid his disappointment, surrendering them to medicine and the Church.

Jessie was more like the volatile Pencarrows than an offspring of this staid and virtuous pair. All the years she would stay in the Sounds, working cheerfully. Riding over the bridle track or sailing the boat into Picton were her simple diversions. But when the summer holidays came round, even though it was the busy time on the farm, Jessie joined her cousins.

At one time, when Kelly was there, they went in force to Duffield. They were happy days for Michael, when the house rang with cheerful shouts and laughter. Jessie and Neil Macdonald, Genevieve, Kelly and Pat Pencarrow, Robin Herrick. It was before her marriage, and Ella and Gentry were then the "moony pair".

Since the quarrel, the house party had never again met at Duffield. Kelly was away inland, and Jessie, Genevieve and Robin had found a happy hunting-ground at Grannie's. This annual forgathering of the Pencarrow young kept their interests centred in each ther, though not to the exclusion of other friendships. Kelly had some personal quality he did not consciously exert which drew and held them, and it was to him now they turned.

The second summer after Grannie died, they all went up to Tapuwai.

Kelly had built a two-roomed whare, and a large shed, and he was steadily clearing the land of its heavy bush. The Tapuwai was part of a large block of Maori lands in the King Country, not far from the Wanganui river. The old Maoris had objected to it being cut up, as it was Tapu, or sacred ground, particularly the valley through which the Tapuwai stream flowed. It was here that Kelly's farm was situated, sweeping up from the stream, over steep spurs and ridges, heavy with giant forest trees. The Maoris claimed that the valley was an ancient burial-ground, and nothing would persuade them to cut the trees or burn the bush or disturb the earth near the Tapuwai stream.

Kelly accepted Genevieve's challenge, rather than extended an invitation.

If you don't mind roughing it, come. You will have bunks of wire netting stretched between four posts, and a mattress of straw and fern. But bring your own bedclothes. The bathroom is a stunning little swimming-hole in the creek near the whare. If you want to be fussy and have clean plates for every course, bring the damn' things with you; I've only two. You will have to toss up to see who gets the kitchen and who the bedroom. The room with the stove has advantages in winter. But during a house-party, sleeping in the par-lour-kitchen-bedroom means being up with the lark, as I can't have you putting on petti-coats while I'm frying the bacon.

P.S.—Bring a couple of bridles; I can borrow a horse or two, but you'll have to ride on sheepskins, or sacks.

P.P.S.—Bring a big cake; remember, no shops under twenty miles, and you may weary of bread and dripping and gooseberry jam.

"Heave ho! Blow the man down,
    And we'll pay Paddy Doyle for his boots!"

A lusty voice rang out from the bedroom overlooking the harbour. It was a rich, vibrant voice, with the dew of youth upon it, and the lighthearted lilt of a sailor.

80

"Come on, Paddy Doyle; look slippy."
Genevieve banged on the door.

Pat Pencarrow came out, smiling a low, attractive smile, that caught up one corner of his mouth. His eyes were blue like Kelly's, but his face had a ripe tan; not burnt by Colonial suns, nor that darker tone of the Anglo-Indian. It was the salt tan of the Blue Water sailor, for he had sailed home round the Horn and out by the Cape more than once since he joined the *Waitangi*, and now considered himself a seasoned sailor.

"Pat, you've got a face like a well-cured ham," said Genevieve.

"You would pick on something disgusting like pig. I was told I was a nut-brown laddie by a lovely lady in a foreign port. Oh, la la!" He was in high good humour.

Pat had grown and developed amazingly since he had gone to sea. Though not quite so tall as his father, he gave the illusion of height. It was a well-knit body, still spare. From the repressed schoolboy, grouped with the Little Ones, he had grown into a cheerful, confident youth. Life at sea was hard, but exciting, and if it had not fulfilled his early dreams he at least had no cause to complain of its monotony.

When he returned from his first voyage home his mother had questioned him closely about the life and conditions at sea, with particular anxiety about his food and clothing, and the language of his mates.

Pat eased her mind under duress, with a felicitous picture that would have staggered the *Waitangi* mess. To his father he was more discreet and less picturesque, but equally far from the truth.

It was up at Tapuwai, under the genial influence of a camp fire with Kelly, Genevieve, Robin and Jessie Macdonald, that he gave a more accurate version of life before the mast. From being a Little One, Pat had rapidly acquired importance, and now joined the Big Ones, taking precedence on account of his travels. His adventures promoted him to an exalted position in their eyes.

Pat's shore leave coincided with the planned visit to Kelly at Tapuwai, and, like all sailors on shore, his one desire was to get astride a horse. Of course he could ride, unlike most Cockney sailors whose exhibition of horesmanship in port so entertained the landlubber.

At first his parents were reluctant to have

Pat go off to the country, but the combined entreaty of the family prevailed.

"Come on, Paddy Doyle!" said Genevieve. "You're going to miss the train, and make a hash of all my lovely plans."

Norah had looked anxious and talked about a chaperon when the children first spoke of their expedition to Tapuwai.

"Oh, Mother, what rot!" Genevieve was afraid that Aunt Kitty might be induced to join them. Not that she would have mattered, but she belonged to an older generation, and her ideas and tastes would have to be considered. Genevieve was a pioneer of the new century. She was not in open revolt against anything in particular, but she felt the cramping influence of the average parent towards its young. Much her father did, she was sure, was merely in the true parental tradition of his period. He could not really believe all that exemplary twaddle. "When I was your age, my boy, I never did that!" Genevieve threatened to compile a list of all the things that Father never did, according to this oft-repeated formula. Once she had asked Grannie if her father had been such a model and virtuous youth, and the answering twinkle in the grey eyes as she evaded a direct answer told Genevieve all she wanted.

Her mother, too, had a few set phrases which were echoed, so she found, in other homes.

"That's no way to answer your father." "A most unladylike remark." "Such unbecoming conduct."

Her easy comradely manner had brought on her wayward head the repeated caution, "Don't make yourself so cheap. Remember, familiarity breeds contempt." They were all copybook maxims, and she wondered if all mothers learnt them off for the edification of their daughters. Genevieve had no burning zeal in the cause of freedom, and even had women in New Zealand been denied the vote, as they were in England at that time, it is doubtful if she would have become a suffragette. She was not jealous of men's powers and prerogatives, though she sometimes envied them, but not politically. Her revolt, if it could be called such, was against the peculiar hypocrisy that seemed ingrained in the relationship between parents and children. Did that transition into marriage eliminate in a night, as it were, all the devilishness that seemed inherent in youth? Or was it mostly a pose on the part of parents? Why couldn't they talk things over frankly and sensibly?

"But why can't we go by ourselves? We're not babies. And we are all brothers and sisters or cousins."

"I don't like it, Genevieve. People will talk."

"People! Who? Cats! And what can they say?"

"That's just it, you never know; about the Pencarrows running wild like Maoris."

"Is that all?"

"You don't understand, Genevieve. You make it very difficult for me."

"If you would only talk candidly to me, Mother, it would be so much easier. Do you imagine we will do anything at Tapuwai that we wouldn't do here? We will live in two rooms and rough it, but, apart from that, do you think we will behave any worse because you and Father and all the aunts and uncles in Christendom aren't watching us?"

"That's no way to speak, Genevieve."

"I know. You tell me that regularly, Mother, but I'm only being frank, and I wish you would be. What's the good of all our careful upbringing and education and religion if you can't trust us out of your sight? They're wasted. If a standard of right and wrong and decent conduct needs bolstering up with aunts—"

"Really, Genevieve, I don't know where you get these shocking ideas from. It was always done in my time; it was considered improper for young people to go off alone. I— I . . ."

Norah's ready tears welled into her eyes.

"I'm sorry, Mother. I didn't mean to upset you. But you're only doing it because others do it. Now be candid. Can't you trust us? Don't you think I have any personal pride? Do you imagine we will create a frightful scandal of some sort? You know we won't. The very fact that we are there alone, on our honour to behave well, will be enough check. Don't you know there's more fun in being bold and bad when you're dodging someone on the watch?"

"I don't know; I really don't. But you're like your father, and I can't argue."

Genevieve got her way in the end, but not until she had worn down her father in a fierce discussion about ethics.

It was not without some trepidation that

Norah saw them off, with saddles and bridles, and boxes of bedding and food.

A fine, hot morning in late January cast a sparkling radiance over the harbour; the faint southerly breeze ruffled the surface which threw back the flashing sunlight like a myriad jewels.

They were all there, Genevieve and Pat, Robin and Jessie.

Their voices were excited, their eyes shone, and little squirts of foolish laughter were checked in deference to the conspicuousness of their position and the feelings of Norah and Kitty.

"Now, be very good, won't you?" Norah said for the twentieth time.

The train steamed out, past the line of trucks and heaps of coal, climbed and crossed the Hutt Road which lay far below. They took a last look at the loveliness of the harbour and the city, then plunged into the long black tunnel that pierced the hills around Wellington. When the smoke from the last tunnel had cleared from the windows they were out among the green farmlands. The rugged coastline was left behind. Night would find them in the King Country.

Kelly met them at the station. The heat of

the day had passed, and the clear mountain air of this higher altitude was like a long, cool drink after the smoky suffocation of a railway carriage.

"Oh, Kelly, this is heaven!" and Genevieve took a deep breath and flung out her arms in a gesture of freedom.

"Heaven, is it? Wait till you see what you have let yourself in for."

"I don't care how rough it is. It's heaven to get up here and away from town. It's stifling down there."

The boys greeted each other with the casual informality that cloaked real affection.

"My God! Look at the circus!"

Pat was delighted at the sight of a string of horses tied to the station fence. There was a horse each, and two for the luggage. They were a mixed team: a chestnut cob, a great raw-boned black, two shaggy ponies, and several nondescript animals with no particular characteristics.

They were standing, one leg easy, tails whisking the buzzing flies that had gathered about their quarters with irritating persistence. A couple were nibbling the grass that remained in reach, thrusting an eager mouth between the palings, while one, with drooping head, slept philosophically.

"Where did you get them?" Robin pushed his Panama hat to the back of his head to accentuate his look of surprise.

"All honestly bought or stolen. Oh, Barker, this is the family," and Kelly introduced them to a tall, lean man who was apparently in charge of the horses.

Geoffrey Polthard Barker was an Australian, a typical Cornstalk in appearance. His ambitious mother, who had died during his infancy, had been responsible for his names. Old George Barker, finding himself left a widower with a fractious infant son, and a large, lonely tract of sheep country in New South Wales, and a five-year drought to further depress him, turned for ready consolation to the nearest source, and quietly drank himself to death. He was a kind, amiable, easy-going man, overwhelmed by circumstances. He hadn't the guts for the fight.

The child, Geoffrey Barker, having no choice in the matter, was brought up economically by conscientious but needly relatives. Five minutes after he entered school, Polthard Barker died, and Potty Barker was born. The name stuck.

It was Potty Barker, having drifted about Australia, doing a bit here and there, on farms, in stables, about the docks who drifted over to New Zealand and out to the King Country. Drift is the term that rightly describes his mode of progression. He went with the tide. Potty made no plans, harboured no ambitions, enjoyed the moment, and left tomorrow to take care of itself.

Over a couple of pints of beer and the buying of the chestnut cob, he and Kelly had struck up a casual acquaintanceship. Kelly wanted a man to help him, and Potty Barker, having no deep-rooted aversion to work in congenial surroundings, the bargain was struck.

He had a lazy grace of movement, the automatic response of a healthy body in fine fettle, and a lazy manner of speech. This lazy drawl with flattened vowels produced a peculiar twang.

"Did you have much trouble getting all this circus up from Tapuwai?" Genevieve asked, as the boys saddled up and strapped the luggage on to the two pack-horses.

"A fair cow," drawled Potty Barker.

Genevieve and Jessie had the ponies. Kelly gave Robin the chestnut cob, Pat climbed on to the big, bony black, and Kelly and Potty Barker rode two of the nondescripts and led the pack-horses.

"Potty, you go ahead and lead. We'll have to push on while it's light," and Kelly glanced at the sky.

"But there's a moon, Kelly; quite a big one."

"Yes, but moonlight doesn't penetrate this bush, fathead," slipping into a childish nickname for Genevieve. "It is dark in broad daylight in some thick patches. And it's only a rough track further on, mind you. But don't get scared, the nags know the way. They all belong to this part. Still, we had better get a move on."

A premature dusk shut down when they entered the heavy bush country of Tapuwai. The horses dropped to a walk and picked their way among the potholes and roots as the winding track led first along a sharp spur of hill then down into the Tapuwai Valley beside the stream. It was here that Kelly had cleared the first few acres and built his whare.

The Tapuwai Valley was practically encircled by high, thickly-wooded hills, broken into ridges and spurs. Some faces lay well to the sun, others had a chilly southern aspect, catching, as it were, the direct icy winds from the South Pole, and having small share of even the summer sunshine.

Kelly had been fortunate, and his land had, for the most part, a north-easterly aspect.

As they rode down the spur, they passed an old Maori.

"'Day, Honi," said Kelly.

The old man stood aside to watch them pass. He did not answer, but shook his head.

"Not a very friendly greeting," said Genevieve.

"The old Maori resents our being here. He told me the day I came that this valley was Tapu. 'You will have te bad luck if you cut te tree, and burn te bush in Tapuwai.'"

"Why?"

"It's one of their old burying-grounds."

"Why don't you do a bit of excavating on the quiet? You might find some valuable greenstone Meres buried with the old chiefs."

"Yes, and get all their ancestral bones crying aloud for vengeance! I've got trouble enough clearing the bush without digging for treasure."

"But you don't believe it?" pressed Genevieve. "You don't believe it will bring you bad luck?"

"No, not exactly. But a couple of the settlers do. Lately there has been quite a lot of talk about the Curse of Tapuwai. Hughes's brother was crushed under a tree and died next day, and Fabian's wife has gone mental."

"Yes; but, Kelly, that might happen anywhere."

"Oh, I'm not worrying," Kelly said confidently. "There are too many real problems without looking for fancy curses. Wait till you hear some of Potty's curses. Now they are real—the meatiest I ever heard."

"Mother warned us against loose talk and unbecoming language before we left," said Genevieve, laughing.

"Loose—was that all? But Pat ought to have a nice variety."

"He has! 'No fo'c'sle talk here,' Father says every time he starts telling us yarns."

"The kid has quite grown up," Kelly conceded.

"He looks terribly dashing in his brass buttons."

"You're like the rest: a uniform gets you."

"It does make a difference, Kelly. But tell me, who is Potty Barker?"

"Except that he is an Australian and helping me to fell, I don't know any more than you. But he is an amusing bird," and Kelly chuckled.

6

THE simple homes of the settlers were built in clearings about the valley, a few miles apart. The land rose sharply behind them, rugged hills covered with dense bush and heavy undergrowth. As everything for their furnishing had to be transported over the rough mountain track on pack-horse, luxuries were scarce. Each little group was dependent upon itself for amusement and entertainment, and visitors were a peg on which to hang some simple backblock festivities. The descent of the Pencarrow clan had been heralded throughout the Tapuwai, and the arrival of so many young people held promise of a richer variety in their simple summer gaiety.

The big burn was the spectacular event for which their visit was timed. The stern business of clearing the land came before dances and picnics. These they could enjoy at any time, but the burn was to be a thrilling novelty, particularly for the town-bred cousins.

Fabian and Hughes, Kelly's nearest neighbours, had been longer on the place. Their properties met at an angle and they were combining to burn off the felled bush, starting at a sharp spur, as soon as wind and weather were right. Kelly had worked hard, but the area he had cleared was much less than that on the adjoining farms.

"If the dry spell holds, the fire should run through quickly and clear it up well," Fabian had said that morning as he passed Kelly going into the station with the string of horses. "I hate a half-burn. It means so much work afterwards, and the grass won't take. By the way, did you see wool dropped a penny at the Napier sales yesterday?"

"Just my luck," and Kelly knocked the ashes from his pipe and swore profoundly.

* * *

"Here we are!" shouted Kelly, as suddenly they emerged from the shade of the bush into a clearing, and below, beside the stream, they saw the rough whare and shed of sawn timber, unpainted, and the gleam of the corrugated-iron roof.

Cold lamb, pickles, bread and butter and strong tea were quickly produced for supper. Afterwards the men smoked and talked while

Genevieve and Jessie unpacked and made their beds.

"Heavens! Every cupboard is full of brown Windsor soap," said Genevieve, as she looked for a place to store the jam she had brought.

"Cleanliness, my girl. I insist upon it. None of your dirty town ways here. You'll find the time-table tacked up on that tree, near the bathing-pool. It's Potty's idea; he's shy."

"Ladies, ten till twelve. Gents at their pleasure," Jessie read from the notice scrawled on a piece of cardboard.

"I'll bathe when I jolly well like," said Genevieve.

"At your own risk. Don't blame me if you encounter a sea-serpent. Potty has a dip every time he comes past."

Half a dozen sawn-off logs, cut from a large tree, made outdoor seats in front of the whare. The girls came out and joined the four men, who turned suddenly from talk of sheep and ships.

It was late before the moon tipped the hills and cast a pale light on the winding thread of stream that gurgled cheerfully as it raced down the Valley to become lost in a dense tangle of trees that overhung a deep gorge.

"What do you want to do to-morrow?" asked Kelly.

"We've no choice, so far as I can see," Genevieve answered.

"What do you mean?"

"Spring clean, of course. The place is screaming for it."

"There you are, Potty; what did I tell you?"

"What did he say"—and Jessie turned to the tall Australian.

"He said I was wasting my time cleaning up for you, and that women had queer ideas. Whenever they move into a new house they always talk about the dirty people who have just left, and have it cleaned all over again."

"Don't tell me, Mr. Barker, that you cleaned out the whare before we came?" challenged Genevieve.

"I did, Miss Pencarrow."

"And do you call it clean now?"

"Like a new pin," he answered unblushingly.

"Then in heaven's name what was it like before?"

"A fair cow," replied Potty with emphasis.

They slept well, and were astir early. The

boys had a swim while the kettle was boiling, and when Genevieve and Jessie came out the bacon was sizzling in the pan under the expert eye of Potty Barker.

During the day the girls put what Kelly termed a "plush finish" on Barker's attempt at spring cleaning. They found the place was really clean; it was the natural grain of the unpolished wood that had misled them in the dim light of the kerosene lamp. Having appointed themselves cook and housemaid, it was a more varied meal than usual which was spread on the white pine table with its American-cloth cover.

They sat outside on the log seats and waited for the men to return. The collie pup frisked around and Jessie scratched his stomach. From the bush came the ring of an axe, and sometimes the notes of a bird. Near by the stream sang its cheerful song. All around was the quiet hush of the mountains.

"I love this marvellous quiet in the morning and evening," said Genevieve. "There is a strange peace about it all."

"In summer, yes," said Jessie, who knew the country in all its moods. "What about the winter: months and months of it, mist and rain and cold? I'd hate the winter here."

"I suppose so. As Potty Barker says, it would be 'a fair cow'." and Genevieve mimicked his lazy nasal drawl.

Fabian came over about dusk to talk over the burn. It was decided to start it in a few days' time if the weather held.

"What a sad-looking man," Genevieve said when he had gone.

"Yes, poor devil. His wife is in a mental home. The loneliness got her badly. She wasn't the type for this life. His mother took the baby." The words came out jerkily, between puffs of his pipe. No one spoke for a moment, and he continued.

"If only she could have got over the loneliness here and found fun in it she would have been all right. She used to sit at the window all day in the winter, when she had finished her work, and there wasn't much to do in two rooms. Not like dairying. She would just sit looking out, Fabian told me, and when he'd go in, dog weary, she would start crying. He's a quiet chap, and at night they would sit and look at the fire. He wasn't much of a talker, but he would try to interest her and cheer her up; tell her things that had happened during the day; how a sheep fell over the cliff. She would just nod her head and say, 'I bet it was glad to be dead.' Then she got to fancying things."

"Like Aunt Vi, in a way," said Genevieve quietly.

"Yes; only she cleared out, instead of going mad."

For the moment Kelly's mind swung back to Duffield. It had been lonely there, too, at first, but different—different from Tapuwai, shut down in a valley, inland. Duffield was high on the coast, near the sea, and it was open country; it had sweep and space. Kelly did not confide to anyone the loneliness, the misery, the hardship of that first winter here. Duffield could never have been like this; never.

Sometimes in the evening they walked up the Valley, or perhaps they rode to more distant parts where the magnificence of the country, green even in this midsummer heat, had a wilder beauty. Robin and Genevieve usually went off together. Potty Barker drifted to Jessie's side. Kelly and Pat were finding a great deal to talk about, and as often as not they elected to stay at home; to smoke and yarn and watch the soft dusk fill with deeper shadows the curves and creases of the Valley.

"It's rough luck on Father," Pat remarked as the brothers sat one evening talking about things at home.

"I suppose you will go into the Union Company when your time is up?"

"They want me to. If I can get in the *Rotomahana* . . ."

"She's a nice old tub," Kelly said affectionately.

"Don't call her a tub," Pat protested, his sailor soul affronted at such a description of one of the finest little ships that was ever built.

"I know she is the pick of them all."

"Do you know that she was the first steamer in the world to be built of mild-steel?"

"No!" Kelly was surprised.

"Yes. And when she struck a reef up Auckland way, and got holed, the photographs they took of the damage when she was docked were sent to the builders, Denny, and it decided the question. It's been mild-steel for ships ever since."

"I like the look of her, those clipper bows and the graceful line of the hull, and the set of her funnel . . ."

"She did over fifteen knots on her trial run

in eighteen seventy-nine when she was launched. But coming out to New Zealand, round the Cape, she did seventeen knots. And she is only a little over seventeen hundred tons. I'd like to get on her, and do the Wellington-Lyttleton run for a while."

"Does she still have the golden greyhound?" asked Kelly.

"Still at her main," Pat answered proudly, as though he were already part of her company.

"That ought to please the family, having you in and out of port. One less prodigal."

"Do all families smash up like this, I wonder."

Pat drew deep delight with each draw of his pipe, but his mind was troubled about Kelly. Tapuwai was all right for a holiday like this. After the sea, and those long voyages round the Cape and the Horn, it was great fun lounging round, swimming in the stream, riding over the bush tracks, seeing a new generation carry a step further inland the work their grandparents had begun on the coast.

The bushwhacker with his axe had become the spearhead of civilization. Trees, trees, trees! Everywhere were forests of giant trees, or else dense, matted scrub. The barren, tree-less cities and towns of modern New Zealand were evidence of that ruthless spirit, not yet eradicated. Trees were the pioneer's natural enemy; they stood in his path and obstructed his purpose. They must be cut down and burnt, and blasted and uprooted before he could make progress or prosper. He brought in civilization with an axe. His descendants have not yet recovered from that influence. Cut, clear, burn—that was the first gospel of necessity. They have not yet learnt that half the beauty of England—of the world—is trees.

They have not begun to plant and nurture trees, to foster and preserve trees, to love and venerate the majesty that has taken half a century, indeed many a century, to grow. Here and there this loveliness has been added to the land; but it will come. One day a generation will arise in this now practically denuded country that will plant wisely and well, and will stay with firm hands the stupid parish-pump authority that will needlessly destroy in thirty minutes what thirty years cannot replace. Pat had been to England in the spring, in the summer, and the first stirring of apprehension had quickened when he saw the ruthless, though necessary, felling of these lovely trees at Tapuwai. As he sat in the midst of it, his mind went back to England and her trees. The forests had gone, but trees remained; individual trees.

Yes, it was good to spend idle days here in summer, but what of the winter? Kelly was reticent about that. Pat had only Potty Barker's "a fair cow of a winter" to conjure scenes of dripping desolation. These were no leafless trees to etch their bare beauty against the cold wintry sun. The dense evergreen forest never changed, winter or summer. A few old leaves died and fell, and new growth came with the spring. In its almost jungle density, the wet moss and maidenhair fern spread a coverlet over the fallen tree and hid its decay. Taller ferns, bracken, supplejack vines, clematis, bush lawyer, manuka, thousand-jacket twined and wreathed both trunk and branch, and the dark green aisles between the trees were pungent with the odour of dampness and growth, that moist, sweet essence of the bush.

Yet in all this wilderness there is no prowling beast or snake. Perhaps a chance "Captain Cook", one of the pigs, now wild, descended from those few liberated by Captain Cook when he first visited New Zealand.

All this beauty Pat would gladly concede to Tapuwai; but what of the future? He felt that even these first years had left a mark on Kelly. He had lost his easy laughter, as if something of the silence and gloom around him had bitten deep into his soul.

"How long do you mean to stay here?" Pat asked at last.

"Always . . . or till I can sell out."

"You're not going to stay here permanently, and make a proper home and settle down; not like Michael, at Duffield?"

Kelly did not answer. Pat took a quick look, and a tender, reminiscent smile, a little sad as for some dear dead thing, flitted across his face.

"Tapuwai isn't Duffield, but it's the best I can do. And I seem to be doing that damned badly."

"Why don't you go back? Gentry is neglecting the place and leaving it all to Michael. You wouldn't know it now." Pat tried to spur Kelly by prodding his most sensitive spot.

"It's no good, Pat. I can't go back."

"Not even if Michael asked you?"

"He did. Look here, how would you like to sail under some cub you had trained, and in the ship you had once commanded? Put it this way. How would you like to stand by and see the thing wrecked by a damn' fool who didn't know his job, and didn't care?"

Silence fell. Pat realized it was useless to talk to him about it. The discussion had brought back memories of Duffield, and shattered the peace of the evening. A gloomy sadness settled on Kelly's spirits. Even when the riders came home, a cheery quartette, it was obvious that he was depressed.

"Haven't had a row, have you?" Genevieve asked Pat anxiously.

"No; just talking about Duffield."

"Is that all? Funny, isn't it, but he gets quite sentimental about it?" But she was relieved.

"A pity he doesn't fall in love. Then he might get over it and settle down. But you couldn't ask a girl to live here, now, could you?"

"I don't know. It's better than Grannie had to start with," said Genevieve.

"Yes, I suppose it is. But somehow that was different. You don't mind that sort of life when there is nothing better. But this is

107

enough to make him melancholy. Poor old Kelly!"

In the morning there was a letter from Lady Pencarrow. It came out with some stores from the post office shop near the railway station.

"What has Mother got to say?" asked Kelly as Genevieve turned the pages. Norah's large, round writing covered much paper, and it took many sheets to convey all the little bits of home news and the many warnings against dangers and indiscretions, wet feet and uncertain meals.

"Uncle Michael has gone to Manawatu for a week. 'He is staying at the Club Hotel and daily inspecting stock with a view to making purchases,'" she read. "Isn't Mother precise? He finds Manawatu very fertile, but flat, and the farmers seem prosperous."

"Anything else?" asked Pat.

"Father has dyspepsia; a slight attack. Mother went to Lady Martin's tea; Meggie bashed her knee—Mother didn't say bashed— 'has an abrasion, her bicycle having collided with a stone on the way down hill'. Here you are, anyone can read it; it's full of the darling's love and forebodings about the fate of her dissolute brood."

"Uncle Michael's after new cattle," said Kelly thoughtfully. "I wonder what he will get." He could not keep the keenness out of his voice. For the moment he forgot the burn on Tapuwai which, weather permitting, was to start that evening. His mind was back at Duffield.

Fabian and Hughes, who were more experienced in these things, were satisfied that conditions were right for the fire. They had had a good spell of dry weather, and there were no indications of a change.

Down in the valley the noonday heat was stifling. Not a leaf stirred, and the quivering air was heavy and stagnant. Even in the dimness of the uncut bush the cool moistness had a peculiar leaden quality. Towards sunset a faint puff of wind came from the south-east.

"Ah!" said Fabian. "That's good. Just enough and in the right direction." But the breeze died away, and the stillness returned.

Hughes was keen to start the burn at once; Kelly, rather a novice, was agreeable, and fell in with their plans. At the point on the spur where they had decided to start the fire it should sweep up Kelly's smaller clearing, and spread to the larger areas that Fabian and Hughes had felled.

The Government which made financial advantages to young settlers, assisted in cutting up large blocks of land in pursuance of its policy for closer settlement. The Tapuwai Stream, though low in summer, was a deep and dangerous river in the wet season. A horse could ford it anywhere in January, except at the swimming-pool. But in winter it was impassable. The previous year the settlers had obtained a grant from the Government to build a wide arched culvert linking the two sides of the Valley. It was a stone bridge, an outcrop of rock providing cheap material, and the settlers did the work under supervision. In this way they got a better job, or more for their money. Though it was actually a bridge, they always referred to it as the Culvert, for the stream was narrow, and ran swiftly between fairly steep banks. It was built with a high arch in order to permit the free flow of logs and uprooted trees in flood time. Otherwise it might be carried away, or the stream obstructed, and the lower part of the Valley flooded. The Culvert linked Hughes with Fabian and Kelly. Though Hughes had land on both sides of the stream, the homestead block was on the opposite bank, and approached by a different route.

Jessie was used to bush fires. She had seen several down the Sounds, but the bush there was not nearly so dense, nor the trees so large.

"I just love it; it's thrilling!" she said excitedly. "Especially when a big tree crashes and there is a great splutter of sparks. Wait till you see the flames leap from one tree to another; it's marvellous!"

Genevieve did not entirely share her enthusiasm. Somehow she seemed nervous tonight; the brooding calm of the atmosphere was highly charged with tenseness.

"A bit of wind makes it more exciting"—and Jessie talked on rapturously as they waited for the moment.

"You didn't tell Mother, I suppose?" said Kelly.

"Don't be silly! Do you imagine she would have let us come a yard if she knew? We had to keep that a dead secret. It was hard enough to get away as it was."

Kelly and Potty Barker went with Fabian and Hughes to the appointed spur where they were to start the fire.

"You stay here—you'll get a good view—and wait till we get back," said Kelly.

"How long?" asked Genevieve.

"An hour or two; perhaps more. I can't say. So long."

Not a breeze stirred, but the timber was very dry and the flames leapt up instantly. Soon a rool of thick smoke rose above the hills and proclaimed to the neighbours that the big burn at Tapuwai had started. The flames roared as they licked up the dry wood and swept through the felled forest and undergrowth.

In less than two hours Kelly and Barker came back, and they boiled the billy for supper, which they had on the banks of the stream, where the lurid light of the fire vied with the orange of the sunset.

"How long will it take to burn out?" asked Robin.

"Three or four days; perhaps a week. Much depends on the wind and the weather."

"You have struck a dead calm for the moment," said Pat, but he turned a searching look towards the departing sun.

"What if it should rain?" asked Genevieve.

"It would be just my luck," Kelly said gloomily.

"You are not thinking of that old Maori

curse of Tapuwai, are you?" There was scorn in Genevieve's tone.

"You can't start an argument to-night; it's too hot," and Kelly evaded an answer.

"How much will be burnt by morning?" asked Robin.

"Get up, my lad, and have a look for yourself," Genevieve suggested.

"Depends," said Kelly. "But it should be well away to the north."

"And we won't get much smoke here?"

"I hope not. But remember I warned you that you might get smoked out."

"I know, I'm not complaining." Genevieve remembered his diffidence about inviting them at first.

"Why did you fell the bush over there first, and leave all this standing near the whare?"

Robin found the whole business interesting, but a little puzzling.

"I cleared the part near Fabian's so as to get it all cleared up in a burn with his. It was his suggestion, and he is a pretty sound chap."

It was late when they left the stream and returned in leisurely fashion to the whare.

"I hate to leave it. I'd like to watch it all night," said Jessie.

"It fascinates me," Genevieve admitted, "but I would hate to be any nearer."

The girls went to bed, but Kelly opened a couple of bottles of beer, for it had been a hot day and thirsty work, as he said. For another hour they sat and talked.

Before turning in, Kelly had a look at the lurid picture at the head of the Valley, with the great curls and coils of smoke rolling lazily upwards and drifting away towards the north. It was a magnificent spectacle, and a touch of awe mingled with his personal interest in it. He had been partly responsible for liberating that amazing power for destruction, which was now ravenously devouring a forest that had stood for a thousand years. A match struck, a torch to bracken, and a conflagration resulted that swept clear the one great obstacle to their progress and the cultivation of the land. It was almost Godlike. As he stood there watching from his door, something of the power of conquest stirred in him. He—Kelly Pencarrow—had helped to set that alight, and it obeyed his will. And while he slept one great force of Nature would destroy another, so that he might prosper and live. Fire would demolish growth. And the ashes would so fertilize the land that for years its productivity would be doubled. The burnt trees, like a conquered people, would yield obedient service to their successor. As he had swung his axe and brought some fine tree crashing to the earth, Kelly had felt this power of conquest; of subordinating the product of centuries of growth to his will. But there was pity in his pride—pride in his strength, in a good day's work, in progress made. But pity for a great one done to death, and doomed to fire or decay. For trees he had always felt a tremendous admiration, even affection. He remembered the ones he had planted at Duffield, the row of poplars, that would lean before the wind. He watched the fire race on. The puny grass that would replace the trees would be nurtured by the ashes of a glory that once was Totara and Rimu and Pine. And the grass would feed his sheep and fatten his lambs . . .

"How is she going?" asked Barker, and his voice shattered the vision.

"Pretty good. Enough breeze to take it right away."

"Come and have a look, you chaps," Potty called out from the door.

"What a marvellous sight!" said Robin, deeply moved, for the deeper dark of advancing night had given an added brilliance to the lambent flame and curling smoke.

Genevieve slept fitfully, her dreams haunted by the flames. At first she was not sure what was real and what merely a dream. Then through the misty borderland of sleep came a sharp tap-tap-tapping. It was the flapping of a piece of loose iron on the roof.

Then Jessie woke.

"What is it?" she asked sleepily, seeing Genevieve sitting up in bed.

"Just the wind; a gale seems to be springing up. Wait, I'll go out and see."

"Is that you, Genevieve?" came a voice from outside.

"Yes. What's wrong, Robin?"

"Nothing—yet. But Kelly was a bit anxious at the change in the wind, and they've gone out to have a look round."

Jessie followed them out into the hot glare, and stood silently watching the fierce glow now fanned by the wind.

"You're not scared?" Robin asked.

"No, why should I be?" Genevieve's hand had felt the rippling tremor under it as she put a casual arm round Jessie.

"Come along inside," and Robin closed the door.

Jessie looked nervous. What if the burn should go wrong? She thought of the terrible possibilities if the fire should spread from the felled to the standing bush, and down into the Valley. They had taken every precaution, but . . .

"What did Kelly say?" Genevieve enquired anxiously.

"Just asked me to stay behind with you. Pat wanted to see the fun; a fire is a novelty for him; he gets his thrills out of icebergs round the Horn."

He tried to speak lightly.

The wind increased to a gale, and an hour later a perfect hurricane was blowing, sweeping across the country, fanning the flames, which leapt from fallen log to standing tree, clearing the whole range in its devastating onrush.

They were trapped in the Valley, the only exit being the narrow winding bridle path, now barred by flames.

Genevieve saw the terror in Jessie's eyes. This was so different from the bush fires they had had down the Sounds.

Robin tried to cheer them, but his eyes were anxious, and his mind was busy planning a way of escape. Several times he opened the door and looked out.

"It's getting nearer," Genevieve said.

"Yes." Robin slipped an arm through hers, and they drew close together.

"Are you . . . afraid?" he asked.

"Yes. I'm terribly scared."

"Don't get panicky; a lot may depend on keeping your head."

"Then you believe . . ." She stopped and looked at him.

"I don't think there is any real danger . . . yet, but . . ." He paused. "There is always the stream."

"Did Kelly say that?"

"Yes."

"Then he knew . . ."

"Just as a precaution, he said to go there if it got too—too hot."

"Where have he and Pat gone?"

"To have a look at things, and round up the horses and any sheep they can. They will all make for the stream. We will be quite safe under the stone bridge, and the water is only waist-deep there."

Potty Barker, nearly blind with smoke, galloped up to the whare.

"Take anything you value, and the food,

and make for the stream. As a last resort, get under the culvert. You should be safe there. But it is backing round this way, and the whare will probably go later."

"Where are the others?" asked Genevieve.

"Fabian's horse bolted and threw him. The fire scared it. He's got a broken leg, I think, and they are trying to get him down here."

"Where are you going now?" asked Robin, as Potty wheeled his horse.

"Fabian's mother is in his cottage, with the baby. She came up to spend New Year and brought the youngster. He is nearly out of his mind about them."

"I'll come with you."

"Hurry, then, we've no time."

"Oh, Robin!" It was a poignant cry that escaped Genevieve. For one instant in the glare they looked at each other.

"It is all right," Robin said, reassuring her. Quickly he turned and kissed her, and, tearing his hand away from hers, put bridle on one of the terrified horses and followed Potty Barker.

For a moment her head whirled, and the blood seemed to leave her heart, then came rushing back. Confused, she tried to drag herself back to the dangerous reality of their position.

"Has Robin gone too?" Jessie, asked, fear now starkly in her eyes.

"Yes, with Potty. Old Mrs. Fabian and the baby are in the cottage, and Fabian has been injured. Kelly and Pat are carrying him down to the stream. Oh God! What a horrible business; and I feel responsible for bringing you all here!"

The thought steadied her. To stand there, nearly blind and suffocating with the smoke that now beat down into the Valley was futile. She pulled her wits together, and decided what to take to the stream.

She picked up any money and watches belonging to the boys, no matter whose; she packed all the food, a kettle, pot and blankets, and with Jessie, who was now trembling piteously, began their move to the stream. She felt better after this; the inactivity, waiting helplessly, tragically, would have broken her courage.

The heat was terrific. The awful glare in the sky, the crackle and roar of the flames, the rush of the wind that swept everything before it, and against which they battled down to the stream, called for conscious effort.

120

Following the track, Barker and Robin made for Fabian's cottage, at the head of the Valley. Robin was riding Old Faithful, a good hack that knew every inch of the country but had no pace. Maddened by the smoke which scorched his eyeballs, Old Faithful snorted as Robin urged him to make speed. The thought of the old woman and the child alone facing that horrible death justified the spur against such willing flanks.

The smoke was rolling in dense clouds, so dense that he could scarcely see, but the lurid glare of the flames which leapt from tree to tree illumined the Valley in a hectic light.

At last they reached the door, and Robin held the terrified horses while Potty dashed into the cottage.

"Here, take the youngster; he's alive and kicking like blazes," and Barker thrust the baby into his arms.

"Down that way, and try to pick up the stream, but go for your life. I'll follow."

Robin held the squirming baby tightly and the chubby fists pounded his face as he fought against the smoke.

Potty Barker followed, with the inert figure of Mrs. Fabian, a small, lean little grey-haired woman, hanging limp in his arms.

Barker's spare frame had a steely strength, and his endurance was phenomenal. There was no track through the thick scrub, which was now alight in several places from flying sparks. The gale, the heat, the smoke, the terrified horse, the awkward burden, all hampered him. More than once he wondered if he would reach the stream.

Robin got through first, his horse stumbling on the rocky bottom of the stream. Barker was not far behind, but twice he had been struck by sparks which had set fire to Mrs. Fabian's clothes.

"Thank God!" said Robin, when Potty joined him. Here they halted and the horses drank noisily from the stream, the water of which was quite warm.

Potty Barker looked down into the face of the woman he carried.

"Dead! Fright, I suppose. I thought so when I lifted her, but I couldn't leave her behind."

"Better push on," said Robin, who was anxious about Genevieve and Jessie.

"Yes. We'll keep to the stream, and let the horses make their own pace. There aren't any snags or holes in this part; it's damned rough going, but they are fairly sure-footed."

122

"A good thing the Valley is clear on either side of the stream down here."

"If it wasn't, it would mean a quick good-bye. I've seen bush fires in Australia, but they were different. It's drier and the timber lighter and it travels faster as a rule. But I've never seen anything like this."

As they turned their horses downstream, the baby struggled in Robin's arms, and howled lustily.

Dawn was unveiling the devastation of night when they reached the stone bridge and saw the pathetic group watching for them.

"Here's your little son," and Robin held the screaming child towards his father, but Kelly shook his head. Fabian was delirious, and his mind wandered. He just babbled incoherently as he lay in agony, a rough first-aid splint and a torn sheet bandage being the best Genevieve could do.

"His mother is here, but she is sleeping—fainted," said Barker, and he laid her gently on the bank as close to the stream as he dared, and spread his coat over her.

Two sheep, their wool alight from flying sparks, rushed bleating down the Valley. Kelly picked up a heavy stick and stunned them, and threw them into the stream to

123

drown. It was the only way. Already his hands were badly burnt trying to save some of them by beating out the flaming wool.

Throughout the night of horror one thought persisted: he was responsible if anything should happen to the others; he had asked them to come. Genevieve had protested that she was to blame; the idea had been hers. That they should time their visit to see the burn was Kelly's suggestion. Potty told him to shut up, it didn't matter now.

As the whare caught and burnt fiercely for a few moments, and then collapsed into a few blazing logs and twisted iron, a dull despair overwhelmed him. It followed the passionate fight he had made earlier in the night to stave off disaster and rescue his stock. He seemed cursed by some evil genius that led him into one disaster after another. For a moment he wanted to cry aloud, and to curse everything and everyone. Then he heard Fabian moan. The dead woman lay, an inanimate ridge on the edge of the stream. The crying child was sobbing itself into an exhausted sleep in Jessie's arms. Genevieve, what was she doing? She was bandaging Robin's hands. What had happened? Burnt, of course. And God, how burns could hurt! His mind was getting muddled. He could see them all, this fantastic group in the strange light, sheltering under the bridge, like figures in some weird drama. He was ruined. His Grannie's money was going up in these flames. She had given him his chance, and he had failed again. Something was wrong with him. Even if they got out alive, he could never come back; never live here again, not after this hell of to-night. He had lost his money, and would have to begin again. Begin again—that is if they got out alive.

Would they, too, catch fire from the flying sparks? What would he do—stun them, like the sheep, and let them drown painlessly; a merciful death. His hands were dreadfully painful; his eyes were scorched. Yes, he could not let them burn, he would stun them, Genevieve and Jessie first, and throw them into the stream. And Robin, and Pat—all of them, and then drown himself. Hell! How these burns hurt. He must not let them burn like this. Murder? Was it murder? Surely it was mercy. If they had to go, better to drown than to burn. Oh God! was he going mad? He looked at Genevieve, and she saw the strange, wild look in his eyes. Could he kill her? Murder Genevieve to save her from suffering?

Jessie found some comfort in the contempt-uous confidence of Potty Barker. He kept assuring her they would get out somehow. It might be a few days, and they would be a bit hungry, but it was marvellous how long you could live on hope—and water.

Daylight showed the blackened ruin all around them. The flames, now having swept everything near, had moved further back, but still imprisoned them. Smouldering ash and blazing stumps marked the track of the fire. Potty Barker looked at it in the queer half light and said with emphasis for the second time:

"A fair bloody cow."

Pat, who had known something of danger at sea, had learnt to face sudden peril with the stoicism of a sailor. Once only at sea had he heard the dread alarm of fire raised. It was caused by a bale of oakum igniting. They had had regular fire drill, and the sailors and single men quickly took up their posts. The single men had to bring up their blankets, dip them in water, and throw them over the fire. They did this, and the blankets were all burnt, and they had no others to replace them

126

for the rest of the voyage. But the fire was quickly put out.

Pat turned his mind from that incident of fire, and remembered how, when lying sweating in the Doldrums, they had often cooled themselves by talking about icebergs.

Both Kelly and Robin, being badly burnt, were suffering intense pain. Potty Barker, more hardened, dismissed his small injury and illumined the long silences with an occasional picturesque oath. Pat had escaped burning, but was almost blind with smoke. The hours passed slowly, and he tried to offer distraction with tales of the sea, cooling tales of storms, of icebergs and lashing rain and the great green combers that swept round the Horn. Some were from his own experience; others were from that wealth of narrative spilled into the pool of the fo'c'sle.

Fragments of it caught Genevieve's attention.

"She ran her Easting down . . ."

What was an Easting? She would ask Pat some day. Not now. It didn't matter, really.

Barker, who had some experience at sea, encouraged Pat with questions.

"Yes, one trip we struck ice, on the homeward run round the Horn," Pat replied. "We thought we were clear of icebergs, as the temperature of the sea was between 45 and 50 degrees, so we stopped taking the temperature every evening. About four bells the lookout saw the glare of something in the starboard light. There was a yell, 'Down helm!' and we just slithered alongside, and as we swung up into the wind you could have jumped on to the ice. Some of the bergs were four hundred and five hundred feet high."

"Ever see one topple over?" asked Barker.

"One big one, like a tower. It went with a tremendous splash."

"Were there many?"

"It took us two or three days to get clear. One night, in a dead calm, we could 'hear' the ice."

"Hear it?"

"Yes. When salt water freezes it seems to leave the salt behind, and when it melts you can hear it effervescing like soda-water."

"Was it cold?" asked Genevieve.

"Not specially. We passed one big berg miles long, and the sun was melting it, and you could see the water pouring down it into the sea. And all around were lots of loose bergs, probably calves from the big one that had broken away."

"What about gales?" asked Potty.

"What about them?" asked Pat.

"Ever strike a bad one off the Horn?"

"A couple. One smashed two lifeboats, the poop skylight and rails. The hen-coops, pigs and sheep were washed overboard, and the fastenings off the hatch were loosened and the tarpaulin carried away. One great wave like a mountain of water came aboard, and I thought that was the finish. But it's wonderful what a ship can stand if she's properly handled. We hadn't dry clothes or bunks for a week that time."

"Better to drown than to burn," said Kelly, speaking for the first time. With the words, the mad obsession that he might have to drown them seemed to fade, banished by his voice. It was as though his mind had been babbling wildly, like poor Fabian, and the realization came as a shock.

Silence fell again, until the baby cried.

"I'll take him now," said Kelly.

"You can't, with those hands," and Genevieve gave the child bits of bread soaked in the stream. He spat them out, protesting lustily against his personal discomfort, and the effort to calm him diverted them from their own misery.

When the housemaid knocked on the door of Michael Pencarrow's bedroom in the Club Hotel at Manawatu, her eyes were bolting out of her head with fright. Her hand trembled as she gave him the early cup of tea.

"What's up?" he asked.

"We don't know. Cook says it's the end of the world; the sun's gone dark, and the sky's gone funny, and it chokes you to breathe outside, it's so hot."

After she had gone, Michael went to the window and flung it wide open. The girl was right; the sky had gone funny. Everything looked queer. The air was hot, and hard to breathe. It was dark too. Occasionally the sun glowed evilly like blood, and the lights that appeared in house windows appeared green. People going to work gathered in groups, as though for mutual protection. It was uncanny, especially as there was no known cause for the phenomena.

"I bet Ngarauhoe is in eruption again," said Morgan, who had called early to take Michael out to see his shorthorn herd. Morgan of Manawatu was a noted breeder of prize stock.

Suddenly the pall darkened, and a strange luminous glow appeared first in the west,

130

then in the north. Cyclists lighted their lamps, which looked like green eyes flitting through the murky heat. The few motorists also moved with headlamps like dragon's eyes.

The post office was bombarded with enquiries. They knew nothing. No reply could be got from the north, as the telegraph wires were down, or out of order. Parents who had sons and daughters living inland waited outside the post office and the newspaper office, impatient for news.

Of the three mountains grouped together, Tongariro, Ruaphehu, and Ngarauhoe, the latter alone was an active volcano. Seven, eight and nine thousand feet, their peaks were covered with the eternal snows. From time to time Ngarauhoe livened up, and dense coils of steam and lava and stones were flung out of the white-hot vomit of a sickened mountain. But the snows remained.

Rumours of a terrible disaster began to spread; they flew from town to town. Supposition became certainty, and the casualty list grew every hour. Hundreds were killed. Townships were wiped out; the flow of boiling lava was sweeping this way—or that.

Sensation-mongers had free rein, and gained momentary notoriety.

A few stolid ones went on with their work. Children held hands going to school, and strangers fell into step for company. Many went to church to pray that the disaster might not overwhelm them all. Hysterical ones, men as well as women, their pale faces green in the uncanny gloom, were sure it was the end of the world, and read prophetic signs.

Michael Pencarrow and Morgan did not bother about short-horns that morning. They hung about town, waiting for news.

By noon an authoritative message was posted up. A bush fire at Tapuwai, caught by a sudden and unprecedented hurricane, was sweeping the country, spreading over the ranges, licking up houses and barns, fences and stock.

The word Tapuwai was enough. Kelly! Poor Kelly!

"Morgan, you've got a motor-car. I've a young nephew at Tapuwai, down in the Valley, and four cousins are staying with him. Would you . . . ?"

"Some of Sir Miles's youngsters?" asked Morgan.

"Yes. Will you take a chance with me? I

don't know how far we can get, but I feel we might be able to do something. Oh God! If they've been caught in it!" and his voice dropped in an agony of apprehension.

They bought a couple of axes in case fallen trees barred the road, tossed in bread and cheese, a German sausage, and a bottle of brandy.

"A coil of rope, too; it's always handy," said Morgan.

It was easy going as far as Hunterville, as a shift in the wind had cleared the pall of smoke. It was not a fast car, but it outdistanced the horses, many of which had an instinctive awareness of danger.

As they went north, news began to filter through. Stories of narrow escapes, of horrible injuries, of the ghastly fate of some settlers who had been cut off by the rapid spread of the fire.

Further still, and they began to meet pathetic little groups, suffering from burns, smoke-blind, in intense pain, trying to soothe their terrified children. Those who lived through the Tapuwai fire were not likely to forget its horror.

The wind had dropped a little, but the fire swept on. Michael and Morgan could go no further, so they helped in the transportation of the injured to the nearest hospital, as fast as they were being rescued.

The evening papers were full of the tragedy. Little reliable information had reached them, but by tapping every possible source they had woven the few fragments into a thrilling epic of the bush.

Sir Miles was nearly demented. Three of them, Kelly, Genevieve and Pat, were there, not to mention Robin and Jessie Macdonald.

Kitty came in from the Hutt, and together they awaited news.

"I was always against it, always," said Miles in self-justification. "It is like a judgment of God on my disobedient children."

"Don't, dear, don't. Perhaps it is a judgment of God on us. God often punishes parents through their children; it is the way they suffer most." Norah's tear-stained face reproved him.

Miles was ashamed of the words the moment he had said them. He did not really mean it, but the habit had grown, and in this pathetic uncertainty he found relief in words —words that absolved him from blame.

Kitty sat dry-eyed, her hands pressed hard

together, all the power of her love centred on Robin in a wordless, heartbreaking prayer. God could not take Robin; not Robin. Once when Elizabeth, his baby sister, died, Robin had nearly gone. He had been spared then; he must be safe now. The long-drawn agony of waiting dragged far into the night. Michael had sent a telegram to say that he was doing his best to get news of them, but so far only settlers from the fringe of Tapuwai who had escaped had arrived in hospital. They knew nothing of even their nearest neighbours. Few held out hope of any escaping from the Tapuwai Valley, which was completely swept by the fire.

Doggedly Michael worked on, his heart sick at the sight of so much suffering. The poor smoke-blind, bandaged figures knew only that they were ruined.

Already funds had been started to relieve the settlers. Clothing and household goods were being sent up to a relief depôt. Money was freely given, and the Government was planning the rebuilding of homes, the replacement of stock and equipment, and the supply of grass seed to lay down pasture.

All night the fire raged. Thousands of people crowded the churches praying for rain, for that alone could check the fire, and, soaking the desolated country, make the work of rescue possible.

In the blackened valley of Tapuwai, beside the stone culvert which had saved them, the horror of the night was visible in every face.

Everything had been wiped out. They had little food, and most of them were partially smoke-blind or suffering from burns.

Fabian was delirious, and they could not give his injuries proper treatment. His dead mother still lay on the bank under Barker's coat.

Jessie gave the fretful, hungry baby some bread soaked in water, and now he ate it gladly.

Genevieve had looked in vain for sticks to boil the kettle and make tea, but everything was burnt, so they drank the smoky water.

The sun shone behind the curtain of smoke, and it was terribly hot. There had been little sleep, and most of their clothes were wet from sheltering in the stream under the culvert.

The day dragged on, and they drank at intervals from the stream, and waited— waited for the coming of night, another night.

How long before help could reach them?
How many would survive?

Fabian died about sunset, and they laid him
beside his mother.

"Poor little orphan," said Genevieve, as
she took her turn at nursing the baby. "If we
get out, we will see you through between us,"
she pledged.

"You bet," agreed Potty Barker.

Kelly felt the terrible burden of responsibility. He sat with his head in his hands, but
looked up at Genevieve's promise to the
baby. He did not say anything. His mind was
past the framing of coherent phrases, but he
recognized the implications in Barker's "You
bet." At that moment Leslie Fabian's sphere
of life was for ever changed.

It was after midnight when the rain began,
at first lightly and then in a deluge. They had
no shelter except the culvert. But with the
rain their hopes of rescue began to revive.

Potty Barker speculated on how long it
would take, as they were uncertain how much
country had been burnt. No one knew
whether Hughes and his family, whose house
was on the other side of the Valley, had
escaped.

They snatched a little sleep despite the

rain. Dawn on the second morning revealed the blackened ashes sodden and cold, but smoke still rose in persistent wisps from the tree trunks where the deep-seated fire had defied even that deluge. As the morning advanced the sky cleared and the sun came out. The unquenched fires began to take heart again, and little bursts of flame thrust out defiant tongues. They could do no harm now—just smoulder and burn themselves out.

Under the bright summer sunshine, it was a lamentable scene of desolation. Save for themselves, not a living thing remained. Horses, cattle, sheep, poor terrified creatures, maddened by the fire, they had dashed to destruction in their terror.

By evening hope faded. It was useless to attempt finding their way across the blackened country from which all landmarks had been swept. Barker and Kelly offered to go, but the girls pleaded not to be left. They might so easily go astray, and they were weak from lack of food and in pain.

"Better stick together," said Pat. "If it's possible to get here, someone will surely come."

When the light began to fail a dull despair settled upon them. Pat had long ceased to talk of the sea. Even Potty Barker's language was less violent.

Genevieve had said her rosary a dozen times, praying for help; for mercy.

They found Kelly was more badly burnt than they had imagined. As he could do nothing to help, he had kept silent.

Just when they were giving up hope a faint "Coo-ee" caught their ear. Barker mustered his strength to reply. Someone, knowing the lie of the land, was leading a rescue party into the Tapuwai Valley.

Food, oil, bandages, stimulants.

Jessie broke into hysterical weeping now that the danger was passed.

"Poor little girl," said Potty Barker. "Let her cry. She will be better afterwards. Women are damn' fine, and the way these girls stuck it out—well, I don't mind admitting I never expected to come out alive."

When Kelly heard of the fate of other settlers he was heartbroken.

"You're not to blame, old chap. Fabian and Hughes are exonerated from all blame. This hurricane was an act of God, if there ever was one. No man could have anticipated it. Not once in twenty years has such a gale been experienced here. It was bad luck, that was all."

But no words could lift the weight from his spirits, and his mind went back to the old Maori and his curse.

"The present owners may be ruined, but this is the best day's work that could have happened to Tapuwai," said Carter, who had led the rescue party. "Look at the years of work, felling and clearing the land, that have been saved. And, with this ash, why in five years' time this will be the richest grazing in the King country."

"Do you hear that, Kelly?" Pat said.

"I'm through! Anyone who likes can reap that harvest. I'm through with Tapuwai."

Michael had telegraphed immediately the rescue party brought the young Pencarrows to hospital, and the good news was rapidly spread through the scattered family. Kitty and Norah admitted to each other that they had practically given up hope, and now wept in happy abandon.

Hughes, who had got out on the other side, said no living thing could have survived in the Valley, but, in spite of this, Michael had never surrendered his faith.

140

While they had waited for the return of the rescue party, who were scouring the smouldering country, Michael had confided to Morgan something of his problem about Kelly. In that confidence which great peril often engenders, he had opened his heart to this comparative stranger, and told him of the hurt and the misunderstanding.

Morgan felt a special interest in Kelly on this account, and after a long talk with him he said:

"I wonder if you would like to give Manawatu a try? My boy gets married next month to one of the Crossleys of Halcombe, and the old man has given them a nice place to start. I'll miss him; he was very keen, and a good worker. He practically managed for me. Would you like to give it a try? You can have his room, and you'll find it pretty comfortable with us. Don't make up your mind yet, you look pretty done in. But drop me a line when you feel fit for work again. Your uncle knows my place; he has been buying some of my shorthorns."

The offer was like a tiny chink of blue in the leaden sky of the future. He could not think much yet, but the fact that he was not really to blame for this catastrophe had lifted a load from his mind.

As he lay in a comfortable bed, bathed and bandaged, and fed, his mind drifted back to their marvellous escape. He was proud of Genevieve. They had been very game. And it was Robin who had saved poor Fabian's baby; Robin and Potty. They must look after the youngster now. It had been wonderful to find Michael there waiting for them. He had never seen Michael cry before, but tears ran down his face as he held them in his arms one after the other, and welcomed them back from the dead.

After a night's rest, and having their burns and injuries attended to in hospital, and their poor half-blind eyes treated, they left for Wellington with Michael. Kelly, whose injuries were the most severe, was eager to get home. Home!

The days of suspense had left their mark on Miles. He had learnt to pray with a new humility. Oh God, spare my children and give them back to me!

Norah had said that it might be a judgment of God on them. At first Miles tried to justify to himself his autocratic disposal of his children's future in accordance with his own plans. It was for their good. He knew best, as he was more experienced in the ways of the world. He was trying to spare them the perils and disappointments that must follow their headlong course. But in the long hours of waiting for news, while hope grew faint, he and Norah had drawn closer to each other. If he had not said all that this trial had meant to him, Norah knew instinctively. She could feel the gentler mood, and could hear the humbler note in his supplication as they said their prayers together—prayers for the safety of their three rebellious children.

Norah hoped the change might be permanent, and that Kelly and his father would find a better understanding when they came together again.

"There must be no talk of old troubles, dear," she said. "No recriminations. God has been good and given them back to us, and I hope we will never forget what a terrible experience they have been through. We must be very gentle and loving, and make it up to them."

"You talk as if I, too, have not suffered," Miles began, but checked himself. It was force of habit. He must be more cautious.

"Of course you have suffered; we have all

suffered. You can ease the pains of imagination, but not actual pain and the terror of facing such a death."

Norah was right. Miles was inclined to exaggerate the sufferings of suspense when he talked to the men at the Club. It was a gnawing ache rather than the excruciating torture of fire. Miles accepted her rebuke with a new docility.

To-morrow they were coming home. Michael had telegraphed that they were all much better, and had endured the ordeal with extraordinary courage. Miles had relayed the message on to Hester in the Sounds. Kitty had come in each day, a tragic figure, but calm in her anxiety. Her father was now bedridden, so she returned each evening to the Hutt.

To-morrow that gay quartette they had so recently said good-bye to would return, and with them three others—Kelly, Potty Barker and Fabian's baby.

They must be very gentle and loving, Miles agreed. Pride would be a small sacrifice to offer in reparation. And he meant it. They would begin again, and perhaps out of this trial might come for all of them a more serene happiness. They would try again. After all, they were closely knit, and it should be possible to find a common ground on which to express their affection and ideals. The tragedy had shown them more clearly in what relation they stood to each other. Unspoken pledges, like unshed tears, are no less potent because they are hidden deep in the heart.

The home on the Terrace had never looked so attractive as when seen in memory through the rush of flames. And to-morrow they would be home. Rain—rain which they had so often cursed when it postponed their pleasures, had finally saved them. You never know your best friends, Genevieve thought, as this idea occurred to her.

Kelly and Michael sat together on the journey down, and, though Duffield was never mentioned, the breach between them had healed. Only Gentry kept them apart. They could walk together again in perfect confidence, and a flood of gratitude warmed Michael's heart when Kelly said:

"I was thinking of you that night; I wanted you to know I was grateful, and I was afraid you'd never know."

Kelly found himself on the dangerous brink of sentiment and quickly escaped to other things. But afterwards he was glad he had said it.

It was after ten, and a glowing sunset had left its memory in the sky caught up by the scattered stars, when the slow train rumbled into Wellington. No one spoke as they came out of the last tunnel and saw the harbour with its rippling ribbons of light at their feet. But Genevieve turned with a gush of tears and touched Robin's hand as though to make sure she was not dreaming.

Potty Barker lifted the sleeping child from Jessie's arms.

"One good thing, there's no luggage," he said, and they all laughed. It was queer, nervous laughter, but it broke the strain.

7

WHEN Potty Barker was offered the choice of a job at Duffield, or one down the Sounds, Jessie was the determining factor. He accepted Macdonald's offer, and Michael was glad. The whole family felt that something ought to be done for Barker, and Michael said he would take him at Duffield. All the same, he did not want him. He was conscious of a curious disloyalty in giving place to Barker, while Kelly went to a stranger.

Michael also realized that, temperamentally, Potty Barker and Philip Gentry would be a source of friction. Potty knew nothing of the position, unless Kelly had told him in a mood of confidence, which was most unlikely. Potty would blunder in on dangerous ground, for he had a profound affection for Kelly; so his decision to go to the Sounds was a great relief to Michael.

Jessie's account of their experience had wakened in her parents a desire to express their gratitude to Barker in a practical way, and here it was.

Kelly took longest to recover, but his father's obvious effort to forget the past and make things easier in the future removed the mental strain that had, in recent years, made their intercourse dangerously explosive.

With the resilience of youth, a few months had almost obliterated the memory of those nights of terror. Miles undertook to dispose of Kelly's interest at Tapuwai, and after the first flush of tragedy had passed wise men echoed the words of Carter, who had led the rescue party. In a year or two Tapuwai would be doubly valuable, so Miles nursed the transaction and Kelly recovered a good deal of the money he had put into the property.

Meanwhile he had gone to Morgan's in Manawatu. It was late in February when he arrived at the farmhouse—a square, brown, wooden house which had lost its original design in the additions that a growing family demanded and increasing prosperity made possible. Morgan believed in quality stock, and his name was high on the prize lists at agricultural shows. This pride in what he bred appealed to Kelly. It was on these lines he had urged Michael to run Duffield. Something of his old enthusiasm returned, and Morgan enjoyed the flash of pride in Kelly's face when something bred on the farm won a high place in show or market.

Kelly worked with the other men and Morgan's younger son, a lad of seventeen. Morgan took off his coat and did a day's work with the rest of them, but with the difference of superior knowledge. He could give them a lead in most things, and the fact that the Boss could and would take his turn at the hardest task was an incentive. Much of his time, however, was spent in the oversight of his many interests.

They had finished shearing when Kelly arrived. The first day he harnessed up and harrowed the home paddock. They started draughting the stud ewes after that, and then dipping. The stud ewes and rams were disposed of first, then came the crossbreds.

It was a dry February, but heavy rain brought on the grass. The rain filled the ditches, and they overflowed, so he spent the next week clearing them out. March came in windy, and Kelly spent St. David's Day sowing oats for green feed where the crop of turnips had been. Mid-March was occupied in repairing fences. After Easter much of his time was taken up carting metal from the river-bed. Load after load he shovelled into the dray, and then tipped it on to the drive and the paths, and round the water-troughs, and spread it evenly. On wet days he oiled the harness.

As the weather grew colder, the milking became less strenuous as the cows went out, but harrowing and crutching, top-dressing, and special attention to the stud stock kept them busy.

On June the twenty-first, as the rain came down in sheets, Kelly mended cow covers, and reflected that the long days would be returning. Having passed the shortest day, they began looking forward to lambing.

They stand on their raggety legs and bleat,
The new young lambs, the little new sheep.

Then shearing would come round again, and the full flood of milking, when the long summer days would be packed full of work.

Kelly had regained some of his old good humour. Morgan, with Michael's confidence to guide him, understood something of Kelly's turbulent moods. He did not press the boy unduly, but endeavoured to make him join easily in the family's social life. At first Kelly kept to himself, but Morgan made a point of joining him at his work, and talking over it as with an equal, and Kelly's interest immediately caught fire and he responded. He brought a keener intelligence to bear on his work, and was the only companionable person whom Morgan had to confide in, and with whom he could talk things over. The others were good workmen, but rough. It was partly due to Kelly's keenness and eager suggestions and scientific curiosity that they fell into this companionable way. Morgan, too, realized that if New Zealand was to take her place in the front rank she must apply scientific methods to agriculture, and he was ready to listen, and eager to learn, and gave his staunch support to every proposal for raising farming from the muck and mud of pioneering days and improving the breed of stock. Unlike many duller men, he did not protest and combat every Governmental effort to bring this about. In this attitude he found Kelly's sharp young mind akin to his own.

Morgan was not Michael—not by any means; but he provided Kelly with the elements of reinstating himself, and afforded a measure of opportunity.

Morgan was a tall, dark man with a greying beard which he kept neatly trimmed. An educated man, but simple in his tastes, he was much ahead of his wife. She was a kindly, capable woman, the daughter of a neighbouring farmer, who had never progressed beyond the limits of her rural environment. Her jam, her garden, her preserves, her family were the centre of her life, and now, fat and complacent, she had no ambition to go outside that limited sphere. Morgan, as president of the Breeders' Association, chairman of the County Council, and an important figure in agricultural matters, made friends with other breeders and farmers, many of whom lived in greater luxury, and whose families figured in some social prominence. Mrs. Morgan avoided them, except if by chance they accompanied the husband on a visit to view some stock. In her own home she was the soul of hospitality—an easy, unconscious hospitality that embraced everyone with small distinction. But when Morgan was invited to pay a return visit he went alone.

One of Kelly's greatest joys at this period was Michael's weekly letter. There had been no communication between them during his life at Tapuwai. But now they had resumed the old intimate interchange of ideas. Kelly had much to write about. He told of his work, of the progress of show sheep and cattle, of experiments they were making, of tests and improvements. Michael made Duffield real again before his eyes. He wrote of the trees Kelly had planted and how they had grown; of new buildings he had put up, of ideas Kelly had suggested long ago that he was now carrying out. He never mentioned Gentry.

Under these new and more pleasant conditions Kelly recovered some of his old cheerfulness. He whistled as he drove his team, and the young draught horse he broke in was the first to bend his will under the legacy of Potty Barker's picturesque oaths. And when Genevieve wrote in the midst of one of Wellington's howling southerlies that it was "a cow of a day", Kelly remembered with affection that lanky frame with its lazy grace and steely strength, and the cool way he took everything that came. He must get Potty to come over when he went to Wellington. A couple of beers with Potty was unique entertainment.

Pat had completed his necessary sea service, and obtained his second mate's certificate before the Examiner of Mates and Masters in Wellington. His parents were eager to see him more frequently than was possible when his ship was trading between New Zealand and London, so he joined the Union Steamship Company as fourth officer on the *Rotomahana*, and sailed under the golden greyhound between Lyttleton and Wellington. It had always been his ambition to serve in her, for she was the loveliest ship afloat and the greyhound of the Pacific. On this ferry service he would have plenty of time at home. No one appreciated the change more than Genevieve. She and Paddy Doyle had found much in common in later years. When Pat was on his nightly trip, there was, of course, Robin, who still lived with them.

The future of Fabian's baby had been temporarily decided. Kelly and Genevieve agreed that it would not be fair to disrupt the family by thrusting a strange infant into their midst.

"They've had their share of squalling brats with us," said Genevieve.

It was Sister Mary Agnes who solved this little problem for them. Why not let her have the baby and bring him up in the orphanage controlled by the nuns, where he would have the company of other children of his own age and every care? Later, the family could provide for him and send him to school.

So Leslie Fabian joined a group of other babies; but, unlike them, he had good friends. Every birthday and Christmas was remembered, not only with toys, but at Genevieve's suggestion they kept a money-box for the baby and dropped in odd coins which were banked for him.

Kelly, who liked a bet at the races, put a little of his winnings away for the baby whenever he had luck, which, however, was not often. But his contributions were not dependent upon racing. The proceeds of one pet lamb each year were also added, and in most cases, where the family shared some unexpected good fortune, a portion was put to the baby's credit.

After its tragic opening, the year softened to a happy close, and as the scars left by the fire faded so the memory of its horror grew dim. Miles, accustomed to the revolt of Kelly and Pat, felt that he was due for a period of peace at home, and relaxed somewhat into his autocratic mood. But his reconciliation with

Kelly was complete. That battle was fought and won, and both bore their wounds. Norah, too, had settled back into a serenity she had not known for years. But it was not to last.

8

ON a Sunday morning early in December, Genevieve stood buttoning her gloves and looking out over the harbour. She had been to church and, with a long summer day before her, felt the radiance that anticipation can throw over a familiar scene. Rain the previous day had laid the dust. Though the sun was bright, a few woolpacks hugged the hilltops, but the air had the crisp, clean taste of spring.

Genevieve wore a long skirt of cream serge with a device in silk braid above the deep hem, a white linen blouse with a starched collar, and a large white hat set with wired bows of white silk. This was pinned to her head with several silver hatpins. She wore, too, a motor veil, two curtains of chiffon on an elastic band which circled the crown of her hat, and were drawn taut down either side of her head and tied beneath her chin.

She stooped and slipped an elastic loop over each foot, and fastened the strap attached to the inside of her skirt with a safety-pin. This was essential when cycling in the wind, for skirts flapped dangerously on either side of the wheel, beside exhibiting much more leg than was then deemed morally safe. The cord of the skirt-guard on her bicycle was new, or she would not have risked her cream skirt. Only the week before a blue serge had been mangled and chewed by the cogs of the bicycle chain where the guard had broken.

Her large hat, like a ship in full sail with its wired silk bows, always inspired Pat to a sea chanty. But it was at the moment a most fashionable creation. And her skirt had been made specially with an inverted pleat at the back, so that each side might fall modestly and completely hide the saddle.

Miles, sitting in an armchair on the balcony, was reading the supplement from Saturday's paper.

"Where are you going?" he asked suddenly, as she caught his eye.

"Out to the Hutt to see Grandfather."

"How?"

"We're biking."

"We! Who are we?" he asked irritably.

"Robin and I."

Miles read a line or two, but his mind was not with the words.

"Good-bye, Father," and Genevieve, satisfied that everything was in perfect order, turned to go.

"You are not to go," said Miles firmly. "I forbid you."

"Not to go? Why?" she asked in amazement.

"That's why!"

"But . . . that's no reason."

"It is enough," and Miles resumed his paper.

"Why can't I go? Why do you object today; you never have before, and I've often cycled out there on Sundays?"

Miles made no reply, but he heard what she had said.

"Why can't I go, Father?" Genevieve persisted.

This objection had come out of a clear blue sky, and left her completely bewildered. But she was determined to know the reason for it, if there was a reason. Perhaps it was just a whim, but she would not be put off. She could see her father was getting angry, so she took great care to be extremely polite—polite but firm.

159

"I have asked you a simple question, very courteously, Father, and you have not answered me."

"Answered you! Answered you! Why should I answer you?" he blurted and blustered.

"It is customary." Genevieve's voice had the maddening quiet of complete composure.

Miles snapped the paper and moved his chair.

"Why do you object to my going to the Hutt to-day? Is it because it's Sunday? Or do you object to me cycling? Or do you wish me to do something special at home for you? Or perhaps you don't approve of my clothes. Or do you object to me going with Robin—"

"Stop! I say you're not to go, and that is enough. Am I to give you reasons for everything I do?" he asked in a challenging tone.

"It would be . . . wiser. If there is some reason why I shouldn't go, tell me. I'm not an idiot."

Miles sprang up, the crumpled paper clutched in his hand. Standing, he had the advantage of height. But Genevieve, with the calm assurance that she was right, did not yield an inch.

"Go to your room. I'll have no more of

your impertinence. I'll have obedience while you live under my roof . . . I'll—"

"What's this, what's this?" Norah came out to smooth things over hearing her husband's angry voice.

"Father objects to me going to the Hutt today, but he won't tell me why, and I want to know; I have a right to know."

Norah made "hushing faces" at her daughter, and looked apprehensively at Miles.

"I think you'd better not go to-day, dear. It will be very hot riding all that way. And it might rain, and you would get your skirt ruined with mud."

Her appeal to feminine vanity fell flat.

"That is not the reason; there is something else."

"Reason or no reason, you'll stop at home," and Miles, grateful for his wife's support, sat down and resumed his paper as though the matter were settled. Norah, eager to shirk an unpleasant task, hurried off to talk to the cook about puddings.

Genevieve paused in the hall, uncertain. All the glory of the summer day had been swept away, and her mood of happy anticipation was clouded. She heard the clang of a bicycle bell. Robin was waiting at the front door, where he had propped the two machines while he pumped up the tyres.

"What's the matter?" he asked as Genevieve came out, her face set and stubborn.

"Father says I am not to go."

"But why?"

"That's just it. He won't tell me. He just roars and says, 'That's why!'"

"It's such a wonderful day, too," said Robin regretfully, looking up at the blue sky. "And the faintest wind, just enough to help us up the valley."

"I know. I thought it was going to be heavenly, and now it's all . . . curdled."

"Well, I won't go either."

"Oh yes you will, and, what is more, I'm going with you."

"But—"

"I know—a row." She paused. "Perhaps it will induce Father to treat me like an intelligent person. It's not as if I am a child and couldn't understand. But for the life of me I don't know what it's all about. We have gone so often since we had bicycles, and on Sunday, too."

Robin disliked crossing his uncle and causing trouble.

"Perhaps if I asked him—"

"For goodness sake leave him alone now. He is in one of those humours when, right or wrong, he would die rather than give in. Let's get away before they call us back."

Robin's eyes brightened with a curious smile of admiration. Genevieve was like her father in so many ways, but more logical. Miles expected to have his dicta accepted without question. Genevieve wanted chapter and verse, and he hated to be nailed down to a statement and made to justify an opinion or prove a theory.

They tried to recapture their usual happy-go-lucky humour, but the discordant note echoed far down the day.

When the family sat down to Sunday dinner at one o'clock Miles had recovered his composure. He took the cover off the roast of beef, and Ellen brought in the dishes of peas and french beans and baked potatoes. Miles lifted the carving-knife and gave it a couple of slashing cuts on the steel to sharpen the edge. Norah moved the vase of roses further from the joint to give him plenty of room to carve.

Remembering the omission, Miles put down the carving-knife and fork:

"Bless us, O Lord, and these Thy gifts which we are about to receive—Where's

Genevieve," he demanded suddenly, breaking off in the middle of Grace.

"She and Robin went out to Grandfather's," said Meggie.

Now dinner was going to be spoilt, thought Norah, and it was such a tender roast.

"But she can't. I forbade her to go," thundered Miles.

"She did. I saw them free-wheeling down the hill."

"Do you permit your daughter to defy me like this?"

They were always Norah's children when they were disobedient.

"Well, dear, if you couldn't stop her, how could I? I didn't know she had gone. I thought she was in her room."

Norah was smitten by a sense of injustice in having the blame pushed on to her, but long years had taught her the folly of demanding that reasonable conduct from Miles which Genevieve insisted upon. Of course, she was to blame in a way over this episode, but she had only done what she thought best. She felt that Miles ought to be consulted and know how things stood.

Silence fell while Miles cut the lovely rich brown roast of beef into rags and tatters and slapped it on to the plates. To-day he took no delight in his carving.

"Pass the peas, please."

"Pass the potatoes."

"Where's the gravy, Mother?"

"Who has got the mustard?"

Subdued voices repeated the accustomed phrases.

Suddenly Miles snatched the table-napkin from his knee and flung it on the table, and, pushing his plate from him, got up.

"It's intolerable," he said.

"Miles, dear, have your dinner."

"I don't want any dinner. I can't eat. It would choke me."

"It's such a tender roast, and you specially asked for beef to-day."

"I asked for beef? I ask for obedience, that is what I ask for—obedience and respect in my own house. To be flaunted and defied by a chit of a girl! I'll see who is master here. I'll . . . I'll . . ."

The door banged.

"Ellen! Ellen, take your master's dinner into his study and a glass of beer. It's very hot and he has a headache. Leave the tray there, even if he tells you to take it away. He may eat a bit when he is alone and it's quiet."

165

And he did, quite a big bit. But even the bottle of beer did not wash away the taste of his anger and the bitterness of this defeat. He knew that he had been wrong to take up that attitude with Genevieve; but, damn it, what else could he do?

Norah hoped he might sleep, as he often did after Sunday dinner. It was cool in the study, and he had a long horsehair couch to lie upon.

At tea-time she tapped gently and went in, taking with her the tray with tea for two of them. Better to get it over without the children. In any case, you couldn't discuss it in front of them.

"Perhaps I was wrong in mentioning it at all," said Norah.

"You were quite right. I would have noticed it myself, only my mind is occupied with other things. But now I see it plainly, and it's got to be stopped. Cousins! It's disgraceful. I wonder Genevieve hasn't more sense, a girl of her age. And demanding—yes, demanding—to know why I object to her going off with him for the whole day."

"I think we ought to tell Kitty. I wonder if she has noticed anything. Mind you, it's only since the fire. They were just like brother and

166

sister before. But when I saw Robin put his arms round her and kiss her, and saw their faces—"

"Stop! It's disgusting. I don't want to hear it all over again. But it's got to be ended here and now," and Miles thumped the table and spilt the milk.

Norah sighed and mopped it up. The tea-cloth would have to be washed, and that crochet frill was so difficult to iron nicely.

"What can we do about it?"

"Robin had better go back to his mother. It's not too far to the Hutt, and there is a good train service now. He can make the change at Christmas, and that's only a couple of weeks off. And when the winter comes—well, we will see."

"Yes, I suppose that's best," Norah agreed, but she was sorry to lose Robin. "We can't forbid them to see each other. It might start a scandal, and we don't want any talk. It's not as if anything really had happened—"

"It's quite enough. God knows how far it has gone. But I'll have no more defiance here."

"Don't you think it might be as well if you spoke to Robin and warned him about—

about—well, tell him that cousins can't marry? It isn't nice."

"I hope you will make your daughter understand and put an end to this very unwholesome state of affairs," he countered.

"Yes, I'll have a talk to her; I suppose I'd better"; but Norah, with the peculiar reticence of the mothers of her period, did not relish a conversation with this very frank daughter on a rather delicate subject. She was afraid Genevieve would make it terribly embarrassing, and bombard her with that inevitable Why? Why? which so maddened Miles. She was also aware that a little opposition was an amazing stimulus to people like Genevieve. Dragging the subject into the open might give it just that impetus they dreaded, and make it a subject for public comment.

"Have you heard, Genevieve Pencarrow and her cousin Robin? . . . Always together . . . the family are terribly upset . . . and Mrs. Herrick is so ambitious for Robin . . . wants him to marry an English girl, I believe . . . No, I don't know how far it's gone yet, but . . . her father is furious about it . . ."

In imagination Norah could hear it all.

It was a long ride to the Hutt, but despite the hampering effect of her long skirt and large hat, Genevieve managed it without fatigue. She was a strongly built and extremely healthy young woman. Tall, the youthful curves of her figure were softly defined under the close-fitting garments which followed the contours of her corseted body.

When they arrived at the Hutt, after several halts by the way, they were just in time for dinner.

"How is your father?" Kitty asked as she kissed Genevieve.

"Scotty!"

Kitty's face assumed a becoming expression, slightly shocked.

"You mean he is a little irritable. Dyspepsia is very trying."

"It's not dyspepsia, Aunt Kitty; it's temper that upsets him."

"But surely you must know, dear, that it is digestive trouble that makes him short-tempered? What was the trouble to-day?"

Kitty understood, but she realized that parents must stand in together if discipline was to be maintained. Still, her eyes looking lovingly at Robin; she had no reason to complain. What she wanted seemed to be just what he desired. This mutual agreement had spared her so much anxiety. So far she had not tried to mould him against his will, nor impose harsh restrictions upon him. She could afford to be indulgent.

"What was the trouble to-day: simply that I was coming out here."

"But why?"

"That's what I asked, and he wouldn't tell me. It's just a sudden fad."

"He let you come in the end, though," said Kitty, still in defence of parental authority.

"Indeed he did not. I just came. Oh yes there will be a gorgeous row when I get home, but if you let a row deter you in our house you would never do anything."

"That is not quite fair," Kitty protested.

Genevieve laughed. "Perhaps it's a wee bit exaggerated. All I want is to be treated as an adult person of reasonable intelligence. If Father said, 'I don't want you to go to the Hutt to-day, because I need you at home'; or 'I object to Sunday cycling, or to big hats or white blouses', or whatever he does object to, I would know where I was."

"He couldn't have stated it better himself," said Robin, and gave her a pat on the back. "You're a regular bush lawyer."

They talked to their grandfather for a few minutes and then dinner was served.

"You never forget me, Genevieve," the old man said as he held her hand in his twisted fingers. "Now be off to your dinner; you must be starving after that long ride."

Afterwards they sat under the weeping ash in a corner of Grannie's garden. It was still Grannie's garden, for her spirit seemed to linger among the flowers she had loved, and they always spoke of them as Grannie's roses.

Genevieve sat on a low garden chair, her hands locked behind her head, her golden-brown hair catching the flickering lights that fell like spangles through the gently rustling leaves.

Robin lay full length on the grass, his head resting on his arms, his face turned towards Genevieve. Kitty was with her father. After dinner he had seemed restless and in pain.

The drowsy hum of bees as they buzzed among the flowers, the gentle murmur of leaves swayed by an erratic breeze, the golden warmth of the December sun, nearing mid-summer heat, washed over them like a sensuous tide.

Genevieve had drawn from the morning's encounter with her father a curious defensive strength. As she sat with eyes closed, her mind leapt from peak to peak of wildest enterprise. The future rose like a mountain range to be scaled, an entrancing vision of sunny valleys and glittering summits, beckoning her, luring her, daring her. She felt she had the mental alertness and the physical strength to do more than potter about at home, indulging in the ladylike occupations of Mount Mellick and macramé work; of covering puttied drain-pipes with bits of broken china; of taking tea in the drawing-rooms of her mother's friends; checking the laundry or watering the maidenhair fern in the wire stand in the hall. The maidenhair had replaced the green parrot.

She liked to pit her wits against her father; against anyone who would give battle. She liked to take his statements and pick them to pieces and look at them inside out, phrase by phrase. His rhetoric, family brand, did not stand such close analysis, and this attack on his infallibility in the domestic sphere annoyed him. Genevieve wondered what a girl could do with her life, apart from the accepted occupations of domesticity. She had felt depressed at first. After the scene with her father resentment clouded everything.

But the exertion of cycling out to the Hutt, with its attendant weariness, then dinner, and now the luxurious restfulness of the summer day had restored the balance and given stimulus to her mind. She no longer felt rebellious. Her tired muscles relaxed, and with this sense of relaxation came a surge of new vigour. An abounding vitality pulsed through her and fired her imagination. As her vivid fancy chased sudden hopes and prospects, the magic of their inspiration played upon her face, which responded to every motion. Like one who draws the blind but leaves the door ajar, Genevieve's face revealed to Robin, lying lazily at her feet, the seething press of ideas that tumbled about behind the closed eyes. Some were too fantastic even to find words to clothe them, but, like a secret indulgence, she dallied with them awhile before tossing them away.

"What's it all about?" asked Robin.

He touched her face with a blade of grass, and she opened her eyes.

"What's what?"

"That sounds like your father," he said. "What were you thinking about? I'm jealous you didn't share it with me."

"Everything: life, the future, and what a

girl can do beside watering the maidenhair fern."

"Swollen with ambition?" he said.

"Swollen fit to bust, if you want to know."

"I do; tell me."

"It's easy to have it in your head, and so hard to put it into words. It's like watching the clouds up there, bits floating about, twisting and turning, making first one shape and then another; a fish suddenly becomes an elephant, and ships take wings and fly like geese."

"Nebulous," Robin prompted her.

"Yes, nebulous; but don't interrupt me, even if you've got the right word."

"All right. Go ahead," and he laughed.

"If you laugh I shan't tell you. I'm serious."

"So am I"; he caught her hand, and she slid from her chair on to the grass beside him.

"Boys get a chance to try what they can do. I was just thinking, you've got your life all clearly mapped out. You want to be a lawyer, and everyone agrees, and you sail through your exams . . ."

"Not too much sail," he protested.

"I know you worked hard, but you wanted to. It's the work you've set your heart on, and from now till you are an old man like Grandfather, I suppose, you will be a brilliant and successful lawyer."

"I like your flattering picture. But go on."

"Pat wants to be a sailor, and runs away to sea. Kelly is determined to be a farmer, and the devil himself won't stop him. Mary wants to be a nun, and she battles down Father's opposition by sheer weight of obedience, and gets her way. But look at me! I don't want to be a nun, and tinkering about the house seems so futile. Yet what can I do?"

"What do you want to do?" An apprehensive note throbbed in his voice.

"That's just it. I don't know. But I want to tackle a job with both hands; something that makes you stretch yourself," and she illustrated the thought with a gesture of striving, and her hand reached and caught a bough overhead.

"Must you do something . . . different?" Robin asked. "Can't you just be content being . . . Genevieve; our Genevieve—my Genevieve?" His voice dropped to a whisper.

They sat with fingers interlaced, and Genevieve felt again the blood pounding in her temples and her heart thumping an exciting rhythm.

175

Both were conscious of the new emotion that drew them apart from the others. At one time, though inseparable companions, they could share openly all that budded and blossomed in their hearts. They had passed beyond that now, and each was aware of it and a little fearful.

"You don't want to go away?" Robin said at last. "I can't imagine what it would be like without you."

"I don't know what I want, but I feel it can't go on much longer. If I had something to do, some outside work to fasten my mind to, I think it would be easier at home. When Father comes in tired out, I'm all bottled up. Oh God, how I wish I had been a man!" she finished passionately.

"I hate to hear you say that."

Robin snapped a twig between his fingers and threw the bits over his shoulder in a gesture of impatience.

"It's only because you get a wider chance. If I could get out and do something—something really useful, or important, I would much rather be a woman."

"I see. Just running a home and managing a husband and a family don't seem important."

"They do. But I haven't got them. I'm just an upper servant with too much time on my hands. That is Mother's job, and I think she does it marvellously. The way she smoothes things over. Can you imagine the house if she weren't there? I can't. It would be Bedlam."

"I don't quite follow you." Robin was still puzzled. "Why can't you be content . . . a little longer?"

A wild urge to claim her, to defy them all, pressed hard. He had no illusions about what such a declaration would mean. All previous family disasters would pale before it. This would not only be in direct opposition to all his mother's hopes for him, and the family's general attitude, but a breach of the code. Almost indecent.

Robin knew his mother harboured great ambitions for his personal and social advancement. Subordinated to the necessities of her own marriage, they were now reviving, intensified for him. The house in Hobson Street had been tentatively mentioned, and to please her he had shared her enthusiasm at the prospect. Some day!

"Some day, of course, you will marry, dear," Kitty had said, "but not for a long time yet, I hope. It handicaps a young man.

And his choice at twenty-two is not as wise as later on. A foolish marriage can do more than anything to wreck a man's career. And I want to have you to myself for a little while, a few years; we have been so much apart, and you are all I have. But I will never stand in your way of a good marriage—a happy marriage. Still, that is a long way off."

"Don't be afraid, Mother; I'm in no hurry to marry."

That was before Tapuwai.

At the moment Robin was content to keep secret in his heart the love he had for his cousin Genevieve. He must be sure of his place in life before he faced the storm. Miles would fling him out of the office and leave him to fend for himself, that was certain. His mother, who had made so many sacrifices for him that he might have his chance, would be so distressed; he could imagine the bitterness of her disappointment. Could he bear to inflict that hurt? She had such high hopes for him; they were the very pivot of her life. Later, perhaps, but not now. He dare not precipitate such a disaster by a premature word. Yet he was afraid to lose Genevieve. If this driving restlessness and curbed ambition could not find some outlet, and the friction at home continued, Genevieve might commit some irreparable folly. Marry to escape? No, not that. But she might become involved in some occupation that, beginning as a part-time interest, might eventually absorb her entirely. Women were like that. Men could keep their business and emotional lives in separate compartments, each ruling in its proper sphere. But women were more single-minded. They could not so readily divide their interests. Training through the centuries had accomplished much for man. Woman had not yet achieved this regulation of her affections, though its coming was already heralded, and her adaptability was soon to be tried.

Genevieve, too, was aware of this changed relationship and its implications. Though the sweets of shy first love, and a quick, stolen kiss were the measure of it, the future left her troubled. She was not sure, despite her wild imaginings, how full might be her portion as Robin's wife.

Unlike many young lovers, who meet and build a top-heavy structure of passion without any base to sustain it, Robin and Genevieve had the solid foundation of years spent under one roof in the intimacy of family life.

The close friendship, the shared secrets, the lash and wound of adolescent tongues, and the sweets of reconciliation had made known, each to the other, how much of strength and weakness they could count upon. Brief flashes had revealed those dark corners where even the rankest natures hide a spark that, controlled, may illumine, but liberated will destroy. Now that sane commonplace of rooted friendship was laced with faery gold. As the wisps of cloud melted and disappeared, so vanished their troubled thoughts before love on a summer day.

Take the flower, and turn the hour, and kiss your love again.

They were startled from their happy dreaming by Kitty's voice calling urgently from the verandah. It had a wild, tragic note. "Robin! Robin! Come quickly."

Matthew Pencarrow was dead.

9

ROBIN stayed with his mother, and a neighbour drove Genevieve hurriedly to town. Kitty was anxious for Miles to come out.

Genevieve walked into her father's study, the morning's scene completely forgotten in this sudden tragedy.

"Father . . ." she began, but his angry voice broke in.

"Go to your room. I'll speak to you later. How dare you disobey me?"

She raised her hand in a protesting gesture, as though to wave aside a futile quarrel.

"Grandfather is dead," she said gently.

"What!"

"It was quite sudden, this afternoon. His heart, the doctor said."

"My God! This is terrible!"

"We sat with him for a while before dinner, and he was in pain then, but he seemed glad to see us. 'You never forget me, Genevieve,' he said. I didn't see him again."

"Quick, call your mother. We must go out at once."

Matthew Pencarrow had been conquered in spirit by physical pain. For years his movements had been hampered and his big frame twisted and cramped by rheumatism. Long after he had surrendered his authority, Bessie's indomitable spirit had held sway. Matthew had lost touch; even the home farm, now capably managed by an experienced farmer, had ceased to interest him greatly.

Kitty—the gay Kitty Pencarrow—the delight of his eyes, who had been more concerned with putting frills and flounces on her gown than rearing chickens—she had been his greatest comfort in these last sad years. She would sit and read to him, and hold the knotted old hand in hers, and turn the pillow and bring what fleeting joy was possible into his declining days. She alone had been with him when the last seizure had caught him up in a crushing embrace. Her arms were round him, her kiss was on his forehead. All the love and gratitude of a stricken old man for his best-loved child were in the eyes that closed for ever.

With the passing of Matthew Pencarrow an epoch ended. He had outlived many of his contemporaries, and the younger generation had taken control of the land which he and his kind had won for civilization.

The Pencarrows gathered for the funeral, and afterwards Miles read the will, which, as previously arranged, made special provision for Kitty. But they all would share to some extent in the ultimate disposal of the estate.

Matthew, who had made his will some years before, while his interest was still keen, expressed the wish that the home farm at the Hutt might remain in the family, and he left it to Michael and Miles, whom he appointed trustees, to make what arrangement they deemed wisest when the time should come.

To part with the old place was unthinkable. That Grannie's garden should fall into a stranger's hands was almost sacrilege.

It was a very hot day in mid-December, and the garden was a riot of blossoms.

Kelly had arrived the night before, and with Robin had stayed at the Hutt. In the evening they walked up and down the garden, smoking and breaking the friendly silence with an occasional remark.

The mignonette sent up a rich, sweet fragrance.

"Do you remember how we used to gather the soft sand from the side of the road in little paper bags for Grannie's mignonette?" Kelly asked, as he stooped and plucked a piece.

Robin remembered.

The magnolias were large trees now, and on a summer evening, after rain, when each great ivory chalice was drenched, the evening air drew an intoxicating perfume that was as heady as wine. The bed of pink and purple stocks and the roses were in full bloom. In a swampy backwater that flanked the main garden Kitty had cleared a pool, and all around it, in their season, grew masses of white arum lilies and blue and yellow iris.

Memories of their childhood, of adventurous days, of Grannie, came thronging back as they paced the garden.

Death pulls up with a jerk the reckless pace of youth. Matthew had been young once, like themselves, but they remembered him only as a twisted old man with creaking joints.

"Grannie stayed the course the better of the two," said Kelly reminiscently. "She was a gallant soul."

"It shows how hard it is to guess the future." Robin, too, was thinking of the past. "Grandfather cracked up quickly as soon as he had to give up work. His authority and power were physical. Without them he fell back. I believe if Grannie had been struck blind and dumb she would still have bossed the show."

"She would," Kelly agreed.

A wave of longing to be back among it all swept over him. He had been a wanderer for years, outside the family sphere. But on this summer night in the garden, with sweet and poignant memories of their childhood spent here, of the touch of tragedies enacted, of the hurts and solace that had come to the souls that had lived within its walls, something of the claim of blood asserted itself. Kelly wondered what his grandfather had done about the old place. To-morrow, after the funeral, they would know.

A few faint stars peopled the dark blue sky, like lonely settlers in a far-off land. The night was heavy with the scent of flowers. It was all so quiet and peaceful. A new longing tugged at his heart; a new urge to take up the thread where it had broken, to carry on the story, to pass it on in turn to younger hands. As they paced the garden in the long silences, Kelly Pencarrow resolved to come home.

When Miles had finished reading the will,

and the expressed wish that this land on which they stood, this soil from which the family sprang, should not pass to strangers, a hush fell on the group.

Miles already knew the contents of the will, as he had drawn it. It was no surprise to him, nor to Michael. Looks were exchanged, but no word was spoken. Who was to carry on the Home Farm? Would Michael come back, and leave Gentry on Duffield? Impossible! Would Gentry take over this property, which was so much nearer town, and so should appeal to him and to Ella also? And would Kelly, once Gentry had left, go back to Duffield with Michael? Would the wheel turn full circle, and the little balls drop into the appointed groove, as ordained by fate?

Kelly previously had refused to work for his grandfather on the Hutt property. It was, he said, already so highly improved that it was a matter of running it under his grandfather's supervision. It lacked scope for his enterprise, and Matthew had passed the stage when he would encourage or sanction experiments. But now he had gone. The place stood tenantless. He saw it in the bright light of this summer day as a thing desirable. Now he had more experience, but no less enthusiasm; his recklessness had been tempered. If he could get a block of hill country, perhaps across the range, or over the Moonshine Valley, and work them in together! To live here, in this hospitable old house with its wide doors and gateway; to enlarge and perfect Grannie's garden; to carry to completion the things she had planned and he had dreamt of; to . . .

"Father, I would like to lease the Home Farm, and buy it later when I can . . ."

Quick, impulsive, Kelly had come back as surprisingly as he had gone away. Before Michael or Gentry or anyone else had time to think or decide, Kelly had claimed his privilege. And he knew that Grannie would be glad that it was he, who understood and shared so closely those secret delights of a garden, who was to be heir to the work of her hand.

"I'm glad, my boy. I'm glad you will carry on the old place. I'm sure it is what they would have wished—your Grannie—" Miles stopped abruptly and blew his nose.

Michael put a hand on his shoulder in the old affectionate way.

"Couldn't be better," was all he said. But to Kelly it conveyed much. It was Michael's phrase of complete approval; the high-water mark of his praise.

The Gentrys offered no comment; it did not impinge upon their lives. Philip would never have consented to live on the Hutt Farm, despite its proximity to Wellington. It lacked the prestige of a sheep station.

Genevieve's eyes flashed with the fire of a sudden inspiration.

"And I'll keep house for the prodigal," she announced. "Kelly, I'm engaged on the spot, and take over my duties with you."

She looked round the big old living-room, mellowed and warm with memories. There would be no ruthless changes, but much that was outworn and useless would merge into a more fitting form for a new generation. Here was a job at hand, to share with Kelly the carrying on of the old tradition. Her face lit with pleasure at the thought.

"You mean it?" asked Kelly seriously.

"Absolutely!"

Delight and relief at Kelly's decision were dampened by this sudden complication. Miles frowned upon it from the first, and Norah, uncertain of what it might imply, urged more mature consideration, but did not oppose.

But Genevieve had caught fire, and the idea of being mistress here, with no niggling restrictions and an absence of her father's irking interference with even harmless pleasures, swept all objections aside.

Kitty would go to town, and that nice house in Hobson Street was at last possible, and Robin would make his home with her. Life had its compensations.

The home on the Terrace seemed suddenly denuded. Only Meggie, a quiet girl of no particular charm or character, and Peter, when he was home from college, remained with Miles and Norah. They became suddenly aware of this new desolation. Desertion, Miles called it. He decided there was no such thing as gratitude in the present generation; not like his day. Kelly's return, long desired, had been dimmed by this break. Miles saw the focal centre of the family being moved back to the Hutt; he felt his waning influence. He had scattered where he might have garnered and retained his position as head of the family by virtue of the affection they bore him. But instead, he had tried to retain his power by force of will, and the strength of his compulsion had driven them from him. Dare he add, even to his own soul, that they had been glad to escape?

He thought of his mother, of the sway she still exercised over them years after her death. He knew, for he was no insensitive man, that something of Bessie Pencarrow's power had finally drawn Kelly home. He might have held them, too, but it was too late now. He could not change. Norah comforted him, and thought the grief was for his father. She, who had changed and adapted herself to the changing phases of her life, like one who follows the shadow cast by a tree as the sun swings high, now planned to meet this new condition. Not having taken up a rigid stand, but only the quasi-infallibility of a mother (fathers alone were free from error), Norah could do this without loss of dignity. Much as he yearned to regain his old place in the lives of his children, Miles could not bring himself to surrender, or admit he had ever been wrong. So he hugged the prospect of loneliness like a winter threat to his soul, and men saw the signs of grief, and commended his filial devotion.

Kelly could not leave Morgan of Manawatu in the busiest part of the season, so he stayed on till the end of January. Robin and his mother had busy weeks furnishing and fitting up their new home in Hobson Street. When the many personal things that belonged to her had been removed from the Hutt, Genevieve took stock of everything remaining, and, with Kelly's approval, planned for the new régime.

Christmas and the holidays had kept things moving, and no one had time to mope or mourn. It was February when Kelly and Genevieve went to live at the Hutt.

Kitty and Robin were established in their new home, and the first faint glow of triumph came when she wrote "Hobson Street" on the cards she sent out for her house-warming party. That this, so long deferred, had at last been accomplished Kitty took for a sign that her other and greater ambitions might yet be realized. But she must be patient, and everything must be subordinated to that fixed objective—Robin's brilliant career.

As Miles and Norah sat alone over dinner the night after Kitty's house-warming, Norah referred to an almost forgotten subject, but one which had lingered dimly in her mind throughout all these changes.

Meggie was not back from tennis, and

Peter was at school, so she could speak freely. But these lonely meals were depressing and Norah could feel the shadows darkening in her husband's mind, and a certain grim, relentless battle to justify his past was barring the way to a permanent contentment.

"Do you think we ought to speak to Kitty . . . I mean to mention about . . . Robin and Genevieve?"

There, it was out at last!

"What! Is that nonsense still going on?"

"I really don't know. With all this upheaval, and moving, perhaps . . ." Her voice trailed away.

"Now that Genevieve has something else to interest her and they don't see each other so much, it might be better to leave things alone," Miles conceded.

"Kitty seems so happy again, with Robin back, it would be unkind to worry her. And it may not be serious. They are both young."

"Yes, better leave it and see," and Miles dismissed an unpleasant subject.

The year that had come in, bringing so many changes to their lives, settled into its stride with the waning summer.

Kelly Pencarrow, now lord of his small estate, struck roots deep into a favourable soil. His wanderings over, his heart at peace, he seemed to stretch himself, mind and body. Always vigorous and spurred by the genial inspiration of Genevieve, the easy folds of habit never enveloped him. But he knew in these pleasant, peaceful years a return of contentment, and, released from the jarring edge of family friction, he prospered and found vent for his ambition.

Genevieve, having assumed this responsibility, showed the qualities out of which success is forged. It was her pride that once again the Home Farm was the central point of family life, as in Grannie's day, and her spirit seemed to hover unseen over the home she had long loved, and to direct their actions.

"Do you think Grannie would like it this way?"

10

MICHAEL came to town more frequently in these days, and always stopped for a meal at the Hutt. He encouraged Kelly to talk over his work, and together they discussed the virtues of various breeds of stock, and alternative methods of increasing production. It was never suggested that Kelly should go out to Duffield. The old sore was never probed with words, and the scar was fading. Michael felt that in due time, of his own accord, Kelly would return to Duffield as suddenly as he had decided to carry on the Home Farm. Indeed, he regarded Kelly's return to the Hutt as coming half-way in more than a geographical sense.

Genevieve's success as chatelaine was not derived from any special passion for farm life. Unlike Kelly, the land did not claim her affection in a personal way. Kelly loved the land because it made an appeal to the spirit of man, the conqueror. Something vital, almost primitive, that was shared by savage and by king, the conquest of his kingdom, and its subordination to his will. That love of the land was a primary quality. He would have been a farmer, and drawn his living from the soil, whatever fortune had befallen him. He was keen and strong enough to bend circumstances in such an essential matter as a choice of life. But the land his forebears had cleared of forest and brought under grass was doubly dear, because of their association with it. For that reason Duffield and the Home Farm were desirable above all others.

With Genevieve it was not so. The new life at the Hutt provided her with an opportunity to try her skill, and do something that was measured against the high standard set by Grannie. It had scope and made her stretch, as she put it.

In Kitty's régime, during old Matthew's last years of invalidism, there was an atmosphere of impermanence; the transition from one generation to another; from Matthew and Bessie to—whom? Kitty's life at the Hutt, after Herrick's death, was only an interlude. She would take up life again when Robin should be grown up and have completed his studies. Then he would establish that long-promised home for her. During these years the centre of family activity had been dissipated.

Genevieve now set herself the task of restoring the tradition established by Grannie, and winning back the old position that the Home Farm had once held. It was a job to hand, and one that appealed to her sense of family. At that time Genevieve would have thrown her abounding energy and ambition into another channel if it had provided the same scope.

Robin, who was made a junior partner in the firm of Kelly, Pencarrow and Herrick, had the joy of rewarding his mother's years of sacrifice and devotion, and if the house in Hobson Street, so long delayed, did not bring with it all its possession had once promised in her impetuous youth, he was not permitted to know. It was sufficient to have him with her, and be the mother of a handsome, much-favoured son.

The break had been a considerable one, and not only had Genevieve and Robin been torn apart by physical circumstances, but the complete change in the ordering of their lives, the shifting centre of their personal interests, had applied a brake as no outside interference could have done. Not that they had changed, but that daily encounter in the leisured summer evenings fed an increasing need in each of them.

Robin realized more clearly that he could not desert his mother at this moment of the realization of her long-delayed dream. They were very companionable, as mother and son, and he was determined to give her the full measure of his love and enrich her life in return for those harsh years of disappointment.

Genevieve led a busy life, unlike the discontented days when Robin was her chief consolation. When they met, as they frequently did, it was with the same eagerness, and between them no conscious change had taken place. Yet they never returned to quite the same plane as they had reached on that summer day when Matthew died. It was partly because they were seldom alone; nor did they seek to avoid the others. They were apparently content to leave in suspense that open declaration, the result of which neither could foretell; they were satisfied with things as they were.

The temporary placidity into which the family had sunk was rudely stirred by the news of Neil Macdonald's engagement. Neil had gone to England to complete his medical course, after qualifying in Dunedin. It was his intention to remain for two years, but his success justified further years of specialization, after which he took a post in London in order to gain added experience. The two years had stretched to seven. How this measure of life abroad would affect him there was as yet little indication. His letters revealed the same self-importance, which filtered through news of his work and achievements; certainly he had reason to be proud of himself.

The quiet existence at Scot's Bay in the Sounds woke to happy activity in anticipation of his return. Donald Macdonald stroked his beard, and all the Scottish man's pride in intellectual triumphs warmed at the thought of his son.

Dr. Neil Macdonald would commence practice in Wellington, and already an excellent hospital appointment awaited him there.

He had sailed by the P. & O. Line to Australia, where he was to remain a couple of weeks before taking ship to New Zealand. It was from Sydney that the surprising news had come in a cable announcing his safe arrival: *"Engaged to be married, particulars on arrival*" was the cryptic addition to this brief message.

Hester immediately wrote to Kitty and Miles, and Kelly passed it on to Michael.

Who was she? If he had become engaged in England, it was strange he had not written and given them full particulars before sailing.

"It is someone he met on the boat, you see," said Genevieve.

"I don't like these shipboard romances," said Norah, quoting the fate of several salt-sea infatuations which had germinated during that six weeks' voyage, but had not survived six months in the commonplace of life ashore.

The indefinite information conveyed in the cable had let loose a shoal of speculation, and according to their individual temperaments, so they filled in the features and characteristics of this nebulous fiancée.

Jessie was sure her brother would marry ambitiously.

"I bet she is a snob. But I'll be bridesmaid, anyway, and I'd like to see her turn up her nose. I'm ready for her."

"Don't say rash and foolish things," Hester protested, but her mother's heart was anxious. "I'm sure she will be very nice, but I wish he had waited a while," she added wistfully. She pictured every type of bride for her son, often with dark doubts, until any certain knowledge would have been a relief.

Miles, too, thought it a queer way to make the announcement. It looked to him as though the boy were preparing them for a surprise of some kind, probably an unpleasant one. Why not say who she was straight out if there was nothing to hide?

Kelly said Neil was the type to fly high; stand aloof, cautiously, and then get caught suddenly.

"Perhaps a designing widow," and Pat, who knew so much more of that emotional insanity bred at sea, smiled wisely, but offered no further comment.

Neil's arrival after such a long absence would under any circumstance be an event in the family, but the glamour and uncertainty surrounding this unknown lady, no doubt accompanying him, gave it an importance based largely on curiosity.

"Mother, this is my fiancée, Erena Joicey-Goff."

All her self-control was needed to keep the exclamation of dismay locked in her heart. Hester looked at the dark girl beside her

200

handsome son. He was every inch the doctor, she thought, and very consciously the professional man. She stifled the cry that wrung her.

Erena Joicey-Goff, a young, beautiful half-caste Maori, combined the breeding of her English father, younger son of a country gentleman, and her mother, the proud daughter of a Maori chief.

So that was it.

The Joicey-Goffs were large land-owners in Gisborne. Erena's father, one of the early settlers, had acquired a large block of land, and added considerably to his estate when he married the daughter of a famous chief. Erena's mother, even into middle-age, retained that native aristocratic bearing which marked out the rulers of this savage race.

Though the Maori had no written language when the white man came, they had a wealth of tradition handed down from father to son, and their genealogical tree was carved in symbolic devices on their dwellings. For hundreds of years they could trace their ancestry, and the records of their battles and victories, their tribal conquests and migrations, were as stirring as the tale of any knights of old.

Their language was rich in poetic imagery, and their flax and feather garments were woven with artistic symmetry of design, while the harmony of their simple colours was evidence of an instinctive taste.

Erena was an only child, and when she was fourteen her father sent her to England, providing the best educational facilities that Great Britain and the Continent could offer. After England, she went to France, Germany and Switzerland, and she spoke her foreign tongues with ease.

At nineteen she was a slim, dark, lovely girl with brown eyes and black wavy hair. Her musical voice had the Maori's alluring quality, a charm that persists long after an early maturity has robbed the women of her mother's race of that ephemeral beauty which faded and sagged at the noonday of life.

Unlike the white man in India, in the South Seas, or the East, whose prestige suffered through an alliance with a coloured wife, the British settler in New Zealand did not invite social ostracism for himself and his family by marrying a Maori. It is true that many parents, who had known the Maori as a splendid savage, but still a coloured savage who had practised cannibalism and enjoyed a feast off his victim's flesh, objected to these mixed marriages. A brown race, but not negroid, the colour and other characteristics were apt to miss a generation or two and then emerge intensified by contrast with their white-skinned sisters. The slightest taint of colour which dooms the negro of America to his gloomy isolation, and the Eurasian mixture which bars the way to social intercourse in the East, found no echo in this young colony. Often the half-caste was prouder of his Maori blood, and the fine record of the warrior ancestor who ruled, than the heritage of culture through the bluer blood of those who merely served.

In other countries the barrier is fixed by blood, and no personal qualities, greatness of character or intellectual achievements can win a way to the white man's world. The British settler in New Zealand set no such bounds. His attitude was in effect: become our equal and we will accept you without reservation; we will judge you apart from your skin. And so it came about that those who achieved eminence they met on social equality. A few intermarried, but not a great number. The dark-skinned Lady bore her title with superb dignity, and entertained the sons of England's king. The men might not aspire to trade, but they could excel in science. Once, in later years, the only man with a university degree in New Zealand's Cabinet was a Maori who had been knighted by the King. And for a brief term a half-caste of beguiling eloquence acted as Prime Minister of this young Dominion.

Though no one dreamt of resenting this equality, where equal gifts and mutual tastes combined to forge a pleasant friendship, the thought of marriage, the mixing of the darker blood in the generations that were to follow, was an unhappy prospect which many parents viewed with keen dismay.

Walter Joicey-Goff was an austere man of military bearing. Widowed during Erena's absence, he had retained until her death a deep affection for his wife.

Some of the Maoris, educated in youth and brought up in British ways, returned in later life 'to the mat'. Periodically they delighted in escape from the strictures imposed by civilization, and returning to their native Pa, squatted indolently on the mat, growing fat and featureless in well-fed idleness, and enjoying with relish the native diet.

Erena's mother had never inflicted this

humiliation upon Joicey-Goff, and however strong the call of her native blood, she conformed to his standards to the end.

Age may repent its youthful folly, but wisdom makes the best of it. If the dark skin of his pretty daughter caused a pang of regret that a headlong passion had brought him this gift, he was determined that in everything else she should be English. He set the standard high, and from birth he kept her from too close an association with her mother's people.

In England her regular features, though dark, might easily pass among those not skilled in anthropological exactitudes as beauty of Latin origin. No hint of colour marred her reception among her English relatives or her friends at school. Now, with many accomplishments and the poise of an aristocrat, she returned home, where her father proudly welcomed her.

From a social and financial point of view, an alliance with the Joicey-Goffs was a desirable one. Personally she had great charm. Only the too-recent habits of her savage ancestors and the colour of her skin made her acceptance among them a matter of reluctance. But in the face of Neil's happiness, and his delight in her, and her father's affection for her, no shadow of this secret regret was permitted to appear.

When they were alone, however, what a spate of talk was released! The Macdonalds, the Pencarrows, the Herricks, all their tongues were busy; some regretfully, others curiously. A touch of malice crept in, for Neil was not the most popular of the cousins.

Miles said it was "a damn' shame".

Hester wept quietly, and Donald found it hard to comfort her, for his own pride was humbled. Once again the prize was struck from his hand.

Kitty was torn between the material advantages and the problem of heredity, and took pleasure in disagreeing with everyone.

Kelly said she was a damn' sight too good for Neil, and the prettiest girl he had seen for years.

"He is mad about her," said Genevieve. "I didn't think Neil could let himself go like that."

Robin did not see what the family were all making such a fuss about.

"I couldn't help thinking of the day you bashed Neil's hard-hitter in at the party," and Genevieve recalled the two country boys in their new serge suits and heavy boots, and those terrible bowler hats.

"He knocks the shine out of both of you now," she said. "The last word in London clothes, and such a fierce moustache."

Kelly, a squat figure in his rusty tweeds, with his unconscious ease, and the great authority of a young squire, tapped his pipe on his heel, and said they would all get growing-pains if they tried to live up to Neil's exalted idea of himself.

"I bet he will dress for dinner every night—"

"For six months, Genevieve, not more," Kelly said, with dry conviction.

"Didn't you want to bash his hat in to-day, when he stood there so conscious of his importance?"

Kelly laughed. "Want me to start another row, do you?"

"You've changed, Kelly; hasn't he, Robin?"

"Getting sense, that's all."

"Sense! If anyone is looking for it, they can have it any time for the asking. But I'm not picking a quarrel for the fun of it, or to entertain you. And isn't it time we had tea? You're a rotten housekeeper, Genevieve."

Genevieve said he had changed. Kelly wondered. Perhaps he had. He looked back on the long years of disagreement with his father, and all the turbulent events that followed. Had he changed? Some of the fire of youth had left him. At times he felt old—older than his years; an age that is estimated in experience. He was like someone who has over-spent his youth, and now in early manhood must economize. Those wild, unhappy years, always at cross-purposes with someone, had exacted a tremendous toll of vitality. Now he was glad to be at peace, like the blue-water sailor come to port. But would it last? Would this period of contentment grow irksome? There was something of the adventurer in his blood. Part of his distaste for law was the prospect of routine days spent in an office. He grew stagnant rapidly, and required the revivifying effect of a storm to lash him into violent activity, in order to save him from the slow poison of apathy. That was the alternative.

The Home Farm, dear as it was to him, offered little more than routine. He had made many changes, bringing it up-to-date. He had an eye for detail, and was constantly planning improvements, but these were all confined within the narrow frame of the valley. At Duffield he had the mountains and the sky and the sea as a backcloth for his picture, and against this vast, rugged magnificence there seemed no limit to what he might do. It was a kingdom to conquer. This was a garden to maintain. For a married man with a family, the Home Farm offered everything. Highly improved is the term that applied to it. It was small and compact, level and fertile, and, except for a chance spring flood, nothing disturbed the round of regular work. The house was comfortable; the garden a paradise. But to Kelly, whose youth had not yet exhausted its wild energy and sobered his fancy by domestic responsibility, there were moments when he felt a spiritual lethargy creep over him in this peaceful routine. He worked hard, but not slavishly, as they did elsewhere.

Genevieve had noticed it. Had they all been aware of a change? A stilling of troubled waters. His parents would be glad. "Settling down sensibly" would be their comment, no doubt. But under this contentment at times stirred a yearning to rush out, to get away, to find himself among the hills mustering sheep as the morning mists rolled back; to have space to stretch mind and soul and fix his eyes on that far horizon. Here he was hemmed in, in a snug and fertile valley, by friendly hills that did not give him elbow-room. It was a cushioned existence, despite the work. Perhaps he was getting flabby. Genevieve had asked him if he did not want to bash Neil for his self-importance. Did he? Once his hand was ready to strike in the wake of any flashing impulse. Too ready. Neil's smug consciousness that he had stepped out of the rut, and was showing a clean pair of heels to his city-bred cousins, might provoke a desire to see his pride humbled. But did it wake in Kelly a desire to bring about that fall? Figuratively speaking, to bash his hat in, and roll him in the mud as in that far-off, famous fight? Perhaps not. He was content to sit and watch it come about through other agencies.

Genevieve's words had sent his mind enquiring through the dark corners of his soul. He had changed, and he knew it now. She had said it as though what she saw were a change for the worse. It was not contempt in her tone, but a challenge.

Kelly, finding that Genevieve was right, decided to stir himself. He had rather shunned social activities. He still loved dancing, but preferred the lesser formality of a country dance to the punctilious demands of the Pencarrow social set.

"Getting slack, that's what is the matter with me," Kelly decided. And Neil was the bait that drew him back.

"Come on, Kelly, we can't have Neil lording it round like this. I'm for keeping that lad in his place. But I think Erena is a darling. I don't wonder he fell in love with her."

Seven years before Kelly was prepared to go bull-headed into every fight. To-day he was content to sit on the sideline and watch the fun. Genevieve had challenged him to come out. He accepted the challenge, and climbed into his starched shirt and white tie for the dance Sir Miles and Lady Pencarrow were giving to launch Dr. Neil Macdonald and introduce his fiancée. As he knotted the tie under his chin it suddenly occurred to him that it was the first big family gathering on the Terrace since Ella's marriage with Gentry, and the quarrel.

To-night he was to meet Gentry in the same room, under similar conditions. Would the others remember? How different things were now. Instead of an impulsive boy, reckless in his blind devotion to Duffield, he was a confident man, self-possessed, with a definite status in the family as owner of the Home Farm. Genevieve's prod had wakened him to a little more self-assertion. No more slacking. To-night he and Neil and Gentry would meet under his father's roof for the first time in seven years.

The prospect suddenly took a new significance, and invested the event with greater importance.

"Well, are you ready?" asked Genevieve, looking him over critically.

"I am; will I do?"

"You really want new tails; you're getting—"

"Not fat; not fat," protested Kelly.

"No, but broadening. The coat looks pinched."

"We shall have it, my girl," he said cheerfully. "If to-night launches us all successfully, and we escape without disaster."

"So you have thought of that, too. I bet they all have."

"I hope they won't expect me to give a repeat performance."

"It will be rather fun to see if they do. But they will remember all right. Father, Uncle Michael and Philip—"

"Why not the others?" Kelly enquired.

"Mother and the aunts are far too busy speculating about the prospect of Erena having brown babies. Mother, poor darling, is so glad their name isn't Pencarrow. Being Macdonald doesn't matter so much—there are lots of Macdonalds—and if they turn out cannibals we can disown them."

"You have a flippant tongue," but he smiled grimly as he realized the transfer of the family problem to a new centre.

This dance was not merely a family affair; the guests included people of importance in Wellington. Though not large, it was exclusive. Norah felt it was imperative that Neil should begin right and know all the proper people.

"People with disorderly but expensive stomachs," suggested Genevieve as they drew up the list of guests.

"You have a very coarse way of expressing yourself," commented her father, who, though not wanting to engage in an argument on the admissibility of such a word as stomach into polite conversation, could not let it pass without some mark of disapproval.

"The tail always follows the head," said

Norah, and Kitty agreed. A few distinguished patients on his list would encourage others to follow.

Hester was coming to see her son the central figure of this important social event. After her quiet life on a farm down the Sounds, she was impressed by the spontaneous generosity of Miles and Norah in arranging the dance.

In Kitty's mind, however, lurked a suspicion that an undue fuss was being made of Neil. Robin had not been given any ball when he joined the firm of Kelly and Pencarrow. She had to admit, of course, that he had not made a spectacular return after an absence of seven years. Robin, too, had walked into a ready-made practice, unlike Neil, who had to start from the bottom. But she was determined that Robin should not be overshadowed. She was going to consolidate for him the position he held already, and for which she had striven. She was glad to share in all the Pencarrow prestige, but she would like to feel that Robin and she had established a place of their own.

Peter, the baby of Miles's family, was facing matriculation at the end of the year, and then Kelly, Pencarrow and Herrick. It was ordained long since, though Miles was aware that he had not the ability of the others.

Peter, so many years their junior, had been rather a spoilt child. He had not grown up in the midst of the family and learnt to take the kicks and cuffs and stand up for himself.

"Don't be a cry-baby, Peter," was too often heard in the nursery. Meggie defended and mothered him, and the older ones either petted or ignored him. He was now a tall, fair youth with thick wavy hair, long lashes and large blue eyes. "A pretty boy", he had been called till his curls were cut.

In his last year at school, with rapid growth and a fair conceit of himself, he held promise of permanent good looks. But he lacked the athletic instinct which might have hardened this malleable material and hammered out a virile man. A soft portion had always been his. Norah could refuse nothing to her baby, and it was to her he always turned.

"You ask Father," he would coax.

"All right, dear, but . . ."

Norah yielded, and many a bedroom battle ensued.

Peter was wearing his first dress-suit, and was recognized as having at last joined the Big Ones. Having won a victory over the suit, he had later persuaded his mother to include a friend of his in the invitations to the party.

"But we don't know her, dear," she protested.

"You ought to, Mother. She's got a lovely voice, and she is Miss Beere's best dancer. Everyone will want to know her after *The Mikado* She is the most marvellous 'Yum-Yum'."

"She won't know anyone here, and it might be awkward for her—feeling strange—"

"She hasn't been in Wellington long, that's why she doesn't know many. But I do think it would be nice if you asked her, and give her a chance to meet people."

Norah sighed. "All right, dear. I'll talk it over with your father."

On second thoughts she didn't; she simply sent out the invitation and trusted to Providence. Talking things over with Miles was not always so simple as it sounded.

Joicey-Goff came with Erena, and on closer acquaintance Miles was impressed by the man's absorption in his pretty daughter. They talked over a whisky-and-soda, while the younger ones danced.

In Erena's presence it was impossible to associate her with ancestral savagery. She had

216

the poise of a princess, and a composure that, without robbing her of youth, indicated absolute control of emotions. Ambition, jealousy, anger might burn behind those fine dark eyes, but some dignity, innate rather than acquired through Western education, would restrain any manifestation of wilder passions. Her musical voice and her soft low laugh had a winning charm that threw into unpleasant relief the flattened vowels of some of the more careless whose ear was not attuned to niceties of tone. Her dress, her fan, her cloak were in perfect taste. In her presence the dark blood was instantly forgotten.

Kelly and Robin danced with Erena, and Neil was proud to hear her praise sung on every side. His adoring eyes followed her, and he relinquished her only that others might learn to appreciate what was his.

Robin and Genevieve danced together several times, and then sat on the stairs, where they drank claret cup and talked about everyone at the party.

"I wonder why Erena fell in love with Neil? He is so smug, so sure of himself." Genevieve said thoughtfully.

"Why does anyone fall in love with anyone?" Robin asked. "Why do I love you?"

"Do you?" She turned a pert nose towards him, then drained her glass.

"Don't I?" He slipped an arm round her waist and drew her nearer. They sat in the shadow and no one could see.

"I'm sure I don't know."

"Oh yes, you do."

"I seldom see you now; you are so busy, I suppose." There was no complaint in her voice.

"Whose fault is that? When I do come out the house is full."

"Is that why you haven't been coming lately?" Genevieve asked, a little quiver in her voice.

"And Mother. I can't leave her too often, and it is not so easy in the winter."

"Does she mind you coming out to the Hutt?"

"Lord, no! She likes me to go. But—shall I tell you a secret?"

"Yes, what?" Genevieve could see the excitement in his eyes.

"We are buying a motor-car. Then I will be able to come out any time. And I'll take you out for lots of runs all over the place. And

218

there won't be people about all the time. We never seem to get a chance to talk like we used—here."

Genevieve was silent. Robin was the most companionable person she knew. Kelly could be moody, but you could always rely on Robin. There was something comforting about him; to feel him beside her was like sitting in the sunshine, a burgeoning of pleasure. She was glad he loved her in this quiet, unpossessive way. She had no answer yet for a hungry passion. There was no fire in his kiss, but it woke in her heart a glowing warmth. It had the tenderness of a young plant; the fragrance of sweet herbs. She wondered if the volcanic emotion that stirred other men and women was something more glorious or more gross. Just to have Robin's love in this firm, warm way filled all her need. And he, apparently, was satisfied.

"Neil can have his dusky beauty; you are a thousand times more wonderful to me. I can't imagine life without you, Veve," and the little throb in his voice made her turn and catch the longing reflected in his eyes.

"These are good days," said Genevieve. "We will both remember them—always."

Something prompted her to speak as

though a ghost of the future had cast its shadow over them.

"But there will be better days—much better," he said.

They had drifted into a softly dreaming mood, and silence fell.

A door opened and voices recalled them.

"Hullo, Kelly!"

"Hullo, Gentry. Have a drink?"

"Right! That's enough, a dash more soda; thanks. How are the young Jerseys doing? Michael said they promise to turn out a good investment."

"The best I've got, so far, from the tests," Kelly answered, glad to find an easy subject. It was the first time they had come face to face—alone.

"Come out to Duffield one day. I'd like you to see those shorthorns Michael bought from Morgan of Manawatu. He is very keen about them, but I'm not so sure. You know his stock well, I suppose."

"I had nearly a year with him. He is a sound man, Morgan. Best judge of cattle in the Manawatu, I reckon."

"Well, come out and tell us what you think."

"If I can fix it . . . I'm pretty busy just now."

Kelly did not commit himself to a promise, but he was glad that he and Gentry could meet so easily. His experience and ownership of the Home Farm enabled him to meet Gentry on equal terms. The rebel, the rolling-stone, the casual farm-hand, the family prodigal had always been too conscious of his failure to desire an encounter before. Now it was easy; too easy. He wondered why he had wasted so many years in bitterness and unhappy enmity towards Gentry. Perhaps if they had left him alone, and not tried to push him into a premature reconciliation, much might have been spared. Now the gentle Jersey cows had done what the family's united efforts had not been able to accomplish. He wanted to laugh aloud. How absurd! For years he and Gentry had avoided each other. They had met seldom, and then protected by platoons of relatives. Now, by chance, they were alone; a whisky-and-soda and the Jersey cows had done it. They could meet without embarrassment. The folly of those years, running away from a shadow—the shadow of a hot word and a quick blow. Kelly saw himself again the

221

passionate boy, blind with tears of rage, rushing from the room. Then all that unhappiness. He thought of Grannie; she was right. It must heal on the inside first. In a way it seemed as if he had insisted on wearing a bandage on a long-healed wound, and when he removed the wrapping even the scar had gone.

"Have another drink, Gentry?"

"Right!"

"Here's luck!"

"Cheerio!"

Robin and Genevieve, looking over the banisters, heard and understood.

When the last guest had gone, and only the family remained, Norah heaved a sigh of relief.

"She is very sweet, Hester," she said to Neil's mother as they joined the others in the breakfast-room, where supper had been served.

It was too late for Kelly and Genevieve to go out to the Hutt, so they were staying till morning. Hester, with Neil and Jessie, also were there. Robin and his mother lingered behind to talk the party over before going back to Hobson Street.

"Are there any oyster patties left; I didn't get one, and I'm ravenous," said Genevieve, searching among the plates and dishes.

Kelly picked up three sandwiches at once and munched between remarks.

"It went off very well, I think," suggested Norah.

"A wonderful party; and what beautiful dresses," said Hester, grateful that all this should have been brought into being for her son.

"Did you have a piece of that rainbow cake, Hester? It's a new recipe I got. Try it," and Norah cut herself and Kitty a slice of the cake.

"You never get enough to eat at your own party," Peter began.

"Not if you are a good little boy, and keep on passing things." Genevieve scooped up a pile of mixed sandwiches, and, tipping them on to one plate, said: "Here, have a good tuck-in now."

"Tuck-in!" Miles repeated the phrase with disgust. "Where do you get such expressions, Genevieve?"

"From my vulgar companions, Father," she answered, a sweeping gesture embracing the room.

223

"You won't hear Erena using an expression like that," he replied tartly.

She would have let it pass but for the smile of triumph on Neil's face at hearing her rebuked.

"She has not been contaminated by the Pencarrows yet; she is still in her native innocence."

Robin caught her eye and flashed a warning signal. He did not know what Genevieve might say; something unkind, perhaps unfair, not out of malice, nor dislike for Erena, but to bash Neil's complacency.

"Any more sandwiches left?" asked Peter, scouting round, as he cleared the plate.

"Guts!" said Kelly.

"Oh, by the way, who was that young person I saw sitting on the table in a most unladylike fashion, Peter? And all you boys were encouraging her. I don't mind laughter, but I do object to that kind of hilarity. Who was she, I say?" and Miles waited while Peter gulped a mouthful.

"That was Maisie Kite." He volunteered the information with great gusto. He took the centre of the ring, as though he expected a burst of applause to greet this momentous announcement.

Genevieve kicked Kelly under the chair, but did not look his way.

Could they never have a party without it ending in a scene? thought Norah, wishing she had sent them all straight to bed.

"Who?" demanded Miles.

"Maisie Kite!" repeated Peter.

"Kite! Kite! Do we know these Kites?" he snapped, lifting his nose as though the very name conjured a bad smell.

"Must you go, Kitty?" and Norah positively pushed Kitty out of the breakfast-room door in order to cause a diversion.

Norah had seen the rising anger in Miles's face and could read the signs. She had yielded to Peter and asked the Kite girl against her better judgment. A nice little thing, she thought her. She had hoped Miles would not notice a stranger among the many he knew, and she had hinted to Peter the wisdom of not thrusting Maisie Kite under his father's eyes at some embarrassing moment. Now she would have to explain away her own omission to consult him. She was very tired. The party had been a great success: everyone had said so. Why couldn't Miles leave it at that? She wasn't complaining, but at least he might have commented on the excellent supper and

225

arrangements she had made. But no, he must hit upon this nice little girl, and start a row because she had a circle of boys around her, making them laugh.

"Good night, Genevieve."

"Good night, Robin."

"Coming, Kelly?"

"Half a shake—any more beer?"

"Good night, Mother."

"Lock the door, dear."

"Put the cake in the tin, it gets stale so quickly, and cover the tarts."

As they dawdled and drifted about before going upstairs to bed, Miles's voice rose once more.

"Who are these Kites, Norah?"

"Yes, dear; just a minute. I want to see if Emily has put the ham back in the safe."

"Kite! My God! What next?" and Miles grunted and damned as he ripped off his collar and tie.

11

ABOUT the time Miles Pencarrow was knighted, and his young brood were still in the nursery, Wallie Kite and his family moved from Waimate to Ashburton.

Walton Kite was a man who had the initiative to begin many enterprises but lacked the perseverance to complete any of them. He would open a little store with a bustling energy that brought him ready trade, but soon his interest waned, and it was left to his wife to carry on until they sold out to avoid bankruptcy. He would dig up the garden—roses, roots and bulbs—and pile them on the path with promise of wonderful changes, but he wearied by noon, and the evening saw Mrs. Kite panting as she replaced the wilted flowers in their old beds, dragging cans of water to nurse them back to life. He always began to paint the kitchen with half a tin of left-over paint that could not be matched, and so left it piebald. And no one could remember the whole of Kite's hedge being clipped at once.

Walton Kite's father had arrived from England on the heels of the Canterbury Pilgrims, who had laid out that lovely city of Christchurch, on the edge of the Canterbury plains. The grey stone cathedral, with its tall, tapering spire, and the elms and oaks and acacias reminded him of England, but he soon left the town for the country. He was one of those who were later to be found shepherding on remote sheep stations. "A university scholar who drank," the settlers said.

In his lonely shepherd's hut, a jar of whisky and the Odyssey were his companions. Hugh Walton might have, and should have, married Mary Kite, but he didn't. He was drowned in a flooded stream before knowing that paternal responsibility awaited him and fulfilling the duty of making an honest woman of her.

The girl's father kept a little country store, in which she had always helped him, but in righteous anger he drove her out, and it was an aunt who took pity on the girl and saw her through her trouble. She called the child Walton, after his father—Walton Kite. But Wallie came more trippingly to the tongue.

The boy had a bad start, and what he inherited from his father was certainly not his love of literature, though a queer artistic strain occasionally cropped out in unexpected places.

When Wallie was a useful age his grandfather relented and took Mary and her child back to the store. The lad could sweep out and run errands, and when he saw how well the boy worked his grandfather felt that his magnanimity had been morally justified.

Storekeeping was Wallie's trade, and though he started several times with a flourish that promised success it always ended the same. His business dwindled, while rivals prospered, so he sold out and moved on.

He had married in the flush of one promising venture a kindly, simple girl who bore him many children. Despite an increasing family and decreasing prospects, Wallie Kite was never despondent. He had survived changes and outlived disasters enough to crush any ordinary man. But he was no ordinary man. His resilience was remarkable. Odd little pockets of ambition still remained concealed in his mind which he revealed to no one. But something of his paternal forebears had come down to him, and though he knew nothing of his father, except that he was a university scholar who drank, he had often felt the stirring of desires and ambitions alien to the Kite tradition. It was, in fact, this something in his blood which started him off from time to time to paint the kitchen or re-make the garden; a desire for something better; an unconscious yearning for his right-ful place in life. But the weakness in his father, combined with the Kite family's reverence for store-keeping, failed to give him the necessary support. He lacked stamina. The first opposition or discouragement, even the first weariness, and he lapsed into his old indolent ways.

His wife had no great gifts except a dogged motherhood and an ability to keep on her feet all day. She was a large woman, with an ample bosom; a great soft cushion that was made for pillowing tired babies. In later years it was a veritable sounding-board for sighs when the babies began to grow up and go their wilful ways. Her light step became a heavy tread, and fallen arches were a lament-able accompaniment to her thirteen-stone weight.

She had been a good wife to Wallie Kite, and he knew it. He was grateful to her for getting him out of many a hole. A shaggy, sandy little man, his eyes still twinkled when some comic aspect of life's tragedy presented itself to his artless mind. They were fine eyes, really, but hedged in with untidy sandy brows. His straight moustache overhung his lip and stood between him and his food. Of the seven children, Maisie, the middle one, was his favourite, and he looked upon her as the hope of the family. She would go far, would Maisie, he had concluded long before the child was aware of a wide world outside the country store.

"A throw-back on my father's side, I wouldn't wonder. She's different from the rest."

She was not a pretty child, but she had a vital quality which made everything she did significant. Something in the way she carried her head and the swing of her body conveyed a suggestion of authority. She had her father's fine eyes and his amused outlook on life. A slap might sting her flesh but it would not tame her spirit.

"Here, Maisie, do these dishes. Me on me two feet all day," and, sighing, Mrs. Kite would sit heavily and fan herself with her apron.

231

"No, finish them properly; and hang up the frying-pan and wipe the pot lids. What! Want to go out! Where are you galavanting now? You ought to be doing your home-lessons."

"Oh, let her go, Mother; let her go. I'll do the frying-pan," and her father would blink knowingly at Maisie, and take the tea-towel, while Maisie scampered off.

Maisie harboured secret ambitions of great-ness. The dull day and its drudgery were for-gotten at night when she entered her real world. Darkness shut out the dingy wall-paper, the cheap lace curtains, the yellow wooden chest and the pealed enamel that hung in flakes on the old bedstead. She closed her eyes to this sordid world, and opened them in an imaginary one where she was a great lady, until sleep claimed her. In fancy she touched the satin of her lovely gown, and in her hair were shining jewels. It was a game she played, a game so real that the drab world of daylight became less positive than the man-sions of her fancy.

Silks and lace and perfume and the richest of gay colours had an irresistible fascination for her. She did not openly lament the lack of these in her life; she accepted it with other

232

hard facts. But it did not entail resignation. The family, as a whole, seemed resigned to its fate. Her mother looked forward to nothing better, and only hoped it wouldn't get worse. Passive acceptance was no part of Maisie's childish philosophy. Trained in the brilliant world of her imagination, she soon began to picture herself filling an important rôle in life, and she saluted herself as a rising star.

Maisie soon realized that money was very important. The odd pennies that came her way were not enough. Her first independent venture in business was the sale of eight empty beer-bottles at a halfpenny each, and that fourpence encouraged enterprise. An empty sack was worth twopence, but they were hard to get without detection. The lead from inside the chests of tea in the store, when collected into lumps, was bought by the old Chinaman who kept the fruit shop and laundry, and proved more profitable.

The trading of these goods was done on secret missions, for no hint was given to her brothers or sisters. The idea was her own, and she was entitled to the fullest fruits of such originality. There would be little profit if the others shared, and, besides, her mother would soon find out, and this profitable trading would come to an abrupt end.

With two-and-ninepence in hand, Maisie decided she could afford a little luxury, but impatience nearly robbed her of its enjoyment. She bought a bottle of scent for sixpence, and the temptation to try it next morning was so strong that she foolishly dabbed some on her hands and soaked her handkerchief before going in to breakfast. She plunged her pert little nose into her hands and drew in a deep sensuous breath of delight. Scent was wonderful, she thought. It made you feel quite different. She was still inhaling it when her mother's voice was raised, calling the family to breakfast.

"Maisie! Where's Maisie?"

"I'm here, Mother," and she hurried out and took her place with the three young ones on the form along one side of the kitchen table. Her father smiled at her and plunged his moustache into the spoon of porridge, drinking it in with audible relish.

Mrs. Kite spooned out the porridge and passed the plates round. Suddenly she paused and sniffed. She sniffed three times, to the north, to the south, and to the east, an expression of distaste deepening on her face.

234

"Did you change your socks this week?" she asked, her eye resting on her husband.

"Yes, day before yesterday," he answered firmly, clearing himself of suspicion.

Maisie, reading signs of danger, looked at her hands and nails in sudden surprise, as though alarmed to find them far from clean, and pushing past her little brother and mumbling something about washing them, she darted out of the door.

With her departure the unpleasant odour diminished, and Mrs. Kite, with one more sniff, resumed the spooning out of the porridge.

Maisie took the scented handkerchief from down the front of her dress, fishing it up by a corner, and planted it in a currant bush in the garden. Such a waste. She took a deep breath before parting with it, and then, resentfully, she washed her perfumed hands with brown Windsor soap.

Examining them with satisfaction, she returned to her breakfast. Maisie was only ten when she learnt this first lesson of caution in a critical and unappreciative world.

Maisie, having an older sister, seldom got a new dress. As Ethel, a big, gawky girl, grew out of her clothes, they were passed down to her. Fortunately Ethel grew quickly, so they were never more than a year old.

It was, however, a source of resentment that these slightly soiled and much faded frocks alone replaced the silks and satins of her dreaming.

At eleven, Maisie was growing into a leggy child; her limbs seemed too long for the slender body and neat, small head. Her hands, red from washing-up and freckled from the sun, looked enormous when thrust through these shrunken sleeves.

Summer brought her a well-washed white frock, which was already too small. The sleeves were tight, and finished meanly midway between elbow and wrist, exaggerating the size of her hands. They were, in fact, shapely hands, but rough from lack of care. The dress fitted fairly well otherwise, but had a skimpy look. Maisie was sorely conscious of her awkward hands in these shrunken sleeves, and she felt that something ought to be done about it. No use asking her mother; she had troubles enough of her own. Maisie had already learnt that it is well to be self-reliant, and decide these personal matters for yourself.

As she looked the dress over carefully, she

fingered sixpence—the profit from the last bit of lead taken prematurely from the tea-chest in the store when no one was looking. Turning the sixpence over, her mind on the great event timed for three-fifteen on Saturday afternoon, she decided to take the plunge. There were no more sacks in sight; no lead would be available for some time, and her mother was keeping a close grip on the key of the cupboard where the beer was stored.

"I'm no wowser," Wallie Kite would say. "I like me glass of beer and five bob on a horse." He said it, not boastingly, but as a man who knows his own mind. But it was not always the mind of his wife, who held the key. And it was only when Wallie showed signs of going out to see a man about a dog that his wife deemed a bottle at home better than six elsewhere. The result of this was to limit the scope of Maisie's private trading.

Her decision made, she tied the sixpence in the corner of her handkerchief and contemplated with excitement the purchase of lace. You couldn't get much lace for sixpence, not wide lace, but she felt that effect, and not quality, must govern this expenditure.

"I want a yard of lace, please," said the shabby child.

"What sort of lace?" asked the little man in the drapery shop.

"Lace for sleeves," said Maisie, her hand weaving a graceful fountain of frilling as she spoke.

The little man peered at her through his glasses, then over them. A queer child; one of the Kites, to be sure.

She sat up to the counter on his one chair like a grand lady ordering the best as he brought out a box of lace all wrapped round cardboard squares.

"About how much a yard?" he asked.

"Let me look at it first," she said imperiously, as though price were nothing to her. But her quick eye caught a wide cheap lace marked sixpence, and she selected this.

"I think this will do; it's just the right width. How much is it?"

The little man fumbled with a clumsy thumb to lift the folds of lace and see the price marked on the card.

"Sixpence," he said at last.

"Is that all?" the child said, as though implying she had expected it to be at least half-a-crown. "I'll take it; a yard, please," and she untied the corner of her handkerchief behind her back so that he might not see she had no purse. The lace was about six inches wide and very coarse, but this did not depress her.

Sharing a bedroom with her two sisters, one older and one younger, there was no privacy in her life. The kitchen and parlour, which were behind the shop, were connected by an ever-open door, and her mother, who, as she declared, was on her two feet all day, was constantly in and out, in and out.

Maisie cut the lace in two, and with a needle and cotton, ostensibly to sew a button on her nightdress, managed to join the lace and gather it without discovery. It was so small she could push it out of sight in an instant. To get the frills sewn on to the sleeves of her dress was another matter. Under pretext of fitting on the dress to see if the hem was right, Maisie put it on, then ran down to the Little House in the garden, and hurriedly shut the door. She dragged the dress off, and by the dim light that filtered in through the mitred boards at the top of the door, and a chink of light through a wide crack, she sewed a frill on each sleeve with a long stitch.

Putting the dress on again, she made play with her hands, delighting in the rise and fall

239

of the lace frill as she swept her arm in elaborate gesture. In the dim light of the Little House the sixpenny lace might have been the best from Brussels. Hearing approaching footsteps, she pushed the lace under the tight wrist-band and dashed back to the house, her heart beating with excitement.

Maisie was a good little girl next day. It was Saturday and she had several weekly duties to perform. Her mother had a "bad head", so Maisie persuaded her to lie down after dinner, and took her in a cup of tea.

"She can do it when she likes," thought her mother gratefully.

"Now you lie there until tea-time and have a sleep," said Maisie. "And here's a nice clean hanky; I'll wet it in vinegar and put it on your forehead."

As she got the handkerchief from her mother's drawer she surreptitiously picked up her mother's brown kid gloves. It had been easier than she thought. White cotton gloves were all she possessed, and there was a glamour about kid, even if they were brown, much too big, and a bit scabby at the tips.

"Lace and kid gloves!" Even to say it to herself gave her a little thrill. The next thing was to get to the railway station by three-fifteen, when the train carrying Pollard's Juvenile Opera Company was due to stop for five minutes, to water the engine. They were opening a season in Christchurch that night and were on their way from Dunedin. They were playing *La Mascotte*. Maisie liked the *La*; it was foreign, she knew, but it suggested something glittering and polished. She was quite disappointed when she found it was only French for "the".

Ten minutes before the train arrived Maisie accomplished a difficult feat, and out-witted the whole family, escaping over the back fence via the Little House.

She was a quaint figure, this little girl of eleven. Her shabby shoes were polished till they shone like mirrors, her black cotton stockings were hitched up taut. The embroidery of her drawers was two inches below her dress, which still showed the marks where the hem had been let down after Ethel had given it to her. The child's slender body was too large for the shrunken garment, which, how-ever, was too big for little Kate and too good to throw away. Not having a sash, she had contrived a bow of pink pongee silk—a gift from the milliner for picking up pins from the floor—another form of enterprise which

241

was paid in "scraps". The brown kid gloves, despite the fact that the fingers were an inch too long, gave her a feeling of elegance, and as Maisie raised a leisurely hand to thrust a wisp of hair from her eyes the lace fell from her wrists in a ravishing cascade.

Conscious that she was attracting attention, but satisfied that envy lay behind the staring eyes, she walked up and down the platform—alone, moving with a disdainful air among the blank, honest faces of other children, most of whom held a parent's hand.

The passing of Pollard's train was a great event for Ashburton and drew a large Saturday afternoon crowd. The company was too important to play in this small town, and the fleeting glimpse of them while the thirsty engine took its drink was their share in this famous theatrical enterprise.

Maisie did not want to stand with groups of other children; she was wise enough to know that she was more conspicuous alone. She had not gone to all this trouble to be overlooked in the crowd.

With a shrill whistle the train came in sight.

"Stand back there; stand back!" The stationmaster came out of his office to assume authority for a brief moment, buttoning his heavy dark-blue uniform as he came. It was a hot day and he had worked in his shirt-sleeves till the train was signalled.

As the engine slowed down and slid into the station, faces appeared at the carriage windows. It was a juvenile company, with a few adult principals. Tired eyes looked out, frowsy girls, just wakened from an uncomfortable sleep in second-class carriages: a few children, some with their hair still in curlrags for the night. But to Ashburton eyes they were smart and brilliant creatures, with their frizzed hair and paint on their faces, and dressed in the gayest of colours.

Her mother called them "Jezebels". It sounded a nice name, but from her mother's face she knew it must be something bad. To the yearning eyes of Maisie they were beings from another world, a dazzling world of light and excitement and applause. She looked at the tired children with envy. Some were younger than she, but she imagined them in spangled dresses with curled hair and belladonna in their eyes to make them shine. She had read about that. She had decided that her next money would go on belladonna.

She went nearer the carriage windows, and

even the hot smell of orange-peel and biscuit crumbs did not repel her. She wished she knew one of them. It would have been more exciting to have been able to claim one of them as a friend. She would have felt nearer to the heart of it, almost as if she, too, belonged to this brilliant company. She dreaded the moment when the station bell would ring, the guard would blow his whistle and wave a flag, and the heavy chug-chug of the engine would take them all away. How wonderful to go away in a train—away from Ashburton! Fancy going to Wellington and Auckland, and over to Sydney; perhaps London. How she envied them their luck.

Maisie's eyes were not exclusively on the little girls. Three young men had got out to stretch their legs a moment and, hatless, walked up and down.

"Chorus boys," she heard someone say.

Their curly hair was plastered with brilliantine, their pointed tan boots were of the brightest yellow; their ties were rich and varied. To Maisie they were romantic figures; elegant young gentlemen, like the ones who peopled her dreams.

She walked along the platform in their direction, deliberately courting their attention, but primly averting her eyes. When nearing them she stole a glance and saw the tallest nudge his neighbour and look at her. Holding herself more erect, and swinging her hips so that the hem of her short dress swayed with her movements, she walked slowly on. As she came opposite she lifted one gloved hand and delicately swept an imaginary tendril of hair from her eyes. As she did so the lace frill fell in its graceful folds. The satisfaction of this gave her confidence, and she raised her eyes and looked straight at the young men.

The tall one smiled and winked.

"Hullo, girlie!"

"Now, there's a fairy queen for you," said the other.

A magic wave of excitement swept the child. Three chorus boys were talking to her, telling her she was beautiful. The comic little figure in the shrunken cotton frock and the cheap lace frills and the incongruous brown kid gloves felt that she *was* beautiful, and with this thought throbbing in her brain and the memory of their flattery and their compliments, she stood as in a dream. The bell rang, the whistle blew, the young men scrambled back into their carriage, and the train slowly drew out of the station.

"Good-bye, girlie!"

The tall youth blew her a kiss.

The train rattled away in the distance, the crowd, pushing and shoving and talking, their brief Saturday excitement over, scattered to lounge about the footpaths and the shop-fronts. With eyes wide open, staring after the vanished vision, Maisie stood as in a dream—a golden, glorious dream.

"I'll tell Mother on you, taking her best gloves, and talking to young men. You do look a sight, don't she?"

So the gawky Ethel had been there too, with her friend, the Jewett girl.

But nothing could shatter the dream. The nagging and slapping would be a small price to pay for so much glory.

Maisie's friendship with Clara McIntosh marked her first real upward step. Clara's eldest sister worked in a dentist's rooms, and when the thumbed copies of the *Queen* and the *Sketch* in the waiting-room were no longer fit to distract nervous patients waiting to have an aching tooth extracted, they became the property of Clara's sister. No matter if they were a year, or even two years old, their pictures represented people whose lives were governed by an age-old tradition. Each year their bridal retinues were equally bridal, they hunted in the same tailored perfection; and when they were presented at Court, minor changes of fashion were nothing compared to the unchanging plumes and veil and the yards of sweeping Court train.

From Clara, by the simple method of purchase, paid not in cash but in kind, the coveted pictures passed into Maisie's hands. What was a bit of blue plush earned from the milliner for picking up pins to this authentic setting for her dreams? She read every line on every page and soaked herself in the printed details. She felt on surer ground about the lives lived by the rich, the ways of Society, and the behaviour in Court circles. It was a strange study for a child, but history and the battles of very dead kings took on an added interest when viewed in the light of such knowledge. This was London, where all the kings had lived. From this deduction the historic dead were more convincingly mortal when viewed in the light of a King's levee.

Some of the pictures she cut out and

pinned to her bedroom wall, and pride of place was given to Queen Victoria in her Coronation gown. To acquire this she had parted with a piece of purple plush.

The gawky Ethel had gone out with the Jewett girl, and Kate was in the shop with her father, earning her two brandy-balls for stacking pounds of candles from a newly opened box. Her mother, who had been on her two feet from early morning, had fallen asleep in the rocking-chair in the kitchen. The family thus accounted for, Maisie closed the bedroom door. Her eyes were bright as she climbed on to the chair, and then to the dressing-table, and unhooked the white lace curtains. Experience had taught her the value of a ready excuse. A large reel of cotton, scissors, thimble and a threaded needle lay conspicuously at hand. The curtain was dusty, but what matter! Quickly she took it down, then with two large safety-pins, and after much striving, she attached it to her shoulders at the back.

She was just spreading her Court train behind her when her sharp ear caught her mother's ponderous step. Which way was it going? She listened apprehensively; yes, she was coming this way. Quick as a flash, Maisie put her back to the wall, and, gathering the curtain in a bunch in front of her, began busily mending a hole.

The door opened and Mrs. Kite's bulk filled the aperture.

"What are you doing?" she asked sharply.

"Just mending the curtain, Mother," and Maisie smiled up with disarming innocence.

"Who tore it, I'd like to know—you?"

"It's been done a long time, but it's only a little hole. I'm nearly finished, but I thought it might get bigger . . ."

Mrs. Kite looked round with suspicion, but Maisie's needle was flying in and out, and she had a convincing air about her.

"Well, hurry up. I want you. And don't let me catch you tearing the curtains again."

She closed the door after her, but, with her hand still on the knob, doubts returned. There was something unnatural about Maisie taking down that curtain to mend it. The knob turned and she put her head in the door again to make sure—just as Maisie spread her lace train behind her and, with a fan of pleated newspaper, made her curtsy to the Queen.

"I'll warm you, my lady, if I catch you at this nonsense again. Take off that curtain, and top and tail the gooseberries out here. I'll teach you to be a fine lady. You'll help your mother, that's what you'll do. Me on me two feet all day, working and slaving and cooking and washing, and you playing the la-de-dah in your room."

It was Clara McIntosh who first discovered the liberating medium of shorthand and typewriting. It opened a new world of opportunities. Maisie borrowed Clara's book and she was not long in mastering the *tee, dee, pee, bee, chay, jay,* and strokes and dots. Clara went to the Technical School at night, and she helped Maisie over the first hurdles. She had already justified herself and convinced her father that here was a new road to wealth before she could get her mother's permission to take up this new-fangled notion and join Clara at Tech. At last she launched herself into this new world which was opening for girls. When she was equipped with several years' experience in an Ashburton office, Maisie, by a ruse, went to Wellington for a week's holiday. But she took a job she had already applied for, and did not return. Her letter was mute witness to her mother's distress and her father's genuine grief. With Maisie's departure went the one bright spot in his life.

"She'll be getting into trouble, that's what she will; working in an office with a lot of strange men, and staying in a boarding-house with no one to know what she's doing. I've a good mind to go up and bring her back."

"Leave her be; leave her be."

Even the little hunger in his heart could not blind her father to the advantage and relief this must be for Maisie.

Hard work, a quick wit, a keen desire to get on, a never-sleeping ambition, were spurs to drive her and keep her on a straight course. All she could save she invested in herself. She had a sweet voice and trained it. She had grace of movement and learnt dancing till she was the star turn at the annual display. She joined the amateur operatic society and learnt everybody's part through sheer love of it all. She filled an emergency with startling success, and now she had been chosen to play Yum-Yum in *The Mikado*, and Peter, a nice youth in the chorus, who had fallen under her spell, had brought her into the Pencarrow circle.

Maisie Kite had caught the rising tide.

12

"**I** WISH you were as keen about your books as about this—this—theatrical rubbish."

Miles, having delivered his judgment, proceeded to carve the duck.

Peter, in a dressing-gown, was being very Japanese. His legs were agile, but tennis was no training for a fan. He flipped and flapped a fan at every opportunity, delighting to snap it unexpectedly in someone's ear and make him jump.

"But, Father, the whole success of *The Mikado* depends upon Peter. He has to say 'Boo' with twenty others in the second act."

"You're very smart, aren't you, Genevieve?" and Peter flicked her ear with the fan.

"Take off that dressing-gown and come to the table properly," and Miles sorted the wing from the leg and expertly sliced pieces from the breast and the plate was passed to Norah, who added the vegetables.

Their jibes and jests left Peter's enthusiasm

dimmed. He talked about rehearsals and "my part", and only his eagerness could have reconciled him to the job of assisting the property-man.

"Second-assistant scene-shifter," Genevieve called him.

No scene could be set, no furniture placed in position, without Peter putting a hand to it. His tireless puppy energy annoyed the veterans, but the Pencarrow patronage was worth enough to justify patience.

Peter marshalled the whole clan for the first night. Sir Miles and Lady Pencarrow sat in the front row of the dress-circle with Meggie. Kitty and Robin preferred the stalls, and so did Kelly and Genevieve.

"I say, Mother, what about sending Maisie a bouquet?"

Peter was still an adorable baby to Norah.

"Dear, I scarcely know her. You send one yourself."

"No; don't you see, it would count so much more coming from you . . . with your card on it."

"In what way, dear?"

"You see, some of them are jealous of her; the other girls. Just because she isn't known and works in an office; well, they're just cats.

And a bouquet from you—they would all know who it came from—would . . . well, can't you see . . . it would be one in the eye for them."

"Who is she, really? I mean, who are her people?" asked Norah.

"She says they keep a little shop in Ashburton. That's what I like about her: she doesn't pretend. And she's had such a hard struggle."

No commendation could have appealed more strongly to Norah than that simple statement.

"Very well, dear. You order the flowers; not too expensive, mind you, and I'll pay for them."

"And you'll write a card; say something nice on it, Mother—something she can read out loud in the dressing-room."

Norah laughed and promised, and Peter went off singing, "Defer-er, defer-er to the Lord High Executioner."

Miles had to acknowledge the excellence of Maisie Kite's performance. She was sweet and shy, yet pert. There was a saucy grace about her tripping movements, and her voice had a lovely ringing quality. He was proud, too, of Peter.

"I wish he would take his work as seriously," said Miles.

"He is easily the best of the men—the chorus men, I mean," Norah agreed, beaming with pride.

There was a great ovation when the curtain fell. Every performer, whether principal or chorus, had friends and relatives in the audience who clapped and cheered.

Norah gasped, however, when an immense bouquet of roses was handed up to the little Yum-Yum. Her practical mind was busy estimating the cost. She should have set a limit and not left it to Peter.

"Oh, Maisie! Who sent you those?"—enviously.

"Lady Pencarrow!" she said, reading the card.

"Do you know her?"—in surprise.

"Oh, yes"—casually. "I've been there to dances."

Looks were exchanged and a certain iciness of manner thawed. After all, she was a success as Yum-Yum, and now, if the Pencarrows took her up, it might be as well to be friendly. You never know . . .

"Let's ask Maisie Kite out on Sunday,

Kelly," said Genevieve as they drove home after the opera.

"Yes, do. She is awfully amusing; doesn't care what she says. Is Father coming? He'd have a fit."

Peter brought Maisie out to the Home Farm on Sunday, escorting her with a triumphal air, as though he shared equally in her great success. Robin came, too, his mother having gone up to Norah's for the day. They were lonely Sundays on the Terrace now, and the noisy young group at the Hutt rather irritated Miles. He had no authority there. His frown could not silence them, nor were they greatly impressed by his assumption of importance. They were very polite, but by force of numbers and sheer youthful vitality they wore him down. It was a position he did not enjoy, so his visits became fewer and more ceremonial.

Peter watched Maisie with adoring eyes. He thought she was wonderful, but being several years her junior she regarded him merely as a nice boy.

The child who had put lace frills on the shrunken sleeves of her hand-me-down dress, and borrowed her mother's kid gloves, had now tasted the wine of applause. She had triumphed over circumstances, beaten down opposition, ignored snubs and slights, and fought her way to the front rank in the limited field open to her. On all sides her performance was acclaimed. She had natural gifts which were ripe for development, and the struggle had stiffened her. Her sense of comedy kept her free from pretence. She did not gloss over her early years, but looked back with pity, not only for the child she had been, but more so for her mother and father, who were doomed and could never escape. Even as a child she had enjoyed the temporary liberation of her daydreams. They had none.

To mark her first success she had bought her mother a pair of comfortable house-slippers with rabbit fur round the top.

"Me on me two feet all day," was a cry that echoed across the years.

"Poor Mother; she'll probably take the fur off the slippers and put it round her neck."

They liked her all the better when she told them about her mother and the slippers. Feeling the genuineness of their sympathy, she went on and related the details of her private tragedy: the bottles and sacks and tea-lead that she sold, and the fate of the sixpenny scent, and the lace. It came rushing out in a spontaneous revelation. As a traveller on a high peak looks down into the valley from which he started, now Maisie, on her first ridge of success, turned a backward glance, and saw in perspective the events of her childhood. It made her proud rather than ashamed. She had started the race with a heavy handicap and won the first heat. Why should she hide the handicap?

"I suppose you came out at a ball at Government House?" she said to Genevieve.

"Yes; in white satin and tight shoes. What a night!"

"My first dance was in the country. I was staying with my grandfather, after the whooping-cough. The dance was in a woolshed, with a rough floor, and all the morning two men swept it and swept it. After dinner they began scraping candles with a penknife all over the floor, and scuffling it with their feet to rub it in. I don't know how many candles they used, but I know I was frightfully shocked at the extravagance. But when it was all covered with little flakes of grease I helped them to rub it in with my feet. Afterwards, they got a clean sack, and I sat on it and they pulled me round and round to polish the floor. Once they stopped for a spell, and then started suddenly; they tipped me over and I had a lump on my forehead as big as an egg. But I went to the dance all the same."

"How old were you then?" asked Genevieve.

"Thirteen. And oh, what a thrill it was! I couldn't dance properly, but I had an instinct to go with the music, and was light on my feet."

"Didn't your grandfather object to you going?"

"Bless you, he didn't know!" and her merry laugh pealed out. "I went to bed with toothache after tea, and got out of the window and went with the baker's boy. But I got a good hiding next day from the my grandmother when she saw the seat of my pants where I'd been polishing the floor with them."

Maisie became a regular visitor at the Hutt. Robin had a four-seater car, so even when his mother came he had room for Maisie and Peter.

Sometimes the Sunday party included Neil and Erena. They had been married in Gisborne, only the Macdonalds going up for the ceremony. The Rev. Hector had come from

259

Dunedin to assist the local clergyman, but it was a quiet affair.

Hector was almost an alien among the young Pencarrows, for he found them lacking in seriousness, and treating life with a levity that could not be justified, so he was glad to return to Dunedin and his parish.

Neil was less enthusiastic about the Sunday gatherings than his wife. Erena was always welcome and had established a definite place for herself in the clan. Neil, however, felt that not sufficient attention was paid to him. No one asked his opinion, and when he volunteered it they did not even bother to contradict.

"Now, when I was in London . . ." was a beginning that should have gripped their attention, but it was usually a prelude to a tale so dull, illustrating his prowess, that it met with an instantaneous, "Just a minute, Neil, I think tea is ready. Tell us afterwards," and Genevieve could rob the snub of its sting with a flashing smile. But the tale was never told if they could help it; not after the first.

In the summer the party was larger. It began earlier and lasted longer. Some came for dinner, others for tea. Kelly had a grass tennis-court laid down, and that was an added attraction. After a hard set they might go for a swim in the Hutt river. It was all so friendly and informal, and a few extra people made no difference. Genevieve saw there was plenty of food, and tea was brewed at intervals.

If by chance the *Rotomahana* was in port, Pat came out, and the genial young sailor was specially welcome.

As hostess Genevieve had something of her Grannie's easy charm. There was no fuss. No one made polite conversation; they did just what they pleased; and the restfulness of the lovely garden and the comfort of the old farmhouse had an atmosphere of their own.

The summer came and went, a gay, happy season for the young Pencarrows. When autumn shut down in the valley, and the chill, short days put a period to tennis and the garden, no surface ripple showed that underneath were stirring new affections and jealousies.

Easter was the last Sunday of summer, and they had all come out: Miles and Norah, Neil and Erena, Robin and his mother, Peter and Maisie Kite. Kelly and Genevieve were sorry that tennis must cease, but the lawn was getting soft.

Later, Michael came riding in; he was not a regular visitor.

"Here's Uncle Michael! How nice. Oh, you old darling, it's good to see you!" and Genevieve went to meet him and her greeting warmed his heart.

"You're Grannie over again," he said, and kissed her, and they came in arm and arm.

"What's brought you down?" asked Kelly.

"I have to go into Wellington to-morrow, so I thought I might as well come to-day and look in here."

"You'll stay the night?" said Genevieve.

"If I may."

Robin's one complaint was that he could seldom manage a word alone with Genevieve. Whenever he proposed an evening's run in the car the wistful look in his mother's face hurt him.

"Will you come, too, Mother? We'll call out for Genevieve; I promised to take her up the Valley."

Norah had seen nothing to revive her suspicions, and Kitty was too blind in her devotion. There was, in fact, no outward change or manifestation, and even Kelly was not aware of the subtle movements and their consequences.

In mid-winter Potty Barker came over for a holiday and stayed at the Hutt. Over a pipe and a beer he and Kelly talked of Tapuwai. It was a subject seldom mentioned; like a bad dream, they would gladly forget it. But now that it had receded into the past they spoke more freely than they had ever done, and each acknowledged the lurking fear of proving a coward at the pinch.

From the past they turned to the future.

"Bible for breakfast was a new diet for me," said Potty, "but Old Man Macdonald isn't a bad sort. Not goody-goodish, but regular in his habits. He didn't like my language at first, but he saw it was effective with the dogs when we were mustering, and as long as I don't swear in front of Jessie and the Missus he's easy."

"How's Jessie?" asked Kelly.

Potty moved in his chair and threw his right leg over the left, and grinned sheepishly.

"It's not quite fixed up, but the Old Man's had his eye on the farm adjoining for a long time. Had an option on it for the boys before they went doctoring and preaching. Between you and me, I think he is going to make Jessie a wedding present of it—see! He wasn't keen at first; thought I was a wandering sort of waster. But I've worked like hell over there, Kelly. Sober as a judge; even say 'please' to the dogs when the women are about . . ."

"Quite tamed!"

Potty scratched his chin. "Almost!" he added with a wink.

"She's a damn' fine girl, Jessie," said Kelly. "Tapuwai proved that."

"I'm not a sentimental sort, Kelly, but there aren't many like Jessie. And I'm prepared to settle down and be a good lad for the rest of my days when she marries me."

"When is it to be?" Kelly enquired, a slap on the back expressing his congratulations.

"Some time next spring."

"All set!"

"I'm buying a ring over here. When I go back the news will be out."

"You don't expect us to fall dead with surprise," said Kelly.

"Well, hardly. But the Missus insists on doing it properly; the real Pencarrow touch; notice in the papers, and letters to all the aunts and cousins."

"I know."

"You're too comfortable here, Kelly. I don't suppose you're thinking of getting married. Genevieve's so damned efficient."

"Not yet. Nothing on my horizon."

"Don't you ever feel you'd like a wife and youngsters—squawking little devils, but good fun?"

"Fun, you call them? I don't know that Father and Mother regarded us as much fun. And we've been a bitter disappointment since we've grown up."

"Now, if we have any children I'm going to let them have a free hand. I think your father was wrong; dead wrong. If he had let you alone you'd probably have been—"

"Never! I'd have been what I am. His opposition only stiffened me because I'm an obstinate swine, I know."

"But you are content at last!"

"Am I?" Kelly said it as though it were a question that often troubled him and for which he had no answer.

"Aren't you? Damn it, you ought to be," said Potty, looking round.

"I know I ought to be, and I am, up to a certain point. But I'm beginning to think that I need a spur. When things go well, I am inclined to slack it. Ten years of this and I'd be a lazy old man, past caring, and resenting any effort to shift me."

"Go on; what rot!"

"I mean it. I can feel it; a sort of fatty degeneration of the will."

"What you need is a wife that nags. She'd keep you moving."

"I'd wring her blasted neck!" and Kelly laughed.

"Any sign of Genevieve getting married?" asked Potty.

Kelly turned apprehensively.

"Genevieve! Good lord, no!"

"Or Robin?" Potty persisted.

"I don't think Robin will marry for a long time. His mother worships him and would spoil him if he were that kind. But he isn't; at least, I don't think so. But she wants to keep him with her, and I see signs of her warning off any girls who take special notice of him. Aunt Kitty has high ambitions for Robin. None of your ordinary Wellington girls would do for him."

"Hope he doesn't come a cropper."

"Oh, he's quite content. Girls don't worry him much—not yet."

"He and Genevieve still as thick as ever?"

"Yes—why?"

"Nothing. But they were very maty at Tapuwai. Cousins, of course . . ."

"You don't mean . . . you don't think . . .?" Kelly began, a sudden light dawning on him.

"Wouldn't surprise me," said Potty, unconscious of the full effect of his words.

13

IT was a wet, cold spring, and the early lambs had a chilly reception. Kelly was busy through August and September, but his losses were few. Michael, however, had been less fortunate. The bleak winds whistled across Duffield, and late snow and drenching rains caused havoc among his lambs.

Ella had caught a bad cold, and as soon as she was well she and Gentry went off to Napier for a week, and then on to Auckland, insisting that it was more important that she should get rid of her cough in the sunshine than that he should be in attendance at lambing.

On a wet Sunday in September a message reached Kelly that Michael had been injured. His horse had put a foot into a rabbit-hole while he was out among the sheep in the dark, and fell, rolling on him. Several ribs were broken, his shoulder bruised, and they were not yet certain if there were internal injuries. He had been taken to the hospital at Featherston.

Michael might be weeks in hospital, and Gentry was in Auckland and could not get back for some days.

Kelly saddled his horse and turned up the familiar road that led to Duffield. Genevieve watched him go, a great joy in her heart. Kelly was going back to Duffield. He had said little; just that Michael had been hurt, and he had better go out and look after things. There was no sign that it was other than an ordinary journey.

As he rode in the drenching rain, the violent squalls buffeting him, his heart was beating at a smarter pace. He was going back to Duffield. It was all quite simple and natural. No one had told him to go; no one had asked or urged him to take Michael's place. It was just the most ordinary thing in the world. Odd that such a circumstance had not arisen before; such a combination of events. He wondered as he rode if the trees he had planted had grown very tall; if they had bent before the wind, as Michael said they would. The place would be changed, he knew; the house had been considerably enlarged and the sheep yards moved back out of view.

It was a good road now, not the rutted track

full of potholes that he remembered. The early dark was falling when Kelly came in sight of Duffield. Through an oblique veil of rain he saw the homestead standing solidly amidst the trees. Yes, the poplars had bent before the wind, but he liked them so. How long? Nearly ten years since he had planted them—nearly ten years since he had left Duffield with Michael that morning to welcome Ella and Gentry back from their honey-moon and attend the party Miles was giving for them.

As he drew near and saw the familiar sweep of hills, the swamp lands near the lake, and heard the bleating of the young lambs, his mind went back to those early years when he had been so happy there, so ambitious, so recklessly experimental, trying to remake it all in a night. Now he had sobered down. His present peaceful existence had drugged that youthful spirit, or perhaps it had overspent itself.

Kelly could not recapture the ecstasy. Here he was at Duffield. He drew rein and sat a moment, hoping that something of the old fire would return. It was like meeting the sweetheart of one's youth, now the matronly wife of another man. He was hurt and disappointed—disappointed with himself. He wanted to yield himself to a sweet sentimental regret; to feel once more the longing for Duffield, to know the stirring of his pulse as he looked at it with pride—the Pencarrow estate.

It had not changed very much. The house was larger, and the garden more mature. The difference was close and intimate, but nothing could alter the landscape—the hills and the sea and the wide stretch of land with its sheep and its cattle. The dusk and the mist obliterated the details which alone had changed, and left the broad outline; the Duffield he had known and loved.

For years he had longed for and dreaded this moment. Now it had come, and he was unmoved. But ten years is a long time.

The occasional discontent he had felt at the Hutt had its roots in the dream he cherished —the dream of Duffield. Now, perhaps, he would be satisfied.

Cold and tired, he rode up to the house and was welcomed by the housekeeper. He saw the head shepherd and talked of sheep and lambs. Weary and a little sad that he had been denied the sweet poignancy of that awakened longing, he slept in his old room.

The storm had blown itself out, and Kelly

sprang out of bed eagerly next morning. As the sun rose over the fresh and lovely scene, he stood at his window, his eyes wandering from one point to another, across the garden, to the far hills, and the snowy caps of the Orongorongs.

The disappointment of the night was less acute. He had asked a man for a boy's emotion. He realized now that had he remained here during these ten years he might feel just as he did to-day. It was a response no less deep for its quiet. Youth passes, and with it goes the vaulting hopes and the wild desires, and in its place comes a slower, less passionate answer to the whip of pain or the throb of pleasure. Duffield had not changed, but he had. He looked at last year's frisky lambs, now sober sheep; the playful puppy, now a trusted sheepdog. Last night he was disappointed to find that Duffield did not stir the old wild ecstasy. To-day a sharper edge stabbed when he realized that he could never again recapture that delight and the fever that was youth. As he stood watching from the window he said good-bye to the boyish Kelly who, somehow, he had imagined still dwelt at Duffield and would come back with his return. Now he knew better. If he were to love Duffield, it was as a man, sane with the sanity of experience, but warmed by the ashes of his youthful ardour; a secret memory to be laid aside from prying eyes; a sentiment to be openly repudiated as men reject such things, but to be treasured unashamed in a quiet corner of his heart—the memory of his first love, Duffield.

Without embarrassment Kelly waited for Gentry's return. It seemed odd that it was he, not Philip, who stood at the door as the car drove up; that he should offer the welcoming hand, and say that tea was ready. If Gentry noticed it, he showed no sign. He had never shared Kelly's feeling about Duffield; was free from jealousy. He was quite indifferent, but it was a surprise to Kelly to know how little the encounter disturbed him.

Now that Gentry was back he could leave.

"Oh, don't hurry away," said Ella.

"I'd better get back. We are pretty busy this month. When does Michael expect to be home?"

"Father wants to come next week, but the doctor says no."

"He need not hurry, now that you're back."

Gentry laughed. "I think he has more

confidence in you. He didn't mind while he knew you were here. He thinks I'm a rotten farmer, doesn't he, darling?"

"Of course he doesn't. But you aren't as keen about things as Kelly. I remember when you were always planting trees and drawing plans for gardens and new sheep yards, and trying experiments with feeding. Father said—"

She broke off, as though suddenly she remembered the termination of that happy period. She looked quickly from Kelly to her husband, and then changed the subject.

"Have a drink?" said Gentry.

"Thanks!"

"Here's luck!"

"Cheerio!"

When Kelly returned to the Hutt, suppressed curiosity tingled in the air.

He had been away a week and the news that Kelly had gone to Duffield had wakened keen excitement among the family.

He arrived in time for tea on Saturday afternoon and found Robin and Pat with Genevieve.

"Don't all rush out and ask him how he felt going back to Duffield," she said, when

Miles thought they might drive out on Saturday.

"No, better not," Norah agreed. "Kelly hates to be questioned. But he will be anxious to know if it all went off smoothly, and there was no . . . incident."

"How's Uncle Michael?" was Genevieve's first question.

"Getting better. He will be home in a couple of weeks. Nothing very serious, but a bad shake up and a few broken ribs."

"Ella's cold better?" asked Pat.

"Never saw her look so well."

"Gentry's luck still holding? Marvellous how he picks winners. He doesn't know a damn' thing about horses," said Pat.

"You only hear what he wins; never what he loses," was Robin's comment.

"Things in pretty good shape up there?" Pat asked casually.

"Yes—fair."

Genevieve's sharp eyes watched Kelly closely. She guessed that the Duffield he had dreamt about all these years, and the place he had just seen, were very different. Whatever had occurred, it had left Kelly undisturbed. They had all been secretly afraid that the visit might make him discontented at the Hutt. As the weeks passed, the result appeared to have been otherwise. Kelly settled down to the summer's work with a new eagerness, no longer disturbed by the sharp contrast between the Home Farm and its limitations and Duffield as his youthful fancy had painted it. It was still the same, but something of the glamour had gone. He would build anew an affection for it, if he must, but based on its solid worth and not its romantic value. As the days lengthened and the sun warmed the Valley, he watched the flowers bud and blossom in Grannie's garden, and in a new and more intimate way made them his own.

14

NOT even the *Rotomahana* and her fame could hold Pat to the coastal trade for long, but in this period he brought both joy and anxiety to his parents. Sir Miles would stand, his glasses to his eyes, watching for the vessel to round Point Halswell into the harbour. Proudly he watched in fine weather, when you could almost set your watch by her, after her all-night run from Lyttleton; anxiously, after a night of storm, when she came through the curtain of driving rain and spray, her lovely, graceful lines cutting the angry waters as she made port.

"Here she is, Norah!"

"Oh, thank God! What a night it has been!" and Norah's sigh was a prayer of gratitude.

When at her best speed the *Rotomahana* struck a particular gait, and the whole ship throbbed and hummed, and the flag halyards of her mainmast would slap the mast in a dancing tattoo. Indeed, an old lady sent up a message one night asking the captain to stop the men dancing over her head.

Pat was on the *Rotomahana* when, twenty-five years after her arrival in New Zealand, she did the night run of one hundred and seventy-three miles between Wellington and Lyttleton in the record time of ten hours, thirty-five minutes.

Whenever the wind howled and raged round the house at night, Norah would turn towards the window that looked out across the harbour. "God help the ships at sea tonight!" she would murmur, and her special prayer was for Pat and the *Rotomahana*.

She had personality as well as grace of line, and a turn of speed remarkable for her size. As she came and left port, people stood at their windows to watch her pass, or paused in their walk to admire her. Newer and faster ships have broken her records, but the memory of the old *Rotomahana* lives on in the port that was for long her home.

On New Year's Day, the *Rotomahana* ran an excursion to Picton. Crossing Cook Strait bears close comparison with the Calais-Dover run between England and France. The temper of the two channels is similar in its uncertainty, and the distance between land is something the same. But there is a longer stretch of sheltered waters, from Wellington to Pencarrow Head before clearing land on one side, and the long, lovely waters of Queen Charlotte Sound before reaching Picton on the other side.

These excursions were strangely attractive, and, once determined to go, no wind or weather could deter the passengers so long as the ship would face it. The most enthusiastic passengers were those who had never been to sea before.

New Year's Day is one of the great midsummer holidays, the Christmas closure often extending throughout the whole week and terminating with New Year's Day.

Potty Barker suggested to Kelly that they ought to come over with Pat for the regatta on this holiday and they could all meet in Picton.

Potty and Jessie had been married three months. It was a quiet wedding, with no fuss, and he was now comfortably installed as owner of the farm adjoining the Macdonald homestead. Marriage had clipped his wings, and though he had found it good to have a home of his own, and Jessie for his wife, an occasional desire to get away and savour again the discomforts and freedom of his wandering life disturbed him. He wanted a man's companionship as well as a woman's love. Old Donald was a serious, trustworthy, deeply religious man. Potty admired his father-in-law, but found him rather discouraging. To do a round of the pubs with Kelly, drinking long beers and spinning yarns; to give vent to that suppressed element that once had been as free as the birds of the air; to have a night out! It was this urge in his soul that had inspired the invitation.

Genevieve was eager to go. Robin, who doubted his capacity to stand the tide-rip off Terewhiti twice in one day, was reluctant. Pat warned them of possible discomfort, but was pleased at the prospect. He always hated these excursions: hundreds of young men and girls, packed on board, starting out gaily in the summer sun, dressed in muslins and big hats, later lying limply anywhere, sodden with sea water and drenched with spray, green-faced and sea-sick, miserable, past comforting, disillusioned with one another, and longing for land—or death.

New Year's Day broke fine, but a stiff breeze from the south-east caused Miles to tap the barometer anxiously.

"Pat has just rung up to know if we are going," and Genevieve banged on Kelly's door. They had come in the night before because of the early start.

"Of course we're going. I am, anyway," he said.

"Take a raincoat and a light rug, dear; you may need them. You know what these summer southerlies are like," urged Norah.

"This is worse than I expected," said Genevieve, as they crowded up the gangway in the midst of a gay and giggling crowd of young trippers who had paid their five shillings and meant to have their money's worth.

"Here, put your things in my cabin," said Pat, "and if you get—"

"Sea-sick!" Robin suggested with an apprehensive smile.

"Yes, sea-sick—here is the best I can do."

"Is it going to be rough?" asked Genevieve.

"No; a bit of a swell on, and a breeze outside," said Pat, offering comfort without conviction.

"Just look at them; there ought to be a notice up forbidding them to eat chocolates and oranges," Genevieve said with disgust.

"They'll learn; they'll know better next

time," said Pat, grinning. "I must be off. See you later."

Wellington harbour was sparkling in the sunlight. A few yachts were already out, their white sails filling in the breeze. Three big liners were loading butter and wool and frozen meat for the London market. The coal hulks, black and clumsy, were moored out of the line of shipping. The little *Cobar* was beating across the harbour to Day's Bay with a freight of the less adventurous.

As the *Rotomahana* left Pencarrow Head behind and turned towards the South Island, which was now a dim shadow on the horizon, the tide-rip off Terewhiti came in great green curlers and lifted her as she hummed her merry tune of speed.

The first rise and fall of the deck and the rhythmic heave of the swell had a disconcerting effect upon Robin.

"You shouldn't have come," said Genevieve.

He smiled grimly, hoping to avert disaster. It was maddening to be so impotent. You could stifle a cry of pain, or endure torture without complaint, but gallant hearts and stout courage are no defence against a heaving stomach.

"Here, come on. You're first man down, and you may as well admit it," said Genevieve, as he turned a sickly green. But he fled. He was not going to monopolize Pat's cabin; that, at least, he could do for Genevieve.

"Where has he gone?" she asked.

"Better not enquire," said Kelly. The heave and surge and the drumming of the engines had begun to undermine his own resistance as he leaned over the rail.

"You'd better go to Pat's cabin," he suggested to Genevieve, as all around helpless victims were beginning to lie down to their misery, and the glamour of young love wore very thin as stewards with brooms and buckets were kept busy.

Genevieve was in no hurry to go to the cabin, as she had something of Pat's love of the sea, but the devastation around her was enough to upset the strongest stomach, and she could see Kelly gradually turning a peevish green and eager to be free of her.

Two hours later, when the *Rotomahana* had entered the Sounds, Genevieve came out of the cabin where she had lain with a splitting headache, but no other physical disturbance.

Kelly and Robin, both looking very conscious of their condition, were waiting for her.

"A bit white about the gills, aren't you?" she said, laughing, but not without pity, particularly for Robin, who looked terribly ill.

"It was an insane idea to come," she added.

"We can thank Potty for this," said Robin.

"You'll be right as rain as soon as you get ashore," Genevieve cheered them.

"Will I? The road will come up and hit me in the face—I know the dirty trick. And we've got to go back again this evening; and it will be much worse; the wind is rising."

"Robin!" Genevieve looked surprised at his pessimism.

"It's no good, Genevieve, I'm not heroic stuff. I look rotten and I feel rotten."

"I had the cabin, and could lie down," she said.

"You damn' well won't have it to yourself this evening, my girl," said Kelly.

"Why?"

"Because we're sharing it—see!"

"I know, you and Potty will drink beer and tell yarns all day, and then—"

"Exactly. And then I'll sleep like a top from here to Wellington. What about it, Robin? Isn't that a good idea?"

"What?"

"Get dead drunk and you won't feel anything."

"I like that," said Genevieve. "I do like that."

"Well, you can do the same," and he laughed.

"Can't you see Father's face if we all came rolling home—"

"In-a-cab," said Kelly.

"Hullo. Have a drop of brandy." Pat dashed along for a moment to see how they fared, and grinned cheerfully at the wreckage. "That'll fix you. It's a glorious day, and calm as a pond."

"Liar!" said Genevieve emphatically.

"It is—look at that," and he pointed to the sheltered waters of the Sound.

"Don't you carry any oil?" asked Kelly.

"What! Castor oil? Might have a drop in the engine-room—"

"Fathead! To pour on—"

"Oh yes, 'the troubled waters', as the poets call them. No, we don't use oil; it might make the ship dirty; and we're very particular on the *Rotomahana*."

Pale and pea-green, the gay crowd that had trooped up the gangway in Wellington now crawled or were supported ashore. Some, too ill to move, lay inert about the deck, which the stewards had attacked with vigour.

"Oh, Gawd! This is wonderful!" was Potty's greeting, as he hit Kelly a blow on the chest that nearly knocked him over.

Potty's delight was so warm and generous, and Jessie was so eager to second his invitation, that it almost made up for the trip.

Hester and her husband were there, too, but Potty declared that this was his treat, and he left the parents to their more sober pleasures while he took his guests to lunch at Allports Hotel.

For a while they watched the regatta and the men walking the greasy-pole, and cheered the Seymour crew to victory, but afterwards, not without some apprehension, Jessie and Genevieve decided to leave the men to themselves.

"I believe they mean it," said Genevieve. "Kelly said if he got dead drunk he could sleep all the way back without being sea-sick."

"He won't do that, but Potty has been talking about a day out with Kelly for ages. He has been awfully good, but I know he finds Father a bit too strict."

"Kelly is used to a drink or two, but Robin doesn't like beer. I'm sure if they do a round of the pubs it will only make them worse. I'll have a nice picnic going home."

"It's only once in a while, and Potty has a pretty tame life down here after all he has done. If he does get a bit tight I'll be able to sail home. I'm a better hand with the boat than he is," said Jessie.

When the *Rotomahana* left at five o'clock on her return journey the sky had clouded over, and hung leaden and cold above the hilltops, and they found the sailors had made preparations for heavy weather outside.

Potty, Kelly and Robin were in a state of hilarity, and laughed foolishly at nothing. Jessie anchored Potty to her side and took his arm. No more drink for him to-day. As soon as the boat sailed she would make for home.

Pat only grinned in that amusing way of his, and agreed with Genevieve that they had better go straight to bed.

"You'll have a nice head in the morning," she said.

"I've got it now," Robin announced pathetically.

"Potty's a good sort," said Kelly, trying to unlace his boots.

"He's a big fool, like yourself," said Genevieve irritably.

"Getting very hoity-toity, aren't we?" Kelly answered with rising indignation.

"Go on, get into bed. Take your coat and collar off. I'll wake you when we get inside the Heads," and she drew the curtain in disgust.

"Genevieve!" said Robin in a feeble voice.

"What?" she answered sharply.

"I'm sorry! Oh, my head!" he added, and pressed a hand to his forehead.

"I'm not wasting any pity on either of you. If you must be sick you might at least stay sober," and she left them.

The wind whined and whistled through the ropes and canvas that protected the huddled passengers on deck. Outside in the Strait a half-gale was blowing, and the great green waves broke with a thud and a swish of spray as the clipper bows cut through them. It was an angry sea, lashed by a high wind that came in spiteful squalls. She pounded her way through the storm, which clutched at her and thrashed her, but the slim, defiant little vessel picked up Pencarrow Light before eleven o'clock, long after she was due, and it was a

288

great relief to Miles to see her lights come up the harbour.

Genevieve had been extended the hospitality of the chief mate's cabin, and, though feeling ill, as she frankly admitted, she had not succumbed. Her head was raging, and she walked unsteadily, and the sight of the seasick passengers in the last throes of misery wakened anew her disgust.

Pat had looked in to see Kelly and Robin, and found them both asleep, but looking a little unsavoury, as he put it.

Genevieve came out of the cabin for a breath of air as they entered the harbour. It was very dark, but lights shone in every bay and from the summer cottages by the water's edge. Chains of street lamps were strung out in glowing loops behind the city and stretched up the hilly background. The whole city was gemmed with lights, and they spangled the terraced homes like stars on a frosty night. The red and green lamps of moored ships sent big wavering ribbons of light across the broken water. Someone had told Genevieve that Wellington at night was very like Hong Kong. She wondered as she looked at it if she would ever see Hong Kong. At the moment she had no desire to travel.

She hated ships and the sea, and wondered what on earth had attracted Pat to such a life. This crossing had dimmed all the glamour of the sea for her. And now he was leaving the *Rotomahana*, because he had grown weary of the nightly ferry trip, and was returning to the New Zealand Shipping Company. He was to fill the place of the fourth mate, who had been washed overboard coming round the Cape of Good Hope on the outward voyage. Back to the blue water service, which is so different from the coastal trade. Genevieve said he had a sweetheart in England, but Pat was silent. Well, he could have the sea if he liked it, but she had had enough.

"You do look a wreck," she said, as Pat brought Kelly and Robin to join her.

"Two bright specimens," said Pat. "I've given them a brandy."

"On top of all that beer?" Genevieve asked.

"It's the only thing I could get. It usually works. Pulls them together for a bit."

Neither made any remark. They were too conscious of their woeful appearance; tousled, sickly, limp.

"I think I'll ring Mother and tell her not to wait up for us. Say we've been ill and will go straight to bed. The gale will provide some excuse," said Genevieve.

Kelly looked grateful, but said not a word. Robin seemed unhappy as well as ill. He avoided Genevieve's eyes. She understood that he was feeling ashamed. It was the first time she had seen him at a disadvantage; he was always so punctilious about his person and his clothes. Then pity stirred her and she put a hand on his arm.

"Any better?" she asked gently.

He was too grateful to make a reply; his voice was not under control.

"Good night, Pat; thanks awfully for a foul trip. Come on, you two."

"Pat's a damn' fool. Fancy anybody wanting to be a sailor," Kelly mumbled, as his shaky legs met the rigid, unrelenting road.

15

"MARY wants you to go over and say good-bye, Pat," Genevieve announced at breakfast a few days before he joined his new ship for England.

"Can't she come over here?"

"They all want to see you. Reverend Mother talks of when she used to give you marbles for being a good little boy—pee-wees and agates, and stonies and glassies and a big tor. And once she tried to play with you, and you said she funked because her knuckle was inside the ring."

"Oh, I've heard all that a dozen times. Must I, Mother?" Pat looked to his mother to get him out of it.

"I think you might. It won't take long, and naturally they would like to see you."

"I'll take you over; pilot you through the rows of adoring schoolgirls."

Self-consciously Pat went with Genevieve across to the convent to see his eldest sister. He would much prefer to have seen her at home. Crossing the grounds they encountered groups of girls in black school uniforms, their hair in long plaits, and with white sailor hats bearing the convent badge. Some shyly, some slightly admiring, others frankly interested, watched him pass.

Pat was getting more like his father, and the tall, blue-eyed, bronzed sailor brother of Sister Mary Agnes was a person of conspicuous interest to the group of schoolgirls who were permitted no romantic licence.

A young nun opened the hall door and showed them into the reception-room, an austere room, cold and polished, with stiff chairs, a large pot of asparagus fern, a mahogany case of big books, and two pictures, one of St. Joseph and the other of the Madonna.

Outside they could hear the slither of felt slippers on the polished corridor, the rattle of the heavy rosary beads that hung from their belts, and the creak and crackle of the starched gamps as the hurrying nuns turned a head to speak to each other in passing.

Presently the door opened and Mary came in with Reverend Mother. Then a tea-tray was brought in by a young nun, who looked shy and was glad to escape. The tall figure of the Reverend Mother, her old face finely wrinkled, her kind eyes smiling humorously, poured two cups of tea. Neither she nor Mary shared the meal with their guests. Pat took the frail cup and a triangle of thin white bread-and-butter, and afterwards a slice of Madeira cake, and tried to respond to the cordiality of their interest in him. But he felt awkward and ill at ease, especially when the nun who had taught him in the infant school arrived, and then the stout little veteran of the music-room came bouncing in cheerfully at the Reverend Mother's call, to speak to her old pupil. His discomfort deepened as the minutes passed.

With a turn of the head and a crackle of gamp, they recalled his childish exploits, his devotion to St. Anthony, his delight in playing his scales with both pedals down, and the inkpot, shaped like a cabbage, he had bought out of his money-box for Reverend Mother's feast day. As the reminiscences flowed simply, embarrassingly, waking kindly memories of an ex-pupil, now a sailor who travelled the world, Genevieve saw Pat's mounting confusion. He looked ready to leap out of the window in his desire to escape.

"I think we will have to go, Reverend Mother," said Genevieve, looking at her watch.

Pat instantly stood up, the prospect of immediate release making him more genial; almost the cheerful sailor they had expected to find him.

"Good-bye; we will always remember you in our prayers," said Reverend Mother.

"Good-bye, Pat."

"Good-bye, Mary."

She gave him a little parcel, with an Agnus Dei and a medal of St. Anthony, and Reverend Mother presented him with specially blessed rosary beads.

"Well, dear?" asked Norah, as they came in.

"You were a dismal failure, Pat," said Genevieve.

"Why do you say that?" asked his mother.

"They expected to see him with his brass buttons—a real sailor—not in these dull, ordinary clothes."

"Rot!" said Pat.

"Mary told me. 'We're so disappointed he didn't wear his uniform' Aren't they childish?"

"Genevieve!" Norah's tone reproved her. She did not like this critical attitude toward the nuns.

"But they are, Mother. They see so little of

the outside world, and they can't help being curious."

"Genevieve, I won't have you talking like that."

"But it's true, Mother. They are curious. It isn't a crime to be curious; it's natural. But they do like to know all about what you're doing, and if an old girl gets engaged or married they want her to trot him up to the convent to be looked over. And Pat's a sailor, and a sailor sounds like a hero to them, and they remember him as a fat little youngster who used to bite his nails. Taking a habit is like putting on a uniform, Mother, it doesn't entirely eliminate human nature; it may subdue it, but curiosity—harmless curiosity— isn't a sin. Curiosity is an incentive to learning. Not to be curious is to be indifferent, and that is much worse. And the nuns are curious, and I don't blame them. When I go over with a new dress, Mary always wants to know if that is a new fashion. And I say Pat was a dismal failure because he didn't arrive in his brass buttons, and he looked a big sookie and wouldn't say a word, and—"

"My God, that girl's got a terrible tongue!" said Miles, who had been reading the paper.

Pat was annoyed.

"Put on your uniform this evening, and slip over to see them for a minute," suggested Norah, who was very proud of her handsome sailor son, and sympathized with Mary's disappointment.

"Oh, Mother!"

"Why not? Put a raincoat over it—"

"And I'll carry your hat in a paper bag," added Genevieve.

"You've too much to say," said Miles angrily.

"Well, you don't hear me so often now; it ought to be a treat."

"That's no way to speak to your father, Genevieve." Norah resorted to her usual phrase of admonition.

Pat took advantage of the swing of discussion to Genevieve, and disappeared.

When he sailed three days later there were Norah's tears and his father's advice to be cloaked by Genevieve's flippancies.

"Good-bye, Paddy Doyle. Bring me a dress from Worth's in Paris, and I'll pay you back when Kelly raises my wages."

"She's paid more than she's worth now," said Kelly.

"All right. I'll take Maisie Kite's advice,

and learn typing and shorthand, and be a woman of independence."

"Say good-bye to Maisie for me," said Pat.

"I will," Peter chimed in.

"Ha! Don't you trespass on Peter's preserves," and Genevieve laughed. Peter got red and tried to look dignified.

Robin and Kitty arrived at the last minute, and had a few words with Pat.

"The whole Pencarrow tribe," said the second engineer to the third as they went below.

16

GENEVIEVE wondered what was keeping Kelly. He was very late. Several times he had gone in to Wellington on Saturday afternoon and arrived back at night a trifle hilarious. Now it was nearly midnight and there was no sign of him. She would not have worried but for the fact that this Saturday night out was becoming a habit. Each time he came home a little later and with more pronounced evidence of how the evening had been spent. The thought flashed across her mind that some barmaid might have got hold of him and captured his fleeting fancy, though it was not like him to be fascinated with that type. She never questioned him. Genevieve knew too well how stubborn he could be; how resentful of criticism or interference. She was anxious tonight, and could not sleep. Perhaps Robin knew where he went, but she could not ask him. It seemed like spying on Kelly. She despised the weakness of many mothers who would not trust their children; that questioning devotion which would not permit them a private thought.

"My children tell me everything; absolutely everything. I dislike secretive people. And it is so much safer."

Genevieve had heard that boast more than once. A frank confidence she entirely approved, but the forced confession of every thought and word and action led to subterfuge. She hated the petty tyrannies and the little lies and evasions it entailed. If she were defiant, it was an open challenge and preferable to dishonesty for the sake of peace.

As she lay awake listening for Kelly's return, nebulous fears began to take shape. Kelly had changed. He needed opposition and difficulties to brace him. Life was too placid at the Hutt; too limited. The farm was well run, but compared with the heart-breaking work he had known in Taranaki and at Tapuwai, and the wide scope that Duffield offered, it became a pleasant routine, and routine was a deadly poison for Kelly. She kept house efficiently; he was not worried by domestic problems. Without conscious effort they had drawn the family back to the old home by some innate gift of hospitality. It was all so easy—too easy, thought Genevieve.

"It's bad for anyone to drift, and that's what is happening to Kelly—and to me."

She was aware that the months were slipping pleasantly into years, and she was quite content, at least until something brought her face to face with the realities of life.

"This won't do," she decided. "Kelly needs a jolt, and so do I."

Her mind drifted to Maisie Kite, and her eager, ambitious fight for the things she lacked. She might learn shorthand and typewriting; it would give her something to do; something to make her stretch her mind a little. She could do it out here in her leisure. She couldn't spend the whole of her life keeping house for Kelly. It had served its purpose, but it was not enough. She had made a success of it, though she had little love for domestic work. Now she wanted to try something else—something more difficult. She was revolving this idea in her mind when the gate clicked. Then she heard Kelly stumble over the doorstep and swear.

"In a bad temper, too," she thought, as she listened to the impatient noises from his room: the banged door and a chair kicked out of the way.

Kelly looked seedy at breakfast next

morning. He was a sickly colour, and had no appetite, but Genevieve made no comment. He was grateful, but could not show it, and a querulous tone hung out a danger signal.

"The whole family's coming out to-day," she said.

"They are—damn them?" he said irritably.

"Yes, but not till after dinner."

That was a reprieve. By afternoon he might feel better. He would hate to sit through dinner opposite his father and mother. He knew he looked wretched, and his mother would be all concern; there would be tears if she guessed right, and medicine if she didn't. His father would recognize the shaky aftermath, and lecture him on sobriety. But tea was an informal meal. He could escape their scrutiny by being an assiduous host.

After breakfast he rode across the farm, and though the summer was waning he had a swim in the river.

Of course Genevieve knew, but she wouldn't say anything. And he could not bring himself to speak of it; not yet. But he could feel contempt in her silence, which stung him more than her most biting words, and they often had a cauterizing effect.

At dinner he looked much better. He had

taken special care in dressing. The sun shone and they could still play tennis, and despite a headache he looked immaculate in his flannels. His white shoes were scrupulously clean, his rebellious hair brushed and sleek. He had made a considerable effort to obliterate the signs of the night's dissipation. But still Genevieve made no remark. She felt it was, in its way, more a gesture of apology to her than an attempt to disguise his appearance before the family. Silently he had offered this apology, and she had accepted it.

Genevieve realized, however, that it could not continue. Whatever had captured his fancy in town and led to these Saturday orgies was a menace. To combat this influence Kelly needed some fresh and vital interest in life.

Her mind was debating the question when the first of the family, Robin and Kitty, arrived. Miles and Norah and Meggie came later, then Peter and Maisie Kite. Michael might be down. If ever he had to go into Wellington on a Monday he usually came to the Hutt the day before and joined the Sunday party.

Kelly greeted his parents with less than his

usual restraint, and showed marked deference to his father's opinions.

"The boy is improving," was Miles's comment.

"He doesn't look too well," said his mother. "A little pale, I thought."

"Nonsense. He is the fittest of them all. Hard as nails, and leads a healthy life; to bed early, not hanging around hotels and barmaids till all hours—"

He caught Norah's eye, and, remembering his own youth and its follies, coughed awkwardly and changed the subject.

Norah and Kitty sat in the garden watching their children playing tennis. Miles was pacing the path puffing at his pipe. The two mothers were indulging in speculations about the future.

"I often wish Genevieve would marry," sighed Norah. With all her large brood, there had not yet been a wedding in the family, and her maternal heart looked forward to grandchildren. It would be so nice to see the next generation launched. It might be good for Miles, also, to find himself a grandfather and see his name perpetuated in a new branch. Neil and Jessie were married—strange marriages both of them. She hoped her own children would do better. Ella, too, had married and now had two little daughters, but no son, to Michael's disappointment. She was a little jealous of the start the others had made.

"Genevieve is very . . . intelligent," said Kitty, choosing her words carefully. She wasn't exactly pretty, being too athletic and vigorous for the approved type of the period. Her frankness and easy comradeship inspired friendship, loyalty, confidence, but it did not bewitch or beguile. There was no coquetry.

"Yes, she has a fine character, so terribly honest, but a sharp tongue," her mother confessed.

"It's a pity," Kitty sympathized. "Men don't like a clever woman, especially if she has a biting tongue; even if she is witty."

"I don't think she is anxious to marry." Norah was instantly on the defensive. "She could have them if she liked, but she doesn't bother."

"Still, she can't go on keeping house for Kelly always."

Kitty's own memories of life at the Hutt before her marriage and her desire to escape came back to her vividly.

"Kelly may marry," she continued.

"Not if Genevieve makes him so comfortable. He seems to be—well—reluctant to move or change, and it's not like Kelly." Norah talked of her perplexities until a chance remark startled Kitty.

"Why do you say that? Why do you say: 'If it weren't for Robin'?"

"What I meant was that Genevieve and Robin and Kelly are always together, and seem satisfied with each other's company. It shuts out strangers . . . other people—"

"I hope you don't mean that Robin's friendship for Genevieve is standing in the way of her marrying—"

"No, Kitty, not exactly. And yet when people see them so much together, they may think—other men may believe . . ." She paused awkwardly.

"Think what? Believe what?" said Kitty, bridling.

"Well, you know, dear; now don't be angry, but, after all, they are cousins, Kitty, and it wouldn't do; it wouldn't be nice—"

"Are you suggesting, Norah, that Robin and Genevieve are in love?"

"Hasn't it ever occurred to you?"

"Never! I never dreamt of such a thing. And I'm sure you're wrong. Robin is very fond of his cousin. They are like brother and sister. I think it is ridiculous to try and twist it—"

"I'm not twisting it, Kitty. But I've been worried about it for some time."

"I think it is most unfair to suggest that it is Robin who is keeping Genevieve from getting married. He likes her and understands her sharp tongue better perhaps than other men. A shrewish wife—"

"That's most unkind, Kitty. Genevieve is frank and outspoken, but she is not shrewish. I'm sorry I mentioned it now, but I thought you ought to know; that you'd be glad to talk it over and see what could be done. I've been wanting to, for a long time . . . ever since I saw him kissing her—"

"Kissing her? What harm is there in that?"

"Yes, but this was different, like a young lover. It was after that Tapuwai affair that I saw the change."

"All that time, and you've let it go on and said nothing?"

"I wasn't sure. I hoped when Robin went to live with you, and they didn't see each other so often, it might be different. But just look at them now."

Robin and Genevieve, who had finished a

set, walked off laughing towards the house, their arms linked. But there was an intimate quality in their laughter; a secret delight in their glances.

Kitty's hands gripped each other firmly, a habit she had when needing control or faced with a difficulty. She had been a fool not to have seen this before. Instead she had felt security in it. The lonely boy might have sought companionship and found love, but in this friendship with his cousins she felt an ally. She wanted to keep him with her. She had been parted from him so much, and had made so many sacrifices, and now she grew afraid of anyone who threatened to take him from her. Some day he would marry, but not yet. He was still young. When he married . . .

In her most secret thoughts she planned a brilliant marriage for him. Someone of good family, well-connected, of charm and beauty and accomplishments; a wife who would help him socially as well as make him happy; an English girl, perhaps, with a title somewhere in the family. You could not speak of these things, but they were good to dream of—in the distance. Now Norah had come crashing in with her disturbing suggestion that Robin was in love with Genevieve. She objected to cousins marrying; there was always the fear of the children being—queer. But, in any case, a dominant character like Genevieve would be the worst type of wife for Robin. She would overshadow him. She was not social. True, she played hostess at the Hutt very successfully, but she hated society and its ways, and would not be a good influence on Robin. She was too self-contained. She would drag Robin away from the world in which she wanted him to shine. Her ambitions were all wrong.

Alarm at the prospect, and anger at Norah's clumsy suggestion that it was Robin's friendship that was keeping Genevieve from marrying, completely spoilt her day. She was glad when Genevieve called them in to tea. It was getting chilly and she shivered slightly. From now on she must be on her guard, and watch for signs for this foolish affection which Norah declared she had seen. No use saying anything. Genevieve was too much like Kelly to brook interference. It would merely intensify the trouble; she must act diplomatically. But it was all very disturbing.

No more was said, but Norah felt a chilly note in Kitty's good-bye. That was all the thanks you got. Still, she was glad she had done it.

One reason for telling Kitty was that she knew how strongly she would oppose it, and how much influence she exercised over Robin. She might be able to break it from that end, and spare her an embarrassing interview with Genevieve, from which she always came out worst.

Two days later Genevieve went in to Wellington and, under Maisie's guidance, bought her shorthand books and hired a typewriter. Maisie had appointed herself tutor, and it meant that she would have a legitimate excuse for going to the Hutt more frequently.

"Why this sudden passion for work?" asked Kelly.

"You never know when it may be useful. When you marry and leave me in the lurch I don't think I'd find life at home very absorbing. It happens to be something I can do here, and it interests me."

Kelly frowned on the idea from the first. He could see no justification for it. Not that it affected him, but it suggested restlessness, and he did not enjoy the prospect of Genevieve leaving him. Maisie's visits were welcome, however. He found her amusing and a refreshing change from the more self-conscious girls whose horizon was bounded by marriage. Kelly was regarded as eligible by many mothers, and the pre-war girl had not the alternative of taking a job. Only necessity justified that, except for a few strong-minded pioneers.

"I'll soon be able to type your business letters, Kelly. 'Dear sir—I am in receipt of yours of the tenth ult. re sheep dip.'"

Norah was greatly distressed when she heard about Genevieve's new fad. Her hopes of Genevieve's marriage seemed to recede further; it was very disappointing.

Robin said he'd give her a job in the office, and Kelly remarked that it was not considered decent to lure domestic servants from their allegiance and put notions in their heads above their station.

"See what it means to have a marketable value," laughed Genevieve. "Once men fought over women merely as wives; now they battle for their brains."

"Brains!" Kelly repeated. "It doesn't require brains to tap out: 'Now is the time that all good men should come to the aid of the party', and let the potatoes burn. Every bit of paper in the house has that silly phrase typed on it."

"Can't you convince him of its useful-ness?" asked Maisie.

"I haven't tried. If he hasn't the intelli-gence to see, it's a waste of time."

"Perhaps you could convince me, Maisie," and Kelly smiled at her. A quick flush coloured her face.

So that's it, thought Genevieve, and she went to the kitchen to talk to the maid about what sandwiches to make for tea.

The idea that Maisie was becoming fond of Kelly took root, and at every turn she found confirmation of it. Of Kelly's feeling she was not at all sure. He never exerted himself to capture a girl's affection, but he was popular with them all. He had shown no preference for any one, and Maisie's amusing company had not awakened any warmer response. Genevieve was sure now that the girl's eager-ness to teach her had its origin in her admira-tion for Kelly.

If Kelly married Maisie! Lord, what a row there would be! Sir Miles Pencarrow's eldest son and this almost unknown office girl! But it wasn't likely. So far Kelly seemed proof against it.

Genevieve liked Maisie; she admired her courage and fearlessness, her staunch loyalties, and her fighting qualities. Kelly might do worse, she considered. However, it was no part of her plan to marry Kelly off, and she knew him too well to try to thwart him. Without making it too obvious she gave Maisie her chance, and left fate to decide the future.

Peter was making a final attempt to get his matriculation, his previous failure having greatly incensed his father.

"No more of this damn' play-acting till you're through," he said, and Peter was torn from the amateur operatic society, causing, he was convinced, considerable loss to the company.

Maisie still played leading rôles, and steadily consolidated her footing in those circles which impinged upon music and the theatre.

Without conniving at the affair, which she knew must meet with violent opposition from her parents, Genevieve, however, devised excuses for leaving Kelly and Maisie together.

"Come on, Robin. I want a walk before supper."

Robin was only too glad of the chance to have Genevieve for an hour, and in that easy manner of human affairs a few repetitions soon became a fixed habit.

Norah's startling revelation to Kitty about the evident love between these two had exercised her for many days. Kitty decided that something must be done, and it was evident Norah would only bungle it if she tried to interfere with Genevieve. She was fond of her niece, but Robin came first—a long way first. Her passionate devotion to him would justify any action to save him. She thought it over from every angle. Should she speak to him direct? She decided against that. It might merely precipitate an avowal, or compel Robin to take a definite stand against her. Better to be tactful. If only she could gradually break the habit of going to the Hutt. If she could get him interested in other girls—not too interested, but enough to break with Genevieve. She looked round her list of acquaintances, and selected two or three families as likely allies. She would endeavour to get invitations for Robin—invitations that would take priority over Genevieve's customary Sundays. But it took time.

Kitty harboured no resentment against Genevieve, and she was not anxious to come into conflict with her. She was a proud and sensitive girl and very outspoken. There would be no silent weeping into her pillow with Genevieve. If she suspected a plot to separate her from Robin she would hurl it into the open without compunction. She would do it more coolly than Kelly, however. Genevieve could keep her temper and that gave her the upper hand in an argument. Kitty was quite honest in her admiration for her niece, and also her affection, but even this must not stand in her way. She did not wish to injure Genevieve; indeed, she had convinced herself that such an unfortunate marriage could only mean unhappiness, and she salved her conscience with the excuse that she was really doing Genevieve a good turn, saving her from the results of a foolish action.

But it was not Genevieve's happiness, it was Robin's future that weighted the scales. With a dominant wife, who shunned society and had original ideas about life, Robin would soon slip back. Whatever the cost, it must be stopped, but she would need to exercise care. If she could make Robin understand that Norah regarded his constant companionship as a stumbling-block to Genevieve's chance of marriage! If she could divert his interest elsewhere, temporarily! Perhaps she could see more of Genevieve herself; keep her close, and send Robin off with the others. She must do something and soon, but better if the break came between themselves and not from outside interference. Never to further her own happiness or ambitions did Kitty extend herself and her resources so exhaustively as in her attempt to separate Robin and Genevieve; to save him for the brilliant future she had planned.

17

"HOW nice, Robin! Here is an invitation to tea at Mrs. MacShane's next Sunday," and Kitty passed the note across the breakfast-table.

"Yes, a pity I can't go," he said.

"Why not? They have a lovely place at Karori. I don't think you have been out there before."

"No, I haven't."

"You'll enjoy it. They are most hospitable, and it is a beautiful garden."

"Perhaps they'll ask me another time. But you go."

"What is to stop your coming too?" asked Kitty naïvely.

"I promised Genevieve."

"Surely you can put that off; it isn't important. You can go out there any Sunday."

"Yes, I know. But I promised to ride over the Moonshine Valley with her next Sunday; it's getting too late for tennis."

"Write a note and tell her. I'm sure she will understand."

"I can't do that, Mother."

"Why not? You can ride with her any Sunday. And you may not get this invitation again. After all, social influence is an important factor in a young man's success. You don't want to lean on Miles's associations always. He, poor dear, is getting very out of things. He seldom goes anywhere now except to the Club, and new people are coming to the fore. You must not stick entirely to the family, dear. You want to go about more and meet people. I've been thinking lately that we really ought to do more entertaining ourselves. Small dinner parties are rather nice . . ."

"Yes, of course; then we could have . . ."

"Don't bother about that now," and she smiled, her handsome face soft and bewitching under the radiance of her absorbing love for him. "Just write a note to Genevieve and tell her you can't come on Sunday."

"I can't do that, Mother," he protested.

"I'm afraid you rather monopolise poor Genevieve. I believe Norah thinks you are spoiling her chance of getting married. You are such friends. Still, it isn't quite fair to her.

318

She is getting on now, well into her twenties, and such a fine character, but not every man appreciates a woman with a witty tongue. They dislike clever women, especially as a wife. A henpecked man with a shrewish wife!''

She said it lightly, laughingly, but a cloud had settled on Robin's face. He was not listening to her now. His mind had caught one phrase. He was standing in Genevieve's way. He was the reason she had not married. Why not tell his mother now that he and Genevieve loved each other and were waiting because of his desire to spare her? They were prepared to miss these early years of happiness so that she, his mother, might have some recompense for all she had sacrificed for him. To bring Genevieve as a bride to share a home with his mother was unthinkable.

He felt his mother's eyes on him and looked up. All the love and pleading of her heart were shining in them. How could he hurt her!

"Robin, dear, don't mind what I said. I'm sure if any man wants to marry Genevieve, though you will miss your old playmate, you won't be selfish and stand in the way. It wouldn't be fair. And I'm sure Genevieve will do the same, when you fall in love . . . later on. Still, I was sorry for poor Norah when she hinted the other day that she would like to see Genevieve married, but no man ever got a chance as you were always with her. I think it better for that reason if you didn't go out every Sunday. Let Miles and Norah see that you are not to blame. It would be kinder, dear. If she still remains single they can't blame you. That is why I am so anxious for you to come to MacShanes' next Sunday. To please me, Robin; just to please me. I don't often make demands on you, dear."

"Very well, Mother. I'll write and tell Genevieve. I'll go Sunday week instead."

He had not made the decision without an effort. Perhaps if the family took that attitude it might be as well. He would explain to Genevieve and see what she thought they ought to do. Neither wanted to precipitate the quarrel they knew was inevitable. Robin particularly dreaded the hurt his decision would inflict on his mother; the shattering of her dreams for him. But they could not wait for ever. Robin feared that Miles might turn him out of the firm. His uncle had been kind and very indulgent to him and he did not want to appear ungrateful, especially as his own family had been such a keen source of disappointment. Robin was eager to repay in loyalty something of the debt he owed for the opportunity and preference Miles had accorded him. But it went deeper than that. In his stubborn attitude towards his own sons Miles had deprived himself of a great source of happiness, but the close association with Robin, both in the house and at the office, had provided him with some compensating devotion. In his gentle way Robin had seen much of the conflict in the older man's soul, and had understood the self-inflicted hurts of pride and obstinacy. But he had seen too the hunger in his heart for the close companionship of his children that once was his, but which he had lost. Knowing this, Robin was torn by indecision when it came to claiming Genevieve, realizing that he must hurt and disappoint the two people to whom he owed so much and to whom he would gladly have made great sacrifices to express his gratitude. He decided to say nothing yet, but to talk it over with Genevieve. A crisis was impending; the present position could not last. In yielding to his mother he was playing for time.

If Miles kicked him out of the firm and he

had to start for himself, it would be a terrific blow to his mother, and the long, slow process of establishing himself would have no assistance from the firm of Pencarrow. He would go to MacShane's on Sunday, but he must see Genevieve as soon as possible. She would know what to do. That was one thing about her: there was no shilly-shallying. She had a fine clear mind, not muddled by sentiment. She would not shrink or shirk in order to shield herself, but she could sympathize with others less robust of spirit. He could not explain in the letter why he was not coming on Sunday, except to say that his mother had got him involved in an invitation to MacShane's, which he had to accept, but he would be out the next Sunday without fail and had something very important to tell her.

"Robin is not coming on Sunday," said Genevieve.

"Why?" asked Kelly.

"I don't know. If his mother were trying to marry him off—"

"Which she is not, and never will," Kelly interpolated.

"You're right. She wants to keep him. But if she were, I don't think those two fat Mac-

Shanes would be her game. They are going out there to tea."

"Business, Genevieve; business. Mac-Shanes are bloated with money; wool-broking. Aunt Kitty's got a shrewd head for business."

"Hoping for litigation, with the Mac-Shanes' end upheld by Kelly, Pencarrow and Herrick, but mostly by Herrick. You're wrong. She isn't as far-seeing as that."

"Well, what's the game?"

"I don't know. But I'm convinced it isn't just a chance social engagement. Robin hates that kind of thing as much as I do. There's something in the wind. I wonder what?" and Genevieve went off to complete the grocer's list before the man called for orders.

Kitty asked Genevieve to lunch and made much of her. It was a day when Robin would not be home, as the Supreme Court was sitting. She was paying tribute to her conscience, but her purpose was fixed and her plans determined.

"How do you like the MacShanes?" Genevieve asked as her aunt spoke of the delightful Sunday party.

"They are very hospitable."

323

"Terribly dull, aren't they?" suggested Genevieve.

"Oh, I don't know. They can afford to do things well, and Mr. MacShane is quite a well-read man."

"I bet Robin was bored. He hates that kind of thing. And the MacShane girls are heavy weather."

"He enjoyed it very much. You see, he must go out more; it doesn't do to ignore changes and new people. He has to make his way and social connections so often lead to new business. The Hartleys were there, too, and we have promised to go over to tea with them. Mrs. Hartley took quite a fancy to Robin and they were most pressing. I don't think your father knows the Hartleys; he is a newcomer, but they are very well connected and quite charming."

"You're a terrible snob, Aunt Kitty," said Genevieve.

"Indeed I'm not, but Robin won't do anything himself. I've got to see that he meets people. After all, is there any harm in choosing your friends with the same discrimination you show for your hats and selecting the ones that suit you best?"

"Score, Aunt Kitty. But is it a case of suiting your taste or your purpose?"

Kitty ignored the hair-splitting.

"The Hartleys are having a big party next Sunday . . ."

"Not next Sunday; Robin is coming out to us; we are riding up the Moonshine Valley."

"Yes, dear, but can't you go some other Sunday? You see, dear, he ought to accept these invitations. You never know where they will lead to."

"Of course he can go if he wants to, but I think it's rather rude. After all, he put me off last Sunday."

"He was going to write to you and explain, but I don't think he has had time yet with the Supreme Court sitting. He has been so busy."

"I see. You want him to break new ground socially."

"I know you understand; you're such old playmates. But is it wise to be so exclusive as a family? I mean"—she hurried on—"fair to you . . ."

"To me! Why to me? I don't understand."

"You know you're an attractive girl, Genevieve, and you ought to be thinking of getting married. But you don't give the men a chance. You and Kelly and Robin are always together. I think your mother feels that Robin is standing in your way; always monopolizing you. It was all right when you were young, but now you ought to be thinking of a home of your own. You won't be keeping house for Kelly always. He will marry, and then where will you be? I hope you don't mind me speaking quite frankly, Genevieve, but, remember, I'm your aunt, and I'm very fond of you. And I would like to see you marry well. If I can help . . . if there is any man you would like to meet, I'd . . ."

"So you and Mother have been talking it over, have you? I see. Poor Mother! She's afraid she's going to have an old maid on her hands. Well, she isn't."

Genevieve looked frankly at her aunt as she said it.

"But I'll marry a man of my own choosing when I do, thank you. I don't want any match-making done for me."

"I'm sure you will. I always think you are cut out to be the wife of a distinguished man; someone of character, probably older than yourself. The kind who would appreciate you more than a young, struggling man."

Cut and thrust, they fenced throughout

lunch. Kitty was prepared to offer her help in obtaining any husband she selected—any save Robin.

Genevieve was angry with Robin for having put her in this position. Yet it was hard for him to withstand his mother. Kitty was trying to buy her off, that is what it amounted to; to bribe her to give up Robin, by flattering her into accepting marriage with one of the several older men of position—rakes, but wealthy rakes, socially established. She was angry that they had discussed her. Without actual words, she and Robin had decided to wait—to wait, to please his mother. It was all so undefined; so clear in her own mind; so muddled in theirs. She knew it would be possible to capture a husband if she wanted to, but she did not. She had seen the wandering eye of a recently widowed doctor repeatedly seeking hers invitingly. It sickened her to be the subject of discussion. "Poor Genevieve, what a pity she isn't married!"

"You needn't waste any pity on me, Aunt Kitty. And you needn't give any parties or invite me to meet some of your precious old men. And you needn't imagine Robin is spoiling my chances, either . . ."

"Ah, but you might be spoiling his." She said it teasingly, but Genevieve knew she had touched the nerve centre of the whole business.

"So he is to be forbidden to come out to the Hutt and made free of all the approved household. I didn't know you were so eager to marry him off" There was a biting note in her words.

"I'm not; I'm not. I dread to think that he will marry some day and leave me. I hope it won't be for years." Her words had the ring of pain.

"And when it is, he must marry a girl of your choosing; I see. Poor Robin! Well, I must go. Tell him he is excused for next Sunday, and any other Sunday if his Mamma won't let him come."

"There is no need to be rude, Genevieve," said Kitty.

"I'm not. I'm being terribly polite."

Kitty, having won the first round, could afford to be generous, but she flinched at the flick of the girl's sharp tongue. Naturally, Genevieve was annoyed, but she would make it up to her. Later she would be grateful. Young people so seldom knew what was best for them, and Kitty convinced herself that her interference was amply justified.

It was early autumn, and the mellow warmth of the day was barbed with the bite of a rising wind.

Coming in from the Hutt she had been quite hot, and under the sheltering flank of the hills, against which the noon-high sun beat down, it seemed as though summer lingered. Here and there the grass was burnt and dry. Beneath the trees where families had picnicked or lovers had lain the tangle of uncut grass was trampled flat to the earth.

No hint of the russet reds of autumn tinged the everlasting green of the bush, but a poplar or a willow tree wore golden mourning for a season dead. The calm lay heavily over the city and the gentle lap-lap of the tide against the Hutt road broke the shimmering stillness of the harbour. A steamer, her two red funnels trailing plumes of smoke, slid from her moorings at the Queen's wharf. No fresh snow had yet fallen, and the mountain peaks were grey under a veil of haze. Seagulls circled and screamed, and Genevieve watched the pattern of their wings against the sky and marvelled at their voracity. Every aspect of the day had its beauty, and under the warm sunlight a radiance lightly touched the life around her, and in her heart was something akin to it.

It was in this happy mood she had gone to lunch with Kitty. Now she bent her head and clutched her hat as petulant squalls tugged at her and spirals of dust and dry leaves whirled into her eyes and her wide skirt flapped about her ankles.

The wind was cold, too, and it had teeth that bit and a lash that flayed. She shivered as she crossed Lambton Quay. Uncertain for a moment, she sheltered in the doorway of Kirkcaldie and Stains's shop. What should she do? Crazy ideas rushed through her mind: to go to the office and see Robin now. She wanted to do something, to find some vent for the storm of anger that Kitty had stirred. Should she go home and see her mother and face her with Kitty's story? She decided against it. She was too angry to be safe. Surging inside her was a tide of rebellion against their plan to order her life—and Robin's. She must not quarrel with her mother, and she could not trust herself to see Robin—not now. Better go home to Kelly.

He might see, but he would not question her. They had always respected each other's privacy. But all this tumult must find an outlet. She did not know what she wanted to do, or what to say, it was all chaotic. But someone was going to be hurt, as she was hurt. She knew that wherever she struck, the blow would recoil, and it was she who would suffer most. Outwardly she looked calm, just a pale, bewildered young woman sheltering in the doorway from the storm, looking far beyond the passersby, her mind remote from everything around her.

She thought of Robin. Ever since he was a little boy they had established a special claim upon each other; a sweet, trusting mutual content; a doubling of joys shared, a compensating happiness, like a friendly hand in the dark. It had never been the sudden wild passion of strangers for each other, but a slow growth of companionship, burgeoning in season, restrained by circumstances, but striking unseen roots deeper with the passing years. Genevieve had accepted Robin and Robin's love as a part of her daily life. His coming stirred no tumult; his departure left no pain. Her love for Robin had been a smouldering fire. Now Kitty's open challenge had fanned it into flame. Never before had Robin been so dear to her, so desirable, or she so conscious of his place in her life as when she stood shivering in the gusty wind on Lambton Quay. For the first time she was jealous, and its pain burst like a fury in her heart. She wanted to cry out to ease the misery that overwhelmed her. She could have beaten her fists against the wall behind her till they bled; it was part of a madness to hurt.

"Hullo, Genevieve!"

His head down against the wind, his coat collar up, Robin was hurrying back to the office from the Court when he saw her, looking pale and distraught, but tensely controlled. She held her emotions in check.

All her love, the new fierce flame that Kitty had stirred to life, flooded her as the blood surged from her heart.

Robin! Robin whom she loved, but Robin who would pass her over at his mother's bidding. She wanted to fling her arms around him and hold him; to claim him now, as never before. But her memory spread before her eyes a note:

Dear Genevieve, I'm sorry, I can't come!

Without a word she turned and walked into the shop.

"Genevieve!" he called. "Genevieve!"

But she didn't even look back.

18

KELLY came in tired. He read the cables and stock reports in the *Post*, and when the roast shoulder of lamb and baked potatoes were set upon the table he gave the carving-knife a slash along the steel and began to carve.

"Come on, Genevieve!" he called irritably, "your dinner's getting cold."

She came in and sat down, making busy play arranging a bowl of mixed garden flowers that stood on the table between them.

"How is Aunt Kitty?" he asked casually.

"All right."

"See Robin?"

"No . . . Yes."

It was absurd! Ridiculous! Kelly put down his knife and fork as Genevieve suddenly left the table and the door closed behind her. He was positive he had seen tears in her eyes. Now he came to think of it, they were a little red and swollen, but he had attributed that to the wind.

Why was Genevieve crying? Genevieve,

who never cried. Perhaps if she had melted easily into tears like her mother Miles might have been more readily appeased. No scathing word of his, no scorching attack, had ever brought tears to Genevieve.

"She's hard; unnatural," her father had said.

"No, Miles, she is not hard; she has the softest heart," her mother always defended her. "But she is more controlled than most girls."

"I call it damned callousness."

Even as a child it had been difficult to make her cry. She would fly into a temper and fight Kelly tooth and nail, and take her bumps and blows gamely, but she was not a soppy little girl who blubbered at every hurt. There was none of the cry-baby about Genevieve.

It was this fact that made it all the more astounding, and Kelly was brought up sharply against the disturbing idea. Something had happened; something very serious had happened to Genevieve. She and Aunt Kitty were always good friends and he could not imagine any quarrel between them to account for it.

Damn it all, why couldn't she say what was the matter and not shut herself up in her room? No good asking her, she wasn't that sort of girl; a bit like himself, and had to be left alone to get over it; hated anyone prying and questioning. She was not a sentimental ass, the sort who is always getting wrought up and imagining things. She had a clear, cool head and pretty sound judgment. That made it the more inexplicable.

Kelly tried to read the paper, the leading article, all about the need for extending the railways of New Zealand and opening up the country. He skimmed it and passed on. Football, racing; no good, he couldn't keep his mind on it. He filled his pipe and went out to the stables, then walked along the garden path. He felt the shadow of impending events like a weight upon his mind.

For a while Kelly walked up and down past Genevieve's window, but there was no gleam of light. He wanted to go in and see her; he was anxious to know what it was that had broken her self-control. She had stood by him so often; he wanted to stand by her now, but he did not know how; she had shut him out. He could not ask her; she would probably tell him to get to hell and leave her alone. He tried to think of some way in which he could show his sympathy and help, but he was quite impotent. Genevieve in the room behind the dark window, crying, fighting it out alone.

He wondered what Grannie would have done; she would have known.

Genevieve was up and out early next morning. Her face was a little pale and strained and her eyes showed lack of sleep, but she had recovered her composure and there was firmness in her voice and manner that offered apology for the momentary weakness of the previous night.

When Kelly was there she was eager to talk —too eager, as though afraid of a silence between them, lest it permit a thought or word not under her control which might endanger her secret.

The Supreme Court finished its session on Friday afternoon, and Kelly, Pencarrow and Herrick were released from the tension of much exacting work. Robin had found the last few days very difficult, his mind torn from the problem of defending a defaulting cashier by his personal unhappiness. Nor had his mother helped. He did not ask her what had happened when Genevieve came to lunch; he did not question her about what they had talked of and over what they had come into conflict. He knew. He did not even mention Genevieve. Nor did he tell his mother of their brief encounter afterwards.

On Friday, at dinner, Kitty announced cheerfully, though he detected a quiver of apprehension in her voice, that it looked like being fine on Sunday and it would be very pleasant out at Hartley's.

"I'm not going to Hartley's, Mother," he said firmly.

"But we have promised," said Kitty.

"You have, Mother. I'm going to the Hutt on Sunday. I put them off last week. I can't do that again."

"They would understand, Robin."

"They might not. After all, they mean more to me than strangers . . . these Hartleys."

"But, dear, you know you ought to go about more and meet people—new people."

"I'm sorry, Mother, but I'm going to the Hutt on Sunday. I've promised."

Kitty wondered if Robin had seen Genevieve since she had been there to lunch; if she had written to him, or complained. No, Genevieve would not do that; she was too proud. Well, it couldn't be helped; she would go alone and consolidate her acquaintance with the Hartleys, and fix another invitation for Robin. She must be satisfied to make the break by degrees; wean him away from the Hutt and its friendly Sunday afternoons.

She had not seen Genevieve since, and though she had gone up to Sir Miles's for dinner, Norah, apparently, had not seen her either, and she was unable to find out how Genevieve was taking it. Of course, she would get over it, like a sensible girl. She must do something for Genevieve; make a generous gesture. Perhaps give a dinner-party for her birthday and see if she could not divert her from Robin. Now Dr. Washburn, not much over forty, a widower for three years, no children; any number of girls would give their eyes to catch him; good-looking, drank a bit, certainly, but had a fine practice. It was just the match for Genevieve. She would talk it over with Norah.

When Robin arrived at the Hutt for Sunday dinner he found Kelly sprawling in a willow armchair on the verandah, reading *Truth*.

"Hullo!"

Robin sat on the step and lit a cigarette.

"I see you got that bloke off," said Kelly.

"Just reading about it. Do you really think he did it, or did the manager pinch the cash and plant the blame on him?"

"He's a crooked swine, if you ask me," said Robin. "I never saw so much bluster in the witness-box, but he caved in when Miles cross-examined him."

"Father can put the harrow over them," Kelly admitted with admiration.

"He's marvellous. No one can touch him if he is really interested in a case. He believes that young chap was just a dupe. He gave old Purley hell, but, of course, we had no case against him. He will lie low for a while after this; he went out of the box like a whipped cur."

They went into dinner after a call from the dining-room announced the meal was ready.

"Where's Genevieve?" asked Robin, as he sat down and noticed places set only for two.

"Oh, she's gone to Featherston. Didn't she tell you?"

"No. At least, I didn't understand that. I thought she was expecting me; we were riding up the Moonshine Valley."

"That was last Sunday, wasn't it."

"Yes, but I had to put it off. Mother had made some engagement for me to go to a rotten party and I told Genevieve I'd come to-day instead."

"She must have misunderstood," said Kelly, "because she told me that no one was coming and I could sleep my fat head off all the afternoon."

"Oh!"

It was a good dinner, the traditional Sunday dinner that Grannie had instituted, but Robin had no appetite.

Genevieve knew he was coming; he had written distinctly that the Moonshine trip was merely postponed a week. Had she done this to punish him? To even the score? Or was she hurt or angry with him, and deliberately avoiding him? Genevieve had never been one to "pay back" an injury, as the children say. She was bigger than that. If she had anything to say she said it, and did not mince matters. It was not like her to go off when she knew he was coming. In the old days she would have met him and faced it out and told him frankly what she thought about him. This new elusiveness, this dodging of a straight discussion, revealed a changed Genevieve, and one he was afraid it might not be so easy to deal with. The other was a com-

341

rade, frank and friendly. Now for the first time he had touched the woman.

Robin did not go out to the Hutt the following Sunday. He had promised his mother, by way of compromise, that he would go with her. He had hoped to see Genevieve and explain it all and make her understand. He wanted to talk to her and decide what they had better do.

Robin realized that he was not being quite fair to Genevieve, and yet he was conscious of his gratitude to his mother for the gallant fight she had made for him when his father failed. Grannie had told him, and he recalled so much now, dim memories from his childhood, which had taken on a fuller meaning seen with the eyes of maturity. Must he be compelled to choose between them? To hurt one? He felt there must be some way out if only he and Genevieve could talk it over. He relied on her to suggest the course; she had clear vision and sound sense. He did not want to write, but to talk to her. Put in a letter it might be misunderstood, and for the first time he began to fear a misunderstanding.

He might write and ask her to meet him in town, but it would be futile to talk to her in a crowded lunch-room, and he could not ask her home. He might run out in the car one evening and chance catching her in, but Kelly would probably be there, and somehow he did not want to confide in him yet. Other secrets they might share, but not his love for Genevieve. It had been such a slow, natural growth that, despite Potty Barker's warning, Kelly had seen nothing to confirm it. Kelly would be decent about it, but it would upset his life. He would hardly share the family's abhorrence of a marriage between cousins. Yet with Kelly you could not always accurately predict.

A week passed and Robin heard nothing from Genevieve. He spent a miserable Sunday afternoon at the Hartleys', and his abstraction rather dampened Mrs. Hartley's enthusiasm and annoyed his mother.

On Monday evening he took the car and drove to the Hutt.

"Where are you going, dear?" asked Kitty.

"To the Hutt. I shan't be late. Good night."

Kitty watched him go with a little hungry fear that she was losing ground. He had not asked her to go. He had gone to Genevieve alone. Not since the day at lunch had she seen her niece, and as the time passed she felt a growing embarrassment at the prospect of their next meeting.

Genevieve was alone when the car came in at the gate. She knew the sound and her heart quickened its pace.

"Hullo, Robin!" She said gaily, in the old, easy manner, but there was a brittle quality in her laughter.

"Kelly is out, I'm afraid. Gone up the valley to see about a sheep dog."

"I'm glad. I wanted to see you."

"How is Father?"

"In great form."

"And Aunt Kitty?"

"All right. Look here, Genevieve . . ." He came over to her eagerly, yet afraid. She met his eyes.

"It's no good pretending, Genevieve. Something's wrong, I know. I can guess what it is . . . you . . . and Mother."

He hesitated, but she did not help him.

"Do you imagine I want to go to their rotten parties?" he blurted out. "You know I don't. You know I wanted to come out to you, but Mother thinks—"

"I know what she thinks."

Genevieve was taut as a bow-string. He felt the hand that lay in his grow steely, and the

344

very warmth seemed to drain away. There was no answering pressure as his fingers gripped hers, and it lay unresponsive, sharpening the edge of her words.

"What happened? What did Mother say? Don't let us quarrel. Can't we talk it over like we used to? Oh, Genevieve!"

He tried to draw her into his arms, but she was not yielding. She sat erect and quiet.

"Tell me, won't you? What did Mother say?"

Genevieve tried to speak of it as though it were a trivial incident. She shrugged slightly.

"Just that I was standing in your way, monopolizing you; preventing you from meeting new and important people. And, I gathered, blocking the way to your brilliant marriage."

"I was afraid of that. But you don't believe it's true? You know there is no one in the world but you, Genevieve; no one. It's just because we're cousins, and the family will make a fuss, and I'm . . . well, you know . . . I owe so much to Uncle Miles . . . and Mother."

"I know; I know it all," she said wearily. "But don't keep saying it over and over again. What are you going to do?"

345

"What are we going to do?" he corrected.

She saw the conflict in his mind, the divided loyalties. The sharp, sensitive face had the look of a hurt child, that sweet bewilderment that asks why it must suffer for a deed that has no ill intent.

Genevieve softened for a moment. She tried to be fair to him. Never consciously would he hurt her, but that very aversion from inflicting pain on those he loved brought to battle his varied allegiance.

Kelly had struck them all blindly in turn in a wild bid for personal freedom. Genevieve shared some of that quality. Robin, inheriting much of his father's gentleness, was destined by the circumstances of his childhood to be more aware of his indebtedness to others than his well-provided cousins. The quarrel between Kelly and his father had worried Robin and he shrank from the open conflict between Genevieve and Sir Miles. But the wounds inflicted were clean; no aftermath of malice poisoned them. Genevieve had profound admiration for her father, despite her keen realization of his faults. And there was no doubt Sir Miles knew his daughter to have much of his own quality, misplaced in a girl, but still something to be proud of though uncomfortable to live with.

Robin sometimes winced at the sharpness of their words when they crossed swords in a family wrangle. Such warfare had been unknown in his own home. He could not remember his father ever losing his temper or speaking sharply either to his mother or himself. He was shrewd enough to know that his mother had learnt restraint by bitter experience. Her overwhelming devotion to, and ambition for, her one surviving child had become the supreme passion of her life, and never had Robin openly defied her. He knew how much she had done for him; that first humbling of her pride when she took a little country hotel so that she might make a home and provide for his future—a future no less successful than the other Pencarrows. His mother had won the first fight for him—his education; his Uncle Miles had made the next victory possible and established him in a profession.

Now his love for Genevieve threatened to destroy it all. He did not shirk proclaiming it because he feared to face hardship. He had too much grit for that. It was the hurt it must inflict on others; the apparent ingratitude to

347

fling it all back in their face and take Genevieve.

They sat in silence for a while, their fingers
interlacing.

"What shall we do, Genevieve?"

"That's just it. What do you want to do?"

"I want you. I love you; there is no one,
and never will be anyone but you . . ."

"Are you asking me to marry you now,
Robin? Remember, you never have."

"Not in words, perhaps, but you have—we
have known for a long time . . ."

"Are you?" she persisted.

"What's the matter, Genevieve? What has
come over you? You were never like this
before."

"Like what?"

"Like this. Demanding exact words."

"It's better to be quite clear about things."

"Were you ever in doubt?"

"Perhaps not, but I might have been mis-
taken. I knew what you were feeling, but not
what you were going to do."

"You think I've funked it?"

"No, not funked. What's the legal term for
being clever enough to keep in with both
sides?"

"Is that fair, Genevieve?"

"Diplomatic covers it, I suppose," she said, ignoring the ring of misery in his voice.

Again silence fell. They were aware that each was playing with dangerous phrases outside a locked door. Who would first open it?

"Genevieve, only those we love have the power to hurt us."

"Of whom are you thinking now?"

"You. I came out to-night to ask if you will marry me; if I may announce our engagement at once."

"And take the consequences?"

"And take the consequences," he repeated.

Her eyes wandered over the room and rested on a portrait of Grannie over the mantelpiece. The grey, starry eyes looked down on them—smiling, trustful, courageous. She looked at Robin, struck once more by the startling resemblance.

"You know what it will mean? Rows and more rows; a real family bust-up this time."

"I suppose so."

"You will hate it, Robin."

"It is the only way. We can't go on like this."

"You're not a good fighter, Robin. I mean, you get squeamish at the sight of blood."

Colour flooded his face and he drew his hand away.

"I'm sorry to fail you," he began.

"You're wrong. I didn't mean it that way. Kelly and I love a scrap; it clears the air. That's the Irish in us, I suppose. You don't."

"I don't mind the fight. I'd fight all hell for you. It's because they have been so damned good to me and I would like to have repaid them first. But it can't go on. I don't know how I got through this week—after you cut me that day."

Genevieve slid her hand over his hair, and her fingers brushed his temples with a warm, caressing touch. He leant nearer to her, and some of the hardness melted.

"I was too hurt to speak. I couldn't trust myself—not there."

A little quiver fluttered behind her words.

"I thought you were angry."

"I was—hurt and angry."

"My darling! Oh, Genevieve."

They sat, their arms about each other, surrendering to the sweet influence of a complete reconciliation, when look and caress and all the mute eloquence of love were balm to the little wounds of fretful, petty words.

"I adore you, darling. You make it easy to face the family row—worth anything."

"We will make it up to them—later. But I think we had better not say anything till after Easter. Let us get that over in peace and then, my dear, we will face the storm together."

"Genevieve! You're adorable. You don't know how happy I am now that we have decided to tell them."

They stood close together, their eyes searching each other's face, as lovers do, and the grey eyes of Grannie seemed to look down and bless them.

"Good night. Go before Kelly comes in; he might suspect something was up; your eyes are shining."

"One more kiss . . . Good night."

19

"AND Peter, what is he going to be?" asked old Judge Lucas.

"I'm going on the stage."

"What's that?" demanded his father.

"I'm going to be an actor," said Peter with a brief burst of courage.

It had become a family habit to break bad news to their father when visitors were present. The alien presence tempered the wind, and Sir Miles was obliged to curb his temper and choose his words.

"You'll do no such thing," he said with fine dramatic force.

"Oh, I've quite decided, Father."

"You've decided! You've decided, have you; and who are you to decide these matters?"

Miles's temper was rising, despite their guest, and Norah made clucking noises of warning and looked apologetically at the Judge.

Old Lucas was not the least embarrassed; he seemed to be enjoying it.

"And why do you want to go on the stage, Peter?" he asked.

"I just love it," said the boy, encouraged by his kindly smile.

"You're coming into my office after Easter, and make up your mind to that, my boy."

Peter had not Kelly's courage, nor Pat's good sense, but he blundered ahead, having taken the plunge.

"I'm sorry, Father—"

"I'll have no painted pimps in this house," said Sir Miles, and he thumped the table and sent the jam spoon flying.

"Painted pimps! It sounds like a headline from *Truth*," said Genevieve.

"Hold your tongue, will you?"

"Miles, dear!" Norah's voice took on its pleading note, and old Lucas's face crumpled up like a merry old apple and his eyes twinkled wickedly.

"You know, we always stage our family rows at meals," said Genevieve, turning to their guest. "We find it a splendid aid to digestion. Look at us; did you ever see such a healthy lot?"

"An excellent idea, and most entertaining," added Lucas.

"Suppressed anger curdles your food . . . ."

"Genevieve!" Norah was afraid that her daughter might disgrace herself by talking openly about food after it had passed beyond the pale of conversation to the region of the stomach.

"Let her go on, Lady Pencarrow. Genevieve always had original ideas," said the Judge.

"She's got too sharp a tongue."

"Not sharp, Father; sensitive!"

"Huh!" he grunted.

"Do you remember that brown redingcot dress you had, Mother, with the plush panel down the front?"

"I do, dear. You always liked to sit on my knee when I wore it."

"Do you know why? I used to lick the plush. And Father had an Irish frieze coat, a harsh, acrid, hairy thing, and I always licked that, too. It was horrible, but I couldn't resist it, and it always made me shudder."

"You filthy kid," said Kelly.

"Merely training a sensitive tongue," said the Judge. "Learning discrimination. I fancy, Genevieve, that you will always lick the plush and the frieze of life."

"You mean . . .?" she enquired, for she could see interest in his faded blue eyes.

"Savour everything."

"I wonder," she said thoughtfully. Her mind plunged ahead. "I'll lick the frieze after Easter," she thought.

It was Holy Week, and the waxing Easter moon grew rounder as each night it climbed a little later over the hills, and its shining face slid in and out of the scudding clouds.

Genevieve stood outside the front door and all the warm mellowness of autumn rose on the still air. Seedpods hung on plants, a few late roses bloomed; the rich, tawny colours of chrysanthemums—yellow and bronze and red—had replaced the summer flowers. Against the north wall, catching the sun, a Virginia creeper was red as blood, and the two tall poplars wore a scanty coat of pale gold. For the rest, the native bush on the hills and in the gulleys was the same, its unchanging green a little dusty and the new leaves now darker with maturity.

Night shut down early in the Valley, the heavy shoulder of the hills blotting out the sun and throwing deep shadows that were her heralds of night.

Genevieve recalled Judge Lucas's words the previous day. She was facing a change, not only in her own life, but forcing it upon the whole family. Everyone had accepted the friendship of the Pencarrow cousins as a natural thing, and few had suspected the changed relationship between Robin and Genevieve. Mothers commiserated with Norah over Genevieve remaining unmarried; hanging fire, as one termed it.

"A pity she doesn't go off; such a disappointment to Lady Pencarrow; no wedding in the family yet, and such a big family, too."

And they all knew Kitty's ambition for Robin, for more than one had tentatively put forward a daughter as a likely candidate in that clever way mothers have. But Kitty was a match for them.

"She would like him to marry an English girl—with a title—that's what she's after."

"Well, there is a title in the Herrick family somewhere, isn't there?"

Genevieve knew it all and could imagine the sensation their engagement would cause. After Easter she had said. That was next week. Just a week more of the peace and serenity here, in Grannie's old home, with Kelly. She wondered how he would take it.

No longer would she play hostess on Sunday afternoons and gather the clan about her as that gallant little lady had done.

Her mind went back over these pleasant years, the comings and goings, the Christmas and Easter parties, the first dinner with lamb and mint sauce and green peas which had become another ceremonial occasion, and a poignant note crept into her memories now that she had decided to leave it all. Not only leave it, but probably smash it all.

Kelly came in from the stables, where he had been looking at a sick horse, and, puffing contentedly at his pipe, stood beside her. There was a warm contentment in the autumn air; harvest was over, the fields and fruits and flowers had responded generously to his work, and the dying season had left its rich bequest to man.

"Kelly, we must have an Easter party—a big one this year. The whole family—Michael and Ella and Gentry, and Neil and Erena. I wonder if Jessie and Potty Barker would come over. A real slap-up party."

"Why so special this year?"

"I thought it would be nice; you never know when some of them might be moving on . . . out of reach."

"Who, for instance?"

357

"Oh, anyone. But it would be rather nice, don't you think so?"

"Righto! You go ahead."

"I'll write to them all to-night."

"Write! A bit formal with the family, isn't it?"

"It's quicker and will save time."

"They usually come out for Easter, anyway."

"Yes, our own crowd. But I want to make sure of them all."

"Full roll call!"

"Exactly."

A queer excitement stirred Genevieve as she wrote the invitations; just friendly little notes they were.

"Do come out for Easter!" was the text. And they all came; all, except Jessie and Potty Barker.

Leaden clouds rolled up on Good Friday, and Saturday broke with drenching rain. At noon it cleared, and the sun came out with a hot burst that sucked up the moisture and brewed an earthy smell, a wet fragrance that an erratic wind blew hither and thither. And the broken, ragged clouds moved away before it like driven sheep.

Genevieve worked with a nervous energy and sang snatches of songs as she salted the almonds, iced the cakes and prepared the poultry. The old servant, accustomed to the recurring feasts of the year, like Kelly, was surprised at the lavishness of her preparations.

"Who are you killing this fatted calf for?" Kelly asked as he came into the kitchen.

"For the prodigal who is departing," she answered soberly.

"I thought it was when he returned that he got the feast. When he goes he gets a kick on the backside to help him, if my memory serves me well."

"This is the story of the prodigal—new version."

Miles and Norah came first.

"You have got a cold, Father," said Genevieve.

"Oh, it's nothing," and he gave a series of rasping grunts to clear his voice.

"He caught it yesterday in that heavy rain. He wouldn't change his boots when he came in," and Norah looked reprovingly at him as though he were a stubborn child.

"I don't hold with all this coddling. Your

359

mother is too fond of red flannel and chest plasters."

Peter, who had suffered a sudden eclipse since his rash announcement before Judge Lucas, was keeping out of his father's way, and he and Meggie were fooling about with tennis-racquets.

Peter's rebellion was short-lived, and with a sinking heart he now faced his father's office after Easter.

You might want to be a farmer and get a job on a farm; you might decide to go to sea and earn a hard living while you trained, but recruits to the Colonial stage, unless with special qualifications, could fall on lean days after the company's tour of New Zealand was over. Sir Miles was determined that lack of financial help from home would soon terminate Peter's youthful ambition. If necessary, he would starve him into submission. "He will come home quick enough when he is hungry."

At Norah's urgent pleading he did not storm and rage at the boy, but talked it over calmly and kindly, and endeavoured not to repeat his previous mistakes in dealing with his children. Peter, who had no great dramatic ability and an indifferent voice, was compelled to surrender.

"I want you with me, my boy. I want one of my sons to carry on after me, and not let the old name die out of the firm. Believe me, you'll be thankful in later years when you know more of life. A wandering actor with uncertain employment, no home, and increasing difficulty in getting parts as he gets older, is a poor prospect for a man. With me, you have a certain future, and as you get older you will realize the value of a comfortable home and a good income. Also a definite place in society."

Miles was surprised at himself. He had never before reasoned with his children, but had issued orders and made demands. Norah was right. He knew it without being told, but he was too stubborn to acknowledge it. He might have won the others if he had kept them close to him and made his appeal with the simple logic he was now employing with Peter, his youngest and least talented son.

They talked as they walked over the hills at Wadestown, and pausing on the height that dominated the city and the harbour, it was as though Miles were offering him all the wealth and honour that the city held if only he would give up this fatuous idea of the stage and buckle-to in the office.

Miles stood, a hand on Peter's shoulder, making his appeal to reason here on the windswept hilltop. He had lost the others—Jack by death, Kelly to the land, Pat to the sea. They had had qualities that Peter lacked, but he clung tenaciously to the last son and the hope that a Pencarrow might yet follow him in the firm.

"What made you think of joining Williamson's Company, my boy?" Miles asked when Peter had accepted his father's plans for him.

"Well . . ."

"Go on!"

"Maisie Kite is joining them. It's all fixed up, but she hasn't told anyone yet—except me."

"A bad influence; a bad influence from the start," and Miles frowned.

"She's a jolly good sort, Father. And you needn't blame her. She tried to stop me; said you would be furious, and I'd start another family row."

"Oh, she did, did she?"

"Yes. But it's different with her. She's jolly good. I bet she will make a hit in Sydney."

"She may! She may! But it's a big world

and competition is keen. There are lots of pretty girls about."

"She isn't just pretty, she's got brains. That's where she scores."

"Yes, cleverness of a kind, no doubt," Miles conceded grudgingly.

Norah was delighted with the success of her little plan to send father and son off for a long walk to talk things over and straighten them out.

Secretly Miles was jubilant at his victory, but he would not admit it. Having made their pact, father and son rather avoided each other. They could not continue on that plane bordering intimacy, where each had revealed a tiny glimpse of hidden feelings. Down on the everyday level again such confidences seemed embarrassing.

So on Easter Sunday Peter and Meggie knocked tennis-balls about on the tennis-courts and waited for the others to arrive.

Michael drove down with Ella and Gentry. Genevieve greeted her uncle with a quick, spontaneous hug, and he kissed her and ruffled her hair, and she clung to his arm as he came in to join Miles.

Gentry and Kelly met easily and talked

sheep and football and racing while Ella was welcomed by Norah.

As the years passed she grew more like her mother. She had Vi's dark elegance, but there was a warmer quality, something of her father that was hidden behind the sleek exterior.

Erena and Neil came next.

"How are you, Erena, dear? Be careful of those steps," and Norah kissed her. "Are you still keeping well? How splendid. It won't be long now—next month, isn't it?"

Genevieve wondered why Robin was so late, but she knew it was Kitty's habit to be either first guest, or last.

"Ah! Just in time," said Genevieve as Robin and his mother drove up in their smart car.

"How are you, Aunt Kitty?"

Genevieve kissed her as usual but felt uncomfortable, as though there were treachery in the kiss. She did not show it, however.

"Hullo, Robin!" she said cheekily.

"Hullo yourself!" he answered lightly, taking the cue from her and not daring to meet her eyes.

The young ones played tennis, then Michael and Gentry went with Kelly to look over some new wethers he had bought. At intervals they feasted, and never had the old homestead seemed more desirable. The spirit of the founders of the family—Matthew and Bessie Pencarrow—brooded over the scene and blessed the continuation of the work they had begun.

Genevieve was commended for her housekeeping and the excellence of her food, and this praise struck a sentimental note. What would happen to the old home and Grannie's garden when she had gone? Who would take her place? Would Kelly marry? He had stopped his Saturday night excursion to town, which, for a time, had worried her. The barmaid's charms were fleeting. As she talked to Michael and Kitty and Ella, and surrounded Erena, the expectant mother, with cushions and care, her mind darted ahead and she tried to see into the future—next Easter and all the other Easters. Where would she be—she and Robin? Would it mean beginning life in some smaller town, working up a practice of his own, cut adrift from the family? She tossed a friendly word to Robin, but they avoided each other, afraid lest even a look might betray their love.

As they sat down to supper of cold chicken and salad, trifle, fruit salad and cream, scones and cakes, a sudden squall blew up and drenching rain fell, drumming noisily on the iron roof and swishing against the windows. An autumn chill crept in with the rain, and Miles shivered.

"I'll light the fire; it's all ready," said Kelly.

They drew their chairs in and the men smoked, and the talk spread from little detached groups until it swept them all into one conversation.

Michael and Kitty and Miles became reminiscent and a well-fed benevolence prevailed. Robin and Genevieve, one on either side of the fire, were silent, and only a chance look, swift and sweet, told of all that lay under the surface.

For one moment a mad recklessness prompted Genevieve to fling the challenge then and there. She felt cramped and fettered by the silence and her innate honesty hated the subterfuge, the deception. They were glowing sparks, those stolen intimate glances, but of a secret word they had had none.

The rain ceased as suddenly as it had begun and the stars came out. The late Easter moon, with a slice off one side, stole over the hills, the lights gleamed in the pools on the path,

366

and mud splashed from the passing wheels on the road.

"Come in for dinner on Wednesday, Genevieve—you and Kelly. Kitty and Robin are coming up, too," said Lady Pencarrow as she kissed her daughter good night.

"Yes, rather. We'll be there."

"Good night, Genevieve. You're Grannie all over again. It's been a lovely party," and Michael kissed his niece.

"Good night! Good night!"

Robin lingered behind and for a moment joined Genevieve, as coats and umbrellas and goloshes were sorted out and claimed.

They stood together in the gloom, pressing close, their fingers locked.

"Good night, darling," Robin whispered.

"Good night."

"Wednesday—shall we?"

"Yes. After dinner; they will all be there."

"Nothing—no one can come between us now. Till Wednesday . . . I love you so."

The last words brushed her ear as he turned to join Kitty, and their clinging fingers parted.

"You put up a jolly good show," said Kelly as he picked up a chicken wing and nibbled bits off it before giving it to the cat.

Genevieve smiled and put the cakes into a tin and saw that the meat safe was secure.

"We have enough cold chicken to do till—"

"Till Wednesday!"

"Till Wednesday!" Genevieve repeated thoughtfully.

Genevieve went into Wellington early on Wednesday morning. She had some shopping to do and decided to make a day of it. Kelly would come in later.

All the morning she kept her mind on the list of purchases to be made for the house and for herself, but as she sat over lunch in a crowded tea room, excitement quickened her pulse. The terrible uncertainty about the family's reception of their decision to marry fluctuated between the prospect of a first-class row and a resigned acceptance in order to avoid a scandal. The latter was too good to be true.

After lunch she rang up her mother to ask if there was anything she could do for her in town.

"Nothing, dear, thank you. But come up early, as soon as you can. Your father is in bed; his cold is worse and he is such a restless patient. I'm expecting the doctor this afternoon. He protests that he is all right and he won't let me put a mustard plaster on his back where it is so sore. So I've sent for the doctor."

"He will bully him into it," said Genevieve. "I'm sorry he is in bed. Perhaps you would rather put us all off till another night."

"Oh no. Dinner is prepared and you've got to come up and eat it now. He will be glad to see you, too."

The doctor came at five and said that he would look in again later. It rather dampened the family to find Sir Miles in bed, and they felt, out of consideration for him, they must not sound too cheerful or laugh too loud; he would interpret it as heartlessness and be very hurt. So they talked in subdued voices becoming to the occasion.

The doctor came again at nine and looked grave. Miles's temperature had risen.

"A touch of pneumonia, I'm afraid, Lady Pencarrow. He will have to be very careful. I'll look in again in the morning. And, by the way, I think you'd better have a nurse. I'll send one along."

"He won't like it, I'm afraid," said Norah, now truly alarmed.

"It will be too much for you and she will

make him take his medicine, even if he doesn't like it."

With a white face, Norah came in to the drawing-room.

"How is he now, Mother?" asked Genevieve.

"It's pneumonia."

"Oh, Mother! Don't worry. I'll stay and help you nurse him," and Genevieve was instantly at her mother's side. "Don't worry; he is awfully strong."

"Not his chest, dear; he is always inclined to get colds that settle there."

Kitty went out with Norah and for a moment Robin and Genevieve were alone. He took her hand and smiled a little sadly. She leant against his shoulder and he kissed her hair and her eyes and her lips.

"We can't now, Robin; not to-night. It's like hitting a man when he's down."

20

MILES rapidly grew worse and doctors called frequently and held consultations in the dining-room. Another nurse was engaged and the whole house was just a hushed ante-room in which they waited anxiously from hour to hour for the crisis.

Norah, with her faith in red flannel and mustard plasters, was a little sceptical of modern treatment and would gladly have supplemented the efforts of doctors and nurse.

"He is not any better, Genevieve. I'm sure if I just put—"

"Darling, you've got to leave it to them now. It's running its course and they are watching it closely. I have implicit faith in Doctor Davies."

"He looks so terribly ill, Genevieve," and the ready tears started in Norah's eyes.

"Lie down, Mother. I'll stay up and, if he wants you, I'll call you. Don't worry. I'm

371

sure it will be all right," and she persuaded her mother to snatch an hour's sleep.

Genevieve did not interfere with the nurse on duty, but she was always at hand, quiet and cool. She was gentle but firm with her mother, who would have slapped on a mustard plaster while the nurse was not looking. In her terrible anxiety she would have tried half a dozen conflicting cures at once.

"Where's Genevieve?" Miles frequently asked.

"I'm here. What is it?"

During these fevered days and nights Genevieve's presence gave him comfort; courage, too, perhaps. After a first feeble protest he had submitted to the nurse, and while the doctors fought for his life Genevieve brought him some spiritual consolation.

"Where's Genevieve!"

"She's here, Sir Miles," said the nurse.

"What is it, Father?"

He moved his hand towards her and in his eyes was a piteous appeal.

Genevieve sat beside the bed and the gentle fingers smoothed the greying hair from the damp forehead, then took his feverish hand in her cool, firm grasp. For a while they sat and no word was spoken, but as he looked up at her the hard protective shell that had grown about him, and behind which he had imprisoned his love for his children, seemed to break. Miles Pencarrow saw the barren years in which he had fought his children in an attempt to hold them and maintain parental prestige in his house. What a harvest of disappointment he had reaped. From childhood he had tried to subdue the sharp tongue and fearless honesty of Genevieve—Genevieve, who he had so often said was callous and unnatural. He had resented her back-answers, but his anger never silenced her.

Now in his extremity he turned to her with absolute confidence. The appeal in his eyes was for forgiveness—for an answering love. Gently, with a tenderness she had not hitherto shown, Genevieve answered him. They had often measured swords against each other, but each treated the other as a combatant worthy of respect. Admiration there had always been. Now, in the dim night-lit room, in the dusky silence, they drew close together —closer than they had ever been. She answered his smile with a kiss and laid her cheek against his hand.

"I wish you had been a son, Genevieve. You would not have failed me. If I—if I go . . .

keep the family together. You can do it. I see my mistakes now, but I hope my children will forgive me. It was for their sakes; I wanted them to have the best of life. I wanted a Pencarrow to follow after me. Robin will, but he is not quite a Pencarrow, and Kitty is terribly ambitious for him. She has plans, great plans, for him, away from here. Don't let them repeat my folly and drive the family apart. I rely on you, Genevieve. You won't fail me, I know."

He spoke with an effort, brokenly, and she did not interrupt him. Afterwards he lay back, his eyes closed, spent by the exertion.

Genevieve sat holding his hand, overwhelmed by the manifestation of his faith in her. Despite their repeated conflict, and moved by the simple declaration of his failure, a confession not easy for him to make, he now placed the onus of carrying on the family tradition upon her; not Kelly the farmer, not Pat of the sea. They had made their choice and he acknowledged their right to do so. He did not say how it was to be done, but upon her he placed the burden of keeping the family together and seeing that Pencarrow followed Pencarrow in the firm.

Her father was strong on family loyalty, but

how was she to do it? She could not ask; she could not argue; she could only accept the responsibility.

Kitty's ambition for Robin! What did her father know of that? He spoke as though some definite scheme propounded by Kitty had actually been discussed between them—something of which Robin knew nothing as yet.

As she sat holding her father's hand, soothing and comforting him with her serenity and devotion, a gentle caress feeding his hungry heart, she wondered how far one's life is one's own, and the limits imposed by loyalty. The pursuit of happiness was a phrase that kept recurring. Was happiness to be captured by direct pursuit or was it merely a by-product of work and loyalty to an ideal and the doing of the ordinary things of life? Her mind was troubled and her soul harassed by doubts and the ceaseless dread that death might win. She pressed her lips to the limp hand on the coverlet, and Norah, who had crept along in her dressing-gown, saw Miles open his eyes and look with infinite love and gratitude at the bent head of Genevieve.

Kelly was sent for and Sister Mary Agnes came from the convent. Pat was somewhere off the South African coast, making for New

375

Zealand and unaware of his father's illness. Peter and Meggie and Genevieve were always on call.

The Last Sacraments had been administered and the priest read the prayers for the dying. Genevieve, dry-eyed, kept close to her mother. Robin and Kitty were in the background, and Hester Macdonald had come over from the Sounds. Michael too, was down, but Ella and Gentry had remained at Duffield.

"I'm sorry I disappointed you, Father." Kelly said it with an effort.

"We were both wrong, my boy."

Miles lay unconscious now and the family waited in little groups scattered about the house.

Genevieve slipped away from the sick-room and Michael met her in the hall.

"Tired, old girl?" he said affectionately.

For a moment she let her head rest on his shoulder. "I could sleep for a week," she replied wearily.

"How is he now?" asked Michael.

"The same. But I can't believe he is dying. I've still got hopes."

"Hang on to them, Genevieve. If he's got the will to live."

"Oh, he's got that all right. He has never funked it. He is fighting hard. I feel positive he will get better."

"And everything will go on the same?"

"No, things can never be quite the same again. Father has changed."

"Will it last?" asked Michael.

"We'll make it last."

Robin hovered about helplessly. He was cut off from Genevieve, but she saw the entreaty in his eyes. Poor Robin! This was making it all so much more complicated. Not now; not now; they must wait.

Miles Pencarrow did not die. He made a slow recovery, and long weeks and months elapsed before he again walked Lambton Quay with his swinging stride, or his voice boomed out in Court.

When Miles was pronounced out of danger the weight of anxiety lifted from the family and the tense atmosphere relaxed. A mild diversion was caused by the approaching confinement of Erena.

"Where is your mother?" Miles asked Genevieve one afternoon.

"She is with Aunt Kitty, deep in speculation."

"Speculation! About what?"

"Whether Grannie's next great-grandchild will be a savage," and she laughed.

"How is Erena?" he asked.

"A bit scared. Aunt Hester is coming to-night. Poor Neil looks like a frightened rooster. You know that smug professional manner he has acquired; it's got its feathers ruffled."

Miles smiled faintly, but there was no rebuke for her levity.

For twenty-four hours even Miles felt that he had ceased to hold the centre of the stage as invalid-in-chief, while the mothers—a term which lumped together Norah, Kitty and Hester—talked wisely in whispers and drank endless cups of tea.

"What's the betting?" asked Kelly, who had come in from the Hutt.

Genevieve grinned. "My money is on a nut-brown boy."

When Norah heard that it was a girl with red hair she drank three large glasses of champagne in an ecstasy of relief, and stayed in bed with a sick headache next day.

Hester had hidden her anxiety beneath her accustomed quiet, but her joy was great when she saw Erena with a tiny daughter who had inherited her appearance from old Matthew Pencarrow.

"When are you coming back?" Kelly asked Genevieve. "The place is like a pigsty."

"Why don't you beat old Kate over the head and make her clean it up?"

"Father is getting on all right now."

Kelly was not given to making an impassioned plea.

Genevieve shook her head. "I'll have to stand by a bit longer."

Kitty and Robin were frequent visitors at Pencarrow House on the Terrace, but in that family interchange there was little chance of privacy. Winter was fast settling in and life centred indoors round the fires. Someone of the numerous group was always prowling in and out, and Kitty seemed never far from Robin. The adoring, indulgent mother kept close, and the intensity of her anxiety where Robin was concerned was almost pathetic. Her whole life and love and hopes centred in him. Not for herself, but for Robin she would have faced any trial—any test. As she grew older there was a lurking tragedy in her eyes: the fear of losing him.

It was not until Miles was convalescent and the doctor ordered him off to Sydney and the

Blue Mountains to avoid the winter that Genevieve and Robin again faced their problem.

"We will have to wait, Robin. He is taking Mother and me with him. Perhaps if I see a chance I may be able to pave the way."

"I wish you weren't going, Genevieve. It sounds beastly selfish, I know, but it isn't that."

The pull between his mother's influence and his love for Genevieve held him midway in an uncertainty that shattered his peace. There was no chance of making a gallant gesture, or being a romantic hero, in such circumstances. All his brave impulses were wrecked on trivial domestic moments. Try as he would, he could not find a compromise, and sooner or later a decision must be reached. Though he deplored the delay, it was a relief to find that events had ordered a reprieve. He dreaded the break with his mother, yet the prospect of Genevieve going to Sydney for three months now woke a new alarm.

A certain gentleness has elements of timidity. At times Robin doubted himself and his ability to face trouble. Was he a coward? Was there some yellow streak in him that accounted for his reluctance to snatch his happiness at the expense of others? The doubt worried him, and had it not been for Genevieve's departure for Sydney he might have felt compelled to put it to the test; to satisfy himself rather than endure this torturing uncertainty: Am I a coward?

In the bracing air of the Blue Mountains, in the enforced quiet, Miles regained his health. He soon wearied of the rôle of invalid and his mind searched about for occupation. He wondered how things were going at the office; if Robin would manage that Burton case properly; if they were setting that Saunders business satisfactorily. He became fretful at times, particularly on wet days.

"I ought to be getting back," he began.

"Why not write to them? I'll do it for you," said Genevieve. "I'm not fast, but I can do shorthand a bit. It will be good practise for us both. It will ease your mind and get up my speed. Come on, try me."

Out of this grew regular morning sessions at which Miles dictated long, detailed and very aggravating budgets for the office. They arrived in masses every week and had to be read and replied to.

Genevieve rapidly improved with practise and her father was delighted at the intelligent interest and wide knowledge she displayed. Poor Norah! He had never been able to discuss his work or his problems with her beyond the most superficial observation. But Genevieve found it vastly absorbing this little by-play of the law; finding means of legitimate evasion, or phrases of subtle compulsion, or building up the structure of argument and the whole architecture of persecution and defence.

Robin's duties were multiplied by the detailed account of cases which he was obliged to forward each mail. Only the fact that he felt himself directing the office personally, though from a distance, reconciled Miles to the long absence.

Peter had settled down in the office, but as he still had the hurdle of matriculation ahead, after two failures, and took scant interest in the work, it was quite evident that he would not justify his father's hopes.

Maisie Kite, as Peter had said, had accepted an offer to join Williamson's, and her first public appearance as a professional was an occasion for much comment. She had a minor part and appeared in tights.

"Have you seen Maisie Kite in tights?"

Norah was profoundly shocked and Kitty mildly caustic.

"But why, Mother?" asked Genevieve. "You've seen dozens of girls in tights—in pantomime and musical comedy."

"Yes, dear, but that's different. We didn't know them."

"What has that got to do with it?"

"It makes a big difference. If she appeared in Australia . . . But here, in Wellington, where she is known! And our boys all know her; it isn't nice. I felt quite hot and uncomfortable all the time she was on the stage, with Kelly and Peter there."

"Oh Mother darling, you are an old prude! I think she looked marvellous; she's got such beautiful legs!"

"Yes, I know, dear; that makes it worse. She stands out so conspicuously."

Norah felt that the family friendship with her should now be on another basis, less personal, but she did not know how to bring this about.

Miles's illness came on the heels of the Williamson season and banished all thought of Maisie Kite, who was then touring in the South. Maisie had the supreme pleasure of passing through Ashburton and greeting her parents and the gawky Ethel during the few minutes' stop while they watered the engine of the train.

Maisie's mind went back to that day, years before, when she had bought the lace for the sleeves of her shrunken dress and borrowed her mother's brown kid gloves and the chorus boy who called her "girlie". Now she smiled at the local youths who stood awkwardly about, hands in pockets, or slouched along smoking.

But Maisie's stage career was a short one. She had the voice and the ability and the gay courage to have fought through to success, but she went down with tonsilitis just before the company sailed for Australia, and she was left behind in an Auckland hospital. The doctor insisted on the removal of her tonsils as soon as she could stand the operation. Whether it was fate or faulty surgery, however, the timbre of her voice was changed. She could still sing, but the quality that might have carried her to the front rank had vanished.

Valiantly she tried to win it back, but soon it was evident that no training or system of production could repair the damage. She faced defeat gamely after the first breakdown with its bitter, bitter tears. It meant going back to Wellington to find another job—an office job once more, her brief dream ended.

"I saw Maisie Kite to-day," Kelly told Robin. "What hard luck! But she's a game youngster. Her eyes filled with tears for a moment when she told me, but she is not sitting down to whine. She can't get back to Murray Roberts'; they have filled her place. But she won't be long getting something to do; she is a pretty good typist."

The mail was in and several fat letters awaited Miles when he returned from his afternoon drive. Letters also for Lady Pencarrow and Genevieve.

Lady Pencarrow was the first to have the news; it was in a letter from Kitty.

"Oh, how dreadful!" she exclaimed.

"What's up?" asked Genevieve.

"Kitty is terribly upset because Robin has engaged Maisie Kite as a typist in his office. She got ill and lost her voice and had to give up the stage."

"I think it was rather decent of him to give her a job," said Genevieve.

"That's what Kitty thought at first, but

now she says the girl is encroaching upon him. That class is always rather pushing, and several times Kitty has met him walking along Lambton Quay after work with her on the way home."

Miles snorted his disapproval. It was not until he read a special plea to him from Kitty to get rid of the girl and suggesting that Maisie Kite was probably trying to trap Robin, and painting a lurid picture of a family scandal—Robin married to a common typist—that the event assumed any magnitude. The thought of Robin marrying was becoming a positive obsession with his mother.

Robin, too, mentioned the matter in his letter to Genevieve.

I've given Maisie Kite a job as typist. Kelly met her very down on her luck. She had to give up the stage because an operation had ruined her voice. And she is a damn' good typist; the best we've got. She has been very game about it all; you can't help admiring her. Now the funny part is that Mother has cut up rough because she met me coming along the Quay with Maisie after work. She says it won't do to be seen publicly with one's typist. A bit rough on the girl, and she is such a funny little beggar, too; she always makes me laugh. I took her into my own office because of Peter, to tell the truth. I don't think he has quite outgrown his puppy infatuation for Maisie, and I thought it wise not to start him off again. I'm being very firm: quite paternal. Now Mother is getting notions about the dignity and the importance of keeping the staff in its place. What a world!

Each subsequent mail brought further news of Maisie's progress in the office of Kelly, Pencarrow and Herrick.

Peter wrote enthusiastically; her presence, though for a great part of the day denied him, had reconciled him to the office. But it did not whet his appetite for work.

Kitty's direct appeal to Miles for the painless but immediate removal of Maisie Kite became an irritating but recurring phase of their correspondence.

I don't like to mention to Robin the real reason, but I feel sure the girl is taking advantage of her position. He says she calls him "Mr. Herrick" in the office, but that makes it even worse to have her addressing him as

"Robin" outside. She was at the Hutt last Sunday when we went out. Kelly had invited her, and I thought it a grave mistake. Not that I am a snob, but it is bad for office discipline. I'm sure, of course, she is quite a nice little thing in a way, and amusing, but after her recent appearance in public in tights, and now this . . . truly, I am very worried.

"I think Kitty is making an unnecessary fuss; that is the worst of having an only child," said Norah, who was annoyed at this trivial affair being exaggerated by Kitty into a problem of major importance demanding Miles's intervention. It was unsettling him, these imaginary pictures of hers; what might be happening in the office during his absence and the subversive influence of Maisie.

Robin's letters gave more and more space to Maisie.

I gave Peter a kick in the pants yesterday for hanging about Maisie in my office when I was out. I came in early and found him sitting on a corner of the table with a box of chocolates. I will say she doesn't encourage him, but I did the big boss act very effectively for me, as she hadn't finished my letters. They both said he had not been there five minutes. She made up time amazingly; she certainly can crack it out on the machine. And she never minds a bit extra; she doesn't work with her eye on the clock. Maisie was out at the Hutt on Sunday; Kelly had asked her and Mother didn't like it.

Having dismissed Maisie Kite from their minds with the putting aside of their letters, Miles continued his programme of daily dictation to Genevieve, which occupied much of the morning. The time was punctuated with questions, for Genevieve refused to pass over anything she did not understand. In this closer intimacy Miles gradually found himself talking to her on a new equality, explaining theories, expounding legal technicalities, ever listening to her shrewd criticism. He discovered that her un-legal, man-in-the-street commonsense often pointed out a weak spot in his argument, and it became a habit, later on, to talk over problems and cases. Not that she knew anything of law, but she was unhesitatingly frank. Once only had Miles openly voiced his admiration. After a busy morning, when she had fought him on a small point in one of the letters he was dictating to

389

Robin and won, he put an affectionate hand on her shoulder.

"I wish you had been a son, Genevieve. It would have made all the difference."

She flashed him a grateful smile and the intimate moment passed. But underneath their growing companionship was the consciousness that they were allies. They might, and, indeed, they would, disagree, but at least they could meet on common ground and talk it out. Miles would not again dismiss her comments as vulgar flippancies or unfilial disrespect. Genevieve had won a definite victory and Miles was proud of his daughter. She would be a woman of character and considerable ability. Perhaps, after all, it would be as well if she did not marry. It would be good to have her near him always. She could not waste her time keeping house for Kelly on the farm.

As the the days of his convalescence drew to a close and he looked forward to his return his mind made new plans—plans for Genevieve.

21

THE usual party which marked all notable events in the family was organized to welcome home Sir Miles and Lady Pencarrow and Genevieve.

The boat arrived in the morning and there was a dinner-party at the Terrace at night. Miles had completely recovered, and the change away from his usual routine had broken some of the fixed habits of recent years. His illness and the nearness of death had recast his values and thrown into truer perspective the events of his life. Great things became dwarfed when seen against the background of eternity, and minor circumstances acquired major importance. To hold the love and confidence of his children seemed a far greater victory than any material success, and yet it was over such matters that he had sacrificed them. In his hearty laugh and the joy at being home again was something of the Miles of former days. Norah saw it and tears of relief slid down her cheeks as she smiled and watched the warmth of his greeting with Kelly.

Genevieve and Robin had adopted a consciously casual attitude towards each other in front of the family and it lacked even the old frank easy comradeship. In a house swarming with relatives—Michael, Ella and Gentry, Kelly, Kitty, Erena and Neil—privacy was impossible. Sir Miles and Lady Pencarrow were there of course, and also Peter and Meggie. It seemed hopeless for Genevieve and Robin to get a word alone. He had gone to meet the boat, and their first interchange had been the foolish remarks shouted from the ship to the shore as she berthed. Even their eyes screened any emotion before the crowd.

They had spoken to each other, a whispered greeting, and, standing close, their hands had met and the fingers locked in a secret caress, while they talked of commonplace things.

It was the first time they had been separated since they had become aware of their love for each other. Each wondered how the other had stood the test of absence and their eyes searched for signs.

In the confusion of departure after the

dinner-party they had watched for and seized a moment alone.

"Good night, Norah! Good night, Miles!"

"Come up for lunch to-morrow, Kitty. You are staying down, aren't you, Michael? Ella and Erena, you come up too, and bring the baby. She must have grown." Norah talked on, extending hospitality to the family. It had been so hard when they were all here together. Miles had done most of the talking at dinner; and there was so much she wanted to say—and to hear.

"Genevieve! Oh, my darling!"

Robin had caught her hand and drawn her into the unlit breakfast-room. For a moment they were content to hold each other close and feel all the flow of sweet intimacy. He kissed her, first gently, reverently, then wildly, and she laughed softly, a little catch in her voice at this new impetuosity, and lifted her face to his in an eager response.

"Soon, darling; it must be soon. I'm growing impatient."

It was the Robin who was a little afraid—afraid of being afraid; afraid to take what he wanted of life and risk the consequences. This was the Robin who held her in his arms, making passionate demands of urgency. He banished all thought of his mother's hurt and his uncle's charge of ingratitude. Might he not be exaggerating the opposition? Surely they must see how great was the foundation of their love, this long, happy companionship.

"Soon, darling, soon!" he whispered, and kissed her again.

"Yes, quite soon," she answered.

She felt strong enough now to face anything with him. Not that the delay had arisen from any weakness on her part. At any time she would have faced the family much as Kelly had done. It was Robin who had hesitated.

Robin felt more confidence in himself, having so far won the battle over Maisie Kite. His mother had been persistent in her demands, but here, he felt, he was quite justified in resisting her. It would be unwise to permit home interference in office affairs. Sooner or later Miles would pass on to him a greater load of responsibility in office management, and it would never do to have his mother, even with the best intentions, deciding who he should or should not employ. Her reasons would be based entirely upon social or financial grounds and divorced from ability. He had been very firm about Maisie Kite and had backed his decision with the soundest of arguments. His victory in this had, to some slight extent, restored his confidence in himself. He had firmly but definitely refused to permit her interference with the appointment of a typist.

At first she had been very sweet, then hurt. Afterwards she veered to the dominant mother, but she stopped short of the folly of claiming authority over his actions.

After he had refused, Robin had been doubly devoted to her, giving in graciously about purely social matters and yielding to her inclinations in other things. The question had then been dropped and Robin was greatly relieved to find that it had not marred the harmony of their relationship. It was a small thing, but if he could do it in small things, why not in large?

Now he was fired by Genevieve's return, and the slow burgeoning of their love had become a pent-up force that clamoured for its consummation.

Soon, they had agreed in that first meeting after her return. Soon it must be. Genevieve felt the new relations with her father would make it possible to talk it over calmly with him; to reason with him and make him see it from their point of view. He would listen to her now.

"Come out on Sunday; come early," said Kelly to Robin. "The 'skivvy' will be back on the job then," and he indicated Genevieve with a jerk of his pipe.

"Don't you be too sure about the 'skivvy' coming back."

"She's getting notions above her station and wanting to be a lady. We'll soon knock that out of you, my girl. I haven't trained you how to run a house to let you clear out now, just when you might be useful."

"You have managed pretty well without me and you've put on at least a stone in weight."

"A contented mind," he said.

"You're getting smug, Kelly, and it doesn't suit you. What you want is a wife."

"You're enough nuisance, but I can get rid of you."

"I'm sacked now," said Genevieve cheerfully.

"Not yet. I'm willing to give you another try. Mother, will you please send my 'skivvy' back to me to-morrow?"

"You had better speak to your father," said Lady Pencarrow.

"I am in demand. I'll put up my price now. Any more offers?"—and as she turned she caught Robin's eye.

"What is all this?" asked Miles, joining them.

"I want my—"

"Housekeeper," Genevieve interpolated.

"I want my 'skivvy' back, Father, so will you please push her out?"

"Ah! That depends, my boy. That depends. I may have other fish to fry for Genevieve."

He said it smiling, as though he had a pleasant surprise up his sleeve.

"Oh! What's this?" asked Kelly.

"All in good time; all in good time. You seem to have managed very well without her so far."

A hush fell and the cheerful banter ceased. Miles had introduced a serious note into the discussion. He looked affectionately at Genevieve, and though she answered it with a smile on her lips, a quick fear gleamed in her eyes, and she saw the anxious questioning in Robin's.

"Come along, Robin. Good night, all. It's nice to have you home again and see Miles looking so well. Good night, Norah. I'll be up

for lunch—at one. Come along, Robin," and
Kitty broke up the group in the hall, taking
Robin's arm as they went out into the wintry
night.

22

MAISIE KITE bit her lip and held her head high. The smile died from her face as Sir Miles Pencarrow said: "Oh, Miss Kite, sit down."

She came into his room in answer to his message, but he went on reading a document and signed three letters before giving her his attention.

Maisie had worked hard since she had been on his staff. She was a good typist—quick, reliable, discreet and obliging. Robin said she was the best they had and she wanted to justify his judgment in giving her the post.

During Sir Miles's absence, with his constant demands to be kept advised about everything, there was a considerable increase in correspondence. Robin's work, apart from this, had been much heavier, and as Maisie's duties were regulated by the volume of Robin's she had extended herself to meet the emergency.

Miles was pleased with the way things had been managed as a whole. He did not endorse every opinion given or agree with some things they had done, but no error of magnitude had been committed, a fact which pleased him, yet left a dim regret that he had been so easily dispensed with.

Once or twice Robin had commended Maisie for her work. But apart from that she knew he was pleased. She was conscious of doing her job well and in her sphere she kept things running smoothly.

The one difficulty she was aware of was Peter's tendency to linger in her vicinity and to manufacture excuses for coming into Robin's office. She successfully dealt with that, however, and even exerted a beneficent influence over Peter's studies.

Maisie had always felt Kitty's hostility towards her. It was not obvious, just a slight chilling of her tone when she spoke; a significant quality in her smile. It was so slight, indeed, that even Kitty herself was not aware of it. Not until she had met Robin and Maisie walking along the Quay one wintry afternoon after the office had closed. Curly wisps of hair flicked Maisie's face, her cheeks were glowing with the wind, and her eyes were bright and laughing as she looked up at Robin. In a flash Kitty saw the menace of this new association; she knew the influence of propinquity in such affairs. From a new direction her citadel was threatened. Kitty prided herself on having checked the growing intimacy with Genevieve.

During her father's illness, Genevieve's absorption in him was complete. While they were in Australia, Robin had been most amenable and had extended his acquaintance with new and important families, under his mother's guidance, distributing his attentions with that easy impartiality that, she felt, was the surest safeguard against marriage.

With the awakening of this new fear in regard to Maisie Kite, Kitty's alarm grew. In her encounters with Robin over it she had met with a firm but courteous refusal.

"She is the best typist we've got, Mother, and I don't see why you should suddenly ask me to sack her."

"It is unwise to mix up one's friends with one's business. It never works. If you make friends of your employees they begin to presume and it undermines discipline."

"Oh, that's nonsense, Mother. It might apply to a cook, but it's different in an office."

"You are young yet, Robin. You don't

understand these things like older people—people of experience. I'm sure your uncle will not approve when he comes back."

"I bet he does. I'm only afraid that he will want her for himself."

"And there is Peter; he is so impressionable, and he was always so—so—"

"Leave him to me, Mother. That isn't your worry. I would back your judgment in many things, but not in the office."

"But, Robin, dear—"

"Please, Mother."

Robin was relieved when his mother ceased to speak about it, and took heart from his little victory.

But Kitty did not yield so easily.

She had lunch with Norah the day after their return, and she painted an alarming picture of the consequences they might expect from having as an employee a young girl like Maisie Kite—attractive in a way, she conceded, and all the worse for that. She had stressed the disturbing influence it was on Peter, the unsuitability of Robin going about with his typist, and the indignity of expecting Miles to meet her on equal terms out at Kelly's. She felt Norah's pulse and decided that, if left to herself, she would have raised none of these objections, not having the acute sensibility to danger that comes of being the mother of an only son. But if it were put to her strongly she might talk to Miles and work upon his vulnerable prejudices.

If Kitty seemed ruthless in her determination to get rid of Maisie Kite, she was not actuated by malice or unkindliness. Always when she was compelled to take action against someone in defence of Robin she planned to make it up to them in some way. She could steel her heart against pity when Robin's future was at stake, and she was relentless in pursuit of her object. Yet she planned some compensation for the injury inflicted, though in most cases she had persuaded herself that her argument was just and her judgment sound and in later years they would all be grateful for her intervention.

At first Miles had scoffed at the idea, but the structure of suspicion that had been built upon so slender a foundation had been strengthened by small incidents in the office; half-heard scraps of conversation and the ring of laughter from Robin's room; the easy manner between them and the assumption of equality that characterized their meeting at Kelly's. He might be "Mr. Herrick" in the office, but it was "Hullo, Robin!" when they met on Sunday afternoon at the Hutt.

Kitty kept hammering away, feeding Miles with further evidences of the folly of letting the matter slide, recounting bits of gossip about them, goading him to take action, until she got her way.

Eventually Miles could see it only through her eyes, and began to interpret every harmless word and laugh and gesture as significant. Kitty confided to Miles alone that she was afraid Maisie might trap Robin into marriage, or, if not Robin, she might get Peter, young as he was, involved in an entanglement to the discredit of the family. She played hard upon Sir Miles's pride. She did not, however, imply that Maisie Kite was immoral because she had appeared publicly in tights, but by inference she suggested that, having grown up in a different and less fastidious atmosphere, the girl probably viewed things—well, Miles would understand.

Kitty urged him not to reveal the true reason for her apprehension and asked if, now that he had returned, he could not reorganize the office, or appear to do so, in such a way as would enable him to dispense with Maisie Kite. Of course, he must give her a very high recommendation and see that she got a good position elsewhere. Kitty had no intention of seeing Maisie suffering any hardship through the change. She tried to be fair to her.

In order to make it easier, Miles took Maisie into his own office, so relieving Robin of any responsibility. He said it was a temporary change as he had decided upon a measure of reorganization. At the end of a fortnight Maisie received a message that Sir Miles wished her to remain behind at five o'clock.

She knew she had done her work well, and it was with expectation of some promotion or a rise in salary that she went to his room.

"Oh, Miss Kite, sit down," he said, and went on with his work. He left that awkward pause to do its work; to give her the first hint of what was coming and prepare the eager young girl, who had come in so hopefully, for the blow that must fall. When he looked up at her he was sorry. He wished Kitty had minded her own damn' business and not stirred up all this trouble. He coughed and cleared his throat, took off his glasses and wiped them, and put them on again. He found it was not so easy to tell her that owing to some changes he was making in the office he was very reluctant to lose her; they appreciated her excellent work. She had been most discreet and satisfactory and he would have much pleasure in giving her a letter of the highest recommendation.

Maisie's brain throbbed. She bit her lip and held her head high. So that was it—she was sacked. Why? All this talk of reorganizing the office was rubbish. She was sacked. Did Robin know? Of course he must. Perhaps not. Sir Miles had sent him off for a couple of weeks' holiday to Napier as a reward for the long months of heavy work and responsibility he had had during Miles's illness. He and his mother were in Napier now. What did it mean? She was not aware of having transgressed in any way.

She could hear Sir Miles's voice saying he would give her a letter of the highest recommendation—personal recommendation. What did she care? She was sacked. Why? Did Robin know? Her mind went round, asking the same question over and over.

Miles ceased to speak but she did not move. Sacked! To begin all over again. She felt suddenly tired—tired from the unequal struggle.

"Good afternoon, Miss Kite."

Suddenly her mind came back to the immediate present.

"Good afternoon, Sir Miles."

She kept the tears back while she put on her hat and coat. Outside the wind howled, a spiteful east wind and she bent her head and plunged along, holding her coat close about her. At Stewart Dawson's corner she paused and stood in the recess for shelter a moment, her eyes now stinging with tears of anger. Blindly she was staring at a row of silver cigarette- and sovereign-cases.

"Hullo, Maisie! Whose birthday is it—mine?"

Kelly stood beside her. "I'd like that one," he said, pointing to a massive one in gold.

She kept her head averted to hide her tears.

"What's up? Maisie! What's the matter?" he asked, suddenly aware of her misery.

"I've been sacked, Kelly."

"Sacked!" he said, puzzled. "Who sacked you?"

"I've been sacked by your father."

"Father! My God! What a damn' shame. Who's at the bottom of this?"

His sudden sympathy lessened her control and she could not answer.

"Here! I've got the car round the corner. Hop in; I want to talk to you about this."

"There's nothing to say, Kelly."

"Oh, isn't there! Come on!"

"Where are you going?"

"Home!" said Kelly. "We can't talk here."

Robin and Kitty got back next day and Norah asked all the family to dinner. Genevieve was still at home, having made first one and then another excuse for postponing her return to Kelly, and her father encouraged her. He did not want her to go back to the Hutt.

Genevieve thought it better not to go until she and Robin had told the family of their engagement. She wanted to be free, as it were, in order to move swiftly if necessary. Miles had insisted upon Robin having a holiday as he looked tired, so once again they decided to defer the announcement.

"It may be the last holiday Mother and I will have together like this, and I want to make it something she will remember, and if we told her now that would spoil it all."

"I suppose you're right," said Genevieve.

"You don't mind, do you, darling? Just two weeks more. You don't think I want to put it off, do you?"

408

"No, it's not that; but something is always happening."

Robin looked brown and well and Kitty was in high spirits when they got back from Napier.

"We've had the loveliest holiday, Norah. Robin is such a darling. I don't think any mother ever had such a son. He spoilt me completely."

Kelly was silent throughout dinner and listened to all the happy holiday talk as though it were of small importance.

The evening was chilly, and a cheerful fire burnt in the grate. Chairs were drawn up, and Genevieve, her elbows on her knees, her shoulders hunched, sat on a stool and Miles rested a lean, brown hand for a moment on her head. Frequently now he made these affectionate gestures, having at last broken through the shell of cold reserve which had shut him in during recent years.

Genevieve smiled back and leant against his knee. Robin sat opposite beside Lady Pencarrow; Kelly and Kitty shared the couch.

"Back to work again on Monday, Robin; how do you like the prospect?" asked Lady Pencarrow.

409

"I don't mind, Aunt Norah. I'm feeling awfully fit."

The remark pushed back Napier and the talk of pleasant doings; of idling in the sun, driving through the English-looking country about Havelock North, and bathing in the shallow rim of the thundering surf. It was now behind them; ahead lay the future—and the office. The sparkle had died down and a flatness marked their words. Then a brief silence fell.

Kelly took his pipe from his mouth, looked at its dark bowl, and deliberately struck a match. He puffed two or three times, then, satisfied that it was alight, leant back into a corner of the couch.

"Why did you sack Maisie Kite, Father?"

The question crashed into their mood like a stone hurled through glass.

Kelly asked it with slow deliberation, having chosen his moment.

"What!" said Genevieve, amazed, sitting up.

Crimson rushed into Robin's face. Kitty was distinctly uneasy and Miles frankly annoyed. Norah alone did not appear to realize the implication.

Kelly waited for his father to answer him.

"Why did you sack her?" he repeated.

For a moment Miles was too surprised to speak—surprised at this attack, for there was a challenge in Kelly's voice. He was angry that what was purely a business matter had been made a personal, almost family, affair. He wondered how Kelly knew; only yesterday he had told Maisie Kite. He had not yet mentioned it in the office, nor had he told anyone at home. They were all unaware of the impending change and the reason for it.

Kitty knew it was coming; he had promised her to fix it up while Robin was away. He decided to give Maisie notice and tell Robin afterwards. He knew it would be an awkward matter to explain, but he could see no reason why Robin should mind. After all, Miles felt he was still head of the firm and his authority was unquestioned.

Kelly and Genevieve saw the quick flush stain Robin's face. So he had known it was coming and had shirked facing it; he had stayed away. Or was it the flush of sudden embarrassment?

"Have you sacked her, Father?" Genevieve turned and faced him.

"Yes." Sir Miles said the one word as

though it were final and left nothing more to be added.

"Why?"

Kelly stuck to his point with a cool deliberation that was a new feature in dealing with his father.

"Why? That's my business."

Miles resented Kelly's tone. Was he to explain his actions to his children? To be cross-examined by them?

Norah's eyes were anxious. She was alarmed at the sudden change in the happy atmosphere and an unknown fear that something unpleasant underlay this sharp questioning kept her silent.

"Did she lie, or thieve, or do her work badly?" asked Kelly doggedly.

"Don't be absurd, Kelly," said Genevieve.

"You don't sack your best typist for nothing," Kelly replied.

"What has it got to do with you?" asked Miles.

"I'm a little curious," he answered, with aggravating quiet.

Robin was taken by surprise and, fearing a scene, said nothing. He knew now that his mother had done this. She had persuaded Miles, and he resented the whole unfairness of it. He could not say anything here; he could not challenge his mother, or dispute his uncle's authority in front of them. He just sat uncomfortable and humiliated, hoping that Kelly was not bent on starting another row.

"Did you know about it, Robin?" Kelly persisted.

He hesitated. To admit that he did not was to throw the full blame on his uncle. After all, it was an office matter, and none of Kelly's business.

"Did you?" Kelly's voice had risen and his control seemed breaking.

Robin looked at his uncle and still hesitated.

"No, Robin did not, if you must know. I am still master in my own office, at least. And I'll have no damned interference from you!"

Miles's temper was rising despite all his good resolutions, and Norah began her clucking noises to warn the children.

"You knew she was going, Aunt Kitty?" and he turned sharply to see the look of entreaty she shot at Robin.

"And if she did, what the devil has it got to do with you?" Miles defended her.

"I thought so!"

Genevieve, tense and rigid, watched them

413

each in turn. There was something behind all this—something she did not understand. Something to do with Robin.

"You don't sack your best typist for nothing!"

What did it mean? What had Maisie done—and Robin? Why all the mystery—Robin and Aunt Kitty sent away for a couple of weeks and Maisie suddenly dismissed?

Robin's eyes were fixed on hers, pleading. He could see the misery in her face, but he was unable to explain.

Kelly let the silence lie heavily, knowing that he had made his point.

Miles stirred uneasily. "Who told you? When did you see Maisie Kite?" he asked truculently, some of the old fire returning. This was the first show of temper since his illness.

"I saw Maisie Kite on Lambton Quay yesterday, after you had sacked her."

"Huh! So she told you, did she? Came bleating to you for sympathy, I suppose. Well, I won't take her back, so you needn't ask me to."

"She didn't come bleating, as you call it, and I am not asking you to take her back; neither is she. I'm glad she is out of it—"

"Why are you so interested?"

It was Kitty's first comment, and there was an edge on her voice.

"Because I'm not a damned snob."

"Kelly, that's no way to talk to your aunt," Norah leapt in.

Genevieve saw a first-class row brewing, and, bewildered as she was by it all, she tried to avert it.

"After all, Kelly, I suppose Father is the best judge of his staff."

"Quite so, but why sack your best typist—for no reason; no given reason? It leaves rather a nasty taste; a suggestion that there was something wrong somewhere."

"Leave it, Kelly. There is no good talking about it now."

Robin's voice had a ring of entreaty. He hated rows, he dreaded scenes, he lacked Kelly's bull-headed determination to face out an ugly situation. He wanted to know as much as Kelly, but not here; not now. It was only making matters more difficult.

"It's all right. I know all I want to now. Good night," and without another word Kelly walked out of the room and banged the front door.

Kitty came round next day to put her side

of the affair to Norah, and she was annoyed to find Genevieve there. She had lunch and stayed to tea, but Genevieve sat on, so she was afraid to mention the matter. Maisie Kite's name was studiously avoided.

"Why, here's Father! What on earth has brought him home at this hour? Heavens, he does look upset!"

"What's the matter, dear?" asked Norah, hurrying to meet him.

"Matter! Good God! Kelly married that Kite girl this morning. Matter!"

"Oh, Miles!"

"That's your eldest son for you; a damn' disgrace. A damn' scandal. My God!"—and Miles paced the floor talking incoherently, while Norah sobbed heartbrokenly.

Genevieve, white-faced, stood drumming her fingers on the window-pane.

"Stop that damned noise, can't you?" snapped her father.

She stopped and slowly turned round.

"Good luck to them both," she said, facing her father. "I hope they will be happy."

"Happy! Happy! How the devil can they be happy; a girl like that? And you're the cause of it," and he swung round suddenly and glared at Kitty.

416

"Me?"

"Yes, you, and you know it. All this damn' fuss about Robin; with your damn' tales. If I hadn't listened to you and dismissed the girl because you asked me to this would never have happened."

The tide of trouble washed over Kitty. She saw Norah's tears and Miles's distress, but in her heart was one great comfort—Robin; she had saved Robin. It might have been he. It was unfortunate that it should be Kelly, but how much worse if it had been Robin—Robin married to Maisie Kite. She was sorry for them, deeply sorry, but she had saved Robin.

"All this fuss about Robin!" The words rang in Genevieve's ears. What fuss? What had been happening in the office while they were away? She recalled Robin's letters, each one with more and more about Maisie; singing her praises. Was there really anything in it, or was his mother becoming obsessed by the fear that every girl wanted to marry him?

Miles could not eat his dinner, and once more the family felt the weight of his anger. All the good resolutions made when he was ill went to the wind. He felt the unfairness of it, a sort of conspiracy to rob him of the full fruits of his family. Just when he had become

417

reconciled to Kelly failing him in the office and had built his hopes upon him carrying on the Home Farm, and perhaps marrying well, and maintaining the family's first association with the land, to receive this final blow. How could they accept hospitality from this girl—go out to the Hutt and find her presiding over Grannie's home, replacing Genevieve? What doubtful strain of blood might she not introduce into the family? Her people were an improvident lot, from Maisie's own account. On and on he went.

Sometimes brooding and silent, then breaking out into a violent tirade against everyone who had had a hand in it—Peter for first introducing the girl; Robin for taking her into the office; Kitty for having precipitated this calamity; Genevieve for defending Kelly's marriage; Norah for her futile tears now that it was too late.

"He'll make himself ill again, Mother, if he goes on like this."

"I know, but what can I do?"

"Get the doctor to drop in casually. He might quieten him down."

"I'd like to, but he would be so angry if I did."

"I'll ring up. After all, it's only a few

months since he nearly died, and an illness like that is sure to have left a weak spot."

"I'd better ask him first," said Norah.

"Miles, dear, I think I'll get the doctor to come along and give you something to quieten your nerves and make you sleep to-night after all this upset."

"I'll have no damned doctor. . . . I'm all right. . . ."

"But it will be better to have some draught than to go on taking more whisky," Norah ventured timidly.

"Good God! Can't I do what I like in my own house? My children defy me, and now you want to regulate what I shall eat and drink. Am I a fool or an imbecile?"

"Miles, dear, don't work yourself up again. It's no good losing your temper. It's done and it can't be undone. We must make the best of it. She may make him a good wife. After all, she has known hard times, and she isn't likely to be extravagant and ruin him. Genevieve is going out to-morrow—"

"I forbid her to go. I forbid any of you to go. I'll teach him a lesson."

"Isn't that foolish, dear?"

"Oh, I'm a fool, am I? Even my wife tells me that to my face."

He was off again, so Norah left him.

"It's no use, Genevieve, I can't do anything with him, but this raging round the house, shouting and swearing and the whisky. . . . I thought that was all over; he has been so different since he was ill. Now he's as bad as ever."

Norah looked pathetic; her tear-stained face seemed to have aged suddenly and she was torn between her disappointment over Kelly's marriage and a dread that Miles would break out again.

"I'll go out to-morrow, Mother, and have a talk to Kelly," said Genevieve.

"Your father forbids you to go; he forbids any of us to have anything to do with them."

"What nonsense! I knew a long time ago that Kelly liked her, but I thought he had cooled off lately. It's the sort of thing Kelly would do, and it will probably turn out as well as most marriages. After all, her mother is dead, and her father lives with her married sister. We are not likely to be inflicted with them. And it was better to do it that way and save all the bother of a big wedding here."

"Better not tell your father you are going out, Genevieve, but I'd be glad if you would.

Go to bed now and get some sleep. Your father seems to be quietening down."

About one in the morning, Lady Pencarrow called Genevieve.

"Quick, Genevieve, get the doctor; your father has had a queer turn."

Genevieve slipped into her dressing-gown and rang up, then went to her father's room, where they waited anxiously for the doctor.

"Keep him quiet, Lady Pencarrow. Don't let him get excited. Another shock like this might have very serious consequences. Smooth things over and don't irritate him unnecessarily; a little white lying, if necessary; you know what I mean—women always do."

He paused.

"So Kelly is married. Well, well! We can't always manage these affairs just as we would like. I know it was a great disappointment to his father when Kelly went farming. He told me all about it. Never mind, Miss Genevieve ought to console him. He is very proud of you, young lady, and you will have to compensate him for this disappointment."

But Genevieve did not smile. Another shock might have serious consequences. Another shock—the shock of being told that she and Robin were to be married. Dare they take the risk? What was she to do? She could not go back to the Hutt now. Never again would she play hostess to the family in Grannie's lovely garden. Maisie was sacked from the office and Kelly was furiously indignant, but his marriage had even more ruthlessly dismissed Genevieve from the Home Farm. Had he thought of that? He had replaced her before telling her that her services were no longer required. Indeed, he had not told her yet. He had offered neither excuse nor apology.

Her father's illness had shattered any immediate hope of her marriage with Robin. Here she was, left high and dry, living at home once more, without any work to her hand, just filling in the days and watching the years slip by, accomplishing nothing, building no future for herself. A mood of black dejection settled upon her and, look as she would, there seemed no gleam of hope. Her father's high ambition for his family might be thwarted, but some perverse fate dogged her, too. Kelly fought for what he wanted, and was the first to strike the blow. Because she and Robin, more merciful, hesitated, something came between them and their opportu-

nity. You need to be ruthless, thought Genevieve. Yet she knew that she could not be
happy with Robin, if by her action deliberately taken, and warned beforehand, she
brought about the evil consequences of which
the doctor had spoken. She must think. Her
head ached, and her heart was heavy. She had
not seen Robin, nor Kelly. She did not want
to see him—not yet. She would have to get it
all straight in her mind first and decide what
was to be done.

She was finishing breakfast when the telephone rang.

"Answer it, Genevieve," said her mother.

"How is Uncle Miles?"

It was Robin.

"Very ill; he has had a slight stroke . . . the
shock."

"Oh, Genevieve!" The despair in his voice
answered her own misery.

She hung up the receiver.

"Robin is coming round; you had better see
him, Mother. I'm going out."

23

MAISIE KITE, now Maisie Pencarrow, woke up in her new home on a bright spring morning and realized that in a few short days the incredible had happened. She had been dismissed from Sir Miles Pencarrow's office, and married his eldest son, and the Home Farm was her inheritance. Here she would in future take precedence over them all.

After breakfast they idled in the garden, Kelly's arm about her waist, looking at the early daffodils. She had known it all, but as a visitor; an outsider. She was the successor to Grannie's famous garden, and though she had never grown a flower in her life she knew that she could not—must not—fail to carry on the work. It was a link between the old generation and the new. She would hand the garden on no less beautiful when her time came to go.

The sky was blue and the juicy freshness of the dawn lingered on till noon. In the orchard the trees were budding and a hint of blush-white marked the birth of a future harvest on the topmost boughs. The sheep and cattle grazed deep in the lush green grass. Birds sang, the lark's full-throated note soaring towards the sun. Busy hens cackled excitedly and cocked a suspicious eye as the lovers passed. A brood of tiny yellow chicks, surprised at being hatched into this amazing world, were being bullied by a truculent mother hen.

The air was sweet with the scent of early flowers and the fragrance of growth. All around life was stirring and the business of living had begun. Plants thrust eager shoots through the soft earth, buds swelled and opened to the sun, birds sang and sought their mates, and gathered twigs and down to fashion a home for the families that were to be hatched. Blind instinct and high intelligence ran side by side. A wild delirious happiness stirred in Kelly. His stormy youth, the calm of recent years, the threatening slackness of which Genevieve was afraid—all were moods of the past. Something of the old boyish ardour that had spent itself upon Duffield had revived, but with it was a richer, warmer glow, the slow-grown love of a man now come to sudden fruition. He was surprised to find how deep were its roots; an affection, half-realized, had burst into full glory.

They had been married the previous day and come back to the Hutt. No trousseau; no honeymoon. But on that first spring day together they had touched the fringe of heaven in the fullness of small and simple things.

Kelly had banished the family from his mind.

"Not to-day—this is ours," he said. "That will come later. But I'm so happy, darling. I could face ten legions of family."

Now they sat in the big living-room so full of memories. They were spent with the very weight of happiness, and in a pleasant weariness they drew close together, the fire making warm patches in the shadowy room. They had not lit the lamp, and the flickering light from the log sent dancing phantoms across the floor. All those sweet hours that are the prelude to marriage had been lost to them; the lover's fondling was a new sensation and not an outworn experience.

Maisie was slim and small; her fair hair had darkened, but the firelight picked out the golden sheen. It waved loosely and grew low on her forehead. Her features had never been

426

regular; fine, humorous, intelligent eyes and a straight brow; a short, neat nose, a mouth wide with an attractive friendliness in its ready smile; a firm chin and throat. She carried herself well; her limbs had an easy grace, and she had quick gestures that matched her ready laughter. Moods passed visibly over her face like clouds across the sun, exposing her mind with transparent honesty. But the long, hard fight she had made had taught her to control her emotions. She had early learnt to take her strokes without wincing, and some innate pride held her silent when she had cause to complain.

Yet all her natural inclination was towards friendliness. The lame dogs knew her for their friend. She was ambitious, but she did not kick from beneath her the steps by which she had climbed. Until her mother's death, Maisie had tried to ease her hard life and tender feet by little gifts. "Me on me two feet all day!" Her childhood was studded with the pitiful phrase, and the birthday gift was always the softest, warmest slippers she could buy. Poor Mother. It had been a dreary life. Maisie hoped that she had found a heaven where the wings took the weight off her feet.

427

Sitting close in the evening dusk, with the pulsing of their new love still throbbing within, their minds sped each on its own mission. Maisie looked backwards over the rugged path she had traversed since her childhood in Ashburton; then forward to the golden days to come as Kelly's wife, the mistress of the Home Farm, the very root of the Pencarrows.

"I will make them love me; I will heal the quarrel," she said to herself over and over again, and stayed her fears with the magic of her love.

Kelly dreamed of the future, having said good-bye to the past. The drowsy warmth of the half-light made for introspection, and the floodtide of their happiness gave wings to fancy.

Then the lamp was lit, and the dreams were replaced by reality.

"Will your father be very angry, Kelly? I suppose it will mean another row."

"Perhaps. But nothing worth having comes easily in this world."

"They will hate me—at first. And your father will be furious."

"I'll love you. Won't that make it up?" and he drew her into his arms, and for a moment

428

they forgot again that the family had yet to be faced.

"How long have you loved me, Kelly?" and her hand slid over his thick, black hair. She had so often longed to do this; now she may.

"I don't know, quite a long time."

"Once I thought you did—a little, but lately you seemed different; as if you didn't care. I've been in love with you for years, only it seemed so—so hopeless."

Her eyes rested on the picture of Bessie Pencarrow over the mantelpiece. She had never seen her, but her memory was still a living force in the family, and she realized how much of the tradition established by her had been carried on by Kelly and Genevieve.

"It will be hard to live up to her," Maisie said simply. "But I'll try."

"You darling! She's going to help us such a lot."

"Do you think she would have liked me?"

"I'm sure she would—you're like her in some ways. She was little and she was game. I never knew such courage, and she always seemed to understand."

They fell silent.

"Genevieve! I can't help feeling I've been

unfair to her. I hope she won't be hurt. . . ."

"She may, at first. But I'm not sure she wanted to come back. I've a feeling that Genevieve was preparing to make some change. She had been very odd about it; always putting it off."

"She may resent my taking her place here."

"She will get over it; they will all get over it. Mrs. Kelly Pencarrow, you'll have a busy time winning them all back, but I'll bet you have the family coming as usual before the year is out."

"I wish we had Genevieve on our side," she said a little wistfully.

"Darling, don't think about the family any more. I want the whole of your attention now. I'm a jealous and exacting husband."

It was quite dark when Genevieve opened the gate of the Home Farm. She stopped to look at the old square house, the light shining from its windows in the quiet hush of night, and a pang of regret woke with the memory of the years she had spent here. She wondered what changes they would make; little things occurred to her—the way she put the cushions on the window-seat and the reading-lamp beside the fire.

She had gone out after breakfast to avoid

Robin. The bright sun of early spring had cast a radiance over the harbour and the hills, and the gorse was golden on the slopes of the Tinakori hill. She had walked for an hour or more, her mind set on some solution. All about her was chaos. Once more the family seemed split asunder and its peace menaced; she tried to get it straight in her own mind before seeing any of them.

Genevieve was hurt with Kelly. He might have told her; surely he could have trusted her. But to dash off in that headlong fashion, heedless of consequences! Maisie she did not blame. Her mother and father were quite wrong in suggesting that she was a designing young creature, out to catch one of the family and secure a position for herself. Long ago Genevieve had suspected that Maisie was in love with Kelly, but of late they had drifted apart. She acquitted Maisie of any desire to marry Robin; but to find herself pushed out, unceremoniously, suddenly dismissed by Kelly when he no longer needed her, made it difficult to overlook.

Kitty she refused to see. She could not forget that her aunt was prepared to sacrifice her—to sacrifice anyone—for Robin. Nothing no one, mattered, provided he was safe. She

431

knew the heights and depths to which that possessive maternal love could attain, and she pitied her for the narrowness of her vision. Might she not, in holding him too tight, lose him altogether in the end? It made her impatient with Robin, this seeming dependence upon his mother. Yet it was that gentleness which appealed to her own firm will.

Now she had to make her decisions as to the future. The doctor had said that her father would recover and that even the muscles which were slightly paralysed would regain their power. But he warned them against a further shock, or anything that might seriously upset him. His long illness had also left his heart weak.

Genevieve's first impulse was to see Kelly and tell him frankly what she thought. Yet what good would that do? It would only widen the breach and cut herself adrift from all association with the Hutt. More and more the burden was being shifted on to her shoulders. Her father had said that he depended upon her now; the doctor had also declared it was for her to compensate for Kelly's defection. Her mother turned to her in every emergency.

Could she, in face of this, marry Robin? Or

must she still wait? Why couldn't she defy them too, and take her happiness where she found it?

A strong sense of family, a firmer fibre that invited responsibility and responded with a curious loyalty, prevented her from following Kelly's course.

Had Robin been a dominant lover, impatient of restraint, she might have yielded to his pleading. There was something almost maternal in her love for Robin. The tall, slim body, the finely cut features, the gentle manner, the timidity where a hurt might be inflicted, was in sharp contrast with her more athletic vigour. She was more robust of mind and body, frank and outspoken, sharp-witted and sharp-tongued.

Now she was learning to control these impulses, to curb her tongue and cloak her hurts. She did not want to pile wreck upon wreck.

She fought it out alone on the windswept Tinakori heights before facing any of them, and she decided to see Kelly first.

Genevieve came in the door and paused.

Kelly and Maisie, taken by surprise, were momentarily embarrassed, and Maisie instinctively looked to Kelly.

Genevieve smiled and put out both hands—one to each of them—but they noticed that her eyes looked tired and her face was pale.

"I hope you will be very happy."

"Then you're not angry with me? Oh, Genevieve, I was afraid."

"Angry, no! Hurt a little. You might have trusted me, Kelly."

She kissed Maisie, and a flood of relief removed the shadow from her happiness. Genevieve was on their side.

"It wasn't that. I thought you had better keep out of it. If you knew . . ."

"I see!"

"How have they taken it at home?" Kelly asked anxiously.

"Pretty badly!"

"Father?"

"Yes."

Genevieve had come to tell them, and in the face of their happiness she was reluctant to dim it with remorse.

"What happened? Go on. We've got to know."

"Father was very angry, and got excited, and raged round the house. Well . . . he's ill now."

"I'm sorry!" It was Maisie who spoke, and

Kelly slipped his arm through hers and drew her to his side.

"A stroke!" said Genevieve.

"Oh God!"

For the first time Genevieve saw Kelly look afraid.

"Won't he ever get better?" Maisie asked in a frightened little voice.

"We hope so."

Kelly looked relieved.

"Is it a bad one?"

"One side is partly paralysed, and he can't speak very distinctly, but the doctor says it may only be temporary."

"And Mother?" Kelly enquired.

"Can't you imagine? Between you rushing off and getting married and Father ill again . . ."

"It's all my fault; I suppose they hate me."

Maisie looked at Genevieve as though pleading for some little word of comfort, and then at Kelly—Kelly, who now filled all her world, and her eyes shone with adoring love.

"It was not your fault, darling, it was mine. I knew he would be angry, but I didn't expect . . . this. Yet it was the only way," he added thoughtfully.

"I suppose so," Genevieve agreed.

"Have you seen Robin . . . or Aunt Kitty?" Kelly asked.

"Not Robin. Aunt Kitty was there when Father came home. He blamed her for having Maisie dismissed; she had made some fuss about Robin."

"Robin!" said Maisie.

"Oh, she is scared to death he will get married," said Kelly. "She watches him like a cat. Funny thing, but once she was afraid of you, Genevieve. I don't suppose you knew, but she had all the family worked up into a fit about the horrible crime of cousins marrying. Then it was Maisie. Who next, I wonder?"

Genevieve found it difficult to sustain the fiction of a foolish fancy. She had to hide the real tragedy that lay beneath in her heart. She envied them their happiness—a happiness they had ruthlessly claimed and defied their world to possess. She seemed to stand alone and very lonely. Even Robin seemed remote.

"What are you going to do now?" Kelly asked the question at last.

"Me? I don't know. Stand by at home till Father gets better, I suppose."

"And after that?"

"Who knows!" She tried to say it lightly, as though it were of no consequence, but Kelly

436

knew there had been some break somewhere.

"When you're fed up with town, there is always your old room here.'"

"Thanks; I'll remember."

"You didn't mean to come back, did you?" Kelly asked, hoping for justification.

She could see that he was haunted by a sense of unfairness in his dealings with her. In Maisie's face, too, was a pathetic eagerness to be acquitted. Let it be her wedding gift to them—peace of mind over that, at least.

"No, Kelly. I've had enough. I'm glad to be free again," she lied.

"I thought so, but I felt it wasn't quite square. You've always been a good sport and kept me off the rocks . . ."

"That's Maisie's job now," she smiled, and spared him further words.

"Good night, Genevieve. Try to make them forgive Kelly."

"They will—in time."

"Let me know how Father is. I suppose I'd better keep clear for the present?"

"Yes. I'll let you know how things are."

"And what about Mother?"

"She would like to come out and see you

both. She cried terribly, poor darling, but you know she soon gets over things."

"Give her my love. No, I'll write to her," said Kelly.

"Yes, do. And Aunt Kitty? Any message for her?"

"I'd like to wring her blasted neck. Yet I ought to be grateful; if she hadn't butted in . . ."

"Don't say you wouldn't have married me."

"I might not have wakened up so soon."

Genevieve turned back at the gate to wave, and saw them, their arms linked, silhouetted in the door against the lamplight.

Tears blinded her for the moment, but she fought them back.

The car she had hired waited beside the road and the sleepy driver cranked up with a shattering noise.

The Valley lay under a light frost, and the crisp air stung her cheeks, but to-night there was no comfort in the loveliness of the sea or the sky. With dull eyes she watched the light-spangled hills spread out as she left Petone and skirted the harbour; they left no image on her mind.

Genevieve had no illusions about the nobility of sacrifice. She was a normal, human woman, who loved with a woman's love and wanted her own life and her happiness. But she was denied it. Next time, perhaps, when all this had settled down, when her father recovered and was reconciled to Kelly and his wife. But there was still Kitty, and Robin's reluctance to repeat Kelly's folly. She began to doubt if Robin would ever reach the point when he would defy the family. Now she had the shadow of her father's ill-health hanging over her. She had been warned of the consequences of another shock. Could they, she wondered, bring about a gradual change in attitude, and instead of making a sudden revelation prepare the family, and meet the position with argument? But she was afraid that at the first hint an alarm might be raised, and all the evil consequences be brought about without accomplishing anything.

Genevieve was drugged with weariness when she got home. It had been a long day, heavy with emotional strain and the burden of decision. She crept into bed gratefully, but sleep would not come. She heard the town clock chime out the hours and the half and quarter hours. It was two o'clock before she slept, and the dreams that haunted her were of an icy wind that blew and from which she could find no shelter and, shivering, she awoke, and with the dawning of consciousness she found herself in a well of black despair.

24

THE spring advanced and the days lengthened. Slowly, like a sleeper awakening, a faint responsiveness returned to the stricken muscles that held Sir Miles Pencarrow a prisoner. Doctors consulted and masseurs worked, and Norah and Genevieve lifted the mental burden in so far as they were able, but Miles knew too well that it was a punishment he had brought upon himself. The shock of Kelly's marriage he had survived. Had he controlled his temper instead of goading himself into a passionate fury, venting it broadcast on the whole family, this would not have occurred. It was not the shock, but the rage into which he had whipped himself. Miles could inspire himself by his own eloquence, convince himself with his own arguments. Now he had lost his powers because he would not exercise control. Deep in his heart he knew this. Had he accepted Kelly's marriage philosophically, as something regrettable but not necessarily disastrous, he might to-day be about his work.

His anger had not hurt Kelly, but recoiled upon himself.

He wondered what Genevieve thought. Had her clear eyes seen the incident in its real light? Did she know that he alone was to blame for his present condition? He found himself becoming more eager to stand well in Genevieve's eyes; to win her approval. Not for the world would he let her know that he estimated her so highly, but he took a secret joy in watching her. He wondered how much she blamed him; how much she guessed of what went on in his mind as he lay there. He could not admit the fault was his, but he no longer railed at Kelly. Not since he was stricken had he mentioned either of them.

That Genevieve went out to the Hutt regularly he must have known. He must also have suspected that a reconciliation had taken place between Kelly and his mother. She could not resist Kelly's letter. It was a new Kelly who wrote: not the stubborn, tongue-tied boy, but a man in love. He was sorry for disappointing them again; for the hurt of his sudden marriage; but he pleaded for a man's right to choose his wife, and the sincerity of his love for Maisie completely won her. He asked his mother to come out, as he could not, under the circumstances, come to her, and something in the direct simplicity of his words healed the wound which, at most, had been superficial. Here was one of her children married at last, and already her mind raced ahead to the grandchildren that might be.

Her life had been one long compromise for the sake of peace, and she was not accustomed to do violence to herself for the sake of a theory.

After the first anxiety over her father had passed, Genevieve began to view the tragedy much as her father was doing. It was not the shock of Kelly's marriage, but his uncontrolled anger, fed by whisky and flogged by his own fiery words. He had exaggerated and distorted a simple act of independence into an irreparable disaster. Sometimes she saw her father watching her, his eyes trying to read her mind. She even caught a subtle plea, "You know, but don't betray me."

When Miles had recovered sufficiently to get up, he still refused to see anyone but the family and one or two old friends. He trailed a slightly halting leg, which seemed, however, to be gradually recovering its powers. It was the twisted face, the little pucker on one side of the mouth, and the difficulty in articulation that hampered his speech which made him reluctant to meet people. He had always been proud of his fine physique and his eloquence. He did not relish the idea of pity. "Poor Pencarrow. I'm afraid he is done. Limping, with a stick, and his face all twisted. You can scarcely understand a word he says." He refused to be a theme for Club gossip.

On warm days Miles drove out but did not halt anywhere.

"I'm a done man, Norah," he murmured pathetically as she helped him dress.

"Of course you're not, dear. You are getting on splendidly. But it takes time."

He liked to arouse her sympathy. Before his wife he could indulge in self-pity, and she spread maternal wings about him and soothed and cheered and flattered him. He never said these things before Genevieve; not that he doubted her sympathy, but he was afraid she would despise his weakness. They met on a fair level of honesty.

Genevieve had tried to persuade her father to go out, to meet people, even to go sometimes to the office. It would distract his mind from himself. But the pride of a handsome man, facing the pity of his fellows, would not submit to this.

Finding him adamant in this, Genevieve suggested that he might give a certain time each day to his work, and offered to act as liaison between him and the office. She knew that if once he got involved in business affairs it would hasten his recovery, though it was doubtful if he would ever again plead in court.

Robin had come to see him regularly, but the subject of Maisie Kite and her dismissal had never been referred to. Miles had avoided it, and Robin could not introduce it. He was therefore completely in the dark as to what had happened during his absence. And he had not seen her since.

It had been the source of the first quarrel between he and his mother. For the first time he had caused her tears, and this fact swung him to the other extreme. Why should he quarrel with his mother over Maisie? The girl was nothing to him. After all, she had come well out of the business. Kelly had married her, and she was mistress of the Home Farm. So the reconciliation was a triumph for Kitty. Not that her tears were false. Robin had never spoken harshly to her before; never told her, in effect, to mind her own business and leave office affairs alone.

Because of her complete absorption in Robin and his life, he was the sole and central figure in her universe. She could not keep out of anything that affected him, and his effort to set up barriers beyond which she might not go had frightened her, and the hurt went deep. It was these tears that brought him back to her, and when the storm was over, and the reconciliation complete, Kitty held her son even more tightly than before, for he was determined to wipe out those tears.

Robin did not go out to see Kelly, but wrote a little note wishing them happiness. When he went to see his uncle each day Genevieve was there, an efficient secretary to her father.

After their first unhappy encounter, when Genevieve suggested that marriage was now out of the question—at least, for the present, and Robin readily agreed—too readily, Genevieve thought—they had not met alone.

Genevieve dreamt of the Robin of earlier days, the gentle, courteous companion, the diffident lover. Nothing could erase those softly radiant years. No wild ecstasy, no sudden thrill of passion, but a warm, satisfying love held in leash by necessity; the grandeur and the glory were to come. She knew herself capable of an ardent and generous response. There was nothing milk-and-watery about her. Now it seemed that they had slipped back from the first heights they had reached, a disquieting mood was upon them. It was a waiting from which the eager expectancy had been drained away, leaving only a sense of frustration; of temporary defeat.

When Genevieve walked with Robin from her father's room to the door there was an uneasy note in their conversation. Robin sometimes tried to stir the ardour, to awaken the old eager love, but her hand lay cold in his, her eyes gave no answering flash. She had not ceased to love him, but there are valleys between the hills, and they walked now in the gloom, their past happiness rising behind them, and the future a peak still wrapped in the clouds of uncertainty.

The daily routine grew more fixed with the summer. Miles's study took on an air of legal activity. He liked to keep a finger on the pulse of things; to know what was happening. More and more he took Genevieve into his confidence. She welcomed the work as something far more interesting than watering the maidenhair fern and counting the laundry. She began to read law seriously so that she might more effectively assist her father. It was a dry but tantalizing test of her mental equipment, and she liked something that made her stretch her mind. It also kept her from thinking too much about herself and Robin.

He had acquiesced readily, a little too readily. The next move must come from him. Not that she doubted him, but she resented his mother's dominating influence. While applauding his devotion, she could not ignore the signs of weakness—weakness under pressure. Had she wished to pit her strength against his mother they might now be married. Kitty would hold her son by almost any means; Genevieve conceded Robin full freedom. She would not fight Kitty for him. He must come to her voluntarily, eagerly. She loved Robin, but she would have no reluctant husband. Had he protested at this further delay, had he shown any desire to make a fight for her, she would still have maintained that it was impossible now, but his importunity would have comforted her. Instead, he had come to her straight from the quarrel and reconciliation with his mother, and at the moment Kitty's influence was in the ascendency.

So Genevieve turned to law and the task of helping her father, and Miles found a deep and compensating happiness in their association. He was proud of his daughter. With meticulous care he explained intricate points of law, and her quick perception delighted him. He began to enjoy the rôle of semi-invalid and the aloof autocracy of directing affairs from afar. Gradually he was recovering, and with the knowledge that soon he would be able to return to his old haunts, a complete and active man, and not one partially dead, he resigned himself to the joy of sharing his days and his work with Genevieve. She might not be a son, but, damn it, she was as good as one!

And so the summer passed. The problem of Christmas was successfully solved by Sir Miles and Lady Pencarrow going off to Christchurch. Kitty and Robin went to Palmerston North for the Manawatu races, and Genevieve had her Christmas dinner with Kelly and his wife. It was a quiet Christmas in the old house, but a peaceful one. Miles did not ask, nor was he told, what

Genevieve's plans were, but he guessed that her loyalty to the old home, and her affection for Kelly, would draw her back again.

Pat's ship arrived at New Year. His easy genial manner had a new importance, and his arrival was a signal for family rejoicing.

Genevieve explained to him how things stood at home, for in letters it was difficult to tell him all the complications. He knew that Kelly had married Maisie, and his father had been very ill. She left him to connect the two events.

"We never do anything in this family without a bust-up," said Pat. "Doesn't Father go out to the Hutt at all, or see Kelly?"

Genevieve shook her head. "They have never met since."

"Can't you do anything?"

"We're giving them time. Maisie is going to have a baby; his first grandchild ought to do the trick. Father won't be able to resist that."

"But meanwhile . . . ."

"It was my bright idea not to try and persuade Father to see them. I go out often and Mother goes sometimes. He knows that, but we never mention it. I'm sure he is burning with curiosity to hear about them, and one of these days he will have to ask. Father is quite a child in some things."

"There will be hell's bells when you get married. You're a fool to make yourself so useful to him. Anything doing?"

Genevieve tried to laugh it off, but for a moment she was tempted to tell Pat. It would be good to talk it over with someone and get it into truer perspective. But the moment passed. She saw Pat was not deeply concerned about her; his mind had travelled across the world. He looked at her, smiling rather foolishly in a way that asked her to guess his secret and spare him the embarrassment of words.

"Go on, out with it. Who is she?" asked Genevieve.

"Do you think it will be safe to tell them?"

"That depends. Is she a fat barmaid or the squire's lovely daughter?"

"Neither!"

"Well, who?"

"Her Father is Rear-Admiral Groves . . ."

"Whew!" and Genevieve whistled. "That ought to redeem the family reputation. Why have you withheld this wonderful news so long? Are you already married, or merely engaged?"

451

"Neither—yet."

"Why not?"

"I only met him once, and he's a bit of a bite."

"Worse than Father?"—and she laughed.

"Now don't be funny. We decided not to say anything to him till I got Father to back me a bit. . . ."

"Can't live on a sailor's pay, you mean."

"She is used to a jolly nice home; an only daughter and all that. And her mother has private means. He would like her to marry a man with a land job; the Mercantile Marine stinks, to hear him talk."

"Are you planning a run-away marriage if Father stumps up?"

"Not exactly. But I'm going to transfer to the Naval Reserve, and . . ."

"I see!"

"I was going to do that in any case."

"What's her name? Have you got a photo? You tire me, Paddy Doyle, you're so slow. I'd have flourished her in the face of the family the minute I landed."

"After Kelly's break, I thought I'd have a yarn with you first."

"Her name, Pat! What's the woman's name?"

"Margaret Groves."

"Is she pretty? Is she dark? It's like drawing a horse's teeth to get anything out of you."

"Here she is," and he produced a photo of a young girl with brown eyes and dark hair.

Genevieve looked at the face; it had commonsense and humour, but was not exactly pretty.

"She'll do," was Genevieve's verdict. "Got it badly, Pat?"

"Don't be an ass."

"When do you tell Father?"

"That's what I want to know."

"Try Peter's dodge, and tell him when there are visitors, and he can't explode."

"I'd like to see the visitor who would stop him if he wanted to."

"I'll tell you what to do. The best time to catch him is the afternoon. We work all the morning, and that makes him feel important and puts him into a good temper; a nice lunch after that will soothe him. I'll keep back anything in the correspondence that might irritate him, and have his favourite grill served piping hot. You walk in half an hour after and there you are."

"Righto! Will you be there."

"No; but within call in case of first aid."

Pat was growing more like his father, a resemblance that flattered him. Kelly was stocky of figure and rugged of features. Pat wore his uniform with much of Miles's air, and as he lost the looseness and leanness of youth the resemblance grew more pronounced.

Sir Miles Pencarrow was delighted at the news of Peter's proposed engagement to Margaret Groves. From what Pat told him, and he did not spoil a ship for a ha'porth of tar, it was an alliance that would do credit to the family. Pat had caught his father in an expansive mood, and he was prepared to give him an allowance which, with his pay, ought to overcome any financial difficulty. He entirely approved of his son's transfer to the Naval Reserve for a time, and even hinted that he and Norah might go to London for the wedding. The latter suggestion, made on the spur of the moment, woke a flutter of excitement in Norah's mind. Genevieve backed the idea warmly, and although the engagement still lacked the tough old Admiral's consent, the Pencarrows made it the occasion for a celebration. They drank champagne at dinner on Saturday, but it was out at Kelly's on Sunday that the prospective bridegroom received the warmest congratulations.

"I'm so glad one of the family has justified Father's hopes," said Kelly.

Pat sailed again three weeks later with the family's blessing and a partial promise that his father and mother would come to London for the wedding. Sir Miles felt it would be a fitting occasion for he and Norah to make the Colonial Grand Tour and see something of England, Scotland and Ireland, and do a London season.

25

MAISIE'S first summer at the Hutt was full of little difficulties. She had never lived on a farm and her instincts had led always towards cities. Her youthful ambitions, which hinged on limelight, fame and personal triumph, had been modified by her fierce early struggle. Her brief stage career had taught her the disillusionment that lay in wait for even high ability. Her marriage was like coming into port after a long, rough voyage, even if it were the wrong port. She had set her course for the city, but it was in the country that her journey ended. She had aimed at the stage, and become a farmer's wife. All that lay between, the years of striving and office work, was merely an interlude, a markingtime, till her great opportunity came.

Her sudden marriage to Kelly had put a period to the past. Now she must adjust herself to a new and strange future, and mould herself to fit without hurt into the place already made by her predecessor, Bessie Pencarrow.

The first Pencarrow mother had set a high standard, and Maisie who never shirked a task, was determined to be a worthy successor. She realized that she had the heavy handicap of Sir Miles's disapproval to overcome, and everything she said and did must stand critical judgment. She moved cautiously at first, feeling her way among the tangle of established customs that formed a sort of tradition. She did not want to transgress, yet she was too free a soul to be merely imitative. She had ideas of her own, and a firm will, and she had no intention of submerging her individuality. Her first task, however, was to bring about a reconciliation between Kelly and his father, though she soon gathered from Genevieve that Sir Miles' antagonism was on the wane. The conspiracy of silence which Genevieve had initiated had proved effective, compelling Miles to feed on curiosity. He would like to have been told how affairs were progressing at the Home Farm and been afforded occasion for criticism or comment. He wanted to be placated by requests for his forgiveness, coupled with reports that events were justifying it.

Maisie made few changes at first, but tried to fit herself into the routine of life and the rhythm of the season. In her eagerness to carry her share of the load she made many mistakes. She killed one brood of young chickens by over-feeding, and disaster followed disaster in the dairy. She knew little of cooking, and lacked Genevieve's light touch.

At first they laughed together over her mistakes, and made a jest of it. But Maisie was shrewd enough to know that by such small things can peace be marred.

Kelly was inordinately happy in this first summer. His marriage had taken up the slack that was threatening deterioration. He took a firmer hold of himself and his affairs. Where hitherto he had been easily content, he became more exacting. To keep things running was not now enough. He planned ahead once more, and something of his earlier ambition lit a guiding lamp to the future.

The summer was hot and proved a fine season. His lambs brought good prices. Wool sold well and butter-fat compensated for the drudgery of keeping cows.

When autumn came all their thoughts centred on the coming baby. Kelly was delighted at the paternal prospect and planned as fantastically as his father had done. Surreptitiously he bought toys and stored them in an old trunk, and he built a wide porch off one bedroom, facing the sun, which was to be the nursery.

It was a frosty night in June when Sir Miles Pencarrow's first grandson was born in Bessie's old four-poster bed. Norah came out next morning, all tremulous tears of pride and good advice. Genevieve held the sleeping baby—a fair-skinned, red-haired Pencarrow—and claimed it as her godchild.

Miles could not restrain his impatience when told it was a boy. At last he was a grandfather. Perhaps here he would find one of his name and blood to follow after him and replace the sons who had gone their own way.

When it came to choosing a name, Maisie suggested Miles. Genevieve wanted Michael, because of the red hair. Kelly felt that his grandfather, who, after all, had made the Home Farm from a rough bush valley, should be perpetuated in the new generation. There was much talk and argument, so, finally, Kelly put the three names into a hat, and Maisie drew one.

It was Matthew Pencarrow who Genevieve

held over the font, and Miles's first disappointment was modified when Genevieve reminded him that there was no Matthew anywhere in the family and they owed it to the old pioneer.

Miles was quite emotional when Genevieve made him take the baby in his arms, and he was glad to see Kelly again. Maisie was not present at the christening, but Sir Miles arranged what was positively a state visit to the Hutt for the following Sunday.

Maisie Kite had given him his first grandson. She was one of the Pencarrows now.

In two and a half years three sons were born at the Home Farm—Matthew, Michael and Miles, commonly known as Matt, Mike and Measle. Sir Miles alone refused to use the absurd nickname that arose from a one-spot scare that was for some hours suspected of being a measle.

"My grandson Miles," he might say, but Measle Pencarrow was the name that endured.

Maisie and her three small sons held Kelly in busy contentment. Matthew was sturdy and positive; Michael Kelly Pencarrow was dark like his father, with the same vivid blue eyes and a restless energy that wore out his mother.

"I'll belt the hide off you, my lad"; but the unblinking blue eyes held no fear of his father.

"Don't say that to him, dear. It sounds so brutal." But Maisie's protest was purely formal. Kelly might threaten to belt the hide off him, but what he did was to toss him high in the air and prod his fat little stomach.

"You're all threats, Kelly, but I do wish you would punish them sometimes and not leave it all to me."

"You won't let me."

"Talk to them. Can't you make children understand that they mustn't do things; I mean explain why it's naughty."

"You ought to have married a lawyer," said Kelly.

"Oh, I don't mean your father's method."

The remark recalled his grandmother's warning. "One day you will have sons of your own, and you will do the same."

Already Kelly found himself planning the future for his boys; one to carry on the Home Farm, one to take on Duffield, for Ella had no son, and one to follow Sir Miles in law.

Their days were busy, but the farm prospered, and Maisie had adequate help with the children. Though the operation to her throat had impaired her voice it had not destroyed it, and she introduced a new feature—music—into the Pencarrow gatherings. Kelly bought her a new piano and encouraged her to sing. She had played, as an amateur, most of the soprano rôles in Gilbert and Sullivan operas, and she knew the scores from end to end. "Poor Wandering One", and "Take a Pair of Sparkling Eyes" were Kelly's favourites. Pat was the only Pencarrow with a voice, but his singing was confined to sea chanties.

"Sing something, Maisie," was a request from Sir Miles which always gave her keen satisfaction. Here was one thing, at least, she could do infinitely better than his children.

In the new adjustment Maisie and her babies became a figure of importance. Three sons was a fine contribution to the clan. Genevieve was a great help in most emergencies. The children worshipped their aunt, and her imagination could meet them on sporting terms, and she took their games seriously.

Having started law to assist her father more effectively, Genevieve went through with it. Soon after Maisie's third son was born Genevieve passed her final law examination. There was some satisfaction in having got through and qualified for a profession, and Sir Miles's inordinate pride in her achievement was some compensation for his earlier disappointments. But in her heart Genevieve regarded it as a barren triumph. It was a cold and empty thing viewed in relation to Maisie's full life. It satisfied her mind, but her heart was not in it. She was not ambitious in that way.

Robin had watched her successful attack upon law with apprehension. The more it filled her life, the less her need of him. They met as lawyers, not as lovers, now, and Genevieve intruded into all their personal relations the fellowship of work. She set it up as a barrier between them; not as a barrier to keep them apart, but as an obstacle challenging him to effort. She wanted him to resent her legal aspirations, to fight her over them, to bully her into surrender, to compel her to throw up the career and marry him. She inflicted on herself so many hurts in trying to wake the fighting man in Robin. All too easily he gave in, and his protests were feeble. He wanted Genevieve, but he was not prepared to stake everything on a decisive action. And while Genevieve, hoping to spur him, built barriers, he, misunderstanding her motive, held back. All the time his mother stayed close beside him, fostering the weak strain in him by making life soft and pleasant.

Miles had recovered from the effects of his stroke, but it had had a beneficial effect upon him. He exerted greater control over his temper, and was more moderate in every way. He was definitely afraid. Twice he had been seriously threatened. He now made the study of health quite a hobby, and periodically was carried away on the wave of some new theory about diet or exercise.

"Too much starch, Norah. That's the trouble. I'll cut it down by half."

"Now, Miles, you know what happened last time you read a book on health; you worried me to change the meals till we all came out in spots."

"The man who wrote that was a damn' fool. This fellow knows what he is talking about; it's common sense. He's sound."

"But you said that last time."

"Well, you can eat what you like, but I'm cutting down starchy foods by fifty per cent."

The period of the nut lunch lasted a week and the relish with which he got his teeth into a juicy bit of steak was conclusive.

"These nut cranks are all mad; damn' rot. A man was meant to eat meat."

"I wish Genevieve would take more interest in her health," Norah said. "She's looking far too thin. Surely there is no need for her to work so hard."

"She is all right. Just leave her alone."

"But she is not all right. She is not a man, and she hasn't got a man's physique. You forget, Miles, women are not made for strenuous mental work. She is getting wrinkles in her forehead from puzzling over those books. I do wish she would marry and settle down. It's not natural, the life she leads."

"Genevieve must choose for herself, Norah. She is a woman now, but damn it, she's got a man's mind. There is not another girl in Wellington could do what she does."

"She would be much happier married, with her babies, like Maisie."

"Pooh! Any little slut can have babies, but it takes brains to do Genevieve's work."

26

"FATHER has just rung up. He won't be home for dinner; he's staying at the Club."

"Now isn't that annoying?"

"And he says not to wait up, he might be late, Mother."

"All this nonsense about a war."

Lady Pencarrow had no patience with disorganizing meals because an Archduke had been murdered in Europe. It was ridiculous.

"It can't affect us out here," Genevieve consoled her.

"Of course it can't. But your father kept me awake till all hours this morning. Since he gave up reading books about diet he has got all this humbug about Germany wanting to fight England. Why she should, I don't know."

"I bet he's down at the Club, telling them all about it. The darling, he does love to gloat."

At midnight Sir Miles came home, looking very serious.

466

"England has declared war, Norah."

Norah woke up and looked at him sleepily.

"Has she? I'm sorry you weren't home; the beef was so tender."

"Dinner! My God! You talk of dinner when the Empire is at war."

"Don't make such a noise, dear. You'll wake the children."

"Wake them! Of course I'll wake them. Genevieve!" he called. But Genevieve was already awake and came in, wrapping her dressing-gown around her.

"We're at war, Genevieve; at war. England will teach those damned Germans a lesson. We'll put the bullies in their place. Three months and they'll be on their knees crying for mercy."

"It won't affect us out here, will it?" she asked.

"It may! It may! We've got to stand by the Old Country. I'd be off to-morrow if I were a young man."

The morning paper was full of it. Scare headlines swept local politics out of sight. Little business was done in town, and people stood about, talking, wondering, speculating.

Men who had fought in the South African

war spoke with the authority of veterans, and their words had weight.

There was great activity at military headquarters. The Territorial system, which recently had been inaugurated for the training of men to meet such an emergency or, more accurately, one nearer home, had not yet reached its full strength. Their equipment was inadequate. The only rifles they had were the old .303 Lee-Enfields, bought from Canada the year before for a dollar apiece. Kitchener had come out in 1910 to inaugurate the scheme and give advice. A few soldiers trained in the English Regular Army were at the head of it, but there were also plump peace-time colonels whose new uniforms clothed a civilian clerk. There was no standing army; this merging of the old volunteer system into the newer Territorial scheme provided for the compulsory registration of all young men between fourteen and twenty-five. Men up to thirty were in the reserves. This scheme, when complete, was designed to train a volunteer army of 30,000 men out of a total population of about one and a quarter million.

The Territorials attended fortnightly drill,

occasional parades, and fired some hundreds of rounds of ammunition each year.

Military training made no great appeal to the average New Zealand youth. He was proud of his uniform in the school cadet corps, which was part of the scheme, but the majority regarded drill night as a nuisance. The annual camp was all right in its way, but in a young, peaceful, free country there were more attractive ways of spending a holiday than in playing soldiers. The military spirit was not strong, and the rigid discipline of army training was irksome to his independent mind. Fight he would but drill he would not. All this fuss about salutes and buttons was a lot of damn' rot. Some, of course, were very keen.

Now England was at war and the test of British loyalty had come. New Zealand was over ninety-eight per cent British, and descendants of English, Scottish and Irish were instantly one in their response. At first there was no real urgency. Only the eager ones rushed into uniform, for few believed that they would ever see the firing-line.

Meanwhile, across twelve thousand miles of ocean, the cables carried New Zealand's offer of assistance, and England's grateful acceptance.

Then men began to enlist in earnest. It would be a great adventure. Things moved rapidly at headquarters, and eleven days after England had declared war two vessels sailed from New Zealand with her first contingent, bound for an unknown destination. On October 15, eight weeks later, they captured Samoa, that valuable German possession in the Pacific. It was the first British victory in the Great War.

Palmerston North, less than a hundred miles north of Wellington, a large inland town and important railway junction, had been chosen some time previously as the seat of military headquarters for the Wellington Province. Three days after war was declared in England a group of young farmers and tradesmen were digging potholes on the Awapuni racecourse, outside the town, and pitching tents for the main body of New Zealand's Expeditionary Force, which was already assembling in little towns and settlements. Young men went to work in the morning as clerks and shop-assistants, as plumbers and butchers, as farmers and lawyers, and came home soldiers at night.

At such a great distance from Europe news came in brief and broken messages, relayed by cable across the seas. People hung about the newspaper offices waiting for official bulletins to be posted. Much wild talk and many rumours gained currency because of the lack of actual news. In a small, remote country, following its peaceful occupation in towns and on farms, where war and talk of war was like a traveller's tale, something fanciful but not touching their lives, it was difficult to visualize the conditions in old militant countries, with their background of conflict, their standing armies, and all the permanent reminder of the danger of conquest.

New Zealand knew nothing of this. Her politicians were not harassed by thoughts of foreign invasion. They were absorbed in purely local problems. Obtaining grants for roads and bridges and the new post office were the test of their ability. Better transportation was the very life-blood of the young country, and the Member of Parliament who kept his eye on the new macadam road and left Europe to mind her own business was the successful man.

In the new communities and bush settlements libraries were few, and the books available were more likely to be a Nat Gould than a serious discussion of international affairs. Little pockets of wider intelligence were scattered about: men who took serious thought, read English reviews, and bought books. They followed the trend of the times and were aware of a wide world outside. But first things come first, and in a farming district work begins early and ends late, and stock reports, market prices and the weather prediction takes precedence over "some trouble in the Balkans", a place as remote as the moon. Of Central Europe they knew little and cared less. The young men on the farms did not bother about such things. Football, horse-racing, sport and work filled their days.

The older men—men who knew England and to whom Europe was something very real —were full of concern and doubtful knowledge. The women wondered, and the wise ones grew afraid.

What would happen? Would the price of produce fall? Would the banks keep a tighter grip upon money? Would our ships carrying their cargoes of frozen lamb and butter and cheese—yes, and wool—get safely to

England? Would we be cut off from the out-side world by German raiders?

Single men were enlisting and going into camp, thousands of them. New Zealand was equipping an Expeditionary Force which was to sail in a few weeks. Other countries deemed months of training all too short, but the spade work had been done in the cadet corps and Territorial camps, and upon this was superimposed a rapid instruction and an intensive military course.

Robin lay awake for hours. To-morrow he would enlist; he must. He was not sure that he wanted to, but once again the terrible fear of being afraid distressed him. Had he been quite sure of himself, he might have been content to talk it over with his mother; with Miles. But he dare not. So many single men he knew already had enlisted, and he had no legitimate reason for holding back. Two men from the office had joined up. Miles, now an ardent militarist, had not approved of their precipitate action as it disorganized the work, but publicly he commended them.

"My own staff, I am proud to say, have not been slow to answer the call."

It was a good example, he felt.

"If I were a young man I'd be off to-morrow." This was his stock phrase. Later he varied it a little. "Would to God that I were twenty years younger. . . ."

"Father commands the 'Would-to-Godders'," Genevieve wrote to Pat.

Robin came of a line of soldiers on his father's side, but he had no great urge to battle or adventure. It was the very absence of the eagerness that had made his friends enlist which had worried him. It was not so much what others thought of him as the idea that he would know himself to be a coward. Every instinct revolted against the horror and brutality of war. He lacked some stiffening, the steel that would stand the test of fire, and he knew it, and, knowing, he was afraid. His fear was not of physical suffering, but of the mental recoil from it. Sensitive and of keen perception, everything was magnified.

He thought of Genevieve, and the years that had slipped by unfulfilled, and bitterly he blamed himself. He saw that weakness bred weakness, and that his mother's influence had been too strong. He would not tell her he was going; he would sign up first and so make it inevitable.

The subject of his enlistment had never

been discussed between them. Kitty skirted the dangerous topic, as though to mention it were to admit its possibility.

"Fortunately, so many young men whose work is not essential are joining up," she kept saying.

This observation, in varying form, was the theme of her comment upon the events that rushed upon them. It was as though she beat her hands against a frightening shadow in the dark.

"If I were a young man, I'd be off to-morrow."

Sir Miles was the burning patriot in private as well as public.

"That would never do, Miles," Kitty said. "The affairs of the country are more important than ever now. We can't afford to send the best brains away. It is the strong, hardy young farmers and workers who will make the best soldiers. They are used to roughing it."

"Well, there's a lot in that," Miles agreed. "We can't all be heroes; some must stay at home."

Robin knew the words were meant for him.

Genevieve heard it and felt the piteous pleading that it cloaked. Kitty was imploring

Miles to hold Robin and to justify his exemption from service.

Not since she had persuaded Miles to dismiss Maisie Kite had Kitty made a direct appeal to her brother. The breach had healed over, but Kitty's influence had waned. She dare not approach Miles now, but at every point she played her cards so that Robin's present and potential usefulness was built up into a structure of national importance.

Robin came into the office after lunch and went straight to his uncle's room.

"That's bad news! Have you seen that last communiqué?" said Miles, looking up.

"Yes. It's pretty bad, all right. I—I enlisted this morning."

"You what?"

"I enlisted this morning."

"Why didn't you tell me?"

"I thought it easier to say nothing till after."

"But it's not fellows like you they want. Damn it, Robin, am I not to be considered?"

"You've said so often that if you were a young man you'd be off to-morrow."

"Yes, yes; I mean, if I were one of these young chaps, doing a job of work anyone could do. Why, you won't get past the doctor. That chest . . ."

"The chest is all right."

"But . . . your mother; does she know? She'll never forgive me for this; never."

"I was afraid of that. But one of us had to go. Peter is too young, and Kelly's got three children. I'm single, so there's no excuse."

"Do you want to go?"

"I don't know." Robin hesitated. "But I'm glad now it's done."

"It will leave me in a bit of a hole here, with Fraser and Atkinson gone."

"There's Genevieve."

"Yes, by God, there's Genevieve! But she can't do the work of three men. I'm upset about this, damned upset! I wish you had talked it over with me first. I had no idea you were thinking of it; not just yet, anyhow."

When Kitty knew that Robin had enlisted her whole world darkened. He did not tell her until next morning after breakfast.

"No! *No!* Robin; oh no!"

Her eyes seemed to grow larger, and her hands clutched convulsively at his sleeve, as though to draw him back.

"I had to, Mother. One of us must go."

"There's Peter."

"He is too young. And, besides, he is very short-sighted."

"But, Kelly—Kelly would love it. He is the fighting kind. They make the best soldiers. And, besides, he roughed it a lot when he was young."

"There is Maisie . . . and the children. The single men must go first."

"Do you mean that because he is married he won't have to go?"

"Not yet. Perhaps not at all. Married men with children can't get away as easily as single men."

"Doesn't he want to go? I am surprised."

"I don't know if he wants to or not. It's not that. It's Maisie and the children."

"Oh, Robin, you're my only son. Doesn't that make any difference? Doesn't that count at all?"—and she clung to him, weeping piteously.

Kitty went first to Norah.

"Can't Miles do something? Buy him out. I don't care what it costs. I'm sure there is some way."

"I don't think so, Kitty. Miles was quite upset about it last night."

"Aren't any of your boys going, Norah? You've three. I've only one."

She was pleading before the gods. Some malign fate was pitting his strength against her. So far she had always won, but this was different.

"Kelly can't, not with that young family. I suppose Pat will go, he is in the Naval Reserve. Miles says he is probably in it now."

"But he is married?" Kitty argued.

"It's different with men in the regular service, the Army and Navy. It's their profession."

"Can't something be done, Miles?"

Kitty had surrendered her pride, and the tears streamed down her face. She had tried to restrain herself in front of Robin, but all day she had sought some way to circumvent his folly; to get him out of it.

"You know the Prime Minister and the Minister for Defence; can't you say that he is essential to you; that you can't spare him?"

"It wouldn't do. I can hardly go on speaking and urge young men to join up and keep Robin back. It wouldn't do. He is single and he has no dependents."

"If he were married, like Kelly, with children . . ."

"Ah! Then he would not be expected to go."

If Robin were married? If he had married Genevieve, or even Maisie—anyone, in fact, she could have kept him. The irony of it; the tragedy! The very means she had employed to keep him was sending him from her. She woke in an agony of despair, and an idea occurred to her. If Robin married now! Would that make it all right!

"Mother! How could you suggest it?"

27

POTTY BARKER came to Wellington to enlist, and with a cheerful grin he turned up at the Hutt for breakfast one morning.

"I've been a good boy for a long time now, Kelly, but it just got me. I put it to old Macdonald on patriotic grounds. He could carry on the farm, and Jessie has her mother to help her with the youngsters. They didn't like it, and Jessie cried, but if it hadn't been a war it might have been something worse."

"I know; it's pretty deadly down the Sounds," said Kelly.

"Deadly! It's a fair cow," and Potty spat with emphasis. "Not that I'm sorry I married, mind you. But a spree in Picton once in a while is the only chance of getting away from it. After that, I can settle down again for a couple of months. But this war, now, it gives a bloke a chance."

"You'll be glad to get back if it's as bad as the Boer War."

"Oh, this'll be a tame show compared to

South Africa. Regular armies forming fours and doing right turn and shooting when they're told, and all dolled up. Now, in South Africa, there was a chance for a little individual fighting, and it didn't matter so much if your buttons weren't clean."

"I wonder if it will be over before you get there?" said Kelly, echoing the popular opinion.

"That's what I'm afraid. But it'll be a good trip."

They fell silent.

"I wish you were coming too," said Potty.

"Yes." Kelly's voice revealed nothing. Potty's enthusiasm had stirred the old adventurous spirit that had been lulled by security and contentment. To be a soldier and go sailing off to Europe with Potty; to see strange cities and come hard up against life! If he were young and single, yes. But with Maisie and the children, and the Home Farm—no. It was just a fleeting impulse. He belonged here.

There were plenty of single men frothing for adventure; let them go. New Zealand had offered men, but it was in supplying food: meat, butter, cheese—yes, and wool, also, for they needed uniforms and army blankets as well—that she could best serve Britain. The farmers were urged to keep up—indeed, to increase—supplies of produce as an essential contribution to the Empire's cause. There had been speeches and editorials in the papers, and articles by men who felt they were authorities on this and any subject. Every day threw out a new prophet, who knew all about how a war ought to be run, and who would win, and when and why. These gave gratuitous advice as only an amateur can, heedless of inaccuracy and the limitations of ignorance.

The farmers must keep up production, for Britain must be fed; also her armies in France; and New Zealand's contribution in food was a vast and vital one.

Miles talked a lot about production. "We must augment and not curtail supplies. Thank God, Michael and Kelly and the Macdonalds can play their part, and help to win the war!"

Philip Gentry enlisted the day after Potty Barker.

"There is no need for him to go," said Miles.

"I told him that, but he wants to be in it. He says I can carry on quite well without him; it's not like leaving Ella and the two children alone."

Michael was uncertain about the wisdom of it, and had come in to talk it over with Miles.

"He is English, of course, and his people will be fighting. Still, there was no need for him to go yet; time enough to take the farmers off the land; the essential farmers, I mean. How is Ella taking it?"

"Oh, she doesn't seem to mind. She is planning to join him in England in a few months, and finish it as a jolly good holiday."

"Huh! I don't like the news we're getting. I thought the English would join up with the French and smash those damn' Germans in no time. They've been preparing for this a long time. We ought to have kept a closer eye on them; ever since I read that book of—"

"Yes, I know." Michael did not want it all over again. Miles liked to pose as an authority, and bolstered his somewhat unmilitary and fantastic theories by reference to his somewhat liberal reading. He had also resurrected an old photo of himself in a busby, taken when he was in the Volunteers, and had it newly framed and hung in his office.

Potty Barker and Philip Gentry had been in

camp three days before Robin arrived. He had been given two days' grace to fix up important matters in connection with a trial that was to come on at the next sitting of the Supreme Court.

Gentry had a commission in the Wellington Mounted Rifles and Robin was lieutenant in the Infantry. They were the type of young men needed for officers.

Potty Barker began his military career by getting gloriously drunk and spending his first night in "clink". Potty sober could be amusing, but Potty drunk was difficult to manage. He was truculent, and all his pent-up hatred of authority was expended upon a newly hatched young officer, the cacoon of whose civilian importance still clung.

From the first day Potty Barker was a marked man and he tasted the very dregs of fatigue duties. His slow sarcasm had a corroding effect on sergeant-majors and the appreciative guffaws from new recruits merely invited longer periods of C.B.

The Awapuni racecourse, which was now a military camp, was fringed with native bush and the darker green of pine trees. A young plantation and ornamental shrubs had begun to weave a pattern of shapely trees in the decorative garden scheme about the lawn and around the saddling paddock. A dry lagoon, obscured by native bush and fern trees, curved in behind the grandstand, which was now an office and the camp kitchen. The hills of Tiritea rose behind the Manawatu river, grey and green and mauve in the changing light, and trailed off south to meet the Tararua range.

Colonels conferred in the jockeys' room and records were compiled where racing stewards had talked of winners and of weights. Raw recruits learnt the difference between left turn and right wheel on the turf track where the best New Zealand horses had galloped before a cheering crowd and white tents filled the oval. Artillery horses were tethered along the rail of the saddling paddock and the horses of the Wellington mounted troops cropped grass in the blood-stock pastures.

A tall, lean captain with a hard eye and a hanging lip cursed the fussy methods of modern warfare.

"All these damned forms and papers and files! Who the hell cares if a man's had measles or wants to know who his aunt married? Can he fight?—that's what we want

486

to know. I'll throw the whole damn' lot into the harbour before we sail, that's what I'll do. I kept the records of a whole company on the back of a biscuit-box in South Africa; these damn' Civil Service clerks and their damn' forms and their damn' files! . . ."

As each new draft arrived every man was obliged to give full particulars of himself, his health, his occupation, his next-of-kin. There were records in duplicate and in triplicate, in red files and blue folders. It all seemed so superfluous then; and it was new to them, this gathering of the personal history of civilians now turned soldiers. It might be necessary—very necessary—later. They signed forms and the sergeant-majors shouted orders, and the officers flicked the heads off the daisies as they crossed the sloping lawn in front of the totalisator.

Potty Barker sat on an upturned bucket peeling potatoes. His head was closely shaved and his long legs in badly wound putties stuck out on either side.

"This is a nice sort of war, peeling spuds all day! Here I've been for a blasted week peeling spuds and carting round dixies of stew. Who the hell wants to be a soldier!"—and Potty flung a rotten potato at a sparrow.

A plumber from Fielding and a man who drove a laundry-van in Wellington were his companions. They accepted the task gratefully. Route-marching on the dusty roads in Bill Massey boots that weighed a ton could not be compared with this life, however dull and monotonous.

Potty's brief career as a soldier had been one series of unfortunate incidents. He hated discipline and had no respect for authority. Corporals and colonels were all one to him; if he had anything to say, he said it.

For a moment he peeled a large potato carefully and a malicious grin broke on his tanned face as he stuck two twigs into it, wound the peelings round the twigs like putties, stuck a little potato on for a head, and with splinters cut from a stick attached a peak cap. With the point of his knife he carved a stupid face on the potato and saluted it as Colonel Spud. It bore a crude but comic resemblance to Colonel Trotter, and was greeted with uproarious laughter. In the midst of this diversion Major Foote and a young lieutenant came from the office near by, and their appearance silenced the laughter, but Potty disdained to notice them.

The young lieutenant, stiff with newly

acquired importance, glared at Potty, and he returned the haughty stare, capping it with a prodigious wink.

Suddenly an inspiration seized him.

"Excuse me!" Potty sprang up from his bucket and intercepted the colonel.

"I joined this war to fight Germans, not to peel spuds all day. If you don't need soldiers, well, I'll just hook it back to the missus and the kids. I'm sick of this blasted kind of war."

Of course it was madness. The penalty for this offence was much worse than peeling spuds, but discipline must be maintained.

The incident, however, had its sequel. Major Foote had the lanky Australian's record looked up, and a black military record it was for so brief a time.

Major Foote knew that soldiers must be rigidly trained and that implicit obedience is imperative. But the army required other virtues than obedience. Courage and initiative were qualities that occasion demanded even in the rank and file.

After his initial failure in camp it was a surprise even to Potty when he found himself promoted to corporal.

Major Foote kept an eye on Potty Barker; the sort of man to undertake a dangerous mission and to achieve his objective, even if his methods were at times rather unorthodox.

Potty nearly lost his stripe a month later. He was spinning a lurid yarn to a little group of his cobbers when a young lieutenant, a pink-and-white youth, came up.

"Here, hook it, sonny. Can't you see we're busy talking?" he said, with a jerk of his thumb in the direction of the officers' quarters.

The boy flushed, hesitated, decided to report the incident, but on further consideration let it pass. Potty's reputation made him diffident about coming into conflict with him at the beginning of his military career. Later Potty realized the boy's forbearance, and a day came, in the heat of battle, when Potty Barker paid his debt.

Potty had his first encounter with Lieut. Philip Gentry in Waddell's Hotel. Mrs. Waddell, a short, stout woman, whose hair miraculously renewed its youthful auburn once a month, sat in the parlour with one eye on the bar and the other on the office. She knew all her customers, and called most of them George or Bert until the war made them into sergeants and colonels. Her one son, Archie, had been among the first to enlist, and this military connection gave her establishment precedence over other hotels. She never made the mistake of under-ranking any man. Captains were promoted to colonels, and privates became sergeants under her benevolent roof. It was not the largest hotel, nor the best, but she ran her rivals on points of popularity.

The first thing any soldier wanted on his evening's leave from Awapuni camp was a drink and a bath. Sweat and sand, small matters to the veteran soldier, were a hardship to the man fresh from a comfortable home.

"Good evening, Mrs. Waddell. Can I have a bath to-night?"

"Indeed you can. You'll find a pile of clean towels on the table outside the bathroom door. Just wash out the bath and leave it ready for the next."

Officers and men were treated alike. Mrs. Waddell had known many of them before a foreign war had inverted the order of precedence. They were all soldiers, poor lads, torn from home and living in discomfort. One thing she could do, and willingly she did it, and that was to keep a constant supply of hot water and clean bath-towels ready for the men on leave. If they had a drink, well and good. If not, it didn't matter.

Gentry had first come with two others, after a hard day's training. He had revelled in the luxury of a hot bath.

"What do I pay?" he asked, fingering his money.

"There's nothing to pay, but if ever you see my Archie, be good to him."

It was, however, a point of honour to leave the bath clean for the next man. She exacted this duty from every rank.

Gentry had had his bath, the second that week.

"Good night, and thank you, Mrs. Waddell," he said as he hurried out.

"Good night, Captain. And don't forget my Archie if you meet him."

A call for more towels sent Mrs. Waddell hurrying upstairs with her bunch of keys.

"Dear me, dear me! that's too bad. I told Maud to put out enough."

A few strides down the road and Philip Gentry missed his wrist-watch. He had hung it on a nail over the bath. He turned and ran lightly up the stairs.

Mrs. Waddell opened the linen press and took out a pile of towels.

"There now, that'll be enough to go on with. Here you are," and she put one into the wet hand that was thrust through the slightly open door.

"I'd like to know the dirty swine who had the last bath," growled Potty. "I'd ring his blasted neck."

"Now isn't that too bad, and I asked him to leave it clean."

"Oh, by the way, Mrs. Waddell," and Gentry came down the passage. "I left my watch in the bathroom. Is anyone in there?"

"Yes, there is."

"I say," began Gentry, "would you mind passing out my watch? I left it hanging on a nail over the bath."

"Here it is, you dirty swine," and Potty's hand appeared round the door—a hand full of wet sand with the gold watch embedded in it.

Choking with rage, Gentry picked up the watch.

"What's your name?"

"Go to hell and find out!"—and Potty slammed the door and a loud splashing drowned Gentry's reply.

When Robin went into camp his mother came to Manawatu in order to be near him. She had failed to get him out of the army

and now concentrated on making everything smooth and pleasant, wangling what
privileges she could obtain from the
Commandant.

"A pretty woman, but a damn' nuisance,"
was her rating at G.H.Q.

"Don't, Mother; please don't," Robin
implored when she told him of the favours
she had asked and the special leave she had
obtained for him.

"But, Robin dear—"

"It's no use, Mother. I'm a soldier now and
it makes a fool of me in camp, all this petting.
I've got to stick it like the rest. Please don't
ask anything else or I'll simply have to refuse
when it is offered. Already I know they are
talking about it; the other chaps, I mean."

Potty Barker was in the Wellington
Infantry, though not in Robin's company.
Occasionally they met, but their common
tastes were few. The Tapuwai incident was
the only link between them—that and Kelly.

Robin and Gentry, both young officers,
though one was foot and the other mounted,
were thrown together more frequently, yet no
great friendship resulted. There is a difference which draws people together and a
difference that keeps them apart. Each had

his qualities and they were both part of the Pencarrow clan, but their friendship struck no roots; it was pleasant but superficial.

Before the main body sailed Robin had leave to go to Wellington. He had gone up to the Terrace to say good-bye before going into camp, and Genevieve had met him with the old frank friendliness, as though they had stepped back through the years to the days before the fire at Tapuwai.

He searched her eyes for an answering warmth, but she met his gaze steadily. The blinds were drawn and he could catch no glimmer of the radiance that had shone for him when Genevieve was first mistress at the Home Farm.

"If only Robin had married he would not have to go."

The words were repeated and echoed through the family. The leash had become a lash. The means Kitty had used to hold him had driven him away. They were all aware of it, and like a thread it ran through their comments on the war.

"If only Kitty had let him marry!"

Whenever any of the Pencarrows met the subject of Robin's enlistment came up for discussion. It did not seem to matter that Potty

495

Barker and Philip Gentry, both married, had gone to camp. It seemed natural. But Robin! That was different.

The first time Genevieve met her aunt after Robin's enlistment she felt impelled to take her revenge.

"You took him from me and now you have lost him. He would have married me years ago and we might have had our children, but you kept him tied to your apron-strings. This is your punishment, the reward of your selfish love."

But when she saw the piteous appeal in Kitty's face, the ravages of that bitter remorse, her heart failed her. It would be cowardly to strike her now. Kitty had driven the wedge that kept them apart, and something had gone out of their love in the long, futile years of waiting.

Now Robin had come to say good-bye. Lieut. Robin Herrick, looking very smart in his new uniform.

"Genevieve, can't we get an hour, some-where, together?"

She shook her head. "You know all I've got to say. It can be said here in front of them."

"I can't. I've a lot I want to say to you—alone."

"Not now. When you come back."

"No, now, Genevieve. I must. To-night, after dinner, slip down to that seat under the kowhai tree at the bottom of the garden. Promise, Genevieve; promise you will."

He clung to her hand.

"Better not. Much better not." But she was weakening. She wanted to yield only to his urgent compulsion. She wanted to feel the whip of his insistence, the crushing weight of his desire; to know herself overwhelmed and to savour that sweet moment, a woman's triumph, when she has decided to yield but delays the surrender.

"You must, Genevieve, you must! It's my last night. I can't leave you like this."

His fingers were steel about hers; he was no longer the diffident lover.

Already the normal restraint was slackening. Sudden and foolish marriages were being arranged in the nervous heat of patriotic fervour. Men, rejected as civilians, became desirable as soldiers. The uniform and training had smartened them up, and the glamour of romance swept sober reason aside.

Life in camp had wakened that latent soldier instinct which Robin had inherited from his father. He fitted easily, and did not feel alien to the task.

In some ways the war had wrought his emancipation; it had liberated him from the tie of gratitude which had made him impotent. A national need had made him free. All his life he had hesitated, weighing his actions lest by them he might inflict some hurt or injustice on another. He was afraid, and knew it; afraid of failing himself in the test, and this fear had deepened in later years. He had been afraid to tell them he was enlisting for fear his mother's tears and his uncle's arguments might dissuade him. He knew now that he must make his own decision and arrange his own life, and not be daunted by the fear of consequences. It was not as they affected himself, but an acute sense of duty, of loyalty, constantly barred the way to his own fulfilment.

In this newly won freedom, sensible of the bitter waste of their golden years of youth, Robin had come to claim Genevieve; to offer a belated atonement for the barren harvest of their love.

On a night in late September, under a grey, moonless sky, Genevieve kept her tryst with Robin, deep in the shadow of the garden, where tree fern and kowhai hugged the mossy terraced bank.

"Darling, will you marry me before I sail? It can all be arranged. Do, Genevieve!"

"No, Robin. Not now."

"Why, darling! It would be so easy now."

"Yes, I know, but I don't want it to be easy."

"I don't understand."

"That's just it."

Robin felt chilled; his arms slackened their hold, and the look of a hurt child, that made his grey eyes seem clouded with tears, woke pity in Genevieve. She longed to say yes; to marry him to-morrow; to still the family's outcry at cousins marrying, but in these troubled times perhaps they would scarcely notice it. Yet it was because it would be easy now that she hesitated. She wanted Robin to demand her, to take her against the conscious opposition of the family, and not slip through unnoticed when their minds were harassed and their attention diverted by the tragedy of war. An obstinate streak in her would suffer the further hurt of denial rather than take Robin now when it could be done so easily. A war-time marriage was a matter of moments. There was no need for a satin dress and a bridal veil and a long retinue of bridesmaids. It was not the lack of these that held Genevieve to her purpose. Fierce opposition she would have faced and married Robin if he had shown the stiffening for the fight. He loved her, he had always wanted her, and he would marry her now because the way was clear and smooth. Yet she hesitated.

"I don't understand, Genevieve. We don't know how long it may last. If we were married now—to-morrow! Oh, my dear, can't you see what it would mean to me to know you were my wife?"

"I don't know why, but I can't; not now, Robin."

"When I come back?"

"I don't know. We must see what happens. It may be a long time and you may change; anything might happen."

He might be killed. She thought of that, and a terrible fear haunted her mind, yet she knew she could not marry him now.

"I want you so, Genevieve?" and Robin lifted her face in his hands and kissed her. "I want you so."

It was senseless to hurt herself and him for a quixotic idea. If only he hadn't said it would be easy! She had gone to meet him hoping to be won and he had spoilt it all. He seemed so glad to evade the storm, and this weak streak in him was the thing she was fighting, and it was also a source of irritation to her. He was of different fibre. If only he had shown a blind unreasoning desire to wreck everything for her she would have counselled wisdom, but been won. So often she had seen him shrink from conflict. He would not attack the fort for fear of the carnage; now he asked her to creep through a gap in the wall.

"I'm a rotten romantic, I suppose," she thought. "But if I married him now—like this . . . No, I couldn't do it."

The feverish excitement that drove others into a war-time marriage restrained Genevieve.

Dry-eyed, amidst the tears, with a chill loneliness in her heart, she saw Robin embark and sail away—away to an unknown destination.

Kitty's tragic misery woke her pity. Ella shed no tears for Philip Gentry, but gaily promised to meet him in London in three months' time, when the war was over.

Jessie broke down when Potty said goodbye.

"It'll be over soon, old girl, and I'll bring you a hat from Paris."

He tried to jest, but even the promise of adventure could not wipe out the years of intermittent content with Jessie and the children down the Sounds. After all, he was a family man now, and it did make a difference when the break came.

Sir Miles and Genevieve were at the Awapuni races when news of the landing at Gallipoli came through.

It was the end of April, and the autumn day was cold in spite of a bright sun and a clear sky. Sir Miles had been making a tour of Manawatu, making speeches to stimulate recruiting and encourage subscriptons to the Red Cross and other funds, and he liked Genevieve to accompany him.

Norah and Kitty were also deep in local activities, gathering funds, organizing committees and laying the foundations of that vast network of useful service that spread its ramifications throughout all civil and military life for many years after the war.

Vague rumours that the New Zealand troops had been overwhelmed in some terrible disaster on Anzac Beach began to filter through.

Genevieve looked across the green space that had, so short a time before, held the camp. She wondered where Robin's tent had been. He had tramped this grassy track where horses' hoofs were galloping. She did not see the colours flash past the post, nor hear the cheering as the favourite won. Her thoughts were on that barren beach where even now, at that moment, had she known, they were fighting a grim, heroic battle to maintain their slender footing; it was a desperate struggle, the withering fire of the Turkish guns on one side and on the other side—the sea.

"Come home, Father. I can't bear it," she said at last.

When they reached Wellington the casualty lists had begun to appear. Now the red files and the blue folders did their work. Days passed, but neither Robin nor Potty Barker's name appeared. Philip Gentry was still in Egypt.

Conflicting stories were circulated, rumours of defeat gained currency and were denied. A terrible uncertainty prevailed. The first casualty lists were heavy, and the deadening

503

sense of the reality of war fell like a leaden weight on those who had regarded it in the light of a great adventure.

More men were needed to replace those wounded and dead. More money, more food. Farmers were urged to increase production still further. Later it became the patriotic duty of older men to buy out the young farmers in order to release them for active service. The laws against land aggregation were suspended, and in this manner many men acquired the beginnings of large estates.

Ella sailed with her children and was already in London. Michael managed Duffield and lent a helping hand to every appeal. He had no son and was himself too old to go, so he gave generously of what he had.

Trentham, up the Hutt Valley, was now a military camp; also Featherston on the other side of the Rimutaka range.

Censored letters brought scrappy news. At Gallipoli there was a constant shortage of everything, and brief messages were written on scraps of torn paper, the plain margins of old newspapers, and the inside of used envelopes. Sometimes the writing was so small it required a magnifying-glass to read it.

Dr. Neil Macdonald was now in khaki;

an important figure at Trentham. Erena's second child, a black-haired, dark-skinned boy, was born while his father was in camp. Some of Erena's dark beauty had faded and she had lost the lithesome grace of youth.

"A damn' shame! . . ."

"Who is she?"'

"That red-haired girl who sings at concerts at camp."

"Does his wife know?"

"I'm afraid she does, but she puts up a brave front."

Erena knew that Neil was unfaithful. He had been caught up in the excitement of wartime enthusiasm. He had a captain's rank with a safe home job, and he had soon yielded to the fascination of a temporary love. Now it was the red-haired singer. His car was always ready to run her back to town after a concert. Women flattered him; they took his own estimate of himself, and that was unduly high. Neil had never convinced the family of his superiority, and the cousins took a keen delight in pricking his pride.

The military activity at his door had disturbed Kelly. From the moment Potty Barker had enlisted and spoke of sharing the adventure together Kelly had been chafing at the routine of the farm. So many married men had already gone, why shouldn't he? Maisie felt his growing restlessness and tried to still it. He was doing useful work on the farm, and he had been told there was no need for him to enlist. But as the months passed, and fresh drafts sailed away to fill the thinning ranks overseas, Kelly grew impatient.

His three small sons, Matt, Mike and Measle, played soldiers and drilled up and down the garden path.

"Why don't you go to the war, Daddy?" asked Matt.

"Hush, dear. Daddy has to stay at home and look after you and grow food for the soldiers," Maisie said hurriedly.

Then one day Kitty asked him if he had thought of going yet. He might take Robin's place, as the poor boy had had over a year of it now.

"Thought of it! Good God! Do you think I want to stick here?"

"Then why don't you go? Philip went and left his family, and so did Potty Barker."

"Yes, but Michael is carrying on Duffield for Philip, and Jessie is with her parents on the farm." Maisie resented Kitty's critical tone.

"It's no good, Maisie, I've got to go," Kelly said.

"But the farm—and the children, Kelly?"

"You could manage without me, couldn't you? It's like this, Maisie, I've got to go. I wanted to from the first, but—well, you know how it was. You've always been a game kid and Michael would be here. He would see you through the busy times. And old Jordon could manage in between, when it's slack."

Sir Miles could not protest as he was hoarse from urging the youth of the country to join up. But he told Kelly quietly that he was more useful on the farm.

Maisie organized entertainments and took concert parties to camp, and she sang with all her old poignancy: "We don't want to lose you, but we think you ought to go."

Kelly was now in camp, a lieutenant of artillery. She liked the navy and scarlet round his hat, and he had a badge made into a brooch for her. The children were delighted to see their father a soldier.

"Daddy, what's that thing you were riding on this morning?" Matt enquired.

"A gun, my son."

"Why's it a gun, Daddy?" asked Measle.

Kelly's training came to an end and he was sailing next day.

". . . Till the day that I'll be going down the long, long trail with you."

A quivering note throbbed in Maisie's voice as she sang, but she checked her tears. Kelly would hate to see her cry publicly. He hated emotional scenes.

Now that he came to leave, an evening melancholy settled on his soul like the close of a peaceful day. Maisie and he walked through the garden and down the path to the pond. His sheep and cattle grazed contentedly on the rich flat pastures beside the stream. They had been happy here. Maisie had won back the family, and if the Home Farm had not again become the focal centre of the family, it had retained much of its homely attraction.

Maisie had found that it was not altogether easy to fit into the Pencarrow scheme without doing violence to her own ideals. If she did not entirely surrender it was because she felt that complete acquiescence would be bad for Kelly. He needed the bracing air of contradiction to keep him from becoming flabby. She contested many of his plans, not with acrimony, but quietly and logically, and her steadfast faith and her splendid loyalty made the victory possible. Maisie was not a blind imitator of Bessie Pencarrow. She stamped her own individuality upon the old home and the family as surely as that earlier mother.

When Kelly had his moody fits and crept into a dark pit to indulge his melancholy she did not question him or ask the reason why. But when, having fought his devils and won, he returned to her, she was waiting for him with a welcoming hand to greet his old cheery humour. This silent understanding was her richest gift.

Like his father, he worshipped his children, but they could not understand his erratic moods, and why the remark that one day won his laughter earned a sharp rebuke on his gloomy days.

Before he sailed Kelly had a talk with Genevieve.

"Maisie will be all right, but you might have a look in sometimes. It's when the youngsters are in bed at night, the time we had together, that she might feel lonely a bit. And if anything should go wrong and I don't come back, see that she gets a fair deal. I've made Father and Michael trustees, but I'd like to add you also. They're getting on a bit,

509

and I would feel easier about her if you kept an eye on things. If anything happened to Maisie—"

"I'll see the boys through. Don't worry about that. But she will be here when you come back."

"A pity you didn't marry, Genevieve. This law business is pretty damn' dull for a woman. I know I'd have hated it. Why didn't you?"

"What a question!"

"I used to think you and Robin might. Potty Barker was sure of it—and Kitty was getting scared."

"Haven't there been enough wild marriages since the war began?"

"But this wasn't a war affair. It was years ago."

"What would you say if I had married Robin?"

"Damned if I know."

"Do you think he is my kind?"

"Not in some ways, perhaps; a bit softer than we were."

"Yes, we're a pretty hard lot, I suppose."

"But Robin's been putting up a good showing at Gallipoli and now in France. He's got the guts all right to stick it out like this. I hope to God I won't funk when it comes to going over the top. Did he ever tell you he was afraid he might?"

"No!"

"Yes, it worried him a lot in camp. He told me twice that it wasn't the getting hurt he was afraid of, but funking it. Probably that's what drove him to be so damned reckless. Captain now and M.C."

Kelly was talking to ease the strain on his own nerves and Genevieve knew the restless signs. She did not interrupt him, but let him ramble on.

So Robin had been afraid of funking it!

So far he had been fortunate, just a short spell in hospital with shrapnel splinters in his leg and a mild bout of fever.

Maisie stood on the wharf beside Sir Miles and Norah and Genevieve, and the band played "The Baby Doll" as the drab troopship, with every inch crowded with horses and men, moved slowly from her moorings and turned down the harbour. It would be months before she could hear from him. A nameless ship, with a simple number to designate it, would one day, if she escaped the submarines, arrive in port. It would probably be three months before that brief cable reached New Zealand stating that the vessel had reached harbour safely.

The town clock had just chimed noon and the summer heat was tempered by a light southerly breeze that fluttered the flags. The cheering died away and the music ceased.

"When will Daddy come back?" Mike asked as Maisie called at Pencarrow House on the Terrace for her three little sons.

"Soon, darling, soon," Genevieve said, but Maisie stood looking out of the window across the harbour, where the troopship had vanished, and stifled her sobbing so that the children might not hear.

28

PHILIP GENTRY was killed on the Somme. A month before he had been to London on leave and spent a week with Ella. They had gone to theatres and danced and made a brave pretence of enjoyment, but the mask was wearing thin.

Ella was doing V.A.D. work with Ann Gentry, Philip's sister, and the children were at school.

"What will you do now?" Ann asked when the first stunning shock had passed and Ella faced the reconstruction of the future.

"I don't know. But I can't go back; not yet. I'll keep on at the canteen."

"Good!" said Ann. She knew there was nothing like work—hard, exhausting work— to keep women sane when their personal life collapsed around them. Ann was nearly forty, but early in the war she had become engaged to a major in Kitchener's Army. He was an old friend, not long a widower, and they had found themselves caught in the emotional wash of the war as it swept deep into the recesses of civil life. He was killed three months later; blown to pieces by a shell. Ann found that to carry on was the sole panacea; it left so little time to think.

Seven months after Kelly sailed his little daughter was born. Maisie had not told him in case the news might add to his present worries. If she and the babe came through safely there was good news, a pleasant surprise for him. If not, he would at least be spared the months of waiting. He knew that Maisie, like so many other women on the farms, was already taking over the work done by the men. The pioneer women had done it, and lent a hand out of doors. Bessie Pencarrow had borne her share of this hardship in their early, necessitous days, but to Maisie and her generation it was something new. As one by one the young men enlisted and labour grew scarce she was compelled to do more herself.

A baby coming, a fact she kept secret as long as she could, complicated matters. Then she told Genevieve.

"I hope it's a girl," Maisie said.

Genevieve felt the piteous envy of a barren love; pity for herself.

"Don't work too hard; take it easier now," she cautioned.

"I'll be quite all right," Maisie said hopefully.

"Are you glad?"

Genevieve touched the wound in her own heart with the words.

"Oh yes. I love my babies. I'll call her Elizabeth after Grannie. I think she'd like it; Kelly would, I know."

Norah was anxious, but Miles was pleased when she told him.

"She is a game little soul," Miles said. He had forgotten his first opposition to her and no one reminded him.

There was courage in the piquant smile when she greeted Sir Miles and a deference in the way she called him Father. It was not until Kelly had gone to France that she had dared that familiarity, and he liked it.

Miles did not mention the subject of the coming child directly to her. He was still hemmed in by the code of his period. One did not speak of an unborn babe to its mother; it was indelicate, embarrassing. Only to one's wife, and then, probably, after the light was put out.

"Oh, by the way, Norah, you'd better keep

515

an eye on Maisie. See that she doesn't do too much on the farm, and—well, you know, advise her."

"I think Genevieve has been talking to her about it."

"Genevieve! What does she know about such things? An unmarried girl."

"Young girls know a great deal these days. It's surprising how freely they talk."

"This war is responsible for a lot and the girls have lost their heads. It's all very well to work for patriotic causes and entertain the soldiers, but I don't like this cheap familiarity. A lot of young—er—"

"Miles, dear!"

But Norah's protest did not stem the tide, although she had anticipated an unpleasant word. She wished Miles would not use it.

Not only servant girls but society girls had got into trouble with soldiers, and some of them had been left unprovided for. A number of these cases had come under the notice of patriotic organizations with which he was connected.

"And the way they brazen it out! My God! The war has liberated the beast in everyone."

"And the best," said Norah. "You mustn't forget, dear, that life is not quite normal.

516

Think what some of the soldiers have been through and what they suffer; the men and women have been very brave, I think—"

"Are you defending these—these—"

"Of course not, but life is so different from my young day. As Genevieve says, it's very stark and real. The old glamour and picturesqueness have gone from war. You have only got to meet one of the hospital ships coming in to realize that. It's your job to keep patriotic fervour at white heat, with speeches and meetings, Miles, but it's terribly sad to see these wounded men and the wreck it has made of their lives. All these young girls left—"

"Do you think I don't know that? But it's no excuse for all this—this freedom between the sexes, and this lack of restraint. I never heard such talk."

Norah did not answer and feigned sleep. It was no use arguing with Miles.

When the little daughter was born in August, such a very little daughter, Genevieve sent a cable to Kelly.

They called her "Elizabeth Genevieve."

The Bessie of Victoria's days had become Betty in the reign of George the Fifth, but she

517

was such a bit of a thing, this fair-haired, blue-eyed baby—they were the vivid blue eyes of Kelly—that Betty soon became Bitty.

Small but wiry, she throve amazingly, and the three boys were her constant bodyguard. She was a month old when Kelly's cable arrived, an excited, happy message, but with the poignant regret that he was not there to welcome his first daughter.

★ ★ ★

For the first two years voluntary enlistment kept up reinforcements for the New Zealand Army and supplied new troops, but at the end of that period the Conscription Act was passed. A complete register of men had been compiled and from this a ballot was drawn for every new draft required.

Each month anxious eyes waited for the fateful telegram. Mothers and wives, tense with dread, feared every click of the gate, every knock on the door. It might be the telegram of notification. War was real enough now. There was no more talk of adventure; of licking the Hun in a few weeks. Fed on war propaganda, ferocious stories of inhuman atrocities which inflamed a lasting hate of the

518

enemy, the men went into camp with full knowledge of what lay ahead. Thousands of wounded men had returned; there was no need for clearer evidence of the effects of a modern war.

First there was their training in New Zealand, then sailing overseas, packed in troopships, zigzagging to and fro to avoid raiders and submarines, with lights shrouded and no knowledge of what was happening around them. Two, perhaps three, months of this intolerable voyage. Then the mud and misery of Sling camp, and after that—the war.

Until the evacuation of Gallipoli they sailed via Suez, and then the troopships were diverted to round the Cape of Good Hope. When America entered the war the Panama route was open to them.

Not only troopships had to face these perils of the long and menaced voyage, but the gallant ships of the Merchant Marine. During the war New Zealand shipped one hundred and sixty million pounds' worth of foodstuffs to Great Britain, and nineteen of her insulated ships were sunk.

* * *

"Maisie is looking very thin, I'm worried about her." Norah took off her hat and blew into her kid gloves before putting them into the drawer.

"What can you expect? She's doing too much. If she would be content to look after the children and the farm; but rushing off at night, singing at concerts in camp and organizing entertainments—it's too much for any woman. My grandchildren have a sufficient handicap in their father being away, without their mother wearing herself to a thread—unnecessarily, I consider. She has done enough of that sort of thing."

Norah was sorry now that she had mentioned it to Miles.

"She feels that she's helping," said Genevieve. "It keeps her from thinking, too. If she is not doing something she is worrying about Kelly."

"She's a bundle of nerves, and we will have her breaking down next and in hospital."

Miles spoke with the positiveness of the law.

"You try to make her take things easy," Norah suggested to Genevieve.

"It's no good; I have tried. She says it's only when she is tired out that she can sleep.

To lie in bed awake and wonder about Kelly is worse.'"

The baby was six months old when the cable came that Kelly had been wounded.

"In the leg, thank goodness. Perhaps he will be out of it now for a while, or come home."

It was a relief to Maisie to get this news, now that it had come. She had dreaded the day when the telegraph-boy would come riding in with a message; and the terrible fear that he might be killed was thrust back. Kelly was wounded in the leg, shrapnel had torn his thigh. He was not classed as seriously wounded, but perhaps it would take a long time to heal, or even incapacitate him for further active service. She hoped so. Better to know that he was in hospital in England with every care, than to live in hourly dread that he might be killed. With the coming of the cable the tension relaxed.

Miles had expected a pathetic outburst when she received the news, but instead, on motoring out with Norah to comfort her, he found her almost glad. He was going to tell her that she must look on it sensibly and remember that Kelly was probably better off in hospital. It annoyed him slightly to find that she had already taken that view.

He saw himself patting her gently on the shoulder.

"There, there, you must not cry like that; think of the children."

But she was not crying. She was pale and showed the strain; it was reaction from the shock—the shock of seeing the telegraph-boy coming up the drive. But she was quite calm.

"Women are queer," he said afterwards.

"I think she is very brave and very sensible," said Norah.

"Yes; a little unfeeling. These young people are beyond me."

Miles's afternoon had not been a success.

They began to talk of Robin's charmed life. He had had several narrow escapes, men standing beside him blown to pieces and companions horribly maimed. The anxiety was eating up all Kitty's reserve strength and the family were very gentle with her.

As men were called up and every office found itself short of staff, Kelly, Pencarrow and Herrick were no exception. Sir Miles bore a heavy strain of patriotic endeavour in addition to his work: speeches, meetings, organizations to deal with the problem of war victims; preparation for training partially disabled men in useful occupations and of absorbing discharged soldiers back into civil life.

Genevieve worked with him and also shared intimately in his legal work. Much that would have fallen to Robin came to her. Sometimes Miles was carried away by his own eloquence, and a few greasy insincerities slipped into a speech. He knew instantly from Genevieve's face that he had struck a false note.

"How did it go to-night?"

"A bit oily."

"I'm getting stale; tired."

"I bet you are. Can't you ease off a little? Take a spell, Father."

"How can I?"

"I suppose not."

After all, there was no spell for the men at the front, and this was paradise in comparison.

Genevieve could feel the strain telling on Robin. He wrote regularly, with little about the war, but the changing note in his letters indicated the wounds of the mind which his body had escaped. Sometimes a cynical phrase crept in, which was so unlike him; a bitter jest about heroes; a sharp criticism of political or military authority. The first fear of proving a coward had gone and also the first secret pride in having been marked out for bravery, though in his heart he knew he was no hero, unless it be heroic to be afraid. He fought on doggedly, but without illusion. The fiery fervour of some new recruit, the gallant attitude towards service, set him cursing with a volubility that Potty Barker might have envied.

All this was reflected in his letters; unconsciously he was revealing raw nerves and the ruin of sustained effort under inhuman conditions.

Robin's promotion to Major was received with great delight in Wellington, and his comment that he would swap it for a swim in the Hutt river Miles regarded as an exhibition of wartime levity which militated against discipline. Miles deplored the attitude; this growing tendency seemed to cut the ground from under his feet and the feet of those who stood for the passing era.

They heard Robin was in hospital for a spell, but no details of injury or illness were supplied. Then back he went for a couple of months and once more his name appeared in the hospital list.

It was Kelly, who was still convalescent in England, with a crutch to ease the strain of a shortened leg, who told them that Robin was a bit nervy; shell-shock, he guessed. He had managed to see him one day.

With the formation of the Rifle Brigade, or the Trents, as they were affectionately called, for they were trained at Trentham, the shortage of men became acute. The constant drain on an under-populated young country had left wide gaps. To retain one man on each farm had been the policy, but the time came when even the last man was taken from the farm and the work was carried on by women and boys and girls. Often one experienced old man would oversee and advise the work for half a dozen neighbours. And these were not compact little farms such as you see in England and on the Continent. They were scattered, hilly, remote, inaccessible; large straggling areas of rough country just being broken in. New Zealand was much larger than England, but her total population was then only one and a quarter million all told.

With the coming into operation of the Conscription Act, a Military Appeal Board was set up, and Michael Pencarrow was appointed the farmers' representative and George McCaw was selected to watch the interests of labour. With a magistrate as chairman they sat in various centres, hearing appeals against the call for service.

Michael fought hard to keep the last man on the farm, but as the German push thinned the ranks it was found impossible to do this. As the first high standard of fitness was exhausted they were obliged to treat and train men who originally had been rejected.

On a hot afternoon in March the Military Appeal Court sat in Palmerston North. Trains from New Plymouth on the West coast and Napier on the East and the Main Trunk Express from Auckland to Wellington whistled as they passed, and the warning bells clanged noisily at the street crossing. As the trains rushed by the Courthouse and slowed down to cross the square, the noise momentarily drowned the voices in the Court.

The vast central square with its trees and gardens, its fountain and its tiny bridge, was cut in four by intersecting roads. A wide paved street enclosed the gardens, and the main business of the town was transacted in the shops that bordered the square on its four sides.

A hot wind blew the dust about in little gritty whirls and outside the Courthouse men and women waited—old men and women who had come to plead for their sons. They were mostly farmers and many had come long distances. Silently, with anxious faces, they waited for their son to be called.

On the Bench sat Mr. Highden, a dark, keen-eyed magistrate. On his right was Michael Pencarrow, his auburn hair faded and tinged with grey, his tanned face lined, his kind eyes a mirror of the pity in his heart. The farmers looked to him for help.

McCaw, a small, iron-grey man, stood for industry and watched the case for the man in trade.

Some appellants had engaged a lawyer to speak for them. The military authorities had a legal captain from their ranks to act as advocate. His keen nose scented the shirker and the malingerer. His thin lips curled scornfully and his bright eyes gleamed behind his glasses as he struck at the carefully constructed edifice of excuse.

"Do you mean to tell me that your mother, a healthy woman of fifty-five, and your brother of sixteen and a sister of twenty-five cannot carry on a country store without you? Do you realize the present position, that every man is needed?"

The magistrate turned to Michael and then to McCaw, and for a moment they conferred.

"George Buckley Smith, your appeal is dismissed. You will report in camp on the seventeenth of April."

A tall, fair youth next entered the witness-box.

"Your name is Henry Oliphant?"

"Yes."

"Your age is twenty-two?"

"Twenty-two last month."

"Your mother is a widow, I understand?"

"Yes."

"How many cows are you milking?"

"Eighty-five."

"Give me the details of the other stock you carry."

Again Michael's fair head leant towards the magistrate, who listened and nodded.

"Adjourned *sine die*."

The next man entered the box.

"Bruce Walton?"

"Yes, sir."

"Your father Bruce Geoffrey Walton, is a farmer at Pohangina?"

"Yes, sir."

"How many acres have you?"

"About six hundred."

"What stock do you carry?"

Again the list of lambs and hoggets and of cows.

"Your father, I understand, is an invalid?"

"Yes, sir. He has been bedridden for three years."

"Your eldest brother, Geoffrey Walton, was killed at Gallipoli?"

"Yes, sir."

"Another brother, Pierce Ernest Walton, is in hospital in England, seriously wounded?"

"Yes, sir."

"Have you any other brothers or sisters?"

"Yes, George."

"How old is he?"

"Just fifteen."

"Any sister?"

"Yes, two."

"Are they both at home?"

"No, sir. One is married and the other is at home. She is seventeen."

"Where is your sister's husband?"

"Fred Compton; he's in camp and sails next week."

(Fred Compton, thought Michael. That would be the little Freddie Compton that Kelly spoke of—the ratty little boy with the big ears, a grandson of the Kate Compton who came out in the sailing vessel with Bessie Pencarrow. Kelly had spent a hard year on that Taranaki farm before Miles would sanction him going to Michael at Duffield. How long ago it seemed now! And Freddie was in camp and sailing next week. Michael decided to look him up if he had a chance.)

"Who is looking after your sister's farm now that her husband has gone?"

"I'm helping her. And an old man of sixty-five, but he isn't much good. He is just a casual labourer."

Again the heads met and the three conferred.

"Adjourned *sine die*."

"What's this *sine die* mean?" whispered a voice at the back of the court.'

"He don't have to go to camp, that's all I know."

Next a tall, white-haired woman, her lined, weather-beaten face quivering with a nervous fear, went into the box.

530

"Mrs. Maud Gresham?"

"Yes."

"You own a farm at Taihape?"

"Yes."

"How many acres? What stock do you carry? How many cows do you milk?"

He took down all the details.

"Your two sons, Henry and Ernest, have been drawn in this ballot?"

"Yes."

"They are your only children?"

"Yes, and good boys, sir, both of them."

"Stand up, George and Ernest Gresham."

Two young farm lads, one twenty-one and the other a year older, stood up. They were shy country boys, bewildered at this sudden interest in them and their affairs. They had been born and brought up on the same farm, and what education they had was obtained at the little school three miles away. They could read and write and add up, and had a little knowledge of geography and grammar, but beyond a cheap detective story or an old Nat Gould their range of reading was limited to the newspaper, and the sporting pages of that. They knew nothing about Germans and Germany and even less about an Archduke who had been murdered in the Balkans.

Where were the Balkans, anyway? Now they had been called up to fight Germans, to leave the farm and go to Europe, which seemed as remote as the moon, and perhaps get killed, and what for? They didn't know and their father and mother didn't know. Sheepishly the two country lads stood there—lean, brown, simple farmers. George stared straight ahead, fascinated by the mental agility of the military advocate who was questioning his mother.

Ernest, his eyes on the floor, his nervous fingers twisted a loose button on his coat-sleeve until it came off in his hand.

"They are both good farmers, Mrs. Gresham?"

"They are indeed, sir."

"Both strong, healthy lads?"

"Yes."

"Which is the better farmer?"

"There's nothing to choose between them."

"One more reliable than the other; or do a harder day's work?"

"I don't think so."

Her eyes looked apprehensively at her sons, as though fearing that one wrong word from her, one foolish or too-trusting answer, might send them from her. She was naturally frank and truthful and had not learnt the art of finesse.

Michael and the magistrate exchanged opinions.

"Have either of your sons been ill at any time?"

"They both had measles at the same time, but it was light."

"Nothing else?"

"Ernest had scarlet fever when he was little."

"Didn't George catch it?"

"No, sir. Only Ernest."

Again the Bench conferred.

A slow goods train rumbled down the line and tooted its whistle impatiently at being kept waiting for signals. A policeman lounging against the door yawned. A blow-fly buzzed noisily against the window-pane.

Five hours they had sat in the stuffy heat while the story of simple lives was unfolded as a part of the tragic panorama of war.

In the hot stillness the tense moment hung weighted for the anxious mother. George stared ahead, his dull, unimaginative mind unable to grasp the significance of the questioning. Ernest, more sensitive, toyed nervously with the button he had torn from his sleeve. The train whistled and moved on through the square with a clattering of couplings. Down the corridor a distant door banged.

The magistrate cleared his throat.

"As there is nothing to choose between them as farmers, Mrs. Gresham, and one of them must go, we have based our decision on the grounds of health. George didn't have scarlet fever. He will, therefore, report in camp on the seventeenth of April. The case of Ernest Gresham is adjourned *sine die*."

29

"YOU look tired, Miles. Why don't you rest?"

"Rest? How can I rest?"

"But you'll be ill again. Don't go out to the meeting to-night. It's still raining; let me ring up and say you can't come."

As he did not answer, Norah slipped quietly away to the telephone and rang.

"There, now; have a quiet evening and go to bed early."

"I'm all right, Norah. I wish you wouldn't fuss about me so."

Miles was glad she had made his excuses for him. He did feel tired, but, good God, when you thought of the boys and what they were putting up with out there!

"Where is Genevieve?" he asked.

"She has gone to the Hutt. Measle has a touch of croup and Maisie was worried. She was afraid it might be whooping-cough and they would all catch it."

"Did Maisie hear from Kelly this mail?"

"Oh yes. He's growling cheerfully, so

that's a good sign. His leg still gives him trouble."

"What else can you expect, with half his thigh torn away? It's a damn' shame he had to go back so soon."

"Still, he has his leg; that's something to be thankful for; not like poor Potty Barker, his left arm completely gone."

"It's time Potty was getting back; he must be due soon."

"I wonder if he will come on the *Marama* with Neil."

"It's more than likely," said Miles.

Norah went on with her knitting. She had knitted them dozens and dozens of socks.

"I saw Erena to-day."

"Did you? How is she?" and Miles put down his paper.

"Much better and much happier. I think when he comes back things will be all right again. You can't help admiring her."

"She's too good for him."

"Oh, don't say that, Miles. Neil was foolish, like so many of the others. He was flattered and carried away, but he isn't bad; just selfish. That accident brought him to his senses."

"He was damn' lucky not to be killed.

What he wanted up the Waiwetu road at that hour of the night, with that red-haired singer—"

"It taught him a lesson. And the scandal—"

"There would have been a great deal more scandal if I hadn't got him on to the hospital ship and away."

"Yes, I suppose so. It soon died down. The girl has a nasty scar right down her cheek. I don't think she will ever lose it."

"Serve her right. I've no pity for her. She knew Neil was a married man."

"They don't seem to mind about that. The war has completely turned their heads."

"It's the uniform. Any man in a uniform will do."

Norah rambled on between plain and purl, plain and purl.

"He used to be such a nice little boy, but his early success and all those years away . . . I'm sure he will turn out well in the end. . . . Erena is still fond of him and I think they will patch it up. . . . Hector was different, but I hear he is quite a good chaplain . . . leaving all those little children of his in Dunedin . . . but he has Hester's sense of duty. . . ."

"He's too strait-laced for me. The very way he shakes hands with you is a rebuke."

"It's just his manner, dear. The clergy get that superior air."

"Any news of Robin?" Miles asked after a pause.

"Just the same. It's nerves, they say."

"This shell-shock is a damnable thing."

"Poor Robin, he has been out so long. If only he had got badly wounded and had a long spell in hospital it would have been better."

"Kitty doesn't know—yet. I mean, she doesn't realize."

"No, she thinks he is resting in a convalescent home."

"It will break her when she knows."

"Go to bed now, Miles, and have a good night's sleep. You've got a busy week ahead with the Supreme Court."

"I believe I will. I wish Genevieve were home. That girl is doing too much. Can't you make her rest more?"

"Now, Miles, how can I make her rest?"

"Er . . . do you think there is anything between her and Major Stanley?" He paused as he folded the paper, one foot on the fender, and looked anxiously at his wife.

"I don't know. I don't think so, dear. The Major is very persistent, but . . . I can't make her out. It isn't as if she had ever had an affair . . . or been disappointed in love."

"She is so normal in most things," said her father.

"I sometimes think that taking up law changed her; it might have something to do with it."

"Nonsense! I never heard such rubbish."

"But it has made her different from other girls."

"She has a man's brain and a man's mind, but that needn't unsex a girl."

"It does take the place of children and a home. It gives her a definite interest in life apart from a husband. And she is as thin as a rail."

"She needs rest. All this rushing about after work, out at night. She should let the idle girls do these things. By the way, when is Peter coming down?"

"First train in the morning. He could have come to-day but for that revue he is putting on in camp to-night."

"I don't like all this damn' theatrical business."

"Still, it is very clever of him to write a revue—all the words and songs. He says they may put it on at Trentham later."

"I hope they won't; it will only encourage him."

"The Awapuni camp is smaller, of course, and he gets more notice there."

"Too much notice, the young pup. He will never settle down properly again after this—never."

"Does it matter, dear? When you think of other people who have lost their sons, we've been very lucky. Even if he won't go back to the office, we have still got him with us."

Miles would not agree, but he knew Norah was right.

Pat was the only one causing them anxiety; he was somewhere in the North Sea, that grim, grey, treacherous waste of sea, whipped by storms, menaced by mines. Beyond that they knew nothing.

Peter was in the Ambulance Corps at Awapuni. He had a clerical job, typing in the Commandant's office. His theatrical talent had fine scope here, assisting the captain, who was an amateur composer of light music, in the production of revues. For the first time in his life Peter felt that his ability was appreciated. He was now out-growing his youthful awkwardness, but his enthusiasm was undimmed. "Side-lights" was his first revue, a medley of topical verse which the captain had set to music, with some dancing and a comic turn. It was a little crude, but had orginality.

Peter arrived in the morning, thrilled with success, and he could talk of nothing but his revue.

"Are you aware there is a war on, my boy?" asked Miles sarcastically.

"Rather, but the men hate you to talk about it. You ask one of the fellows about the war and he'll knock your head off with his crutch. Tell him who won the football match or get a dirty one on to the sergeant-major and he'll listen all day. They want to forget about it, and that's our job, to help them to forget. Now in my revue—"

"Oh, damn your revue!"

Peter still worked through his mother, and her influence was efficacious with Miles. He wanted to get on a hospital ship and go to England.

"Father can fix it if he likes. You ask him."

"Yes, Peter, but why must you go? Why aren't you content to do your share in camp?"

"Oh, Mother, don't start that! Just one trip on the hospital ship; I'd see London and do all the shows in that ten days. But don't mention that to Father."

Peter got his way. He sailed on the next hospital ship and did every show in London.

On the way out, with a freight of sick and wounded, Peter again staged his revue. On a calm night in the tropics all the men who could be moved were brought in to form the audience.

Peter, slim and fair, was the leading lady, with a stately elegance but far too much leg.

Pinker, who had been badly gassed, made a bouquet of paper flowers, which was handed up at the end of the show. Peter bowed and curtsied and blew kisses until the clapping and whistling had ceased.

Two days later Pinker died and Peter took his bouquet of paper flowers and fashioned a wreath. As the grey canvas coffin slid into the sea a gaudy wreath of paper roses bobbed up and down on the face of the Pacific and drifted away into the West.

Potty Barker came home on the *Marama* and Jessie brought the children to Wellington to meet him.

"Well, what do you think of the war now?" asked Miles.

"A fair bl—"

"Potty! The children!" Jessie reminded him.

Potty grinned. "A fair cow," he finished mildly.

"Glad to be home again, I bet," said Miles heartily.

"The Sounds'll do me for the rest of me natural."

He put his arm round Jessie and gave her a bearish hug.

"How about it, old girl?"

But Jessie, in her happiness, seemed bereft of words, and the children had not yet become accustomed to this strange father with only one arm.

Neil had returned on the same ship, a much subdued and chastened man. He had seen so much of suffering, of silent courage, and the human wreckage of war, that his own importance had shrunk as something pitiable.

Erena met him without a trace of bitterness; the same calm, quiet dignity marked her manner under every circumstance. She had forgiven him and was prepared to begin again, and Neil was grateful for her silence.

The Armistice came with the summer. The

eleventh of November had seen the blossom in the orchards give place to the budding fruits; the gold of the kowhai along the Hutt river had faded and fallen, but the manuka's white, starry flower frosted the windswept trees. The long days had come again, and the early roses were in full bloom.

After war's dark night, the coming of peace had the glory of a summer dawn. Was it true? Was the war really over?

The Pencarrows held a family rejoicing. Michael and Miles were there, but Peter was again in camp at Awapuni, and Potty was shearing his sheep down the Sounds.

Robin was still in a convalescent home in England, and Gentry was dead. Pat was somewhere in the North Sea, and Kelly was at the front when the mad, delirious news came through. The war was over; he could come home at last.

As the news of the Armistice swept through New Zealand, so swept that devastating epidemic of influenza that some people thought was plague. Starting in the north, it came south like a prairie fire, sweeping every town and settlement, and finding in these healthy victims a fertile field for the propagation of its deadly work. Men whose years had accorded them immunity from the war were the first to be numbered among the dead. Hospitals were full and halls and homes were used to take in the sick and the dying. Shops were closed, hotels locked up, and liquor was supplied only on a doctor's prescription. Men and women who had organized work for war's necessities now turned their energy to fighting this new evil. They made a daily round of every house, knocking on the door, and if they did not receive a response they broke in and brought help. Relief depots were opened, and those who could not go out nursing supplied soups and foods. All barriers were down—social, financial, religious. Workers stood in queues, waiting for their daily instructions and the food and medicine that were to be distributed. Catholic nuns nursed staunch Presbyterians, the Salvation Army brought succour to the Jews. Anglican and Wesleyan, it was all one in this crisis.

The deadliness of the curse claimed most of its victims among the strong.

Late one night a call came through from Duffield; Michael was down with it.

"I'll go," said Genevieve. "Poor darling, we can't leave him out there alone, with just that silly old housekeeper to look after him."

Five days later Michael was dead.

Genevieve stood alone in the moonlight and listened to the surf in Palliser Bay, a slow, dull, rhythmic sound as the breakers crashed in from the Straits. All else was silent, and to her it seemed the silence of death.

Just when the war was over; when everything was coming right. Kelly had been spared and would soon be back; and Robin. Those strange letters from Robin; so unlike him: querulous, childish, then a glimpse of the old gentleness. His nerves, they said. Too long a strain on so sensitive a mind. The continued horror and the noise, and the shock of bursting shells. He was out of it now, but, somehow, he could not get his mind away from it. Perhaps, he, too, would soon be coming home.

But Michael had gone—dear, faithful Michael. It would cloud the happiness of Kelly's return not to find Michael here! Gentry and Michael both gone. Duffield without an owner!

Genevieve shivered and the cold hand of fear touched her. Who next? From what new direction would fate strike? Surely the world had borne enough in these years of war without this terrible calamity. It seemed as though those who had escaped the war, and prospered by it, must yet pay the price.

Peter wrote from Awapuni:

They have turned Devine's Hall into a hospital for orphan babies, and we chaps from camp do duty at night. I've never seen so many babies before, but it's very different from nursing soldiers. I can fill a bottle and change a napkin with the best.

It was after Easter when Kelly reached home, a thinner, older Kelly, with grey streaks at his temples and a decided limp as he walked.

The three small sons had grown into schoolboys, and his little daughter Bitty, whom he had never seen, was three years old. All those lovely baby days had been denied him.

Maisie had told the child about her father and she had grown to know him from photographs. But, frightened by all the excitement around her, she turned from Kelly's outstretched arms and hid her face on Maisie's shoulder.

"Darling, this is your Daddy."

But Bitty clung fast.

"She is excited, dear. She doesn't understand," Maisie said, but she saw the disappointment in Kelly's face as Bitty turned away.

"Wait till we get home, dear, and you'll have the joy of courting your daughter and winning her away from me."

Kelly with difficulty curbed his impatience to hold the child and feel her response, but he knew Maisie was right.

"Daddy! Daddy! Daddy!"

It was good to have his boys about him, asking awkward questions, and telling him foolish things. And Maisie! It was strange to come back to a wife after nearly four years. It was hard to think coherently, to understand all the changes, and to realize that Michael and Gentry were dead . . . and Duffield was his.

His father kept talking and his mother wept happily and asked if the socks always fitted. Genevieve was the quiet one now, and she and Maisie seemed to share a silent understanding. They had grown close together in these sad years. He was bewildered by it all.

"Let's get home, Maisie. I can't stand any

more," he said when Miles wanted them all to stay on to dinner.

"I think we had better go now, Father. It has been a long day for the children, and they are too young to understand," said Maisie. "And I want Kelly all to myself for an hour," she added, smiling frankly.

A month later Robin arrived. From his letters, and from vague reports and rumours, and also from what Kelly said, they had been prepared for a grave change: Robin afflicted with nerves, irritable, querulous, restless. They had glossed it over when talking to Kitty.

"I shall give the rest of my life making it up to him," she said, and a fanatical light of renunciation shone in her dark eyes. His affliction had given him back to her; made him more dependent. If she could not have him whole, she would have him broken, but he was her son; absolutely hers now. She had filled her days and years since he had gone to the war working with a feverish intensity: sewing, selling, organizing and visiting hospitals. She had built up for herself a new world of activity; a wider circle of friends. It was a purposeful activity, not the lighthearted participation that found in it amusement. Anything that helped win the war helped Robin. He was a part of the war, the centre of the whole tragic disaster for her. If Robin came home, the war would have ceased without an Armistice. Not that she was forgetting the others and what they, too, suffered, but it was on a different plane; as different as their toothache from hers. Robin's war was something immeasurably nearer.

Now he was home, and she would spend her life making up for these years of suffering; this waste of pain and the hideous memories it had left. She would wipe them out and fill his mind with everything that was pleasant and gay. Soon he would forget and be the same gentle, happy, smiling Robin; her son again.

Robin sat beside his mother at the dinner Miles gave to welcome him. It was pathetic to watch her, and Genevieve could see the growing irritation as she plied him with foolish questions about honours and medals. "Oh, for God's sake, Mother, how do I know who awards the damn' things? . . . I'm sorry"—and he ran his fingers jerkily over his forehead and his eyelids twitched.

Genevieve noticed how the sensitive features had sharpened; the twitching eyelids, the jerky movements of his restless hands, the drawn-down corners of his mouth—they all betrayed a tension that was braced in defence. A sudden noise, a menacing hush, a direct challenge, a stupid question, and his slight control weakened and his composure gave way. It was obvious that he was aware of his nervous condition and was riding himself hard to get safely through the first meeting with the family.

Without revealing her motive, Genevieve lifted the burden of attention from him and drew it to herself. Out of that habitual quiet into which she had taken herself, and to which the family had now become accustomed, she emerged with a flash of the old cheeky impudence. She talked at random and carried them to the end of the intolerable meal.

Afterwards she stood with him on the balcony, looking out across the harbour. Her voice was smooth again, and the jarring note of jest, having served its purpose, disappeared as she spoke of odd little homely things, everyday affairs. She did not offer sympathy or probe old wounds. It took on the calm of a commonplace meeting.

Genevieve was afraid that his mother's posessive devotion and desire to sacrifice herself for him would exasperate him and fret his nerves. Even in this first hour he seemed glad to creep under Genevieve's calm for shelter from it.

"Tell me about yourself, Genevieve. You're thinner."

"And older; four years older."

"It's not that; you've changed. What is it? But I suppose I needn't ask; it hit us all, even you out here."

They could not talk of intimate things, but slid along the surface, afraid that any deeper touch might stir a wound. They had longed for, and dreaded, this hour, and now it had come they stood apart, a gulf between them.

There was no talk of Robin's return to the office. He was not in a fit condition to resume the heavy routine of indoor work.

"He ought to have a long holiday first, Miles," suggested his mother. "He has earned it. I'll take him away after a couple of weeks' rest at home, and I'm sure he will get back his normal strength. Just motoring about the country, away from all thought of war; drifting idly from place to place, like we used to. I remember that fortnight we had at Napier after you came back from Australia; he was simply adorable to me then. Perhaps he would like to go to Napier again."

Robin was not enthusiastic about the proposed long tour with his mother; he was not very keen about anything.

Kitty began her life's devotion, which she was offering in recompense, by thoroughly antagonizing him. After the strain of meeting the family and the constant talking to old friends he felt the need of quiet. He liked to lie down and close his eyes and relax in a kind of ecstasy of exhaustion.

He had gone to the office in the morning to see the staff, and he had had lunch with his mother and two women whom Kitty had met during her wartime activities. She had talked so much about Robin they were impatient to meet him. He had held himself on a firm leash while they talked of their collections and committees and all the work they had accomplished.

After lunch he crept away into the dim drawing-room and flung himself on a couch, his feet trailing over the side, his head awkwardly placed on a cushion. It was cool and quiet here. A bowl of flowers sent a fragrant message across the room; a faint breeze stirred the curtain. In the distance he could hear the dull rumble of a shunting train. A beneficent peace spread over him and all the jangle their foolish conversation had stirred died away.

He was growing drowsy when Kitty tiptoed into the room and drew the heavy curtains, lifted his feet and placed them on a cushion and wedged another cushion behind his shoulder.

"Oh, for heaven's sake, Mother, can't you leave me alone? Let me have a minute's peace," and he sprang up and flung the cushions on the floor.

"But, Robin, you looked so uncomfortable that way. I only wanted to—"

"I know; I'm sorry. But if you'd only leave me alone for a while. I can't stand all this fussing and the talk of those silly women . . ."

"But, dear, they are both very nice, and did such splendid work during the war. I thought you'd like to meet them; they were simply dying to see you. Now lie down again, and I won't disturb you. . . ."

"I can't now. I'm . . . I'm . . . Oh, I don't know . . . I think I'll clear out for a walk."

Kitty's blind devotion could not learn its lesson; she had lost all sense of proportion. At the end of two weeks at home, when she proposed a lovely long holiday away together, Robin looked at her with a haunted terror in his eyes, like some timid animal at bay.

"Oh no, Mother, I don't want to go. I'd hate it."

"Just the two of us, Robin. You could do just what you liked, and go wherever you wanted to."

He thought with dread of those long days together, and his mother's hungry love, and now this almost sacrificial devotion rasping where it was meant to soothe and intensifying the discord between them.

"No, please, Mother, I'd rather stay at home."

Robin asked his uncle if he could come back to the office, but Miles shook his head.

"Not yet, boy. There is no hurry. I want to see you quite fit again before you start work."

"I'm all right."

"You want to steady down a bit first; rest and amuse yourself for a month or two . . ."

"But I can't. I'm getting miserable doing nothing but loaf around. I'd be much better working."

"Kitty is wonderful," said Norah with admiration.

"Kitty's a damn' fool, if you ask me," said Miles. "If she would only leave him alone and not coddle him. She's making him worse, that's my opinion."

Genevieve listened, but said nothing. It was quite obvious that Kitty, in her desire to help, was only retarding his recovery. Sometimes, when he came up to the Terrace, he seemed to be quivering with tense emotion, like a frightened child. It was usually after a quarrel with Kitty, when her mothering had nearly suffocated him and her deliberate soothing had spurred him to a quick anger, and he rushed away. At the end of an hour he quietened down.

"Like a ride?" Genevieve asked casually. "Kelly has a couple of hacks."

"I haven't been on a horse for ages."

"One is a crock, but the other is a bit fresh."

It was a challenge to him. Would he dare to ride it?

"We could run out in the car to the Hutt, and get an early start. I like riding this weather; it's keen and there's not much wind."

"I remember you always liked riding on a frosty morning."

"I'll pick you up at eight to-morrow. I think it's going to be fine."

Genevieve had assumed his acceptance. She did not plead; not one word about it being good for him; no sympathy; no poetic nonsense about the beauty of the morning. Either you felt these things, or you didn't.

"I'm sorry you can't have Joxer, he's mine," said Genevieve, as a kicking young bay was saddled. "I'll lend him to you one day if you're very civil."

Kelly's children were a little shy with Uncle Robin because he did not know how to play with them, but he went up in their estimation as he rode off with Aunt Genevieve.

"Robin always looked well on horseback," said Kelly.

"Better to have lost an arm, like Potty, than to be like that," said Maisie sadly.

"What would you have done if I came back like that?"

"Just loved you," and she tucked her head against his shoulder and he gave her a rough caress.

It was sunset when the two riders came in the gate.

"Where the devil have you two been? I nearly sent the police out to search for you horse thieves."

Kelly's greeting expressed his relief.

"We went through the Kahutarawa Gorge, and had lunch at Waikane."

Robin looked pale and was very silent. After tea they motored back to Wellington.

"What did you two talk about all day?" asked Peter. "I can never get a word out of him."

"Why fantails make fans of their tails; wouldn't you like to know?" said Genevieve evasively.

They rode out again the following week, a crisp day with all the sharpness of early winter. This time they took lunch and built a fire beside the stream, and made billy tea, and all the little frayed edges of Robin's humour seemed to plait themselves into a pattern of peace. The river ran surging past over large, smooth, grey stones, and a belt of tree ferns fringed the steep bank on the opposite side. The thin sunshine had only the warmth of a gossamer cloak, and they kept the fire burning to supplement its heat.

"I like this," said Robin, his head thrown back, listening to the hushed sounds of the bush and the muted harmony of river and birds and trees.

Genevieve put her hand on his and his fingers closed over it. It was the first step back to the old relationship.

"Robin, will you marry me now?"

"A wreck like I am! No, Genevieve. It's good of you, but that's just pity."

"You're wrong; it's not pity."

"You're not in earnest, Genevieve. You can't know . . ."

"I've never proposed to a man before, so I don't know anything of the art of persuasion. Once you wanted to marry me."

"It wouldn't be fair to you . . . like I am . . ."

"Don't you want to?"

"You're offering me heaven, Genevieve."

"Then you will?"

"It won't be easy for you . . ."

"Did I ever ask for it to be easy?"

The horses cropped the long grass by the bank. Robin and Genevieve sat beside the little fire as the sun sank lower and talked of the past . . . and of the future.

"If only we could get married without a fuss and everyone swarming round us . . . the family objecting or giving good advice." He looked pleadingly at her.

"There will be none of that," said Genevieve firmly.

Genevieve dressed for her wedding with a beating heart. Once she had rejected it because it was too easy. She had wanted Robin to fight for her, to take her by compulsion. Now she was marrying him; almost taking him by force. Everything had been left to her to arrange. She knew what she was undertaking, and went calmly about her secret preparations. If Robin remained at home with his mother he would never recover. He was still young, and underneath was the same Robin she had loved. She had felt him respond to her touch. She did not offer him sympathy or dependence upon her, but by assuming his strength she inspired him to effort, and her cool, good sense checked exhausting emotion. In time they would find something of the lost radiance of their youthful love.

Genevieve went to her marriage confident in the future; confident that she was doing right, and also undisturbed by thoughts of a family row. Her parents would be angry and

Kitty distraught. But it had to be, and this was the only way.

On a fine cold Saturday morning in June, Robin and Genevieve were married, and Kelly and Maisie signed the register as witnesses. They drank a toast and cut the cake, and Kelly, with Maisie and the children in the car, left for Manawatu. He said that he wanted to buy stock from Morgan.

Robin and Genevieve entered by the big hospitable gate to the Home Farm, and in these familiar surroundings began a new life. Kelly had lent it to them for a week.

On Sunday evening they watched a passing squall drive up the Valley, drench the country in a curtain of rain, then pass on over the hills, leaving the stars shining clear.

They stood close together, their arms linked, their fingers interlaced; soothed and spent.

"Pen Herrick!" Robin said it softly, wistfully.

"Who is Pen Herrick, dear?" asked Genevieve, her mind turning to his relatives in England.

"Before she died, Grannie asked me if I had a son to call him Pencarrow. She said, 'I think Pen Herrick would be a nice name for him.'"

Two brief letters, one to Sir Miles and one to Kitty, were delivered on Monday morning.

Robin and I were married on Saturday.

Genevieve and I were married on Saturday.

When they had recovered from the shock, and Norah had wiped her eyes, she said, "Perhaps it will be all for the best," and sighed.

Miles was too upset to trust himself to speak about it.

"Madness! Madness!" was his curt remark.

Kitty was prostrate, and Norah spent the day consoling her.

"Now it's done, it can't be undone. We will have to make the best of it."

But to Kitty it was a devastating final blow. She had lost Robin now; lost him absolutely. She must step back and Genevieve would take first place in his life.

"He was all I had," she repeated over and over again, and the piteous cry was the echo of her tragedy.

Kelly went up to the Terrace to discuss with his father his future plans for Duffield, but "this foolish marriage", as Miles referred to it, was the subject of their conversation.

"It's the best thing for both of them," said Kelly. "Aunt Kitty would have driven him mad, and it's marvellous how Genevieve manages him. I believe they've been in love for years. That's probably what's been wrong with Genevieve lately—worrying about Robin—and we didn't know."

The family was becoming reconciled to the idea, for they could now talk of it calmly, but they had not been to the Hutt and Robin and Genevieve had avoided the town.

"Give them time and they'll get used to anything; even Father will," was Kelly's advice.

"You ought to know," said Genevieve.

Kelly smiled tolerantly, remembering his own violent youth.

In August Kelly was taking over Duffield. Ella was remaining in England to educate the two girls, so that Kelly would, at last, be master of Duffield, the paradise of his boyish dreams. He would come to it now, a married man, not an ardent youth, scarred in battle, with many bitter experiences behind him; but with Maisie and his four children. How different!

He was nearly forty, with a touch of grey in his hair, and the tempo of his pulse was slower. His affections had an enduring quality, not the wild, reckless passion of those early years. He brought knowledge, an ampler vision, and a serene mood to the planning of this new life.

"How will you like it out there, Maisie?" asked Norah.

"We will be sorry to leave the Home Farm, but Kelly will love it; he always wanted Duffield."

"But you?"

"If he is happy, I'll be happy." She said it simply, with steadfast faith.

The Hutt Valley was becoming a residential area for city people. All about Trentham and Heretaunga were fine homes with lovely gardens, and the Home Farm was now too valuable to keep merely for grazing. Kelly proposed cutting it up for building sites, retaining the Homestead and Grannie's garden, with an adequate acreage to preserve its privacy, and selling the remainder.

It was Genevieve's idea that she and Robin should buy the Homestead. Here, in this peaceful garden and pleasant old house, Robin would get well. A car would take them swiftly to town and soon he would be able to work for a few hours each day.

"No more law for me. I'm through with it. I kept your job warm till you came back. Now you've got to get to work. I won't have a loafing husband around the house all day," and she laughed and ruffled his hair.

He smiled wistfully; it hurt to see his effort at response, but Genevieve knew that he needed effort to brace him now more than ever.

It would not be easy to win through, but it would be worth while.

"I've licked the frieze all right," she thought as the old Judge's remark of long ago came back to her mind.

Robin and Genevieve waved good-bye from the Homestead gate on a grey morning in August as the Kelly Pencarrows left for their new home at Duffield.

Kelly cloaked his impatience with a businesslike air, but the children were shrill with excitement. It was something new, and new things promised adventure.

565

Tears misted Maisie's eyes as she turned to look at the kind old house, her first real home, squatting comfortably among the trees. Her coming had thrust Genevieve from the place. Now, in her turn, she was leaving it to Genevieve. She would again be mistress here.

"Not so fast, dear," and Maisie lightly touched Kelly's arm as he took the curves of the Rimutaka in reckless haste.

A wind sprang up and drove the clouds out to sea, leaving the sky a clear blue except on the horizon. Spring was turning in its bed, like a sleeper walking. An early lamb was bleating on the hill. Duffield came into sight over a brow of the hill, and Kelly slowed the car to see it standing foursquare to the seasons, its screen of dark pines protecting the garden and the poplars he had planted long ago leaning before the wind.

"I hope Ella will sell out to me," he said impulsively.

"Is it wise to take on so much?"

"I'll soon be able to pay it off; wool's high, and prices are good all round."

"But will it last, dear?" asked Maisie cautiously.

"Of course it will. And there won't be any

more wars for a hell of a time, believe me."

"Be content, Kelly dear. Don't load yourself with too much. Remember, you can't work as hard as you used to."

"Nonsense! But if Ella marries that chap in England he might come poking out here. I'll buy her out, and then Duffield will be mine. And I'll do what I damn' well like with it. I'll make it the finest place in the Wairarapa. I want it all—now, and for my boys after me. I hope there will always be a Pencarrow at Duffield."

Maisie saw the old ambitious light shine in his eyes as he looked at Duffield spread out before him.

"I hope so, dear."

But the winds of heaven laughed in the trees.

THE END